TEMPERATURE
RISING

D1366635

By

John Avanzato

KCM PUBLISHING

A DIVISION OF KCM DIGITAL MEDIA, LLC

Credits

Temperature Rising by John Avanzato

ISBN-13: 978-1-939961-26-6
ISBN-10: 1939961262

First Edition

Publisher: Michael Fabiano
KCM Publishing
www.kcmpublishing.com

KCM Publishing
a division of KCM Digital Media, LLC

Books in the John Cesari series by
John Avanzato

Hostile Hospital

Prescription for Disaster

To my sons who taught me how to be a man

Joseph, Michael, Benjamin

Cheryl

Thank you for all you do

Contents

Acknowledgements

I would like to thank those who took the time out of their busy lives to read my manuscript and advise me. Your time and effort is greatly appreciated.

Jean Chamis RN

Lois McMichael

Sally Webster

Lori Matts

Linda Champlin Sharp

Karen Hillery

Michelle Pedersen Robbins

Mara O'laughlin

Mary Townley

Donna Marchitell RN

Anthony Avanzato DO

Michael Babyak

Amy Secor FNP

Joe Jaffe MD

Ed Kirwan

TEMPERATURE RISING

Oath of Office for the President of the United States

I do solemnly swear that I will faithfully execute the Office of President of the United States, and will to the best of my ability, preserve, protect and defend the Constitution of the United States.

Article II, Section 1, Clause 8

Prologue

*I*t was a cold, gray day in late autumn when I heard the news. A friend of mine from the old neighborhood had tracked me down to tell me. I was a first-year medical student in Buffalo sitting in anatomy class when the secretary from the main office came to find me. There were no cell phones back then so I had to go to her office to answer the call, and it had hit me hard. I caught the first flight I could back to New York and here I was.

The ground was moist and the air was damp and I felt empty inside as I gazed at the headstone and freshly dug earth. I held a bouquet of red roses in my hands and stood alone at the grave site in St. Raymond's Cemetery in the Bronx. I had missed the funeral by a day and felt bad, but I had made my peace with this woman while she was still alive and took comfort in that.

Sister Mary Catherine O'Reilly had finally passed on after a protracted illness and now slept with the angels. She was a tough, old-school, take-no-prisoners Irish nun and had been my seventh grade teacher. She ran her class with an iron fist, and she didn't just represent the Catholic Church; she was the Catholic Church, and I doubted that the pope himself would have commanded more respect had he shown up. As a child I feared her; as a teenager I respected her; and as an adult I loved her. She had been like a second mother to me and in fact, she and my mother conspired frequently to keep me on the straight and narrow. The phone line from the convent to my house burned constantly with news about my activities, both in and out of school. If I was seen cavorting with the wrong types my mother would know about it almost immediately and certainly before I had time to dream up an excuse. If I was having trouble with schoolwork, then miraculously the next day Sister Mary Catherine would slow things down for a quick review of the subject. She had a fearsome reputation but I don't remember anything ever happening to anyone who didn't deserve it, including me.

The fact of the matter was that although everyone thought she was a mean and crotchety old woman, she really loved to teach and to be with children. Looking back, I came to understand that her reputation was a carefully cultivated act to maintain discipline and order in an unruly class from an unruly neighborhood. Beneath the ill-tempered exterior was a devout, kind, and generous woman of faith who loved every minute of what she was doing. In fact, I never saw a bigger smile or happier look on her face than when she was handing out candy to us kids on the holidays, like Easter, Christmas and especially Saint Patrick's Day.

It was on a musty fall day just like this that Sister Mary Catherine had finally hit her stride in my education. She prided herself on the fact that she wasn't there to just teach us math and history but to mold us into moral and responsible adults. When the opportunities arose, she jumped on them.

Laura Abbondanza was a girl in my class who sat right next to me and lived one block away from the school. I walked by her house to and from class every day. She was the most beautiful twelve year old in the neighborhood— at least to me she was. I was too scared to talk to her and for the same reason avoided eye contact at all cost. She hated me and let me know it every chance she could. She and her friends regularly and mercilessly tormented me during lunch, recess, and any down time during our studies. I took it more or less on the chin because what else could I do? The humiliation and attacks began to escalate when one day she deliberately tipped an open milk container onto my lap as she walked by my lunch table. Everyone there erupted in laughter at my expense. From that point on it wasn't unusual to have a piece of crumpled paper or an occasional pebble from the schoolyard tossed in my direction.

It came to a head one Friday afternoon as we were settling into our desks after a break. She watched me as I walked down the aisle to sit. She had a look in her eyes that if I had understood anything at all about girls, would have caused me to run away, but I didn't see it coming.

As I neared, she suddenly kicked me in the shin and just as quickly withdrew her saddle-shoed foot, pretending nothing had happened. I winced and saw red. Those who saw, laughed and I turned eight shades of scarlet with embarrassment and anger. Without thinking about consequences, I launched a retaliatory kick into her bare leg causing her to scream in pain and surprise. I had never responded to her provocations before, and she was stunned. So was everyone else in the class including Sister Mary Catherine who had seen me but apparently had not seen Laura.

Laura began crying hysterically and Sister Mary Catherine came charging down the aisle, grabbed me roughly by the ear, and hauled me to the front of the class to stand by her desk while she checked on Laura's health. Once it was determined that Laura would live, Sister Mary Catherine escorted me to the principal's office, reprimanding me the whole way. I tried to explain that I was actually the victim but she wasn't particularly interested and neither was the principal, Sister Margaret. It was Friday and I was given Saturday morning detention with Sister Mary Catherine, a fate worse than death. Mano a mano for an entire morning; eight a.m. to noon. By the time I got home both nuns had already called my mother and she was waiting for me by the door to yell at me some more.

The next morning, I arrived promptly at eight and was greeted by Sister Mary Catherine in full nun's habit, which I assumed she wore seven days a week. I took a deep breath, accepted my fate, and sat in my usual desk, staring at the blackboard. It felt strange to be the only one there on a Saturday. Sister Mary Catherine told me to write one hundred times in my composition book that I would not hit girls, and I got started while she stacked boxes of supplies into a closet in the back of the room. From time to time, I glanced at the wall clock hoping to speed up time, wondering how I could possibly survive till noon.

After thirty minutes, Sister Mary Catherine took a break from her labor and came over, sitting sideways in the desk in front of me. I looked up at her weathered, bespectacled features. I never thought about how old she was or how long she had taught, but if you had asked I probably would have guessed a hundred years or more for both. She had kindly clear-blue eyes, and there was something about them that I couldn't put my finger on exactly, but they almost seemed to glow. Looking into them, I knew she was a kind person despite her reputation.

She asked gently, "John, do you know why you're here today?"

I nodded. "Yes, Sister. Because I kicked Laura."

"That's part of the reason, yes, but not the whole reason. You're here because I like you and I believe in you. I think you're special."

I was confused now and stared at her.

She continued. "John, right now you are a boy but one day you'll grow up to be a man. When that day comes, you will be bigger and stronger than any girl you will ever know and that is why it is important for you to learn right now that you must never hit girls. Your muscles and your strength are a gift from God to protect the girls in your life and never to hurt them. Do you understand what I am saying?"

I didn't but nodded in agreement anyway.

"Do you remember the story of King Arthur and the Knights of the Round Table?" she asked and I smiled. It was one of my favorite stories.

"Yes, Sister, I do."

She smiled. "Well, that's what you are going to be, John, a knight in shining armor, protector of the innocent and the weak. That's what men are supposed to be. Not all are cut out for that task, but I know you are. You're here in detention today not because I want to be mean to you but because I want you to remember what happened and the things we're talking about right now."

"Yes, Sister, but...?"

"Yes, John?"

"What about Laura? She lied. She kicked me first."

She nodded and looked at me in a kindly way. Her eyes exuded a comforting warmth. "I know she did, John. I saw the whole thing, but it was you I was worried about. You struck a girl in anger and you should never do that. I spoke to Laura and her parents after school yesterday, and she knows what she did was wrong and she's very sorry. From now on John, when a girl makes you angry, I want you to promise me that you will count to ten before you say or do anything back, and while you're counting, I want you to think about the knights of the round table and what they would do, okay? Will you promise me that?"

"I promise."

She hesitated, choosing her words carefully and then she let out a deep breath. "John, sometimes when a girl likes a boy and wants him to notice her she does things that may seem odd to get his attention."

"Like kick him and throw things at him and make fun of him?"

She sighed. "Unfortunately, yes. That doesn't mean it's right, mind you. That's not what I'm saying at all, but these things happen and she was wrong and I told her so."

I thought about it a little more. "Laura likes me?"

She nodded. "Do you understand better now?"

"I think so." I didn't, not then, not really, and not for many years after, but eventually it sunk in.

"Okay, John, you can stop writing now. Why don't you read one of the books from our collection? I'm going to take a rest before finishing up with those boxes back there."

She went to her desk and pulled out some test papers to grade and I grabbed a book from the small bookcase off to the side of the room that housed a selection of novels for the students to borrow and read. I picked out *The Roman* by Mike Waltari, went back to my desk and started reading.

At nine thirty, there was a knock on the classroom door and Sister Mary Catherine stood up to answer it. It was Laura and her parents, and she was holding a paper plate covered in aluminum foil. She looked at me and smiled, and I froze, staring at her, as she walked over to me.

She said, "Hi."

I said, "Hi."

She handed me the paper plate so I closed my book and took it from her. She said, "I'm sorry for kicking you and getting you in trouble. My mom and I baked something for you. Why don't you take a look?"

I was speechless as I uncovered the plate and discovered a beautiful large chocolate cupcake covered with vanilla frosting and multicolored sprinkles. It smelled and looked out of this world. I didn't know what to say. I just stared back and forth from the cupcake to Laura and back again.

After a time, her mother called to her, "We should leave now, Laura."

"Bye," she said, turning and walking back toward the door.

Just as she reached her parents, I stood up abruptly and stammered, "Laura—wait."

She turned back and they all watched me. My heart pounded in my chest and I could barely breathe. I meant to say "I'm sorry" but instead blurted out, "I like you too." Embarrassed, hormones and emotions exploding in every direction internally, I felt like I was going to keel over. I started to tremble and then to cry. "I'm sorry I hurt you, Laura. It won't ever happen again." Her lips started to quiver, she sniffled, and then she started to cry. She ran back and threw her arms around me, pressing her face into my chest, and we stood there sobbing.

After they left, Sister Mary Catherine came up to me and said, "You can go home now, John. I think we've been here long enough."

I looked at the clock. It was only ten.

I threw my arms around her. "Can I help you with the boxes first, Sister?"

****

It had started to rain now as I looked down at her headstone. I fell to my knees in the mud, overcome with emotion. I placed the bouquet of roses I had brought at the base of the stone and said, "Rest in peace, Sister, and give 'em hell up there."

As I walked to my car, I thought about what a better world it would be if only we had more ornery, Irish nuns.

TEMPERATURE RISING

BY

JOHN AVANZATO

Chapter 1

A scantily clad girl with short blond hair twirled and gyrated around the pole in rhythm to the pulsating music piped in overhead. She wore black high heels, a red G-string, and pasties. The pole was decorated in red and white garland in honor of the holiday season as Christmas was only a few days off. Vito and I sat in comfortable leather chairs just a few feet away in the dark VIP room of the Kit Kat Club, a very nice gentlemen's lounge on Second Avenue in Manhattan, in which we were silent partners. There was a small table between our two plush seats, and we sipped Johnnie Walker Blue from crystal tumblers as we watched her dance.

I placed my glass down. "Tell me again why we always have to meet in places like this, Vito?" There were three or four clubs scattered around the city that we rotated through, holding our meetings.

"Self-preservation is the name of the game, Cesari. You should know that. If we're going to run the rackets together in lower Manhattan then we have to be disciplined. The feds are always listening and aiming cameras in my direction and probably yours too. These clubs are noisy and crowded. It makes it a lot safer to talk in here. Besides, I'm banging the chick in charge, Heidi, so I trust her. If an undercover fed ever walked in the place, he'd stand out like a sore thumb because the cheap bastards never want to tip the girls properly. Heidi would let me know right away."

Vito and I had grown up together in the Bronx, and were on and off again friends and business partners. When we were off, we were really off and had even tried to kill each other several years ago, but we had patched things up and were now on the same side.

As we talked, the girl in high heels and holiday pasties slinked over like a cat to where we were sitting. Up until then, it wasn't even clear that she knew we were in the room. She spun around twice and then slowly performed a full split in front of us. She paused for a few seconds before rising and sauntered back to the pole to continue her routine.

Vito was impressed. "Not bad, Cesari, huh?"

"She's very talented for sure. Okay, let's get down to business. I'm going to Disney for a week with Cheryl." I raised my hand. "Before you say anything, it can't be helped. She's been begging me to go and I ran out of excuses."

He shook his head in frustration. "Fucking Cesari, this is our busiest time of year and you're taking off. You kill me. You got to get your priorities straight. People are borrowing, gambling, and spending like crazy. It's almost impossible to keep control of things right now. The whorehouses are filled to capacity every night of the week. The girls are exhausted and I barely got enough guys trying to count all the money, and you're going to see Mickey Mouse. Some business partner you're turning out to be."

"All right. Calm down. I told you it couldn't be helped. Besides, I'm supposed to be the silent partner, remember? I'm a gastroenterologist first and helping you is my second job, remember? This is the slowest time of year for my department because nobody wants to have a colonoscopy right before Christmas. The hospital practically ordered me to take the week off. Look, if there's an emergency just call me down there. It's not like I'm going to China. It's a short flight from Orlando, and I can be back to hold your hand in two hours."

I hadn't noticed while we were thus engaged that the blonde had meandered back to us and facing away, bent over directly in front of me. Startled, I wasn't quite sure what to do. I had brought a wad of twenties with me, but given the position she was in, the question was where to place one. She didn't give me much time to think it over as she gently lowered herself onto my lap, turned sideways and wrapped an arm around my neck. She had very nice breasts.

She looked at me and purred, "Hi."

I said, "Hi…miss?"

"Candy…" she cooed and nodded at the red and white decorated pole. "Candy Cane."

"Of course." What else could I say?

"Do you like me?"

"Very much, Candy." She gave me a big smile and wiggled on my lap.

"How much do you like me?"

"A lot, but maybe we should just stick to dancing for now, all right?" I scrunched my nose a little and nodded at Vito. "Me and the big man over there need to talk a little first." I squeezed a folded twenty into her cleavage.

"Thank you." She stood up, bent over one last time, glancing back at me from the side, smiling, and then walked back to the pole.

"Jesus, Cesari, how do you do that?" Vito asked, incredulity in his voice.

"Do what?"

"I'm in here every week, and she never flirts like that with me."

"Maybe it's because you got a thing going with her boss, Heidi. She probably doesn't want that kind of trouble. Or maybe you're just too ugly for words." Maybe ugly wasn't the right word. More like scary. He was a large, muscular man in his late thirties with sharp features and an oversized head that had a permanent scowl etched into it. His icy gray eyes made him seem more like an arctic wolf than a man.

"Just the same, Cesari, I want the name of your aftershave. And one more thing…?"

"Spit it out."

He hesitated. "What do I do or say if I run into Kelly?"

I sat there quietly, surprised by the question. Kelly was my ex-girlfriend. She had dumped me six months ago. She wasn't too fond of Vito because she was with me the time he tried to kill me.

I chuckled. "I'm not sure why you need instructions for that? Just act naturally if you see her."

The idea that Vito actually cared about my personal life was amusing. I was still in love with Kelly but she'd had enough of my questionable lifestyle and suspicious relationships with people like Vito. She was a nurse and had worked at the same hospital with me,

St. Matt's on Third Avenue, but after the breakup she had left to work somewhere else. I'd guessed she was having as difficult a time dealing with the separation as I was. She changed her cell phone number and didn't leave a forwarding address. She'd cut me off like a gangrenous limb.

Vito said, "I know, but she makes me nervous."

Now I did laugh. "She makes you nervous because you like her, and you feel weak around her. I know. I feel the same way."

"Yeah, but what if she asks about you? Should I tell her about Cheryl? Black women have tempers."

I had to admit, Kelly always was a little quick on the trigger. I didn't know if it had anything to do with her skin color though, but he did have a point. "Look, she dumped me, not the other way around. I'm sure she's expecting me to carry on with my life."

"Yeah, well. Maybe she is and maybe she isn't. Who caused the breakup is a matter for interpretation any way. Just because she walked away doesn't mean she wanted it to be that way."

"Well, it's not your problem so just be nice and tell her I'm fine. You don't need to go into any details of my personal life. Keep the conversation casual if it happens, and for God's sake, whatever you do, don't bring up the dog."

"Cleopatra? She's still pissed about that?"

Cleo was the 250-pound English mastiff that had saved Kelly's life and mine from one of Vito's hitmen. A judge had ordered the dog put down because she had killed the guy by ripping out his throat. Among other issues Kelly had with me was that she felt I hadn't done enough to save Cleo from lethal injection.

"Not pissed but an open wound to say the least. Just don't bring it up. She fell in love with the dog and it hurt a lot."

"All right, I won't bring it up."

"Besides, I can't believe you, Vito. At the most, Kelly's 110 pounds dripping wet and you're what, 260 pounds? And you're afraid she might lose her temper?"

Engrossed in conversation, I hadn't noticed Candy Cane returning front and center again, only this time she seemed a little pouty. She got on her knees and spread my legs apart, squeezing in between. She held my hands and looked up at me with seductive eyes. "You're not paying any attention to me," she whined.

I smiled. "Well, Candy, we're just going to have to fix that."

I heard Vito somewhere complaining.

"Fucking Cesari, how do you do that?"

Chapter 2

The bus stopped precipitously, and we lurched forward in our seats, kids and parents screaming. I looked at Cheryl for support, panic written on my face, but she appeared unconcerned. I turned my legs to the side, allowing passengers to stampede past as they dashed to the exits.

She grabbed my hand, dragging me out of my seat. "C'mon, let's go."

"I don't know about this."

"Don't be afraid, Cesari. I'll take care of you."

Outside, the temperature was a balmy seventy degrees, not a cloud in the sky. I stared at the mass of humanity racing by and winced as a baby stroller ran over my foot.

Cheryl chuckled. "You're not such a tough guy down here, are you?"

"I didn't know I was a tough guy anywhere. Where did all these kids come from?" At least eight buses had unloaded their travelers at the same time, lending to the confusion.

"What did you expect to find at Disney World the day before Christmas? Hurry, to the left, quick. That's where the shortest line is."

"I can't believe I let you talk me into this. Why aren't these kids in school? Don't they have truant officers in Florida?"

"Stop complaining. You're having fun." She was as thrilled as any one of the kids. Her blue eyes twinkled with excitement, and her cheeks were flushed.

"I am?"

We hustled to the extreme left of the massive crowd, waited patiently in line, walked through the turnstile, and entered the Magic Kingdom. It was barely nine a.m., the park was already packed, and I felt my social anxiety rearing its ugly head. This was about to be the longest day in my life.

Passing under the archway and fighting our way through the maze of people lining Main Street U.S.A., we eventually reached our destination and took a place in the line, which was already one hundred deep. Tuning out the screaming hordes as best I could, I glanced around, people watching. Cheryl beamed with joy. She hadn't been here since she was a kid and was thrilled to relive the memories. We had just arrived in Orlando last night, and this was the first day of a much needed week-long vacation.

She had been trying to get me to come with her to Disney for a while, and I finally caved. She was an attorney and had used all her powers of persuasion on me, although looking at her now in short shorts, I was pretty certain that she could've talked me into going anywhere with her. Guys are weak like that, and I was weaker than most. She had long blond hair and curves in all the right places. We had dated sporadically for the last few months, but our relationship had gone back for several years so we knew each other very well; too well to believe that this would be permanent, but we were adults and good friends and accepted the opportunity for happiness when it presented itself.

"Cheryl, tell me again why this particular ride is so special."

"My parents brought me here to celebrate my tenth birthday, and this was my favorite ride."

"You do realize that, barring parents with toddlers, we are the only adults in line, don't you?"

She slipped her arm through mine and smiled. "Yes, isn't it romantic?"

After only forty-five minutes, we passed through the gate and buckled up. I waved to the two kids sitting opposite us, and the car began its slow twirling movement up and down as it circled around its axis. Disney music played in the background, and everyone cheered. A minute and a half later, the ride came to a halt, and we piled off, allowing the next group on.

I was not impressed. "So that was the famous Teacup ride?"

"Wasn't it great? Want to go on again?" she beamed.

I studied her face carefully for signs of heat stroke. It wasn't particularly hot, but who knew? "Maybe later, okay? Let's walk around a little."

She whipped out a map of the park and gazed at it while we strolled along. When it came to vacation, she was pretty hard core, and I resigned myself to spending the entire day going on kiddie rides with her. On the other hand, the park had its perks. A babe dressed as Snow White approached us smiling. She was a knockout.

"Are you having a magical day?" She asked with a slight Spanish accent. She was about twenty years old, five feet four with stunningly beautiful features, and hair so black I couldn't help wondering if it had been given a little help to achieve that color.

"I am now, miss...?"

She curtsied. "I am Snow White." She smiled, but didn't seem happy and maintained eye contact just a little too long.

"Yes, you are, aren't you?"

"Are you Prince Charming come to rescue me?"

I smiled. "I'll be whoever you want me to be, sweetheart."

Cheryl looked up from her map. "Okay, Prince Cesari. It's not even noon and you've already found someone to flirt with."

I looked at Snow White. "I guess we know where Grumpy is."

She laughed politely. "Be careful, I heard the evil queen is lurking about." Without warning, she stepped close, placing an arm around my waist, pulling me toward her with strength I wouldn't have guessed at first glance.

Surprised by this move, I froze, waiting to see what would happen next. I looked into her eyes and saw—nothing. The lights were on but no one was home. That was peculiar. We stood there as if waiting for someone to snap a photo. The whole thing felt a little weird, but this was Disney, the home base for unusual. Cheryl didn't like what she saw but got into the spirit of the moment and snapped a quick picture with her smartphone.

I gently disengaged myself from Snow White. "Thanks for the tip about the queen."

"God bless you, Señor," she said and hurried away.

I watched her. "That was kind of strange, wasn't it?"

Cheryl looked at me crossly. "Listen, you. No more of that, okay?"

"What did I do?"

"You know exactly what you did."

"Seriously, don't you think that was odd?" I persisted.

"What, that she didn't ask you to call her later?"

"Well, that too, but I was referring to what she said. 'God Bless you, Señor.' She stepped out of character. I thought they weren't supposed to do that."

"Relax, Cesari, you're on vacation. So, she stepped out of character. C'mon, let's go find a cup of coffee, and then I want to see Cinderella's Castle." A half hour later, after slowly struggling our way through the throngs of people, we arrived at the Main Street bakery, which was mobbed to overflowing.

"I don't know how much more of this I can take, Cheryl. Everywhere we go is a thirty-minute wait, and I'm already exhausted from banging into people." I looked around. "No chance of getting a seat in here."

"I agree, it's pretty bad, but that's part of the fun."

"Oh, I see now. Then it's okay." She didn't see me roll my eyes.

Twenty minutes later, we picked out some pastries to go with our coffees. I reached into my left back pocket for my wallet, but it wasn't there. I checked the other side without any luck. My mind raced as I tried to remember if I left it back at the Old Key West apartment where we were staying. No, I definitely remembered placing it in my left rear pocket as I always did.

I turned to Cheryl. "I can't find my wallet." The long line of people behind us was starting to get restless as they sensed another delay.

"Okay, I'll pay the bill and then we'll look around." She handed the cashier a twenty, while I scanned the floor and patted myself down again.

"When did you see it last?" she asked, coming up behind me.

"I know I had it when we left the apartment, but I'm not sure after that."

"You're sure you had it when we left this morning?"

"Definitely. I counted out my cash and then put it in my back pocket."

"Hmm. Well, let's not panic. We'll retrace our steps from this morning and see if we can find it. I don't see how it could have fallen out of your pocket, but stranger things have happened. Stay calm. I'm sure it'll turn up." We ate the pastries and sipped our coffee as we ambled back to the park entrance to start the day over.

"You don't think I was pickpocketed, do you?" I asked casually, thinking about the hundreds of people I must have bumped into since I woke up this morning.

Cheryl raised her eyebrows. "No, c'mon. In Disney? Ninety percent of the people here are under the age of ten."

"I guess you never read *Oliver Twist*?"

"Oliver who...?"

"It's about a gang of underage pickpockets. Almost everyone in this park fits their description."

She laughed. "I was kidding. Of course I know the story of Oliver Twist. Now, will you stop? It's more likely sitting on the table back in the apartment where you forgot it."

"Just a thought."

"You're not in the Bronx anymore, Cesari. There aren't pickpockets lurking on every street corner here so stop worrying and relax."

"I resent the implication that I would be more likely to get pickpocketed in the Bronx than at Disney."

She refused to debate the issue any further as we scanned the ground, walking back through Main Street toward the entrance, retracing our steps. At the main gate, we continued our search for the wallet, crisscrossing paths, and after a time, our somewhat odd behavior attracted the attention of the park's security.

"Is everything all right?" A uniformed man asked, coming up behind me.

I turned around. "No, not really. I can't seem to find my wallet, and thought I may have accidentally dropped it somewhere. We were just checking all the places we had been this morning. Cheryl continued scanning the ground while I spoke.

He was nice and seemed genuinely concerned. "Sorry to hear that. Have you checked lost and found yet?"

The thought hadn't occurred to us. "No, I didn't even know there was one. Where would that be?"

He turned and pointed to the stroller and wheel chair rental concession on the far side of the entrance. "Right over there. If anybody turned it in, that's where it will be."

"Thank you. We'll go check it out."

"You're welcome and good luck."

I grabbed Cheryl's hand and headed over to lost and found. We knocked on the door and a cheerful girl greeted us. She couldn't have been more than eighteen years old. "Hope you're having a magical day."

"Well, not so far," I said. "I lost my wallet and was wondering if anybody turned it in."

She smiled broadly. "I think today is your lucky day. Someone turned in a brown wallet not more than ten minutes ago."

I glanced at Cheryl. "You're kidding?"

"Never underestimate Disney magic." She turned around and retrieved my wallet from a plastic container on a shelf. When she returned, she asked, "Can you tell me the name on your driver's license?"

"John Cesari. Dr. John Cesari."

"That would be it. What kind of doctor are you?" She handed me the wallet.

"I'm a gastroenterologist."

"What's that?"

"I take care of intestinal disorders."

"Like irritable bowel syndrome? My doctor says that's what I have. It gets worse when I'm nervous or upset. She told me I should eat more fiber like fresh fruit and vegetables."

I nodded and smiled at her. "Yeah, I would have said the same thing."

"She wants me to have a colonoscopy. What do you think?"

"I think I'm on vacation and don't want to have to charge you for a consult. Well, thanks for the wallet. Take care and good luck with the fiber."

She smiled. "I understand. Bye, and have a magical day."

I placed the wallet in my pocket as we walked back into the park. Cheryl said, "That's pretty darn amazing, if you ask me, Cesari. Only in Disney could you lose your wallet and have it show up in lost and found an hour later. Did you check it to see if anything was missing?"

I was so relieved at finding the wallet, I hadn't, so I pulled it out again. Everything seemed in place; credit cards, driver's license. I didn't see my New York State physician's photo ID though, but I couldn't quite remember the last time I actually did see it. That was something I might have left in my hospital locker back in Manhattan. I wasn't sure. Besides, why would anyone take that and leave the cash and credit cards? I pulled out the cash to count, and as I did I noticed a small folded piece of paper taped to one of the bills.

Cheryl asked. "What's that?"

"I don't know." I pulled it off the bill and unfolded it. "It's a note."

"Well what's it say? Maybe somebody wants a reward for turning it in?"

I must have looked concerned as I read it because Cheryl asked. "What's wrong, John? What's it say?"

I showed it to her, and she read it out loud. "Prince Charming, please help me. I am in great danger. Meet me in Cinderella's Castle at noon. God bless you, Señor."

She laughed. "It's just a prank. It sounds silly."

"A prank? Kind of a sick prank, don't you think?"

"Just rip it up and forget about it, Cesari. I'm sure it's nothing. Who on earth would leave a note like that if they were really in trouble?"

"Snow White for starters. She called me Prince Charming and said "God bless you, Señor," just like in this note."

Cheryl looked at the note again. "Well isn't this your lucky day? A come-on note from some hot Disney chick."

"Seriously, Cheryl, what do you think we should do?"

"I think we should just forget about it."

"I really don't think we should. It doesn't seem right."

She snapped her fingers. "I got an idea. Let's show it to the management, and maybe they'll comp us a drink for our trouble." She was very proud of herself.

I chuckled. "That's my girl. Always thinking, but as much as I'd like to laugh this off, there's something troubling about this, and in fact, there was something troubling about that girl too. She didn't seem right."

"So what are you getting at? Snow White pickpocketed your wallet to leave you a rescue note?"

"I'm not getting at anything, and I have no idea who wrote this note or why, but what if it was Snow White and she really is in trouble? You know, when we ran into her, my first impression was that she was nervous or agitated about something. The thought crossed my mind that maybe it was her first day on the job."

"Well, I didn't see that at all, but I wasn't staring at her the way you were. Besides, if she needed help or was in danger, why didn't she just say something or go to park security?"

"You're asking me to explain why a woman dressed as Snow White would act unpredictably?" I looked at my watch. "It's eleven thirty. Rather than spend an hour explaining this to security, let's go over to the castle and see what happens. You wanted to see the castle anyway."

"I'm game, but what if Snow White didn't write the note, or what if nothing happens at the castle? I'm not going to spend the whole day chasing down a prankster."

"I agree with you and I don't know why but I think she wrote it."

"You think she wrote it or you *hope* she wrote it? You know, Cesari, you have a pathologic need to rescue girls in distress."

I chuckled. "I rescued you, didn't I? If I hadn't asked you out, you'd probably be sitting around every Friday night watching TV wearing a terry cloth robe with your hair up in curlers."

She punched me playfully. "Yeah, right. Look, I'll bet you ten dollars this was just some joke."

"Well, I'm placing my money on Snow White."

"That's fine, but if she shows up that's all you better place on her. It's funny that you never seem to want to rescue ugly girls."

Chapter 3

At one p.m., Cheryl sat next to me on a wood bench. "Ready to give up?"

I nodded. "Yeah, I guess you were right. It was just a prank." We had searched Cinderella's Castle up and down, including the bathrooms, restaurants and shops, and for the last forty minutes, I had cruised back and forth in the main corridor maintaining as high a profile as possible. It was Christmas Eve, and wading like that through the sea of humanity had started to take its toll so I sat down to rest when Cheryl came over.

"Don't be disappointed, Cesari. There will be other damsels in distress for you to save."

I chuckled. "Yeah, but I wanted that one."

She poked me. "You better watch it."

I stood up, shrugged it off, and pulled her up, off the bench. "Okay, let's put it behind us. I'll drop the note off with security later just to let them know they have a comedian in the park. Where to now?"

"Lots of places. I assume you're not interested in the merry-go-round or Dumbo ride over there?"

I turned my head to the main attractions in this part of the park, the Dumbo ride and the old school merry-go-round next to it. It looked like a sixty-minute wait with toddlers and preschoolers. "No, thanks. What else is over there?"

"Peter Pan and It's a Small World. Are you hungry?"

"Not really. That danish we had was enormous. I can hang on if you can. I wouldn't mind another cup of coffee though."

"I'm fine too. Let's go to It's a Small World and then get another coffee."

"Sounds good."

We battled our way through the crowd over to the ride and simultaneously gasped when we saw the line, but thankfully the weather was nice and it seemed to move along at a fairly brisk pace. We took up position and marched slowly forward with the others. Eventually we reached a sign that read "thirty-five minutes from this point," and I groaned. A street entertainer came by and offered to perform a card trick for us, but when I went to pick a card, water shot out from the flower in his lapel into my face. Everybody in line thought that was very funny. He was lucky I was in a good mood because a guy could get hurt doing stuff like that. I could be real funny too.

As we entered the boat, Cheryl asked, "Are you mad at that guy?"

"No, why?"

"You're being awfully quiet. It was just a joke, and it really was kind of funny."

"I know. I'm laughing on the inside. That's the way we Sicilians are; very quiet laughers. We almost never kill people because of things like that."

She giggled and snuggled close to me. "I'm so glad we came to Disney. I can't wait to exchange presents tonight. Where do you want to eat dinner? On property or off?"

I thought about that while watching the other passengers in our craft settle in. It's a Small World was one of the older, simpler rides dominated by an endlessly looping sound track of catchy Disney music that had a way of making you feel good right down to the core. The boats were shallow-bottomed barges, fifteen feet long and six feet wide, holding between ten and twelve guests in rows of four. The ride wound lazily around an indoor moat about two and a half feet deep, and the crafts floated along propelled forward by a gentle man-made current. On either side of the water were mechanized puppets representing children from various parts of the world singing and dancing to the music. With a lurch, our vessel moved forward and the fun began before I had chance to answer her question about dinner.

We meandered slowly along the water, listening to the music and enjoying the show. The boat slowed and occasionally stopped at steep turns and bends. About halfway through, near the Polynesian exhibit, the vessel came to an abrupt halt as it collided with the one ahead of us. Water splashed on several of the passengers, but no one was injured, and everyone laughed with excitement.

Exuberant chatter could be heard above the din of the soundtrack as we waited patiently for the ride to continue. Gradually, other sounds started to drift toward us from the cars ahead. First there was confusion, then shouts, and finally— a bloodcurdling scream.

All the passengers jumped in alarm. "Oh my God, what's happening, John?" Cheryl clung to my arm tightly, her nails digging into my flesh. In front of us, we watched as panic-stricken adults and children jumped out of their boats into the water wading as fast as they could past us toward the rear of the column. Smaller children were either carried or sat on top of their parents' shoulders.

"I don't know." I glanced around and saw our boat emptying quickly as well. Fear was as contagious as any virus. "No one yelled 'fire,' and I don't see any smoke." The lights were turned down for the ride, but it wasn't pitch black.

"John, I'm getting very nervous. I have a bad feeling right now. Maybe we should join them and get out of here?"

"Cheryl, let's just stay calm. So far, all I see are wildebeests stampeding without a good reason."

After the last of the passengers passed by, I handed Cheryl my cell phone, stepped out of the boat, and found myself thigh high in cold water that made me grimace.

Cheryl said in alarm, "Where are you going? Don't leave me here all alone."

"You'll be fine. I'm just going up to the front to see what all the fuss is about. You don't want to come in here though, it's freezing."

"This doesn't seem very smart, Cesari."

I smiled. "If you wanted smart you should have said no when I asked you out."

She shook her head. "Hurry back and be careful."

"I will."

I struggled my way through the brisk water toward the lead boat, which was hidden from view beyond the next turn, and as I progressed, the cheerful music played eerily in the background. Making the turn, I saw the vessel swaying gently in the water. It was completely empty and otherwise ordinary. Walking slowly up the side of it toward the front end, I scanned around carefully, not sure what to expect. Eventually, however, I saw it sticking out of the water by the bow—a human hand, floating in the water and still attached to its arm. I didn't notice any voluntary movement of the hand and became alarmed, moving quickly and bracing myself for tragedy. I hoped I was in time but doubted it. The air smelled of death.

The water was too dark to try to see anything beneath the surface so I felt my way down the arm to the shoulder, and suddenly realized what had happened. The body had wedged under the low-lying boat blocking its movement, and the water was too shallow and the current too weak to power the vessel past. Did one of the guests decide to go for a swim or fall overboard? The hand was small and delicate, and I guessed it was a woman under the water. I maneuvered myself underneath her armpits and tugged, trying to pull the body away from the boat but was unsuccessful. I wasn't sure why. I tried again with a little more force and felt garments tearing. A third and much more forceful effort was rewarded with success, and I felt the body give way and float with me to the surface. I hauled her to the side of the canal, lifted her onto the stage, and felt for a pulse. Not finding one, I decided to perform cardiac resuscitation, but my instincts told me it was too late. Cold and blue it was obvious Snow White wasn't going to wake up no matter how many princes kissed her. She was still in her costume.

Fuck.

Once liberated from the obstacle, the parade of boats started to move again. Cheryl's was five back and soon approached. She looked very anxious and her eyes grew wide when she spotted me pumping on Snow White's chest and giving her mouth-to-mouth resuscitation.

"John, what should I do?"

"Stay in the boat and call for help. Tell them we have a drowning victim in full cardiac arrest." I returned to my chest compressions and watched as she drifted by horrified.

"Is that who I think it is?" She called out.

I nodded. "I'll catch up with you outside."

Ten minutes later, an EMS crew from Disney found me near total exhaustion and took over CPR. I watched them intubate and shock her as a rescue worker assisted me out through one of the maintenance doors at the back of the stage.

As I approached the main entrance I saw Cheryl waving to me with the flashing lights of police and emergency medical vehicles a short distance behind her. Disney security swarmed the area, pushing the gathering crowds back. By now, word had spread throughout the park that something bad had happened, and soon, the news vans would arrive. This was Disney, and anything that happened at Disney was big news. Snow White drowning in the It's a Small World ride was going to be very big.

Two burly guys wearing sport coats approached Cheryl and me. One offered his hand to me. "I'm Detective Diaz, and this is my partner, Detective Rodriguez." They both flashed badges. "We're with the Orlando Police Department. We'd like to ask you a few questions if you don't mind. The emergency medical techs said you found the body."

They looked like nice guys. "Sure, but do you think I could get a towel to dry off and maybe a couple of coffees. We've had quite a shock."

Diaz was about an inch shorter than me at five feet eleven; maybe 220 pounds, stocky, clean shaven, and in his late thirties. "Fair enough. Why don't you come this way?" We walked over to one of the EMS vans, and somebody produced a towel, which I used to pat myself down. Cheryl sat down on the rear bumper.

We gave him our statements about what happened in the ride but left out the part about the note or even that we had met the victim earlier in the day. No point in making this complicated.

Detective Rodriguez handed us black coffee in Styrofoam cups. Diaz wasn't happy and had a perplexed look on his face. "Let me see if I got this right. Everyone was running away from the lead boat, but you went toward it. Tell me why again."

I sipped my coffee and answered. "I didn't see any obvious danger, and I was curious."

He nodded. "And then you saw a dead hand floating in the water and instead of panicking like everyone else, you decide to extricate the corpse. You're a pretty brave guy."

"Like I said, I'm a doctor. I wasn't trying to be a hero. It's just that I couldn't be completely sure she was beyond help so I felt I should at least try to do something."

He nodded again and took notes. "You don't know who she is and never saw her before?"

"No."

"Okay, Doc. You're both free to leave, but we may have more questions for you later. How can you be reached?"

"We're staying at the Old Key West resort, right here on Disney property. We'll be here all week, in room 2525. I can write down our cell phone numbers for you."

"Thanks." He handed me a yellow pad to write on.

"So what do you think, detective?" I asked casually taking another sip of the hot liquid.

He thought it over. "Right now, based on what we know, it looks like it was probably an accidental drowning. Sounds like she fell into the water and her dress got snagged on something and then the boat came along and pinned her underneath, but we're a long way off from any final conclusions. God only knows what she was doing there in the first place."

I wrote our phone numbers down and handed him back the pad. "Will that be all, detective?"

"Yes, and Merry Christmas."

Chapter 4

*I*t was close to six by the time we got back to our room and threw ourselves on the bed, emotionally exhausted. I searched the television looking for clues. It was chaos at the park when we'd left, but it hadn't made the news cycle yet.

I said, "Interesting. There's nothing on the news about it."

Cheryl was depressed and sighed. "I guess maybe she really did write that note."

I lay back and watched the ceiling fan spin slowly around. "Yeah, I feel so bad. Like maybe we could have done something."

"John, it's not your fault or my fault. We don't even really know what happened. She may have committed suicide for all we know or maybe it was just a tragic accident."

"She didn't commit suicide, Cheryl. Why would she have gone through the trouble of stealing my wallet and leaving me a note asking for help?"

"Who knows? Maybe it was a metaphorical cry for help, not an actual one. If she was mentally unstable, then it would be almost impossible to try to rationalize her actions."

I thought about that. "Maybe true, but no one tries to drown themselves in two and a half feet of water. Not even crazy people."

"How do you know she drowned herself on purpose? She may have overdosed and fell in. She might even have been dead before she hit the water."

"Should be an interesting autopsy for sure. I wonder if I should have told the police about the note."

She rolled onto her side, looking at me. "Well, as an attorney I'd have to say that it wasn't the smartest thing to do, but it's not going to bring her back, so forget about it. If you say something now it will certainly raise eyebrows."

"Yeah, you're right. The last thing I want is for the Orlando police to start poking around in my background."

She rose off the bed, checked the time, and pushed me. "Let's get ready for dinner. There's nothing we can do by moping around."

I stood up and walked toward the bathroom. "Sure, how about Bongo's on the West Side? I read about it online. It seems like a great place for Cuban food, and I could use a strong mojito right now."

"Sounds good. Why don't you call to make a reservation?" She opened the closet door to retrieve that evening's outfit.

I glanced at my watch. "It's probably too late now."

"Try anyway, will you? At least we'll have an idea of the wait time."

I googled the number while she dressed.

****

The taxi dropped us off at the entrance to Disney's West Side, and we walked past Planet Hollywood on our way to the restaurant. The West Side was Disney's attempt to placate older teenagers and adults who grew weary of all the children's entertainment in the rest of the parks. There was a multiplex theatre, a House of Blues, a cigar store, many New York–style street performers, a Wolfgang Puck restaurant, and of course, Bongo's.

As we strolled leisurely toward it, hand in hand, I asked, "Do you have any regrets about leaving the DA's office?"

"No, I worked there ever since graduating law school. It was time for a change."

I nodded. "Well, I'm sorry, anyway."

She stopped walking and put her arms around me. "Look, Cesari, I'm a big girl, and I know what I want. If those assholes at the DA's office don't like my friends, they can blow it out their ears, okay? So don't feel guilty."

She had been an assistant DA in lower Manhattan and was considered a rising star in that department, but politics dictated that she choose her bedmates wisely. My associations with underworld figures both past and present had caused a firestorm for her at the office, and she decided that no one had the right to tell her whom she could or couldn't sleep with. So one day she flipped them the bird and took a job with a small law firm. Now she defended the bad guys rather than trying to lock them up. The difference was, as she put it, now she went to bed feeling dirty but woke up feeling rich. She was doing very well. It was amazing the piles of cash people could come up with to prevent themselves from going to jail for assorted heinous crimes.

We entered the crowded restaurant and made our way to the check-in girl at the podium. I asked. "Table for two, please?"

"I am sorry, it's at least a forty-five minute wait unless you would like a seat at the bar. We serve the full menu there as well."

Cheryl looked at me. "I thought you called ahead."

"I did. That's exactly what they told me on the phone, but I figured we'd try anyway."

She rolled her eyes. "Cesari, I'm starving. Let's sit at the bar, and promise me we won't talk about what happened at the park. I don't want to spoil Christmas Eve dinner. It's already been a rough day."

"Agreed."

The restaurant was decorated for the holiday, and strands of green and red holly draped back and forth across the room and wound up the staircase bannister leading to the second floor. The wait staff wore green elf hats and greeted us cheerfully as we walked past a Christmas tree toward the semicircular bar in the back of the restaurant. The high-backed leather swivel stools were very comfortable, and we adjusted ourselves in front of the mosaic-tiled countertop.

"We got lucky, Cesari. These are the last available seats."

"Yeah, look at how crowded it is. I think a forty-five minute wait is a bit on the optimistic side." A pretty barmaid named Sonya approached, handed us menus, and took our drink orders. We waited for our mojitos and perused the listings.

I said, "I think I'll have the hangar steak with sweet plantains, and maybe five or six mojitos. By the way, did I mention that you have great legs, counselor?" She wore a strapless, red satin holiday dress with a low neckline and black heels. Gold earrings, necklace, and a silk shawl finished off the top half, accenting her long blond hair and blue eyes. She sat with her legs crossed and way too much thigh exposed. Not that I would ever complain about something like that.

She smiled. "No, you didn't, and thank you. You don't look too shabby either. You should wear dress clothes more often." I wore a navy sport coat, slacks, and white dress shirt, but no tie. I drew the line at ties.

"You know, Cheryl, this is my first Christmas outside of New York."

"Really, how does it feel?"

"Like I need snow."

She giggled as the bartender set our drinks down and took our dinner orders. Clinking our glasses, we toasted to each other's health and prosperity. My drink was a tad too sweet, and I gulped it down like soda, immediately signaling the girl for another. I looked at her very seriously. "You can feel free to put some rum in it this time, Sonya."

Cheryl tapped me with her toe. "Do you get an endorphin rush being an asshole, Cesari?"

Sonya took it well, though. "I'll make the next one stronger for to match the big, rough, tough, American cowboy man." She pursed her ruby lips and exaggerated every word, her accent getting thicker with each syllable, causing Cheryl to burst out laughing.

She said, "Thank you for putting him in his place, Sonya. My drink is perfect."

"Gracias, Señora. I'll be right back with your drink, bub."

I turned to Cheryl. "Thanks for siding with the help."

She leaned in close, smiled, and whispered in my ear, "I can't wait to get you home, Cesari. I got plans for you."

"Humph. Making me feel bad in public doesn't exactly turn me on."

She glanced around furtively and slid her hand between my legs. "Does that turn you on?"

I looked in both directions too. "It's a start. I'll need a few more drinks, though, and then we'll talk."

She drew her hand back and punched me in the arm. We both laughed.

"You're incorrigible, Cesari."

Our meals soon arrived, and we dug in. The aroma of the charcoal-grilled hangar steak and Cheryl's paella filled our senses. "Feliz Navidad" played in the background, and before long we ordered another round of mojitos.

I looked in her eyes. "Except for the fact that a girl died this afternoon, I would say that it doesn't get any better than this."

"You promised not to ruin the night by talking about it. People die every day. You're a doctor. You should know that."

I nodded. "Roughly seven thousand people die every day across the U.S. but I'm sorry. You're right. I really am having a great time. This was a great idea, and I promise I won't bring it up again."

"Thanks." She got serious all of a sudden. "What about you, John? How are you really?"

She trained her eyes on me, and I knew exactly what she was getting at. "If you mean do I ever think about Kelly, the answer is yes, sometimes." I didn't see any point in lying. Cheryl was a grown-up and knew all about Kelly and me. It was no great secret that Kelly and I had been very close. "But if you're asking me am I over her, then the answer is also yes." Now I was lying. The pain was terrible and every day.

She searched my face looking for the truth. "I don't know what I'm getting at. I was just..." I put my arm around her and pulled her close, kissing her long and slow.

"Does that answer your questions, counselor? Why don't we just live in the here and now. It's more fun that way."

"Yeah, maybe." She smiled." I shouldn't have brought it up. Forgive me?"

I smiled back. "Depends on how nice you are to me when we get back to the room."

She lowered her eyes coyly, batting her lashes, and in the sultriest tone she could muster, whispered. "I am going to do things to you, you've only dreamt about, big boy."

I chuckled. "Perjury can get you disbarred. Did you know that?"

We finished our meal and paid the bill. I only managed to get down four mojitos and one shot of tequila, two mojitos short of my original goal, but what the heck, I needed to remain somewhat sober after a promise like that. We thanked Sonya and staggered out into the cool Florida night. It was almost eleven p.m. and sixty degrees.

"Oh my God, Cesari, look at all the people. The crowd is ten times worse than it was just a few hours ago."

"Man, you got that right." We jostled our way through the mob toward the exit.

"Do you want to catch a cab or take one of the Disney buses?"

"Let's take a cab. I don't feel like waiting for a bus."

As we walked into the parking lot, we saw the line for a taxi was at least twenty deep ahead of us. Looking over to the bus stop, we saw the Old Key West bus pulling up.

Cheryl grabbed my hand suddenly. "Change of plans, Cesari." She took off at a gallop dragging me toward the bus stop with her. We got there just in time and were the last ones to board. Out of breath, tipsy, and stuffed to the gills, we found some empty seats in the rear.

The bus doors closed, and the vehicle lurched forward, but seconds later it came to an abrupt halt as two well-dressed men banged on the windshield and door to gain access. The driver opened the door and chastised them gruffly. "I'm not supposed to stop the bus once it starts moving."

The men apologized, walked toward the rear exit, and remained standing, holding on to the metal poles by the door. They both wore dark suits, ties, and highly polished dress shoes. They seemed out of place.

One more mojito and I might not have cared, but as the bus careened around a sharp turn, one of the men's jackets opened, and I thought I caught a glimpse of a shoulder holster. I put my arm around Cheryl and nuzzled close. "Don't look now, but those guys who just got on the bus are armed."

She kissed me. "I love it when you play spy. Maybe we can do that when we get back to the room. You know, I can pretend to be a Bond girl or something, and you can be Roger Moore."

I was offended. "There's no way I'm going to be Roger Moore. I'll be Sean Connery or nobody. As far as I'm concerned, he's the only real man that ever played the role."

She chuckled. "Okay, Sean it is."

"But seriously, I think I saw a gun."

"So, this is Florida, everybody's armed here. Even better, it's Christmas Eve at Disney. They're probably security. I feel safer already knowing they're on board with us. You never know where Al Qaeda might strike next."

I looked at her seriously, trying to determine just how drunk she was. "You're really not concerned?"

She shook her head. "No, not really. I mean look at them. They're probably cops."

They were in their mid-thirties, clean shaven, well built with bland all-American features. She was right. They looked like feds. One of them took out his smartphone and told the other to pose. He pointed the camera at his friend with us in the background, and snapped a photo.

Cheryl was watching them too. "See, Cesari. They're on vacation like the rest of us."

I didn't like it. "Unless the point was to take our picture for some reason."

"My goodness, but you are exceedingly paranoid tonight. I wonder if Sonya slipped something into your drink besides rum."

I put it out of my mind partly because there was nothing more I could do and partly because my mind was semi-ossified from the alcohol. By the time we arrived at our stop, the two men, Cheryl, and I were the last remaining passengers. The two of us got off and strolled to our room while they stayed on the bus.

Once inside, I flipped the light switch on but nothing happened. It was pitch black in the room, and I assumed that housekeeping must have drawn the curtains closed while we were out because I would have expected some ambient light from outside to filter in.

"The light isn't working, Cheryl. Stay here and I'll find the floor lamp. Give me a sec."

She closed the door behind us, locking it, and followed me into the kitchen. As we stepped forward into the room, we heard the unmistakable ratcheting sound of a shotgun chambering a round. Cheryl reached out for me instinctively, and we froze in our tracks.

A powerful flashlight suddenly pierced the darkness, blinding us as a deep voice ordered. "Please sit down on the floor with your hands behind your heads and there is a chance no one will get hurt."

Cheryl didn't say anything so I placed my arm around her for reassurance. We sat slowly down on the tiled surface of the kitchen floor, and I hazarded a question. "May I ask what this is all about?"

"I told you to place your hands behind your head." The voice was polite and seemed highly educated with perhaps a slight Spanish accent. This wasn't your typical home invasion.

Cheryl was starting to get indignant. "Who are you and what do you want? This isn't fair." She had raised her voice and in response there was muffled sound.

Cheryl cried, "Ouch!" And I saw a tranquilizer dart sticking out of her chest. She looked at me wide-eyed with fear as I pulled the dart out of her quickly, leaving a tiny dribble of blood to stain her dress. "Johnny, what's happening…?" She stared at me confused for a few seconds and then her eyes rolled up as she lost consciousness, collapsing into my arms. I gently laid her down into a more comfortable position, cradling her head in my lap.

"That was unnecessary," I said calmly.

"I'll decide what is unnecessary. Understood? Besides, I am an excellent marksman and could just as easily have put the dart in her eye. Now put your hands back behind your head."

I clasped my hands behind my head. "Understood, but her question was reasonable. What do you want?"

"I want to know why you killed my baby girl today, Dr. Cesari?"

Chapter 5

I didn't see any point in pretending I didn't know what he was talking about. "I'm very sorry about your loss, but I didn't kill your baby girl. In fact, I tried to save her. Besides, the police think it may have just been an accident."

"It was no accident Dr. Cesari. I don't believe that for a minute and neither do you. That doesn't even make sense given where they found her. So please, don't insult my intelligence again."

"Look, I know what you're saying but all I can tell you is that I'm here on vacation, and that's all. I didn't kill anybody."

"Then why was your New York State physician's ID found in her possession?"

He caught me off guard with that and I momentarily hesitated. "I didn't even know my ID was missing until just now. I don't know the reason for that, but maybe I dropped it when I pulled her out from under the boat." I heard Cheryl's breathing next to me. She was out cold.

"You didn't just drop it accidentally so choose your next words carefully. Why was your ID found on my dead daughter?"

"How do you know I didn't drop it? You weren't there."

The voice got angry. "Because it was tucked inside her bra, *pelotudo*. Now, you get one more chance to answer the question before you get a dart in the neck and a ride in the trunk of my car." I wasn't sure what *pelotudo* was but it sounded a lot like asshole.

"Wait, wait, I remember now." I stammered. "Earlier today, I lost my wallet, and when I recovered it at the lost and found, the ID was missing. I couldn't remember whether I had left it in New York or not.

Maybe your daughter found it and was planning on returning it to me. A lot happened today, and it slipped my mind."

I felt the tension ease a little as he digested that. "You lost your wallet or was it stolen?" He seemed genuinely curious.

"I don't know. The thought crossed my mind that I had been pick-pocketed, but none of the money or credit cards were missing. In retrospect that's probably when my ID went missing, but I don't see how this is important."

"My daughter is found dead in one of the park rides with nothing on her but your ID and you don't think how she may have gotten it is important? How can I be sure she didn't grab it while she was fighting you off?"

"That's not what happened, and once again, I'm very sorry about your loss, but I just happened to be there when she turned up. It's not clear to me why she would put the ID in her bra." This wasn't going well at all.

"I'm going to ask you another question, and you'd better give me the right answer." He paused, and a floor lamp turned on, illuminating the room, revealing a well-dressed middle-aged man with a graying beard sitting opposite me on one of the dining room chairs. He held the dart gun in his hands, and next to him was a tall, statuesque woman, maybe thirty years old with long black hair and sharp features. She was attractive in a dangerous way and looked as if she had just stepped off a catwalk. Dressed completely in black—shoes, jeans, and turtleneck—she looked like a sexy commando. She held a pump-action shotgun, with a flashlight and laser attachment, trained on me. It wasn't an ordinary shotgun you might buy at Walmart. It had a tactical scope and silencer. This chick was loaded for bear. She reached to the end of the weapon and turned the flashlight off.

They both studied me carefully. The man said, "Did you have a relationship with my daughter?"

What did he mean by that?

"No, I met her for the first time this morning. We were walking through the park when we ran into her. She was in character and took a picture with us."

"Did she try to speak to you or contact you after that?"

I took a deep breath and let it out slowly. I really didn't want to tell him about the note. It could easily be interpreted the wrong way, like maybe we knew each other better than I was letting on, but I was rapidly running out of options. His questions were getting very direct. "Can I put my hands down? They're getting tired."

The girl with the shotgun came to attention aggressively, taking a step closer to me. "I wouldn't."

The older man said, "Consuela, let us not overreact. Go ahead, Dr. Cesari, relax your arms, but don't move otherwise. So did she try to contact you?"

I looked at Cheryl who seemed all right. I nodded. "I think so. When I recovered my wallet from the lost and found, there was a note in it that I believed was from her saying she was in danger and asking me to meet her in Cinderella's Castle. I believed the note was from her because of the language that was used. We went to the castle and searched but couldn't find her. We eventually concluded that it must have been a joke."

Consuela flashed an angry look in my direction. "He is lying, Raul. Marguerite would never do that. We should kill him now, please."

Jesus Christ, she wanted my blood for some reason, but Raul looked puzzled. "Patience, Consuela. I agree, it does seem unlikely for her to do that, but then again, who knows?"

I squirmed. "I don't understand. Which part is hard to believe?"

Consuela took another step and the barrel was inches from my face. I thought about making a move to disarm her. It was tempting but too risky with Cheryl lying there unconscious. She said, "Marguerite would never ask to meet anyone in the castle."

I must have looked bewildered. Did these two just fall off a truck loaded with LSD? "And why is that?" I asked calmly.

Raul stood up. "Because, Dr. Cesari, my daughter hated Cinderella."

I was speechless. Maybe the girl did commit suicide, after all. If this was her family, it's quite possible she was genetically insane.

"Do you still have the note, Doctor?"

"It's in my wallet. Can I get it?"

"Are you armed?"

"No."

"Then show it to me, and please move very slowly. As you can see, Consuela has her own opinion on how to proceed with this interview." I retrieved the note and gave it to him. He read it, and his features changed. He seemed older as he handed the note to Consuela.

"Consuela, put the gun down. The note is truly from Marguerite. It is in her hand-writing and style of speech. She always ended her conversations with "God bless you, Señor or Señora." Even with me she would say that."

Consuela was unconvinced. "This note does not prove that he is innocent."

"No, it does not, but it certainly means that until this morning he had not met Marguerite. I believe you, Dr. Cesari, and I owe you a debt of gratitude for at least trying to help my daughter. I have heard how you tried to resuscitate her." Consuela reluctantly lowered the weapon, although she remained vigilant.

"May I stand, and move her off the hard floor?" I pointed to Cheryl.

Raul said, "Yes, we will help you."

Together, we carried Cheryl over to the couch and lay her down more or less comfortably.

"So who are you?" I asked as we sat around the living room.

"I am Raul Varga, and this is Consuela my—assistant."

I nodded and noticed that she sat to one side of me with the gun pointed casually in my direction, just in case. She wasn't taking any chances. "I meant who are you really, and how did you get into my apartment?"

He hesitated. "I do not have an official title. Suffice it to say that I wear many hats, one of which is general consultant to Disney Corporation."

"You work for Disney?" I was incredulous.

"Not exactly, Doctor. Let's just say that we are mutually invested in each other's ongoing prosperity. I advise Disney on—certain global business opportunities as they arise so that they might be in a position to take advantage of the situation, and they in turn reward me handsomely including giving me wide latitude of operation when on their properties both here and abroad."

I let that sink in. "It sounds like you're a pretty big deal. So how important are you? You know, compared to the guy who runs Disney World here in Orlando, let's say." I was genuinely curious and he didn't seem to mind talking, but why should he? He had all the guns.

Both he and Consuela smirked. He said, "If I thought the man who ran Disney World needed to be fired, I'd have to call someone first to find out his name."

"Okay, that's pretty big, but why does it give you the right to break into my room on Christmas Eve? And where did you get military-grade weapons? Did they just happen to be lying around Epcot?"

"I am sorry about the intrusion, but try to understand. As the night unfolded, I was considering the possibility that you were the deranged murderer of my daughter. As far as the weapons are concerned, consider this. Theme parks are only part of what Disney does. To say the least, it is an extremely diverse organization."

"Are you telling me that Disney is in the arms business, and you just happen to travel armed to the teeth?"

"Disney is like any other business and likes to keep its mind open to profitable enterprises, and men in my position cannot afford to be too cavalier about their personal safety."

"And you were going to kill me yourself, just like that? Wouldn't that have been a little risky?"

"If I only wanted to kill you, it would not have been Consuela and I here, but rather several of my more unpleasant employees who are now waiting for me in the car outside. I wanted to ask you personally about my daughter. What kind of mood she was in? What she said to you before she died? Did she ask for me? Was she happy? Did you make her happy? Why would you kill someone who is obviously so harmless?" He began to choke up.

Consuela placed a hand on his shoulder. "Raul...don't do this to yourself."

"I am all right, Consuela. As far as killing you goes, don't be so outraged. What would you have done to the man you believed murdered your daughter?"

He had a valid point. I sighed. "I understand. So what's this thing with Cinderella? Why did Marguerite hate her?"

He sighed deeply, and I saw the worry lines of a grief-stricken father etched deeply into his face. "It is a long story, and considering what you have been through, I feel you have earned the right to hear it. Marguerite was a deeply troubled young woman. As a child in Buenos Aires, she had a perfectly normal life until about thirteen years of age, when she developed an obsession with Disney characters, particularly Snow White. Little by little, she became convinced she was Snow White. We took her to the best psychiatrists in my country and then yours, but little helped, and her delusions grew." He turned his head away almost overwhelmed by his emotions.

Consuela said softly, "It's okay, Raul."

"My darling, Consuela, it is time to let it out. I have held it in way too long." He turned back to me. "When traditional psychotherapy failed, and to my everlasting shame, I had my daughter institutionalized for a whole year in Zurich, where she received experimental electroshock therapy. Those maniacs almost killed her when they provoked intractable seizures."

Consuela said, "Don't blame yourself. It was not your fault. You did not know what they were going to do to her, and those doctors at that clinic will never hurt anyone—ever again."

"I know Consuela. You did the right thing. You are a great comfort to an old man."

I sat there mesmerized. These two were off the charts crazy—and dangerous.

"Anyway Dr. Cesari, I no longer had it in my heart to keep my beautiful little girl locked up like an animal so I decided that, rather than break her of her delusion, I would contain it."

"By pulling strings and getting her a job as Snow White?" I asked.

"Exactly. She could walk around the park all day in character, and no one but a select few would know the truth. I had people keeping an eye on her for me, of course, and periodically, Consuela and I would drop in to check on her."

I nodded. "So you have eyes on her? Then they must have seen her approach me this morning."

"Yes, but they didn't see her pick your pocket. She was very good at that sort of thing, and spent much time with the magicians here learning sleight of hand. And she approached many men, not just you; that was part of her complex delusion. To her, every man was a potential Prince Charming who would one day rescue her. When she would meet someone new, she would pass him a note like she did to you and ask him to come save her. It was her way of testing their worthiness. She only did it the first time she met someone so unless you saved that note from a previous encounter, which I don't think is likely, you must have just met her for the first time this morning like you said."

I sat there quietly. "So what would happen when they came looking for her?"

"Most wouldn't. They usually thought it was a prank and ignored it. Those who did would be rewarded with a kiss, and then she would run away. As she matured, however, her desire for more than just a kiss grew, and she would occasionally...."

"He doesn't need to know this," Consuela advised.

He nodded but continued anyway as a tear ran down his cheek. "Her antipathy for Cinderella developed out of what the psychology books call sexual competition. She believed Cinderella was trying to steal her prince from her, which is why it would have been very strange for her to ask to meet you at the castle, or as she called it, *the lair of the beast.*"

I thought that over. "So for her to ask me to meet her there meant something had changed recently with the way she saw things."

"Yes, Doctor. Something had changed. She had been sending out distress signals for the last several months, but we have had a difficult time interpreting whether they were real or just a changing pattern to her delusion."

"What do you mean by distress signals? Do you mind sharing with me? I might be able to help."

They looked at each other and Raul nodded. Consuela said, "Did she mention to you anything about the evil queen?"

"Yes, she did. She said, 'be careful, the evil queen is lurking about.' We thought she was talking about the queen in the story of Snow White."

"No, she was talking about me," Consuela said. "She called me the evil queen because I was always checking up on her to make sure she was all right. I have an apartment on Disney property to be near to her. She hated my being around because it threatened her delusion, but at least she allowed me into her life to some degree. Well, for the last few months, she had been claiming to have finally found the real prince charming, and that he was going to take her home to his castle. As you might imagine, we weren't sure what to think. Many men had taken advantage of her over the last few years, and there was very little we could do to intervene other than make sure she regularly visited her doctors."

Raul continued the story. "Mental health is a—complicated issue as I'm sure you are aware, Doctor."

"I'm very aware of that." I had been to many psychiatrists myself over the years. "And you thought maybe I was one of her lovers, and that maybe she had finally hooked up with a psychopathic killer?"

"Exactly. At first, we didn't lend too much credence to her ranting about prince charming until the last few weeks when she started behaving very erratically, even for her. She genuinely seemed afraid of something or someone. My first reaction was that her condition was deteriorating and she was becoming paranoid. Last week, one of the park's guests complained to management that Snow White had offered him sex if he would help her escape from the park. She did this in front of his wife and three children. I was in Baghdad with Consuela at the time, conducting—delicate business. We returned as soon as we could and had barely got off the plane when my sources inside the Orlando Police Department alerted me to the news of my daughter's death and the fact that your ID was found on her."

"You have people inside the Orlando P.D.?"

"I have many friends inside the Orlando Police Department. They, like everyone else in this state, owe their financial well-being to Disney and therefore, in no small part, to me. I was able to persuade them to allow me to speak to you first before they brought you in for questioning."

"What do you mean, 'Bring me in for questioning'? They already questioned me."

"That was before they found your ID on my daughter's body."

I didn't like where this was heading. "What would they have done if you had killed me?"

Consuela chuckled. "Then the crime would have been solved. They already believe that you killed her, and so over-whelmed with guilt were you, that you committed suicide, taking your lover with you. Most police see the world simply, in black and white. Open and shut cases appeal to them. Especially the Orlando police, whose pension is almost entirely funded by Disney."

Jesus, was there anything or anybody Disney didn't have in its pocket? I sighed deeply. "Well, I'm sorry to hear all of this, and I wish I could help you, but I don't know what more I can do to shed light on what happened today."

Raul sat back, crossing his legs, mulling things over as he rubbed his beard. "Dr. Cesari, I think maybe we can help each other, if you are agreeable."

I fidgeted uncomfortably in my chair. "And how is that?"

"My daughter Marguerite saw something in you that made her think you could help her, and your actions in the park clearly confirm her instincts in that regard. I would like your assistance in finding her killer."

"I don't think you understand. I'm just a gastroenterologist not a private investigator."

"Dr. Cesari, you are no more just a gastroenterologist than I am just another suit working for Disney. I believe you are much more than that. In the hours leading up to our arrival here, I performed a back-ground check on you. You have an arrest record for assault, extortion, and numerous other violations of civilized behavior. There are many in the New York law enforcement community who believe you have literally gotten away with murder."

I gulped. "I was never convicted, and that was before I went to medical school."

"You are still associated with a Mr. Vito Gianelli, a well-known New York underworld figure, are you not?"

He did his homework. "Yes, I am, but only because we knew each other from way back, and I don't see how that means I can help you."

"What it means is that you are not only capable of discretion but are used to bending the rules to achieve an end, and I find that quality frequently helpful in delicate situations such as this."

"What are you getting at?"

"I will not allow my daughter's killer to stand trial and make a mockery of her condition for the entire world to laugh at."

"I'm not an assassin for hire."

"I do not want you to assassinate anyone. I will take care of that, but I think you are in a position to aid me in the investigation, and I am in a position to persuade the Orlando police that you had nothing to do with the crime. This is Disney and they will be eager to find closure so that business can continue as usual, which means that you would make a convenient scapegoat."

"You seem to be forgetting one thing—that I'm innocent."

"The world's prisons are filled with innocent men and women. I don't think that argument would be much of a defense in this situation."

"You're being awfully cynical, don't you think?"

"Am I?"

"Don't you have plenty of resources at your disposal? Why do you need me?"

"I cannot actively participate in the investigation of my daughter's death. That would be seen as inappropriate as well as a conflict of interest. I, too, have people I have to answer to. It would also attract unwanted attention to my business interests both here and abroad. No, I need someone competent on the ground who can report back to me. I will supply you with as much information as I have, but after tonight, we will never meet again. Consuela will act as a go between when necessary. Do you accept my offer?"

"What offer?"

"In exactly one hour the Orlando P.D. will be coming to pick you up for questioning. You lied to them about ever meeting my daughter before finding her body, and yet there are surveillance photos of you talking to her in the park earlier in the day. Your physician's ID was found in an intimate location on her body, and you were the last one to touch her before the police arrived. One might conjecture that you were using that time to search for your missing ID. Add that to your criminal past, and it wouldn't be too hard to convince either the police or a jury of your guilt."

I fidgeted uneasily in my chair. "Or I help you find the real killer, and you dispatch him yourself in which case I'm an accessory to premeditated murder."

"Let's not split hairs, Dr. Cesari. If a man deserves to die and then is found dead, is that really murder? It is moral ambiguity at best. Besides, the question of your guilt would only come up if someone finds out, and I have no intention of speaking of this ever again—to anyone. What about you Consuela?"

She pointed the shotgun at me. "Let me kill him now, Raul, I beg you."

I looked at him. "I thought this was the happiest place on earth."

Chapter 6

*M*y head throbbed and my vision blurred as Detective Diaz wound up to hit me again. This time he punched me on the left side of my jaw, and I spit blood to my right. "That's for lying to me, *culero*." That sounded a lot like *pelotudo*.

"It was a misunderstanding. I didn't realize it was the same girl." I was sitting in an interrogation room at the Orlando police station on Hughey Avenue in downtown Orlando. I had been there since two a.m., when they came and picked me up in a squad car. Raul had warned me not to name-drop or I would never see daylight again.

The door opened and a redheaded guy walked in. "That's enough, Diaz. Get Rodriguez and file your reports. I'll take it from here." He turned toward me. "Okay, Cesari. Let's get something perfectly clear from the start."

"What's that?" I asked shaking the cobwebs from my head and licking blood from my lip.

The room was quite small with two chairs and a table. He sat down opposite me on a metal folding chair that groaned under his bulk. "I don't like you. I think you're a punk from the Bronx, and I'm not sure what mail-order school you got your degree from, but you're in my town now, and you lied to my detectives yesterday. You know what that means?"

"Why don't you spell it out for me?" He was a big guy, in his forties, with graying hair and a nose that looked like it had been broken once or twice. He was a little out of shape and wore a suit and tie. I guessed he was in charge of the investigation, but I didn't see an ID badge.

"It means that if I feel like it, I'll squeeze your balls so hard, your dick will fall off."

"Okay, so now that we understand each other, if your guys would stop punching me, I'll try to cooperate."

"You'll cooperate whether they stop punching you or not." To emphasize his point he slapped me with the back of his hand.

My face stung from the blow. "Haven't you ever heard of the United States Constitution?"

"And haven't you ever heard of probable cause?"

"Look, I've told you all I know, and I'm sorry I misled the officers yesterday, but it was unintentional. There was a lot of confusion, and I made an honest mistake. I met the girl briefly, and we took a photo together like thousands of other park guests. I forgot all about it. How she got a hold of my ID and why she held onto it is as much a mystery to me as it is to you. That's all there is to the story." I didn't think it would aid my cause to accuse Sow White of being a delusional pickpocket.

"Let's take it from the top one more time, Cesari. Tell me what happened from the minute you woke up yesterday morning, and don't leave out any details."

"Are the handcuffs really necessary?" My hands had been cuffed tightly behind my back for the last two hours, and I had lost feeling in them ten minutes ago. It was almost four a.m., and I was worried that the tranquilizer Cheryl had been shot full of would be wearing off soon. Raul said it would last anywhere from two to four hours. My absence would only add to her confusion and fear when she woke.

He looked like he was about to slap me again when his cell phone rang. "Hello, Conley here." He listened for a minute, and his features darkened.

"The fuck I will. This is my collar, and no one can make me do that!" he yelled into the phone and listened some more. Frustrated, he hung up and turned to me red in the face.

"Who the fuck are you?"

"Just a punk from the Bronx."

He studied me carefully, clearly trying to decide whether to hit me again, but he seemed to get himself under control. "Why did the chief of the Orlando Police Department just order me to release you on your own recognizance?"

"You'd have to ask him that."

He suddenly slapped me again, and I guess I pushed him too far that time. He said, "Come with me, asshole."

I "accidentally" walked face first into the still closed metal door on the way out, and Conley smirked, "Sorry about that, but you should be more careful."

Handcuffed, he led me to an office two flights up where I met Chief Patterson. The handcuffs were removed and Conley, in one final act of defiance, pushed me roughly into a chair. Patterson sat behind his desk and glared at me without saying anything. He was fat, ruddy-faced, fair skinned, and bald. He looked about mid-fifties and like he drank at least two martinis with a twenty-ounce medium rare T-bone every day for lunch.

"That'll be enough, Conley. You can leave now."

He slammed the door on the way out. "I'm Chief Patterson, it's almost four-thirty in the morning, and I don't get it."

"Get what?"

"Why half the fucking state of Florida is awake talking about you."

"I have no idea."

"Do you know how many times in my career the mayor has called me at this hour and ordered me to get out of bed?"

I shook my head.

"This is the first. And do you know why?"

"I really don't."

"Because the governor woke him up, that's why. All to tell me to let you walk out of here scot-free, immediately. Which begs the question of just who the fuck are you? And why does anyone give a shit about whether you spend the night in lockup?"

"Maybe everyone thinks I'm innocent and that you should be out looking for the real killer?" I tried to sound reasonable.

He slammed his hand down on his desk and yelled, "Don't play games with me you Snow White murdering wop son-of-a-bitch!

You're as guilty as sin and you know it. You murdered that poor girl, and you're going to pay for it. I don't know what's going on right now but I'll sort it out soon enough. Do you have any idea what you've done, you stupid fuck?"

"Please enlighten me."

"You murdered one of Disney's most beloved characters in the world's most cherished theme park. Snow White is the symbol of all that is good and great about this country."

Oh brother, another Kool Aid drinker. I swear to God, the water supply in this state must be contaminated.

He continued. "The entire country is going to be out for blood over this, and the fact that you did it in the middle of the day on Christmas Eve with thousands of little kids watching is only going to fuel their anger. Do you have any idea the kind of shit I'm going to get for letting our only suspect loose? I'll be shocked if everyone doesn't just cancel their reservations and leave Orlando. Maybe that was your plan, to destroy Disney? Maybe you're one of those anti-American loons who just can't leave things alone and let people be happy. Maybe you're a terrorist? Maybe you're a goddamn liberal? I don't know."

This guy was a little overtired. I swallowed a salty mixture of saliva and blood. "I'm sorry about what's going on and the effect it may have, but I really am innocent. I feel as bad about what's going on as anyone else."

His ruddy face turned eight shades of purple as he stood up, towering over me. "If you say you're innocent one more time I'm going to come over there and strangle you myself, and the mayor can go fuck himself."

I didn't say anything.

"This is the deal, asshole. The mayor wants to treat this like an unfortunate work-related accident until the official autopsy report comes back in a few days. If it's declared a homicide, we are going to reconvene this little discussion again, only next time we're not going to be so nice."

He reached down and retrieved a plastic bag with my cell phone, wallet, and belt in it. He tossed them on the floor in front of me and picked up his desk phone, calling in a uniformed officer.

"Uncuff him and escort him out, and I won't be upset if he trips down the stairs on the way." I cleared my throat to speak, but he signaled me that I had better not, so I didn't.

"Get the fuck out of my office, Cesari, and don't leave Orlando." As I turned to exit the room, he added, "Have a magical day, asshole."

I took a cab back to Old Key West and found Cheryl on the sofa, sitting up, looking half awake and very confused.

"My chest hurts, and what happened to your face? In fact what happened, period? I can't seem to remember anything since dinner last night, and why am I still wearing my dress?" She rubbed her eyes, yawned, looked down, and saw a spot of blood and the dart hole in the dress. She got upset. "What the hell happened to me? Hey, wait a minute. I'm starting to remember now. There were people here when we got home, weren't there?"

I sat next to her and gave her a gentle kiss. "Yes, there were. Why don't you clean up while I make us some coffee, and then I'll fill you in. It's a long story. There's going to be a bruise on your chest so don't be alarmed. There's an explanation for that. Merry Christmas, by the way."

"Oh yeah, I almost forgot. Merry Christmas."

Chapter 7

Sipping her coffee quietly, Cheryl mulled over the situation. We were sitting on the terrace watching an old couple struggle down the fairway of the public golf course that ran through the heart of the Old Key West resort. When we first learned the apartment was just off of one the fairways, it seemed like a great idea until errant golf balls started bouncing on the tin roof of the building. It was disturbing to wake up to a sound that was very similar to someone beating on a metal trash can with a bat. Even worse was that our apartment was situated on the first hole. People hadn't even had a chance to warm up, and the ones we were observing at the moment were worse than the usual. The woman waved to us as she swung and missed for the third time.

I looked at Cheryl. "How hard can it be to hit the stupid ball?"

"Obviously, you've never tried. It can be very frustrating."

I grunted, neither agreeing nor disagreeing.

Cheryl sighed. "Okay, enough with the small talk. It's not making me feel any better. Let's review what we know, who are the players, and what can we really do?"

I nodded. This was our third time around. "This guy Raul and his assistant Consuela were waiting for us in the room when we arrived home last night."

"Assistant?"

"That's what he called her but they seemed a lot chummier than that if you know what I mean."

She nodded. "I get it. So he's the asshole who shot me with the dart?"

"Yes."

"And he claims to be some sort of advisor or consultant for Disney, but he's actually some shadowy mover and shaker?"

"The impression I got was that we'll never find his name on any official Disney payroll, if that was his real name."

"Great, and his daughter was crazy and really believed she was Snow White?"

"Even worse, the Consuela woman is just as nuts and likes to play with guns. He had to talk her out of killing me. She was really into it."

"Humph, and she doesn't even know you."

"Thanks. By the way, you speak a little Spanish, right?"

"I can count to ten pretty easily, why?" She actually minored in Spanish in college and had spent six months abroad to gain proficiency.

"What do *pelotudo* and *culero* mean?"

She laughed. "*Culero* and *pelotudo* are the equivalent of asshole. *Pelotudo* is what somebody from Argentina might say, and *culero* is what they would use in Puerto Rico and Cuba. Why?"

"Oh nothing, I was just curious. Just brushing up on my Spanish is all."

"Uh huh, right. So, where do we stand right now?"

"Well where we stand right now is that the Orlando police believe that I'm the killer. They're calling it an accident pending the autopsy report but no one believes it. Raul has friends in very high places because they woke up the chief of police at four a.m. and ordered him to release me. I'm not supposed to leave Orlando until they say it's okay, but I'm not sure they can really stop me. I haven't been charged with anything but that could change in a heartbeat pending the outcome of the autopsy, which will be expedited because everyone wants closure on this thing as quickly as possible. If it's ruled a homicide then the only thing that will save me is if I can figure out who really killed her."

"You would think that they would be rooting for this to be an accident and not murder."

"Not necessarily. Believe it or not a murder that can be solved quickly would be better for business rather than suggesting the rides themselves can be dangerous to your health. Remember, no one expects to drown on a kiddie ride."

Cheryl shook her head. "Oddly enough that sort of makes sense."

"It sure does, especially if the murderer is some lowlife from the Bronx with a prior criminal record. I can just see it now, 'Don't worry folks, we got him and he's rotting away in some cell in the Everglades.'"

"Well, as long as you put it that way. So what's the plan?'

"It's quite simple. Raul doesn't think I'm guilty, and he wants me to cut through the red tape to find her killer, but either way, for the sake of public appearance, someone's going to go down for the crime and both the police and Consuela have voted me that guy, unless of course by some small miracle, it really was an accident."

"How much time do you have?"

"Raul is giving me a week. That's all he's going to be able to hold off the police if the autopsy shows she was murdered. If at the end of that time, I can't turn over to them a credible suspect, they're going to charge me with her murder and Disney is going to throw every ounce of its might into convicting me with Raul's blessing. Someone has to go to jail so it might as well be me, but that's not the best part."

"Oh, there's more?"

"Consuela assured me that if by some strange twist of fate I manage not to get convicted she may come find me in the middle of the night to make sure justice is carried out."

Cheryl finished her coffee and placed the cup down in front of her. "Does this mean we're not going to the Animal Kingdom today?"

Her hair was still wet from the shower, and she looked cute. Pissed but cute. I said, "If you don't mind, I think I've already met enough animals for one day."

She was not amused. "Very funny. So where do we begin?"

"Before he left, Raul gave me the key to Marguerite's apartment here on Disney property. It's taped to the underside of the kitchen table. I didn't want the police to find it, and I wasn't sure how aggressive they were going to be when they came for me."

She looked around. "It doesn't look like anything's been touched."

"No, the officers who picked me up were very civilized. They called me on my cell phone, and I met them outside when they arrived.

They didn't even ask for you. It wasn't until I got down to the station that things got—uncomfortable."

She came closer and inspected my face more carefully. "Does it hurt?"

"Only constantly."

"I'll make an ice pack for you. Maybe you should lie down. You must be exhausted."

I was, and I soon passed out on the couch with a plastic bag filled with crushed ice on my face. Cheryl was curled up in a nearby chair reading a novel when I woke several hours later. I jumped up, blinked away the sleepies, and ran my hand through my hair. "What time is it?"

She looked at her watch, glanced at the wall clock, and then stared at my wristwatch. "Almost four, sleepy head. How do you feel?"

"I'm starving and my face hurts."

"Why don't you clean up, and we'll go find some place to eat."

I showered quickly and shaved, observing my bruised face in the mirror. When this was over, Detective Diaz and I were going to have a long talk. Dressed in jeans, sneakers, and a cotton T-shirt, I grabbed my windbreaker and met Cheryl in the living room, ready to go.

"Where to, Cesari? And don't say the Magic Kingdom. I'm not ready to go back there."

"Okay, then I won't say it, but that's where we have to go unless you want me to spend the rest of my life in prison. We can grab a hot dog at Casey's on Main Street, and then I want to start interviewing some of Snow White's coworkers. They might know something."

"What do you hope they'll tell you that they haven't already told the police?" As we walked outside, the bus to the Magic Kingdom stopped in front of us and we boarded, taking seats in the rear, facing forward.

"If you mean the keystone cops in Orlando, do you really think they were listening carefully to anybody after they found my ID on her? I doubt it." We watched as other guests took their seats. The last two passengers to enter the bus were the same two men I saw the previous night when we left Bongo's. They were dressed a bit more casually today, two-piece suits instead of three, and sat opposite each other toward the front rather than standing by the rear door. Maybe I was getting paranoid, but they just didn't seem right.

I was about to put it behind me when Cheryl leaned close. "Aren't they the two guys we saw yesterday? The ones you said were armed?"

"Yeah, I was just thinking the same thing. Quite a coincidence, no?"

"Maybe—maybe not."

"Then why'd you bring it up?"

"I don't know. I guess they do seem a little odd, but it's probably nothing."

"So they're not following us?"

She looked at them carefully. "They can't be very bright if they are. I mean who wears a suit at Disney? Now that I think of it, that's a terrible disguise, so therefore, they can't possibly be following us."

I liked her explanation. "That settles it then. Let's forget about them." We arrived at the Magic Kingdom at six, grabbed a couple of hot dogs, and meandered toward Cinderella's Castle. The park was just as crowded despite the recent tragedy, and there was no outward sign that anyone was letting the tragedy ruin their vacations. It was Christmas at the Magic Kingdom, and everyone was having a grand time.

Looking around while I ate, I was impressed. "Boy, Disney doesn't miss a beat. It's barely twenty-four hours since Snow White is found dead, and it's back to business as usual. It seems as if no one even knows what happened."

She took a bite of her hot dog. "Maybe they don't."

"Maybe they don't what?"

"Maybe they don't know what happened."

"How could they not know? There were dozens of witnesses, news vans, and police vehicles."

"If Disney can wake up the governor at four a.m., don't you think they can squash a negative news story, at least temporarily until all the facts are in?"

Interesting. I hadn't thought of that. Maybe that's why I didn't see anything about it on TV last night. The death of Snow White had consumed my life, and I just assumed it had everyone else's as well. I pulled out my cell phone and googled Disney, Orlando, and Snow White. Nothing unusual. A few hits on Snow White's latest appearances and some minor changes to her gown. There was going to be another limited DVD release of the classic movie. That was it.

"You're right, Cheryl. There's nothing in the news about her death. I mean, this should have been national news if not international. Man, these guys have clout to be able to shut down a story like this."

"Which means you'd better be worried if they decide to come after you."

"I already am worried. Still, everyone who works here at the park must know what happened, and what about all those guests that were on the ride?"

She wiped a bit of mustard from her face. "That's a tough one. How do you keep so many people so quiet? I don't know."

We entered the castle and walked around aimlessly browsing through shops, hoping for an idea. I picked up a Mickey key chain and paid for it at the register. The middle-aged woman gave me my receipt.

I said, "It's a shame about what happened yesterday."

"What happened yesterday?" the cashier asked.

"You know, what happened at It's a Small World."

She looked at me blankly. "I'm not sure what you mean, sir. Was there a problem at the ride? I heard it was closed down temporarily for a scheduled maintenance, but that was just for a short time."

"Oh, is that all it was? That must have been it then. We'll try again today. Well, thank you."

"And you have a magical day."

I turned to Cheryl perplexed. "You have got to be kidding me. They're telling everyone the ride was shut down for maintenance and people are buying it?"

As we talked, we walked over to the Dumbo ride, which was packed as usual. A guy was selling peanuts nearby and I purchased a bag. "I guess all the employees are pretty upset today, huh?"

He nodded and glanced in both directions. "Who wouldn't be? I don't mind working Christmas but the least they could do is pay us double time. And then they warn us not to wish anybody Merry Christmas because it might offend non-Christians. Can you believe that? Mickey Mouse is dressed up as Santa Claus, Christmas music is being piped in continuously to every corner of the park, there's a fully decorated Christmas tree in every store, but I could get fired for saying 'Merry Christmas.' It's just not right."

"No, it isn't. Well I hope your day looks up."

"Thank goodness it's almost over. Well take care and enjoy your peanuts."

I started to walk away but hesitated and turned back to him. "Hey, pal?"

"Yes, sir?"

"Merry Christmas."

This brought a big smile to his face. "Thank you and the same to you."

We spent about a half an hour talking to employees like that, but none of them knew anything about what happened yesterday or knew Snow White personally.

Cheryl said, "Fascinating. Either no one knows or this is the best cover-up the world has ever seen."

"This is truly peculiar. I would've thought that, at the very least, the employees would have been buzzing about it. Let's head over to It's a Small World."

"So what do you think?" Cheryl asked.

"I'm not sure. They could have offered people bonuses, free park passes, anything to pretend that nothing happened. Employees might have the fear of termination hanging over their heads if they opened their mouths, but I didn't sense fear. Their reactions seemed truly genuine. I really don't think they know anything."

It was getting dark out as we got on line for It's a Small World and clambered into the boat when our turn came up. I watched people's reactions carefully, scanning from boat to boat. People who knew of yesterday's events would certainly search their environment for something, anything. That would be human nature. No one seemed apprehensive or unusually inquisitive about their surroundings. When we reached the turn where I found Snow White, the boat slowed, and everyone sat patiently until it returned to speed. All attention was focused on the singing puppets to each side, and everyone seemed happy. I would've thought heads would have lurched to the sides of the vessel to scan the water for another corpse, but that's not what happened. I looked around to see if there was something amiss, some clue perhaps, something that may have been overlooked.

I sighed as we exited the ride. "Well, that didn't help too much."

She understood and had been observing with me. "I know. No one on the ride seemed aware or concerned in the slightest."

"Just another example of Disney magic. C'mon, let's head over to Snow White's apartment. It's dark enough and hopefully no one will notice us. It's almost seven, and I want to be back in time for the parade at nine." Out of the corner of my eye I saw the two guys from the bus again, hanging out by the entrance to the ride eating cotton candy.

"Cheryl, I hate to keep bringing it up but those guys are definitely following us. There they are again."

She looked over in their direction. "I guess it is kind of odd that every time we turn around we see them."

"That's exactly what I mean."

"I don't know, Cesari. I guess you could just ask them."

I chuckled at that thought. "I got a better idea. Let's go to the Haunted Mansion. You told me it gets very dark and crowded in there."

"Yes, it used to scare the heck out of me as a child. What are you thinking?"

I was thinking that I'm probably not as good a pickpocket as Snow White, but in a dark, crowded room where people are expecting to be jostled, I just might be able to get one of their wallets. But I said to Cheryl, "I'd like to get a closer look at them without raising their suspicions. Maybe even take a pic or two with my cell phone."

She rolled her eyes. "And what if they see you doing this?"

"What are they going to do? Shoot me in the Haunted Mansion? The worst that will happen is that they'll know we're on to them. On the other hand, if they don't follow us there then maybe I was wrong about them to start with."

"What about Snow White's apartment?"

"It will have to wait. Besides, if these guys are tailing us I'd rather not lead them there."

Chapter 8

The wait time to enter the Haunted Mansion was nearly thirty minutes so we amused ourselves by reading the inscriptions on the faux headstones that lined the pathway in. Some of them were quite humorous. We noticed the two men take up position several paces behind us, and I wondered if both would enter the attraction or if one would wait outside. It would be better if I had to deal with only one at a time. Although I had practiced pickpocketing many times as a child growing up in the Bronx, I was never adroit enough to be any good at it. Certainly, the noise and confusion inside would give me the advantage.

As our group entered, I saw one of the men drift off the line and walk back to the entrance to keep an eye out for any unexpected exit on our part. By the time the doors closed, they had packed us into the dark, circular room like sardines with at least a hundred people nose to nose. I slowly maneuvered over to his position as he pretended to ignore us, staring away at one of the macabre decorations that lined the walls above. Loud, haunting music played overhead, and every now and then a child screamed and then laughed.

Cheryl and I had maneuvered ourselves to within inches of his back. Suddenly, the room went pitch black, and we were jolted by deafening, sinister laughter. Now was the time to act. Cancelling the idea of pickpocketing the guy, I decided to go with a more traditional method of investigation, so I made a tight fist and blasted him as hard as I could in the back of the head. Without a sound, he lurched forward unconscious, and I quickly grabbed him, preventing him from falling on top of anyone. Supporting him under the arms, I laid him gently down on the floor as other guests gave us room, sensing a problem in the dark. No one could really see anything, and there was too much noise to attempt an explanation. I searched him quickly, relieving him of his wallet, cell phone, and handgun, which I placed in my waistband under my windbreaker. By now people were screaming for real as they realized someone was seriously ill. The lights came on and the doors opened seconds later. I looked up at Disney personnel as everyone gave us a wide berth leaving as quickly as they could.

I told an employee. "I don't know what happened. He seemed really nervous and I think the stress caused him to pass out."

"Is he breathing?" the young man asked, genuinely concerned. Good question, so I checked him for a pulse and respirations.

"Yes." He seemed okay. I felt the back of his head, and found a lump the side of an egg. "I wouldn't move him until an ambulance gets here though."

"We're not going to touch him. We have policies about stuff like this."

There was chaos all around us now, with frightened park guests milling about with confused Disney employees unsure of what to do or where to go. No one had taken charge yet.

A big guy with a mustache stepped forward from the crowd. With an air of authority he said, "I'm a dentist. Maybe I can help."

The Disney kid nodded. "Thanks, I'd appreciate it."

The guy looked at me and asked. "Do you know him?"

"Never saw him before. What kind of dentist are you?"

"I'm an orthodontist."

"Ever take care of something like this before?"

"No, but how hard can it be?"

I didn't respond to that, but as he evaluated the situation, I stepped aside, grabbed Cheryl by the hand, and hustled her quickly toward the door, whispering, "We can't go out the same way we came in. The other guy will be waiting for us."

We pushed our way through the crowd and saw a sign that said "Employees Only." I said, "There, let's go." We made a beeline toward it, entering an empty hallway as all the attraction's workers had mustered to deal with the crisis. Meandering through the underbelly of the attraction wasn't too difficult as the law required all exits to be well demarcated, and we rapidly found our way back into the park, well off to the side of the main entrance where pandemonium had ensued.

Cheryl was flushed and out of breath from excitement. She punched me in the arm. "What the hell was that? I thought you were just going to snap a few photos. You didn't say anything about killing him."

"I'm sorry. I acted impulsively, but this worked out better because now I have a weapon in case Consuela decides she's been too lenient with me."

"You stole his gun?" Cheryl asked incredulously.

"And his wallet and cell phone. C'mon, we need to move quickly."

We practically ran toward the park's exit. Out of breath she asked, "Is that guy going to be okay?"

"What are you worried about him for? I think I broke one of my knuckles on his skull."

"I'm serious, Cesari. You just assaulted someone."

"He'll be fine. He's young and healthy. Besides, you didn't see anything in there. It was too dark. Just keep saying that over and over to yourself, all right?"

We caught the ferryboat to the Fort Wilderness Lodge, where Snow White had a one-bedroom apartment on the tenth floor. On the way I took out the guy's wallet for inspection.

Glancing at Cheryl I said, "Uh-oh, this isn't good at all, my dear."

"Who is he, Cesari? Don't keep me in suspense."

"He's a federal agent."

"Uh oh."

"Worse than that. He's Secret Service." I showed her his ID. "Phillip M. McIntosh, age thirty-two."

She took the ID from me and studied it, looking very concerned. "Why would Secret Service agents be following us?"

"That's a very good question, and I don't have a very good answer. The Secret Service does many things besides protecting the president, like investigating counterfeiting. Have you been counterfeiting or threatening the president behind my back?"

"Counterfeiting?"

"Yes, they're the chief protectors of our currency as well as high-ranking politicians, ex-presidents, and serious candidates for that office."

"Well, then this doesn't make any sense. Why would they be following us? Do you have any idea how much trouble you can get in for what you just did?"

"That's why it's very important for you to develop amnesia. You can blame it on your birth control pills. There is scientific evidence to support that."

She chuckled. "Oh, I see."

I turned on the iPhone I swiped from Phillip M. McIntosh and watched as it booted up. The home screen lit up without any password requirement, which made me laugh. "I thought these guys were supposed to be obsessed with security?"

I scrolled through his contact list, recent phone calls, and photos, showing them to Cheryl. There were multiple long-distance, grainy pictures of Cheryl and me at various places on Disney property, including a photo of us talking with Snow White. I scanned through his text messages and found several with the subject heading of "Cesari." One of them read, "Identity confirmed, please advise." Another said, "Watch closely. Boss man wants to know all activities." The sender's identity was blocked.

"What do you think this means, Cesari?"

"It means they were following us for sure, but why, and who is the Boss man? They can't possibly be talking about the president."

We both laughed at that as the ferry docked at the Fort Wilderness campground and we disembarked. It was dark out, and I discretely dropped Phillip McIntosh's handgun, wallet, and cell phone over the side into the water. I decided that I'd rather take my chances with Consuela than risk getting caught with a federal agent's pistol. A short distance away we caught a connecting bus to the hotel itself and soon entered the grand lobby. There were large plush sofas and chairs scattered about the large room, accenting an enormous fireplace. Giant wood beams and posts along with moose antlers and bearskin rugs created a rustic feel. The elevators opened onto the tenth floor and we found Snow White's room at the end of the hallway. I took out the key Raul had given me and looked at it, hesitating.

"What's the matter?" Cheryl asked.

I glanced up and down the hallway at the other doors. At its core, the Fort Wilderness Lodge was really just another expensive hotel. "Why is hers the only room with a real key lock and not an electronic one?"

"I don't know. Maybe, it was because she was nuts."

I grunted, opened the door, and we entered a large living room, astonished by what we saw. "This isn't an ordinary hotel room, is it?"

"Cesari, will you look at this? It's unbelievable." The room had been decorated like a dollhouse with bright pastel colors and oversized stuffed animals everywhere. Giant plastic candy canes leaned against the walls, and the sofa cushions were the shape of giant M&Ms with the logo embroidered in the center. The room itself was larger than any five hotel rooms I had ever been in put together. There were several doors leading off the living room and we explored them.

The first led into a full-sized kitchen, complete with a six-foot-long rectangular wood table, refrigerator, sink, and dishwasher. Mickey Mouse mugs and cereal bowls filled the overhead cabinets, and the walls were painted with images of the seven dwarves. The floor tiles were muraled to look like the enchanted forest.

Cheryl glanced at me. "This is bigger than most kitchens in your average suburban home."

I nodded. "They must have knocked down the walls to the other rooms on this floor to build this. C'mon let's check out the rest of the apartment. This may take a little longer than I thought to search this whole place. It looks like they may have given her the entire tenth floor."

The next door led into what could only be described as a playground. There was a swing set, an adult-sized rocking horse, a teeter-totter, a ten foot square sand box, and shelves filled with board games, jump ropes, and various sized rubber balls. This room was easily the size of a small gymnasium.

"Oh my God, John, this is so sad. I feel so bad for this girl."

I sighed. "I agree. She was pretty far out there, wasn't she?"

The last room was the bedroom. If we were surprised by what we saw in the other rooms we were totally let down now.

"I guess our expectations got too high," I said looking around her perfectly ordinary sleeping quarters. It was larger than most hotel rooms for sure but unusually normal considering what we had just seen. There was a queen-sized bed, a couple of matching night tables, and a small flat-screen TV on the bureau at the foot of the bed. A door led off to what I presumed was the bathroom and off to one side, there was a large closet with sliding doors. The carpet and walls were a drab off-white.

Cheryl opened one of the night table drawers. "What do you think?"

"I don't know. It doesn't seem to make sense."

She was very puzzled. "It doesn't make sense at all, Cesari. If she was trapped in the mindset of a little girl, then her bedroom decor would have been very important, if not the most important thing to her. This is extremely institutional. Except for its size, it looks like the kind of room a businessman might choose to stay in."

I walked over to the bathroom and looked in, finding a standard toilet, tub and shower. The room was modestly sized and most unbefitting a delusional Snow White. Cheryl had slid open the closet door and was examining the wardrobe as I joined her. There was a long row of identical Snow White dresses with matching shoes lined up on the floor beneath. There were no sweaters, shirts, coats, or rain gear.

Cheryl looked at me. "She must have other clothes somewhere. She can't have played Snow White 24/7, could she?"

"Yeah, and what about pajamas and stuff like that? Let's look around, check the night tables and the bureau. There has to be some signs of a normal life."

The bureau and night tables were empty. We went back to the living room and playroom and found nothing. In the kitchen, we found an empty refrigerator and bare cupboards. It was as if no one lived here at all. There were no radios, magazines, cell phone chargers, makeup kits, or toiletries.

Cheryl suggested, "Maybe Raul and Consuela had the apartment scrubbed?"

I thought about that. "But why give me the key and suggest I look around?"

"Once again, maybe they're all nuts."

"Hmm, definitely a possibility. Then why leave all the Snow White costumes?"

"I have no idea."

We went back into the bedroom and looked in the closet. It was large and held forty Snow White dresses on hangers. There were twenty identical pairs of shoes lined up neatly in a row on the floor directly beneath the dresses. Not one was even slightly out of place.

"Pretty neat, don't you think? What's that mean?" she asked.

I shrugged. "Maybe she was a bit OCD. I don't know. Should we search the dresses and shoes?"

"For what, more secret messages?"

"Maybe. The girl's dead, Cheryl. There has to be a reason. I can't believe she was the victim of some random maniac who got the urge to kill her in broad daylight. Maybe she was being stalked and left a clue somewhere. Let's put the dresses on the bed and search them. Same with the shoes." We removed them a bunch at a time and piled them onto the bed. Along the back wall of the closet was a mural of Snow White and the Seven Dwarves, which was mostly hidden from view by the dresses.

Cheryl studied it, observing, "Well that's cute."

"Yeah, this is all so adorable," I said sarcastically as I bent over to pick up a pair of shoes in front of me. Doing this, I noticed a space between the bottom of the back wall of the closet and the carpet. It was very small and subtle and I traced it to either end of the room. With my hands I felt along the edges of the wall to see if there was anything different about it but didn't find anything.

"What are you doing?" Cheryl asked.

"There's something strange about the back wall. It doesn't come flush to the floor. There's about an eighth of an inch space between it and the floor, and it runs along the entire length of the closet."

"What do you think?"

"I don't know." I bent down to look more closely at the gap, tapping on the wall in various places. "Could just be shoddy carpentry." I took out the room key and slid it partway underneath. It fit easily and didn't bump into anything.

She looked around. "Nothing in this place looks shoddy if you ask me."

"Well, I don't know then. I don't see any screws or hinges and I couldn't tap out any studs. Maybe it's attached at the sides and at the top but why? That's certainly a peculiar way to construct a wall, especially one that's ten feet wide."

"It is what it is, Cesari. C'mon, let's search her clothes."

A careful inspection of the dresses and shoes failed to reveal anything of interest, and we replaced them in the closet. When we were done, we sat on the edge of the bed together in front of the television thinking things over. I was puzzled. It seemed to me the apartment ought to have offered up more than it had.

"Why would somebody remove her things?" Cheryl asked.

"Maybe to get rid of fingerprints or DNA evidence, but then why leave the dresses? I mean if you're going to scrub an apartment, then you scrub the whole apartment, right? You don't leave stuff. Something doesn't make sense."

"I agree, but then where are her real clothes. Crazy or not she must have had other clothes somewhere like pajamas, underwear, sweaters, and things like that. For God's sake there weren't even any toiletries or towels in the bathroom."

"Very strange."

She nodded. "So, who else would have known about this apartment?"

"Certainly Consuela and God knows how many other people here at Disney. I mean, I'm sure Snow White didn't clean and maintain the place herself. Everybody on staff here must have known about the apartment. Then there's a whole range of lovers she had. Raul hinted at her indiscretions with strange men. She may have brought them back here."

"Agreed."

I scanned around the room again thinking about its plainness. There was a remote control for the TV on one of the night tables, and I picked it up out of curiosity. It was pink and the buttons were oversized, decorated with Disney characters. Aiming it at the TV, I pressed the power button but nothing happened. I pressed it again, and again no response.

Cheryl watched me. "Let me guess. We're in a dead girl's apartment, and now we're going to watch TV?"

"Just trying to put myself in her shoes, you know? See the world through her eyes but the remote's not working, so relax." I put the device down, walked over to the TV, and pressed the power button manually, but still nothing happened. I looked at the back of the set and saw the usual cable wires. There was a power plug, which was not plugged in so I reached down and inserted it into the wall outlet. The TV turned on, surprising me because I hadn't pushed any buttons yet, but I looked back and saw Cheryl holding the remote.

She said, "This is the most fascinating remote control I have ever seen."

"Why is that? Because it's pink and there are Disney characters on the face?"

"Well, I do kind of like that, but no, because there is a second power button on the back."

Turning it over, she showed me a small, discrete button in the middle of the device that I hadn't noticed a moment ago. It was set in flush with the rest of the surface.

She aimed it at the TV and depressed the button. Nothing happened, so she tried again with the same result.

"Maybe it's for the lights." I offered. "Or music or to lock the doors?"

She aimed it randomly around the room, pressing and releasing the button until eventually we heard a muffled mechanical sound emanating from the closet. I went over and pulled open the sliding doors again. I pushed aside the dresses and saw the back wall slowly rising upward into the ceiling. When it had fully retracted, we walked through the opening into another large room. I found a light switch on the wall and flipped it on.

"Wow," Cheryl said. "Would you look at this?"

We stood at the threshold of a massive bedroom, dominated in its center by a ten foot square canopied bed. The carpet was plush and felt nice underfoot. There were two large country French–styled mahogany armoires on opposite sides of the room and a matching bureau on the wall facing the foot of the bed. A large gas fireplace with a marble mantelpiece stood majestically to one side. The bed was high off the ground, and we observed a step stool on the side of it to assist entry. Over the bureau, a large flat-screen TV was mounted on the wall.

"Look at this bedding and canopy, Cesari. It's gorgeous. I've never seen anything so beautiful, and look at the wall coverings. They really are fit for a princess."

She was right, but something was different here than elsewhere in the apartment. This room wasn't childish or delusional. Despite its over-the-top décor, it seemed quite mature and sophisticated. It was more like being in the home of an eighteenth century French countess rather than an obsessed Disney brat.

The bathroom was also very large, with a separate sauna and steam room. The marble tub stood on golden legs and had ornamental brass figures. The mosaic tiled floor reminded me of the ancient Roman exhibit I had seen at the Metropolitan Museum of Art. This girl had it all. You could get lost in this bathroom.

The walk-in closet would easily qualify as an apartment all by itself. In it, there were rooms within rooms. Apparently, she did have normal clothes and lots of them, depending on the mood she was in or the month of the year. There was the blue room, red room, yellow room, and green room. There were rooms designated winter, spring, summer, and fall. There was a room with wall-to-wall shoes. Each room had its own dressing table and full-length mirror.

I looked at Cheryl. "Oh God, we don't have time to check all this stuff out. It would take years."

"The girl liked her clothes, that's for sure. So I guess she wasn't totally obsessed with being Snow White. I'm sort of happy that at least she liked to be normal some of the time."

"I'll say. Look at this." I had entered a room without a label on the door.

Cheryl stood behind me and chuckled. "Way to go girl."

We stood there observing walls of lingerie, ranging from subtle camisoles to raunchy leather, and racks of sex toys. I smiled at Cheryl. "I know what you're getting for Christmas next year."

She pushed me. "I still don't know what I'm getting this year. Some Christmas this is turning out to be." She looked around the room wide-eyed. "Snow White wasn't fooling when she brought someone back to this apartment."

"But why the secret door?"

"If you had a room full of slutty lingerie and sex toys wouldn't you want to keep that a secret from prying eyes? On the other hand, maybe she wanted to be sure she could trust a guy before she took him on the wildest ride of his life. That would kind of make sense too. I mean, she couldn't have known these men very well when she made the decision to bring them here. They passed the first test by responding to her distress note, but then they came here and probably had to pass a second test before they got to this level. Make sense?"

I laughed. "I love the way you think. It's very refreshing. So, did I have to pass some kind of test to get into your pants?"

She smiled. "Of course and I would add, that you did so only by the skin of your teeth."

"Well, I'm glad we cleared that up. So what if a guy didn't pass the test and decided he wasn't going home either? What did she do then?"

"What do you mean, what did she do then? Every woman on the planet sooner or later has to deal with that situation. You bite, kick, scream, and threaten to tell his mother. That's what you do."

I nodded and glanced at my watch. "Damn, we're going to miss the parade at the Magic Kingdom. We have to hurry."

"What's the big deal about the parade?"

"I want to speak to Cinderella, and that's the easiest way to find her. She's the highlight of the show. I'd like to know what she thought about Snow White."

"Well, the park will be open late tonight because it's Christmas. Even if we miss the parade, she may hang around to give out autographs and take pictures." We walked back into the main bedroom, and I watched Cheryl made a beeline to the bed, climbing onto it.

"What are you doing, sweetheart?"

"Come up here with me, Cesari, we may never get a chance like this again."

"Whoa, I don't know what you're thinking, but I'm not getting any of my DNA on that bed. Besides, we got things to do."

She laughed. "I didn't mean that. Let's just lie down and pretend we're royalty."

I joined her on the bed, and we lay there staring upward. "Damn. She was one sick girl, wasn't she?"

Cheryl shook her head. "She certainly wasn't the Snow White I grew up on."

We stared at ourselves in a full-length mirror overhead. Something caught my eye so I stood up on the bed and with my hand outstretched could just barely touch it.

"What are you doing?"

"There's something there."

"Like what?"

"I don't know for sure. Help stabilize me."

I went to the closet and brought one of the chairs out, placing it on the bed and leaning the back against one of the posts for support. With Cheryl's help, I gingerly climbed onto the chair, wobbling gently but more or less securely. There it was; a thin black electrical cable that I traced over the back edge of the mirror. The mirror was suspended by wires to the ceiling, and I could move it a little, allowing me to see behind it.

"You're not going to believe this."

"Please don't say it."

"There's a video camera up here."

"I told you not to say it. Please tell me it's not on."

"Hard to tell from this angle, but I don't think so."

"Thank God."

I came down off the chair, and we both got off the bed, suddenly very uncomfortable. I started searching the room again. "Help me look for other cameras, Cheryl. There's bound to be more. Anyone sick enough to install one would certainly want to make sure they didn't miss anything."

After a few minutes, we found two others, one in the bathroom behind the mirror over the sink, pointing at the tub, and another over the fireplace mantle, hidden behind a wall painting and aimed across the bed.

"Why would she do this, Cesari?"

"Who said she did?"

"What do you mean?"

"Maybe someone who knew about her secret life was taking advantage of her, which means it could be any one of a number of people. I think it's time to talk to Raul again. It seems he didn't tell me everything there was to know about his little girl. We also need to find out who our friend in the Secret Service works for, and not necessarily in that order."

Chapter 9

*I*t was after ten by the time we reached the Magic Kingdom, and we had just missed the end of the parade down Main Street so we cruised over to Cinderella's Castle hoping to catch a glimpse of her, and maybe a word or two. Just outside, I asked an employee if there was any chance we could meet Cinderella, and he pointed toward the interior of the castle where she was taking photos with guests. We found her and waited patiently in line with about twenty little girls and their parents. As our turn came up, Cheryl and I stood to either side of her while the photographer snapped a shot.

"Is there any way we could talk to you more privately?" Cheryl asked. "We're with a modeling agency out of New York and have a business proposition you might be interested in." We had decided it would be more disarming if Cheryl did all the talking.

Cinderella eyed us curiously. There were several other children waiting to be photographed after us. "Wait until I'm finished here." She pointed to a corner of the room. "Over there."

We walked over to where the photographer stood. "It's all right, Al." She called to him.

Twenty minutes later, she came up to us. "Look, I don't get off for another thirty minutes and I can't afford to lose this job. Can we meet somewhere for a drink?" Up close we could see the makeup caked on and the weariness in her eyes. The costume looked like it could get pretty warm.

"Where'd you have in mind?" I asked.

"How about the Dublin Road? It's the Irish pub on the West Side, and I know it doesn't close until two a.m."

"Sounds good. We'll see you there in about an hour?"

"All right, Mr.....?"

"Cesari, John Cesari and Cheryl Kowalcik."

We shook hands and left the castle. Cheryl said, "C'mon, Cesari, if we leave now we'll beat the crowds at the bus stop."

We hustled out of the park and hopped the bus to the West Side. Inside, the pub was nearly filled, and we were lucky to find an empty wood booth with high-backed bench seats. It was a noisy bar-restaurant, with a wood-beamed ceiling and Irish music playing in the background. The bartender was dressed in a green Santa outfit, and we ordered a couple of Guinnesses while we waited.

"Nice place," I noted, scanning around.

She nodded in agreement. "Pretty authentic too. I've been pub hopping in Ireland and they've done a decent job at recreating that atmosphere."

"You've been pub hopping in Ireland? I don't recall you ever mentioning that."

"It was before I met you. I went with my boyfriend from law school."

"Your boyfriend from law school? I don't recall you ever mentioning him either. Didn't we meet while you were still in law school?"

"Oh, please. Did you think I didn't date anyone before I met you?"

For some reason this news irritated me. "On Christmas Day, this is what you choose to talk about, old boyfriends? I can't believe this."

"Stop it, Cesari. You're being ridiculous. Forget I said anything."

"How am I supposed to forget about it? You can't just bring up stuff like that on Christmas and then say forget about it. You probably had sex with the guy too."

"Okay, stop it. That's enough."

"Oh my God! You did."

She folded her arms in front of her and looked angry. "I think we should change the subject."

I took a sip of my beer. "Fine."

"Fine."

Halfway through the second round of Guinnesses, Cinderella walked in, holding a shopping bag, scanning the room. I waved to her, and she joined us at the table, ordering an Irish coffee. She was very attractive; early twenties, blond hair, fair complexion. She sat down next to Cheryl, opposite me, extending her hand. "I'm Shauna."

I said, "Hi Shauna. It's a pleasure, and thank you for meeting with us. You remember our names?"

"Yes, John Cesari and Cheryl Kowalcik. I can get you my resume tomorrow. What did you have in mind?"

Cheryl and I glanced at each other. "First of all, I want to be honest with you. We didn't ask you to meet with us about a modeling job in New York."

She looked puzzled and then upset. "Then what do you want? Are you two perverts or something?"

Cheryl raised her hand. "We're investigating the death of a young woman, and we thought you might be able to help us."

"Me? How can I help and why should I help you two anyway? You just lied to me and tricked me into coming here. I don't have time for bullshit like this." She stood to leave, but when I showed her a hundred dollar bill, she hesitated.

"We're willing to pay for the information, Shauna. Cheryl and I think you may have known the deceased, and we're just trying to figure out what happened. Her family hired us because they think the police aren't interested in the case." She eyed the money and sat back down. The waitress brought her coffee and she took a sip, calming down.

"So who died?"

"A Disney employee who played Snow White. Her name was Marguerite Varga. Did you know her?" She reached out for the hundred dollar bill, grasping one end as I held onto the other.

I said, "We need information, Shauna."

"And I need to pay the rent."

I let go of the bill, and she tucked it away, chuckling. "Well, Mr. Cesari or whatever your name really is, you're out of luck. I didn't start working for Disney until this morning, so I don't know anybody there yet, let alone who might have died or why."

Cheryl and I looked surprised. "Really?"

"Yeah, I applied for the job six months ago and was placed on a wait list. I was serving pancakes at Denny's last night when the call came that they needed a replacement Cinderella as soon as possible and would pay $250 per day to take pictures with kids and wave from the floats. The next thing I know you're offering me a modeling job in New York. Thanks for bursting my bubble."

I said, "I'm very sorry about the deception, but discussing homicide is a tough way to break the ice with someone. Do you know what happened to the previous Cinderella?"

"When I arrived this morning, I asked but no one said anything, and I was too busy trying to learn my way around, you know?"

"Yes, of course. Did anything or anyone seem odd to you? I know you were probably very busy, but did anything catch your eye?"

She thought about it. "I don't know for sure, but the woman in charge of the cast members, that's what they call us, Helena Mantrelli, was awfully uptight about something. I thought it was because I was so new, but she spent a lot of time on the phone during the lunch break. I heard her talking in Italian or Spanish to someone long distance. I was eating in a corner of the cast members' lounge, and one word she kept saying over and over struck me as funny."

"What was that?"

"It sounded a lot like 'baloney,' which seemed peculiar, but it was the only word that seemed familiar to me. 'Baloney' or 'balona,' or something like that. I'm not a hundred percent certain. By that time in the day, my head was already swimming. It just seemed odd, is all."

"How do you know she was talking long distance?"

"When she hung up, she grumbled under her breath that the call was going to cost her a fortune so I just assumed that it was probably an international call."

I nodded. "That's it? Nothing else at all unusual?'

"Hey look. I just worked a twelve-hour day wearing an inch of makeup, someone else's clothes, and glass slippers, and you want to know if I saw something unusual? That's all I got, mister, but if you really want to know about the other Cinderella you should go talk to Helena. She looks like she's been working there a hundred years. Now I got to go. There's a party going on at the House of Blues down the street and the place is supposed to be crawling with guys."

It was then that I noticed she had a small pillow in the shopping bag next to her. Curiosity got the best of me and I pointed at it. "Is it a pajama party?"

She chuckled. "Oh that. I always bring my own pillow when I go out. It's a lot easier on the knees when you meet someone you like."

Cheryl's eyes went wide with surprise, but I didn't show any reaction. I had been practicing medicine long enough to have heard just about everything, and nothing surprised me anymore, especially when it came to girls. It was my feeling that modern women were just beginning to come out of their shells and that it might take decades for the situation to level off. I said, "Well Shauna, it's been a long day and I want to thank you for your cooperation. We're just trying to do the right thing for this girl and her family, I hope you understand that. You've been very helpful so far and we appreciate it. How about I give you my cell phone number, and now that you know what we're interested in, you can call us any time. I'm willing to pay for any information you can find out." I reached into my wallet for a fifty and handed it to her.

"What's this for?"

"Consider it a retainer."

"Kind of a small retainer, isn't it?"

I glanced at Cheryl and handed her another fifty.

She said, "Thanks."

She finished her coffee as I wrote down my number for her on a napkin. "By the way, is there a way we could speak to this Helena person? I mean do you have her phone number or know where her office is?"

"You could go back to the Magic Kingdom. She should be there well past midnight. She told me she doesn't leave until all the cast members have turned in their wardrobes. Her office is on the top floor of the castle, and you can reach it by going up the spiral staircase that's in the center of the building. There's a private elevator but you won't be able to use it without proper ID. Cinderella's dressing room is up there too so she can make a grand entrance coming down the staircase. Other cast members change in the basement."

"Well, once again, thank you for your cooperation, Shauna."

"Good night and thanks for the drink."

She grabbed her pillow and left. I paid the bill and took Cheryl by the arm. "C'mon, we've got fifteen minutes till the park closes."

Chapter 10

By the time we arrived at the park entrance, the fireworks were over, it was after midnight, and they wouldn't let us in. Hordes of people were streaming past us at the exit, but there were still thousands of people in the park slowly making their way out. Battling our way upstream, we were hailed by a park attendant.

"I'm sorry sir, but the park is closed now and once you leave you can't come back in."

Worry and fear etched our faces. "I know, but we lost our son in the crowd. He's only five and may have wandered into the souvenir shop over there or maybe the bathroom. Please let us check."

Cheryl frantically searched the crowd behind the attendant. The Disney employee shot to attention, suddenly concerned. If there's one thing no Disney employee wanted, it was to be on the wrong end of a missing child situation. He thought it over briefly and said, "Okay, go ahead, and let me know if I can help. There's a security guard up there as well."

"Thank you so much."

We ran past him into the park and soon lost ourselves in the crowd, making a beeline for the castle. Main Street was jammed with people and strollers, and the cacophony was deafening. The worst part was at the castle itself as people tried to get a last glimpse before going home. Inside, we quickly found the spiral staircase and made our way past the red velvet cordon unchallenged. The staircase was very wide at the bottom and progressively narrowed during our ascent. After three sweeping turns and thirty steps later, we reached the top, entering a business-like hallway with fluorescent lights and potted plants. There were three doors, two on the left and one at the far end on the right. Each door had a placard; one said "Dressing Room," one said "Cast Director," and the last read "Security." I hoped that Helena Mantrelli was going to be reasonable. After all, one her employees had just died under rather suspicious circumstances.

We glanced at each other. "What if there's someone in there, Cesari?" Cheryl asked, indicating the security office down the hall. We hadn't anticipated that.

"We'll just have to be subtle, I guess. You know, act like we're lost."

"Great. We just walked deliberately up five flights of stairs past a cordon and we're going to pretend to be lost? That's subtle all right."

We knocked gently on the cast director's door, but there was no response so we tried again.

I lowered my voice. "Darn it. She's not here."

"What do you want to do?"

"Let's go in and wait for her. I know it's late but she's got to show, right? The park isn't even close to closing from an employee point of view. We just have a few questions. I mean, she of all people can't pretend she doesn't know what happened." I turned the handle and was thankful the door was unlocked. We entered the dark room, fumbling for a light switch.

Cheryl whispered, "I found it."

As I closed the door behind us, light flooded the room. "Oh God," I said.

Helena Mantrelli lay slumped over her desk with a bullet hole in her left temple. Her left hand lay limply by her side, and on the floor next to it was a small caliber pistol. She looked like she was in her late fifties with graying hair. Her head was turned toward us with her glassy eyes and mouth wide open.

Cheryl stood frozen in place, slack-jawed. "Are you okay?" I asked.

"We should leave now, Cesari. This has just gone from really bad to worse."

"All right, let's stay calm. I agree, this is bad, but let's think it through. Why would she commit suicide?"

Cheryl looked at me like I was crazy. "Because she was seriously depressed. I thought you were a doctor."

"I get that, but here—on Christmas? I don't know if I buy it."

"What are you suggesting?"

"I'm suggesting that it seems a little too convenient that the person who could tell us where Cinderella might be is suddenly dead."

"Maybe she felt guilty about murdering Snow White? I don't care. What I care about is getting out of here—now."

"You're right. Just give me a minute. I want to see if she left a note. If she did, it might help answer some of our questions."

We walked closer to the body. I didn't see anything helpful on the desktop nor in the drawers. "I don't think it's a smart idea to touch anything, Cesari."

Not listening, I picked up Helena's purse from the floor beside her and searched it. Holding up her wallet, I opened it, sifting through for anything of interest. Next, I found her phone and scrolled through her contacts, recent calls, and text messages.

"Look at this. She has Cinderella listed as Cinderella under C. Her real name is Lola Lovely. Okay, that's a start. She made quite a few calls today too, at least three to Europe, judging by the country code."

"Cesari, I don't think we should stay here much longer, not with security down the hall. You're already in enough trouble with the local police. This would be very difficult to explain." She was right. I put the wallet back but kept her cell phone.

Briefly searching the rest of the room, we didn't find anything else that could help us, so we left as furtively as possible. Outside, the park had quieted down considerably, and there were only a few stragglers like us making their way toward the exit. It was almost one a.m., and the last bus out of the park was just about to leave. We jumped on, thanking the driver for waiting.

"Where to now, Cesari?"

"I don't know about you, but I'm all pumped up."

"Yeah, I do sort of feel an adrenaline rush. So what do you think really happened up there?"

"I don't know. Obviously, it looks like a suicide, but what a coincidence. All this going on, and she suddenly decides this is the right time to pop herself in the head. Damn, that's too crazy for words."

"Aren't they all?"

I looked at her, puzzled. "Who—and what?"

Very seriously, she asked, "Aren't they all crazy? You know, people who kill themselves?"

I was startled by that generalization. If it had been anyone else, I might have accused them of shocking ignorance. "No, not at all. When I said that's too crazy for words, I was just being tongue in cheek. I didn't mean it literally. Mental illness is not the same as crazy, and I'm sorry if I suggested that. Many people are depressed, many with good reason, but it doesn't mean they're insane. Some just need help getting through a tough period in life, and others simply can't cope for whatever reason. Many respond to anti-depressants, therapy, or both. Unfortunately, some don't see any point in living and commit suicide, but even then, they are usually completely rational."

"Oh, I'm sorry. I didn't mean to sound like that."

"I understand. It's okay, and I didn't mean to cop a holier than thou attitude. It's just that I get that a lot in the office, and it can be upsetting. Many people won't seek treatment because they are afraid they are going be labeled crazy, and you may have forgotten, but I was in therapy for years before we met. I told you about it."

"Yes, I do remember now, and I'm sorry for being insensitive."

I smiled. "No need to apologize. Besides, a lot of people really do think I'm crazy."

She laughed. "Well, I'm not one of them." She leaned over and gave me a kiss.

As the bus rocked and rolled itself back to Old Key West, I pulled out the iPhone and dialed Lola Lovely's number but no one answered. Cheryl watched me. "What are you doing?"

"Trying to reach Cinderella, but she's not home. No voicemail available either."

After two more attempts, I gave up and scrolled to the foreign number that Helena had dialed. "What country code is that?" Cheryl asked, looking at the phone with me.

"Don't know, but it can't hurt to give it a try, and she won't have to worry about the charges anymore." I dialed the number and waited.

"*Pronto*, Helena?" asked a woman's voice in Italian. I looked at my watch. They were six hours ahead, so it was almost seven thirty in the morning in Italy.

"No, this isn't Helena. I am sorry. *Parla inglese, Signora*?"

"*Si, si*, but of course I speak English, I have been to America many times. How may I assist you and why are you using Helena's phone?"

"I am a friend of Helena's. Can I ask how you know her?"

"I am her sister, Carmella. What can I do for you?"

"She was in a car accident this afternoon, and is now in surgery. I have been trying to reach friends and family to let them know.

"Mamma mia, I can't believe it. I just spoke to her last night. Is she going to be all right?"

"Well, it's pretty serious, but right now she can't speak to anyone."

"Oh my God. Poor Helena, and she always hated to drive. Did she say what I should do with the girl, Lola?"

"Actually, that's one of the reasons I'm calling. Before she went into surgery Helena asked me to call you to make sure that Lola is okay. She had some personal items she wanted me to send to her. Do you know where I could find her? Is she staying with you?"

"I am expecting her but she hasn't arrived yet here in Bologna. Right now she is staying at Helena's country home in upstate New York. Her flight doesn't leave out of Rochester until the day after tomorrow. I'm surprised Helena didn't tell you that. The accident must have confused her. Poor thing."

"You are very right about that. She was very confused and very worried about Lola. Could you please tell me the address to Helena's country home and maybe I can overnight mail these items to her for the flight."

"Wait just one moment and I check."

A few moments passed and she continued. "She is staying at 815 Marble Town Road, Geneva, New York. There is no landline there. We use only cell phones now."

"Well, thank you for your help, Carmella."

"You're welcome. Will you call me to let me know how Helena is doing?

How did I answer that? "I'll do my best but I think that you should brace yourself for the worst."

I hung up and turned to Cheryl. "Vacation's over, darling."

"I figured that out a while ago. Where are we going now?"

"Geneva, New York. The heart of the Finger Lakes."

Chapter 11

*I*t was dawn and we were both sound asleep when the plane touched down at the Rochester International Airport. We deplaned, shivering from the fifteen-degree weather. We had left most of our stuff in storage at the hospitality house in Old Key West and brought with us only the essentials for a one-night stay. It was the day after Christmas, and the airport was deserted. With only one carry on, we didn't have to wait for luggage and proceeded directly to the car rental kiosk, leasing a new, blue Honda Accord.

"Let's grab some coffee and hit the road, okay?" I asked.

"The sooner we get out of here the better. We're not dressed for this."

We had heavy sweaters and light jackets because when we left Manhattan it was a balmy forty degrees and we hadn't anticipated traveling anywhere but back home so we hadn't packed scarves, gloves, hats, or heavy winter coats. We found the car, and it started promptly while we clutched ourselves for warmth. I plugged in the address and pulled out of the parking garage. The roads were clear and thankfully the weather was cooperative, cloudy but no precipitation.

I turned to Cheryl. "Should I stop somewhere for better clothing?"

"No, we'll be fine." Her courage was returning with the rising temperature of the car. "I thought the Orlando police told you not to leave town?"

"If they didn't want me to leave, they should have locked me up."

She chuckled and shook her head.

We sipped our coffee while we drove. The town was about a forty-five-minute ride, and we soon reached exit 42 on the New York State Thruway. Once off the main highway, the roads were not nearly as clear. It had snowed the night before and so we proceeded cautiously. We headed with care south on Route 14 into Geneva and eventually meandered over to Marble Town Road, where I pulled the car to a stop on the shoulder. We were on a deserted snow-covered country road. There was a solitary brick home set back from the road about a hundred yards ahead.

"Is that it?" Cheryl asked.

"According to the GPS, it is."

"So why hesitate?"

"Just trying to think of what to say."

"Just tell her the truth. 'Helena's dead and you might be next so why don't you cooperate?'"

I laughed. "Oh, okay. Why didn't I think of that? That shouldn't scare her too much."

"Cesari, there are already two dead people. Maybe she should be scared."

I considered that for a moment. "I don't have a gun. Do you?"

"Of course not."

"Well, what if she does?"

"I can't believe this. You're afraid of Cinderella?"

"I'm afraid of any girl who might be looking for a husband."

She shook her head again, and I put the car back into drive and pulled into the semicircular drive in front of the house. There were no other vehicles in view, but there was an attached two-car garage to the left of the main entrance. To the right was a path leading to small side porch set back fifty feet from the front of the building. We studied the house for a few minutes, looking for signs of life, and saw none.

"It's barely nine a.m. She's probably sleeping."

I grunted. "Yeah, probably." I sighed deeply, not wanting to leave the warmth of the car. "Oh well, let's do it."

We got out and trudged through two inches of snow up to the front door. I pressed the door buzzer and waited, watching Cheryl shiver. There was no answer so I knocked loudly with an equally unsuccessful result. I stepped back and looked around, thinking about what to do next.

While I was thus occupied Cheryl stepped up to the door and turned the knob. It opened quietly. She looked at me. It was too cold to argue so we stepped inside, kicking snow off our shoes. The first thing we noticed was that the house was warm, indicating that someone was living there. That was a good sign. There was an old wooden staircase with green painted steps to our left and an entryway to the living room on the right. The hardwood floor creaked a little as we walked through the house but that couldn't be helped.

I whispered to Cheryl. "This shouldn't scare her at all."

"I didn't feel like waiting out there. It's too cold. Nice house."

There was a baby grand piano, a plush sofa, a fireplace, a beautiful oriental rug, and several oil paintings adorning the walls.

"Yeah."

Advancing cautiously into the home, we passed a bathroom, a small study, and eventually reached the kitchen and main dining area toward the rear of the house. We discovered a second stairway there leading to the second level as well as a stairway to the basement, but no signs of Cinderella.

Cheryl looked at me. "What should we do?"

"I don't know. It's bad enough that we're inside the house. If we go up to her bedroom she will really freak out."

She nodded in agreement. "But this is rather urgent business, right? The woman who owns this house is now dead. She needs to know that, and we can't just sit around hoping she'll show up. Besides, we need to know why she suddenly decided to take a trip to Italy."

"Very valid points, but it still won't stop her from freaking out, and going back to my original point—what if she's armed?"

I pulled out Helena's cell phone and scrolled to Cinderella's phone number, dialing it. It went to voicemail again. "Damn."

"Nice try, Cesari, but I think we have to go up there and get her."

"I don't suppose you'd want to go up there alone? It might be less threatening to her, and I'm not sure I feel comfortable entering her bedroom if she's sleeping."

She thought about that. "You're right, but what if she's got a gun?"

"If I hear a shot I could go get help." I gave her a weak smile.

She smirked. "You're coming with me." With that she grabbed me by the arm and together we went slowly and quietly up the stairs. It was a large house, and upstairs we found four bedrooms and two bathrooms, but no Cinderella. One of the rooms reeked of pot and looked lived in. The bed was messed up and a pair of jeans lay on the floor beside it.

"Well, there's her stuff." I observed, noting a small suitcase to one side of the room, which I rummaged through while Cheryl checked out the bathroom.

A minute or two later, I joined her. "Anything here?"

"Yeah, a toothbrush, mouthwash, and makeup kit. There was shampoo and a razor in the shower stall. She's not the neatest girl is she?" The floor was wet and there was a towel lying crumpled in the middle of it.

"What do you think?"

Cheryl shrugged. "I've no idea. It certainly looks like she arrived safely and spent at least one night here. From the stench, I'd say she had a very relaxing evening."

"I agree. Okay, let's check the rest of the house and garage while we talk it over."

We didn't find anything in the basement other than canned vegetables, the furnace, a water softener, and some tools on a peg board. The entrance to the garage was just off to one side of the kitchen and we entered, turning on the overhead light. It was pretty clean and organized. There was a car with a protective cover on it in the center of the room. There were shelves with paint cans, garden equipment, and lawn chairs stacked neatly around the perimeter.

"Now what, Cesari?"

I was very disappointed but took solace in the fact that she would undoubtedly return before too long. I looked at Cheryl. "Her stuff is upstairs, right?"

"Yes."

"Okay, so maybe she went out last night, partied hard, and decided to stay at a hotel rather than drive home. Or maybe she met someone and went home with him?"

"It's possible. She's young and probably wouldn't have wanted to be alone. So what do we do, wait here all day for her?"

I let out a deep breath. "I'm afraid so. I mean look around. There are no signs of a struggle. She must have left voluntarily."

"I'm hungry. Let's see what's in the fridge and the pantry."

We found pancake mix, a stick of butter, coffee, and sugar.

Cheryl said, "The pancakes will be edible but a little lacking without any eggs or milk for the batter, but water will work. Look around for any maple syrup or equivalent."

I found a new bottle of Mrs. Butterworth's syrup and placed it on the table. Opening one of the overhead cabinets, I pulled out two plates and coffee mugs and made us place settings.

"How's it going over there?" I asked, watching Cheryl busy herself by the stove top.

"It's going great. Found her pans and spatulas. Want to get the coffee started? She has a basic electric drip pot on the other side of the counter."

Soon we settled down to a decent meal of pancakes and maple-flavored syrup. "Not bad for a lawyer," I said.

She smiled. "Thanks. Coffee's pretty good too."

After breakfast, we settled on the sofa in the nearby sunroom and turned on the television. Within minutes, we fell asleep in each other's arms.

Chapter 12

*W*aking to the sound of a trigger cocking several hours later, I looked down the barrel of a small revolver in the hands of a beautiful, though somewhat disheveled, woman in her early twenties. Strawberry-blond hair, big blue eyes, and full lips, she could've stepped off the pages of a magazine. Even unkempt and without makeup she would be a gorgeous Cinderella. She looked very nervous.

I said, "Take it easy, girlfriend, we're not here to hurt you."

"Who are you and why are you here at all?" she asked.

Cheryl woke at the sound of our voices, saw the gun, and remained silent. I said, "We've been looking for you, Lola."

Her features registered surprise. "Why and once again, who are you?"

"My name is John Cesari and this is my friend Cheryl Kowalcik. We've got some bad news for you. Helena is—dead. It may have been suicide."

She caught her breath and took a step back, nearly tripping over a coffee table. Cheryl and I slowly sat upright on the sofa.

She gasped, "Suicide? That doesn't make any sense."

"Why is that?" I asked.

"She was planning on meeting me in a few days."

Lola looked like she was going to start crying, and then she did. Cheryl stood up, walked over to her, and put her arms around her. She lowered her gun hand and without uncocking it dropped the weapon to the floor, causing it to discharge loudly. We all jumped and held our breath, but thankfully no one was injured. The bullet plowed harmlessly into the floorboards.

I studied the hole in the floor. "I believe they call that patina in real estate lingo. Actually adds to the value of the home." I picked up the gun and pocketed it. It was a .22 caliber.

Everyone breathed a sigh of relief, and we all took a seat. Cheryl said, "We are sorry for startling you like this. It's just that you didn't answer your phone and we just arrived from Orlando and were exhausted."

Lola had regained her composure. "But who are you exactly? Are you the police or newspaper reporters?"

"No, we're neither. But we are concerned citizens searching for the truth, and we are concerned about you," I explained.

"Well, if you're not the police then I don't have to talk to you."

"No, you don't, but we do believe you are in danger, and we might be able to help you if we knew a little better what was going on." I crossed my legs as we spoke and tried to appear confident. "Let's be realistic, Lola. You're on the run, and Helena and Snow White are already dead. We think that whoever is behind their deaths might be looking for you as well."

She looked horrified. "Snow White's dead too? I didn't know that. How?"

I was surprised to hear that and filled her in on Marguerite Varga's death, causing her to start crying again. I had just assumed that was why she was running.

"Oh God, Oh God…I didn't know. What's happening?"

"I guess I'm a little confused, Lola. You didn't know Snow White was dead?"

"No. Really. I didn't."

"So why were you skipping out to Italy to stay with Helena's sister."

"It was Helena's decision. I had Christmas Eve off and she called me frantically that afternoon and told me that I might be in big trouble and had better do everything she said. I was in Rochester before midnight with a plane ticket to Bologna already purchased for tomorrow morning. She told me to turn my phone off and to not talk to anyone I didn't know and that she would explain everything better when she joined me in Italy in a few days.

"Wait a minute," Cheryl interjected. "You're telling us that you have no idea why Helena ordered you to get out of Orlando, hide out here, and then run to Italy. You didn't even question what the reason might be?"

Lola was quiet for a while before speaking and it was clear she was hiding something. "I had kind of expected a call like that for some time. Helena had warned me it might happen one day. I just didn't expect it on Christmas Eve."

"But if you didn't know you were in danger why do you have a gun?" I argued.

"Since when does exercising my constitutional rights require an explanation, especially to two people who just broke into someone else's home?"

I was getting frustrated—and impatient. "C'mon Lola. What are you talking about? You must realize how ridiculous this sounds and besides, the door was unlocked so we didn't break in."

She suddenly stood up, hostile. "You said you're not the police, right?"

We stood as well. "No. We told you that already."

"Then I don't have to tell you a goddamn thing, do I? And you have no right to be here. Now get out, the both of you."

Cheryl said calmly, "Lola, we'll leave but I think you're making a mistake not confiding in us. You're obviously in danger and although putting distance between you and the source is smart, it may not be a permanent solution."

"I want you both to leave now, and leave the gun. It's not yours."

I took the .22 out of my pocket and emptied the bullets from it onto to the floor. I looked at her sternly. This was no joke what was happening, and I was growing angry as well as impatient. "I wouldn't try to take that on the plane, sweetheart."

"Cesari, take it easy. She's upset," Cheryl scolded.

"She's a spoiled brat." And with that I walked past her toward the front door. "Let's go, Cheryl. We wasted our time."

Surprised, Cheryl watched me storm by. She turned back to Lola, "If you change your mind, please call me. He's upset but he really does want to help you and so do I." She handed Lola her business card and we left into the frigid air of upstate New York. In the Honda we shivered and drove off.

"What was that all about, Cesari?"

"Just thought I'd give the old good cop, bad cop thing a whirl."

"Well that didn't go too well, so where to now?"

"We'll need a place to stay, while we wait for her to change her mind."

"You sound very confident that she will."

"I'm extremely so."

"Why?"

"Because I have her passport in my pocket. I found it in her suitcase and took it as a precaution. When she packs her belongings tonight she'll realize it's missing and give us a call. So we need to rent a room somewhere, find some real food, clean up, and maybe get to know each other if you get my drift?" I winked at her.

She smirked back. "I get what you mean all right, and you need to calm down because I'm tired. So why didn't you just tell her you had the passport?"

"Because she was too indignant and would just have gotten angry. Besides, this is better. It gives her time to cool down and think things through. By tonight when time is running out, panic will settle in when she realizes her passport is missing."

She chuckled. "And what if with all this excitement, she forgets to check for it?"

"Well, then she's not going to Italy, is she? Which I'm not sure is the greatest idea anyway."

"A lot of ifs here, Cesari."

"I know but she's our only lead right now."

We checked into a small hotel in the center of town across the street from several mom and pop restaurants and a banquet hall called Club 86. Once in the room we showered, toweled down, and stretched out on the queen-sized bed. It was close to three p.m., and we were running low on fuel. I was also running low on ideas. What if we didn't find out anything helpful? There were now two dead bodies on Disney property, and I was the chief suspect in at least one of the deaths. Cinderella was being a pain in the ass, but she might come around to my way of thinking once she calmed down. While I thought things through, Cheryl had reached over and pulled my towel off.

I said, "Hello."

"Got a problem?"

"No, but I thought you were tired."

"I am." She crawled around to get closer.

"Isn't playing with me like that going to make you more tired?"

"No, it's just mindless activity. Sort of like playing Solitaire or Candy Crush."

I chuckled. "Are all girl lawyers like you?"

"No, but most of the guy lawyers are like you—big dicks."

I hoped that was meant as a compliment, but doubted it. I was trying desperately to come up with an equally witty response but blood flow to my brain was being diverted elsewhere so I simply focused on breathing and staying conscious.

My cell phone went off loudly disturbing the mood. Cheryl looked up and I said, "Don't stop."

I reached over to the night table and picked up the device. I was hoping it was Cinderella, but instead it was Vito. I whispered gruffly into the phone. "What do you want? I'm busy." Cheryl picked her head up again and I pushed it back down.

"Fucking Cesari, is that how you greet a friend?"

"Yes, it is. I'm kind of occupied at the moment. I'll call you back."

Ignoring me, he said, "Don't you watch the news, Cesari? Snow White was found dead at the Magic Kingdom and her boss committed suicide right in Cinderella's Castle. They've closed the park while they're investigating. I was just calling to see if you knew what was going on. It sounds like all hell is breaking loose down there." This surprised me but I guessed that after they found Helena's body, Disney or Raul or both could no longer suppress the story.

"Oh my God," I moaned into the phone.

"Take it easy, Cesari. You can still go to Epcot."

Cheryl looked up grinning.

I didn't say anything as I caught my breath.

"Cesari—you going to be okay? You don't sound well."

"Yeah, I'm fine," I said hoarsely. "What else are they saying on the news?"

"Just that they have several persons of interests and leads they're checking out. The usual bullshit when no one knows anything."

Cheryl had snuggled up to me and whispered into my free ear. "My turn."

"Look Vito, I'm actually glad you called. Can you do a background check for me on some guys I ran into at Disney? I need to know who a guy called Raul Varga is and another guy named Phillip M. McIntosh. Whatever you can find out will be helpful, but let me give you a heads up. McIntosh is Secret Service so be discreet with the inquiry."

"What are you into, Cesari? I thought you were on vacation?"

"I'll fill you in when I get back, but it looks like my vacation is going to end a little early."

"You're involved with this Snow White shit, aren't you? You're a piece of work, you know that?" he laughed. "You can't even go to Disney without killing somebody."

"I didn't kill anybody, but I'll tell you all about it in a day or two when I return. Just get me the information, all right?"

"Sure, Cesari. Give me twenty-four hours. Meanwhile, while I got you on the line. Guess who I saw in Little Italy on Christmas Eve?"

"Why don't you tell me?"

"Kelly. When was the last time you saw her?"

"I don't know, three, four, five months ago. I can't remember. Why?"

"Nothing. Just asking."

"Vito…"

"No big deal. I was in a cafe grabbing a coffee and she walked by. She didn't see me and I didn't say anything."

"So?"

"She was looking a little plump is all. She was wearing winter clothing so maybe it was my imagination."

"What's that supposed to mean? Are you trying to piss me off?" He knew I still had feelings for Kelly.

"Look, forget I said anything. Call me when you're back, all right?" He hung up and I tossed my phone onto the night table. He could be a real asshole sometimes. I looked at Cheryl, who had taken her towel off and started without me.

I said, "Hey, that's my job."

"Don't worry about me. You have your friend Vito you can play with."

I rolled on top of her, holding her wrists over her head. I kissed her forehead, then her eyes, her nose, and then her lips. I slowly worked my way downward, kissing, licking, and nibbling while she giggled.

Chapter 13

Around seven, we decided to venture out for drinks and dinner. The temperature had dropped into the single digits, and the wind had picked up, making it feel even colder. We left the hotel and trudged across the street trying to decide between two small Italian restaurants, one called Pronti's and the other the Deluxe. We flipped a coin and chose Pronti's, mostly because it was slightly closer and we were freezing. Once inside, a hostess seated us at a small table by a window. It was Friday night and the place was packed.

"Cesari, we've got to get some real winter clothing."

"I know. We should've stopped somewhere earlier today. I wasn't even thinking about the weather when we left Florida. It's too late tonight but maybe first thing in the morning, okay?"

She nodded, looking around. "It's a cute place."

I was still shivering from the cold. "Sure. It looks great."

We ordered Manhattans, straight up and studied the menu.

"So I guess we're not going back to Disney?" Cheryl asked.

"Vacation's over, kiddo, sorry. As of twenty-four hours ago I went missing, and you have no idea where I am. God only knows how many people are out looking for me right now, and I have no intention of letting them find me until I'm ready to be found. Now that it's all over the news I can't be sure that Raul will be able to keep the Orlando police off my back. The public pressure will be mounting for them to arrest somebody—anybody."

"When will the autopsy report be done?"

"I can't be sure. In a high-profile case like this they will want to have their ducks in a row before saying anything but I'm guessing in a day or two. America knows something happened so they can't drag their heels too long on it."

The waitress set our drinks down in front of us and took our dinner orders. We hadn't eaten since morning and were ravenous. We ordered fried calamari for two as an appetizer. I had the baked manicotti with a side of sausage and Cheryl had the linguini with white clam sauce. I asked the waitress to bring a bottle of Chianti with the entrées.

I continued, taking a sip of my Manhattan. "There are too many people out there who are interested in me and not in a good way. I don't want to wind up like Snow White."

"What about me, Cesari? I don't want to wind up like Snow White either just because I'm with you."

I chuckled. "And I don't want that either, which is why it might be a good idea if we took a break from each other for a while."

"What's that supposed to mean? Are you dumping me—again?" She didn't look happy.

"Take it easy. No one's dumping anybody, but it will be harder to get hit by a stray bullet if you're not standing next to me is all I'm saying. And that was a cheap shot. I didn't break up with you last time. I got—nervous."

She rolled her eyes. Cheryl had a habit of getting too close too fast, and I didn't like to play house until I was ready to play house. A couple of years ago, before I met Kelly, Cheryl had badgered me to move in with her and I had bolted like a jackrabbit.

"Fine, but if you treat me like you did last time then I'm really going to give you something to be nervous about."

"Okay, I already have two weeks off from work, and, after tonight, I'm only going to use cash. It's too easy to track credit card activity. The people we're up against are very sophisticated and have probably already figured out where we are so we have to keep moving."

"That's just great," she said sarcastically. "What about cell phones? Can't those be tracked too?"

"No doubt about that. Once I get you back to Manhattan, it's going to be radio silence except for emergencies, okay? Besides, I'm going to need to be under the radar because if I can't figure out what's going on to everyone's satisfaction, I'm taking off."

"What's that supposed to mean?"

"It means, if the autopsy comes back that Snow White's death was a homicide and I can't figure out what really happened, I have no intention of returning to Florida to face murder charges. I'd rather take my chances with Cinderella in Italy than face a rigged Disney jury in Orlando. Besides, I have family in Sicily that are just as dangerous as Raul. At least the playing field there will be a little more level."

The waitress served us our dinners and I plunged in enthusiastically, Cheryl just picked. "Everything all right?" I asked.

She shook her head. "No, everything's not all right. This is so far out of control I don't know where to begin. One minute we're having the greatest time of our lives and now you're talking about fleeing the country. Don't you understand? You didn't do anything wrong. You're an innocent man."

I stopped eating and starting laughing. "Are you going to sit there and tell me that you think everyone in prison is actually guilty of the crime they were accused of? John Grisham wrote a great book called *Innocent Man* about a guy who spent years on death row awaiting execution because the cops framed him. Apparently, that's not that uncommon, and I have no intention of letting that happen to me. If they want to fry me, they're going to have to catch me first. I'd rather be on the run swearing I'm innocent than in jail swearing it."

She sat back from the table and folded her arms. "I'm not hungry anymore."

"Oh come on. It's only a worst case scenario."

She let out a deep breath. "You always were a wild ride, Cesari."

"That's better. It's more fun to talk about sex."

"That's not what I meant, and can you be serious for more than three seconds?"

"My record is four seconds, but I'll try."

She let out a deep breath, unfolded her arms, and finally started eating. "Mm, this is very good."

"Yeah, mine too. Look, I know you're going to be worried so I'll figure out some way of getting in touch with you. Maybe I'll just pick us up a pair of cheap cell phones with prepaid minutes."

"And if I don't hear from you? Should I assume you've left the country or are dead?"

"Or in extreme circumstances, but I don't really think there are many choices here. I can't just walk around waiting for them to pick me up whenever they choose. I'd like to be proactive about my future."

She nodded. "I do understand. I'm just frustrated. And what am I supposed to be doing while you're running around incommunicado?"

"That's the spirit. Actually, I may need your help a lot before this is all over, and as of this moment I am formally petitioning you to be my personal attorney. I want you to open a case file on me and document everything that's happened to me since arriving in Orlando. As of this moment, everything that transpires between us is covered under attorney-client privilege."

"Everything?" she asked, finally cracking a smile.

"Especially everything."

The waitress cleared our table and offered us espresso and homemade cannolis, which we took her up on. By the time we finished, it was close to nine thirty and my cell phone rang.

"Cesari here."

"What do you think you are doing?" hissed Consuela.

"I'm having dinner, and how did you get my phone number?"

Ignoring that she asked, "Why did you leave Orlando?"

"Raul asked me to find out who killed his daughter. He didn't say I couldn't leave Orlando to do it."

"So what have you found out?"

"Only that there's a lot more going on than you and Raul told me about."

"Like what?"

"Like, I'd rather not talk about it on an unsecure phone. Maybe we should meet?"

"I think you should return to Orlando as soon as possible or I might have to come looking for you."

"Ooh, that sounds sexy."

She hung up.

Bitch.

Cheryl looked puzzled. "Consuela?"

"Yes, I think she just wanted me to know that I'm not that hard to find."

"How'd she get your number?"

I shrugged. "There are lots of ways to get somebody's cell phone number but more than likely she got it from the Orlando police."

"Do you think she's here?"

"Couldn't possibly say, but it only reinforces in my mind the need to turn our phones off and stop using the credit cards. By the way, we'll be driving not flying to New York after we're done here. If we try to fly anywhere, we'll definitely show up on the grid."

"And our luggage in Old Key West?"

"Call them in a few days and see if they'll ship it to New York. Tell them you had a family emergency, and with all the stress you simply forgot it. It sounds dumb but plausible and they won't care anyway."

"Fine. Look, it's getting late. What do you propose we do? Cinderella may not check for her passport 'til morning and we can't sit here all night."

"Let's go back to the hotel and find an ATM machine. We'll withdraw as much cash as we can and then we'll go hang out in the hotel bar while we wait. I'm betting she calls tonight."

Returning to our hotel, we found the bar there to be intimate and nearly empty. We ordered a couple of cocktails and sat at a small table. "I'm sorry about all this, Cheryl. I know it's not the vacation you've been dreaming of."

She chuckled. "No, not exactly, but I'm a big girl, and I'm not as cynical as you about the legal institutions of our country."

"I wish I could feel the same way, but I don't. And after my experience with the Orlando P.D., I'm fairly convinced every cop there would happily perjure himself on my behalf. That is, if Consuela didn't kill me first."

We waited until midnight and when we didn't hear from Cinderella, we decided to turn in. I was disappointed. We both stripped and hit the sack hard.

I looked over at her in the dark and whispered, "Hey."

"What?"

"Want to fool around?"

"No, isn't once a day enough for you? I want to go to sleep."

"I just thought that since you were now officially my lawyer, it might be more fun. Sort of like role-playing; I could be the hardened Al Capone type and you could be the tough take-him-down attorney."

She shook her head, exasperated. "Shut up and forget that we even shared the same room or I might get disbarred."

"What are you saying? We can't sleep together anymore?"

"I'm glad you understand."

"Why not?"

"For the same reason you can't sleep with your patients. It's unethical. You would be taking advantage of them in a stressful situation where they may not be able to make rational judgments."

"So if you gave me a blow job right now, you'd be taking advantage of me?"

"Exactly."

I laughed quietly to myself. She had more excuses at the ready than any woman I had ever known. I thought about jumping on her anyway, but I had tried that trick before and knew I'd have better luck with a porcupine. It didn't matter because at one a.m. her cell phone went off abruptly causing us both to jump up. I quickly turned on the lamp next to me as she answered it.

"Hello. Yes, this is she. Hi, Lola." Cheryl was quiet as she listened. "Okay, stay calm. It's probably nothing. Don't move, all right? We're on the way. Do you still have the gun? Good. Keep it near you." She clicked off.

"What's up?" I asked as I got out of bed and started dressing.

"A car just pulled into the driveway in front of the house. She was up packing and searching for the passport. She hadn't yet pressed the panic button about that when she noticed the car lights. There are two men in it and they're just sitting and talking."

I pulled my sweater over my head as I thought it over. "What do you think?"

"I think she's in trouble and we'd better get over there fast. She turned all the lights off and is hiding in the dark in the upstairs bathroom with the .22. She's nearly hysterical."

"Okay, let's go."

Cheryl touched my arm. "Should we call the police?"

I hesitated. "I don't know. It might be a false alarm. Maybe the car just got lost and the two guys are trying to figure out where they are. If the police come, Cinderella's trespassing and it won't be long before they figure out that the owner of the house is dead. Then she's really not going anywhere, and if someone were trying to hurt her, she'd be a sitting duck."

Cheryl nodded. "But we don't have any weapons."

"Nonsense. You always have weapons if you look around."

Out in the parking lot, I searched the trunk of the Honda while Cheryl warmed up the car. I found a twenty four inch long tire iron. One end was curved and designed for removing lug nuts and the other end flattened to pry tires off their rims. It weighed about three pounds. It wasn't a gun, but it would certainly make someone pay attention. I got in the car, fastened my seat belt, and Cheryl drove off, slipping and sliding along the frozen asphalt of the parking lot. It was close to zero degrees outside and without gloves the metal bar hurt to touch.

Chapter 14

The plows had cleared and salted the main roads, and driving wasn't nearly as treacherous as when we had arrived in the morning. In less than fifteen minutes, we approached our destination, and just as we turned onto Marble Town Road with the house still a hundred yards away, I told Cheryl to stop the car and turn the headlights off. We were hidden from view by trees, and at this late hour there was no other traffic on the small country road.

I said, "I think it might be better if we approached with the lights off. What do you think?"

She was apprehensive. "But I can't see anything." The heater was blowing full blast and I dreaded the thought of leaving the car.

Nodding, I said, "Look, the house is a straight run from here, and there is a little light from the moon. Let's give our eyes a few moments to adjust."

After a minute, she seemed a little more confident and said, "All right, let's give it a shot." She gently pressed on the accelerator and the car inched forward slowly.

After fifty yards of progress, I said, "Stop. I see something."

In the distance, I made out the brake lights of a car in the semicircular driveway. The headlights were off and exhaust fumes sifted up into the frosty night air, but I couldn't see who or how many guys were in the car.

"She said there were two men, right?" I asked.

"Yes, but that was twenty minutes ago, in the dark from the upstairs window. She could've missed a couple in the back seat."

I thought about that. How many men would you really need to take down one Cinderella? Judging by our encounter this afternoon, they might need more than one carload. I said, "She also said they were just sitting and talking. I wonder why?"

"Like you said before, they don't know if she's armed and since she really is, maybe they're smarter than the average ruthless murderers you're used to."

I looked at her. "Take it easy, counselor, that was prejudicial and leading."

Ignoring me she continued, "Or maybe they're just not sure this is the right house and they're trying to establish that right now. Maybe they're waiting for further instructions. You know, like how to make her death look like an accident or suicide."

"Or maybe they're inside right now drowning her in the bathtub—in the dark."

"Okay, Cesari. You convinced me, we need to do something."

I cradled the tire iron in my lap while I considered battle tactics. The metal was just starting to warm up, and I cursed myself for not picking up a pair of gloves while we had the chance.

"Okay, turn your emergency flashers on and slowly pull into the driveway behind their car. I'll get out and pretend we're disabled and need help. If there is no one in the car then we know they're in the house up to no good or else the lights would be on."

"What if they get out of the car together with guns drawn?"

"Why would they do that? They're not expecting trouble. They're the hunters not the prey. They'll be on the alert of course but will think we're a couple of local yokels who ran out of gas or something."

With lights blinking, we came to a halt a few feet from the rear of a gray Ford Taurus, which we could now see had New York plates. I turned to Cheryl. "Look, I'm going to approach the driver side. If he gets out and things look dicey, turn your brights on to blind him. I would also consider ramming him at full speed so keep the car in drive and your foot near the pedal."

I stepped out of the car with the tire iron hidden from view, tucked up the right sleeve of my jacket. It was really cold out and my ears started to burn almost immediately. It was times like this that I was glad I wasn't bald. Crossing in front of the Honda, I jogged quickly to the driver's side window of the Taurus. There was a thirty year old clean-shaven guy watching me in his side view mirror. As I neared, he rolled down the window a few inches and I could see that he was alone in the car, but Lola had seen two guys. Not good.

He appeared unconcerned as he asked, "What can I do for you?" He had his left hand on the steering wheel and his right buried in the pocket of his parka. From his appearance and demeanor, I suspected there was a pistol aimed at me. He seemed way too confident and nonchalant; the way people do when they're pretending. Okay, that solves what he's up to, and it also meant that the other guy was already in the house creeping around in the dark. Not good.

"Hi. I'm sorry to bother you, but my car keeps stalling every couple of hundred yards and the engine lights are all on. My girlfriend and I are afraid to keep driving like that in this weather and our cell phone's dead. Do you think you could call triple A for us? We'd appreciate it. As you can see we're not dressed for the weather."

This threw him off balance because now it was clear we weren't planning on leaving anytime soon. He eyed me carefully as I hopped from one foot to the other for warmth. If his friend was in the house murdering Cinderella, he certainly didn't like the idea of leaving two witnesses behind, especially if they could ID him and his license plate. Even worse would be for him to call triple A on his cell phone, leaving a digital fingerprint, telling the world that he was here. His brain worked overtime as he thought it through. Letting out a deep breath, he came to the only possible conclusion that made sense. I could see it in his eyes; he'd have to kill us both.

He said, "I'm pretty good with cars. Let me take a look." He rolled up his window and stepped out of the vehicle, his right hand still in the pocket of his parka. He took a step toward Cheryl in the Honda and I understood his thinking. Pretty slick move. He thought to shoot the driver of the car first and then take his time with me. No chance for either one of us to get away.

I stayed to his right and a half step behind as I let the tire iron slide discreetly down my sleeve. Grasping it firmly in my right hand as we walked toward the driver's side door of the Accord, I slowed my breathing and tried to envision the coming violence. At one in the morning, watching the Honda's flashing lights and preoccupied with his own strategy, he didn't notice my clandestine behavior. He was about two inches taller than me and appeared in good shape. As we approached, Cheryl saw the tire iron and understood something bad was going down. She suddenly turned the brights of the car on, blinding him, and simultaneously put the car into reverse backing away. Startled, he froze and instinctively drew the weapon out from its hiding place as I raised the tire iron, smashing it down onto the back of his head. The blow caused him to fall face forward, unconscious, into the snow and ice covered ground, his pistol sliding a few feet away. Cheryl quickly put the car in park, cut the lights, and got out to help me.

"Is he dead?" she asked, worried, watching as he lay motionless on the ground.

Kneeling down to check I said, "No, he's breathing just fine. Help me put him in the trunk of his car for safekeeping. The other guy must be in the house. We have to hurry."

I popped open the trunk using the lever by the driver's seat, and we hoisted him inside. I removed his belt and tied his hands behind his back with it. Then I searched him for other weapons and found none. He did have a cell phone, however, which I threw into a snowbank.

"Don't you want to know who he is?" Cheryl asked.

"Not really," I said, bending to retrieve the tire iron. "I mean, what difference does it make if the guy trying to kill you is named Harry or Bill or Ted?"

I turned the Ford's engine off and also tossed the keys into the snow. Whoever was in the house wasn't going anywhere tonight. "Cheryl, get in the Honda and drive down the road until you're out of sight. Keep the lights off and wait for me. I'll call you when I'm coming."

"What if you don't come?"

"Then you won't have to worry about whether having sex with me violates your legal code of ethics."

Despite herself, she chuckled. "You're such an asshole. Please be careful."

Watching her walk back to the car, I picked up the discarded pistol, examining it. It was a Sig Sauer p228 just like the one I took from the guy in Orlando. I popped the clip and saw that it was loaded with .357 magnum ammo. That's pretty serious ordinance, which meant that this guy intended to kill whatever it was he was shooting at even if the other guy was hiding behind a door or in a car.

I was starting to shiver from the cold and decided I had better get moving before I was too late to help Lola. The front door was unlocked as before and I entered, noting the house to be nearly pitch black and eerily quiet. I decided to go up the front staircase with the painted steps, which was on my left. It had been just over half an hour since Lola had called, and maybe fifteen to twenty minutes since the other guy had entered the house, assuming they had talked over strategy for a few minutes first. His progress would be slow and methodical not knowing where she might be or who might be with her. He may have started in the garage and basement and was slowly working his way upward. Still, he would surely have found his way to the bedrooms by now. If I went up the front staircase I could get to her room first, since it was closer to this end of the house, assuming he did what we had earlier—gone up the second set of stairs in the rear, which would be a more natural approach especially if he was coming from the basement or garage. I was making a lot of assumptions.

I took my shoes off to minimize the sound of my steps and gently ascended the stairs, gun in one hand, tire iron in the other. My heart pounded and I had a bad feeling about a lot of things. Like why would anyone want to murder young women who play Disney characters? And could a guy like Raul really be involved with Disney? Then there was the Secret Service...

At the top of the stairs, a glimmer of light caught my attention at the other end of the hallway. He was flicking a small flashlight on and off as he progressed from room to room. He was two bedrooms away and moving in my direction. He stopped to enter one of the rooms and I seized the opportunity to enter Lola's room, which was less than five feet away. I closed the gap quickly, quietly turned the knob, and entered. It was very dark but I remembered the layout from my visit earlier in the day. Lola was hiding in the bathroom with the .22, and I certainly didn't want to be the first one to open that door right now. Without some type of warning, she would undoubtedly make noise and most likely shoot before looking. Better to leave her there, so I took up position behind the door, which swung inward, and waited, my pulse throbbing in my neck. I no longer felt cold. I no longer felt anything. I didn't really want to hurt anyone, but for some reason these guys felt the need to murder a young girl who did them no harm, so there it was.

A few moments later, the door opened slowly toward me and he stepped stealthily into the room as I crouched, ready to spring into action. The flashlight clicked on and off briefly as he stepped forward. The door blocked my view of him, and I assumed he was scanning the room. The light flicked on and off again as he approached the bed. I heard him rustling the sheets, checking to see if she was there. This was the last bedroom before the staircase down, so he must have been puzzled as to her whereabouts. Expecting to find her sound asleep, he may even have been getting a little suspicious. He grunted ever so slightly in frustration but then turned his attention to the bathroom, and I felt him freeze in place as it dawned on him that maybe his presence wasn't as much of a surprise as he had thought.

As he crept away from me toward the bathroom door, I came out from my hiding place and silently stalked him. I was the lion hunting the leopard hunting the antelope. He hesitated in front of the bathroom door and I read his mind. He was wondering if it was possible that she might be armed.

I had to act now. The minute he touched that handle the room was going to explode in gunfire. Her nerves were frayed, and she was surely stressed out beyond all comprehension by this point, not knowing for sure what was happening.

Trouble was I could barely see his silhouette in the dark room. If I shot and missed, it might penetrate the door and kill the girl I was trying to save. I put the pistol in my waistband and moved in quickly with the tire iron raised over my head. Closing in like that, I could make out his form better. His left hand reached for the bathroom doorknob. His right held the gun. I brought the tire iron crashing down hard on his right forearm, breaking it. The sound of snapping bone was sickening but not nearly as much as the blood curdling howl he let out as he staggered backward in pain and shock. His weapon fell harmlessly to the floor as multiple gunshots burst through the bathroom door at us from Lola's .22. One hit him somewhere in the torso, giving him something else to moan about as he fell backward into the wall. I ducked to the floor unhurt but now out of position.

He was wounded but probably not fatally, and he might have a backup weapon. Another shot burst harmlessly through the bathroom door, shattering a pane in one of the bedroom's windows. I heard the guy across the room cursing in pain. I pulled my pistol out and shot blindly in the direction I last heard him moan, rolling quickly to my left as I did. A return shot in my direction answered the question of whether he had a backup weapon.

In the dark, it was impossible to tell exactly where he was, but with his wounds he probably wasn't that mobile at the moment. I pondered the situation as I lay on my stomach staring into darkness and then had a thought. "Lola, turn on the light, now!" As I shouted to her I rolled quickly back to my right, narrowly avoiding another shot in my direction.

Seconds later, beams of light shone brightly through the bullet holes in the bathroom door, and I saw him scrunched up in a ball trying to hide behind a bureau. He realized what had just happened but it was too late. As he tried to crawl away, I lined him up in my sights and fired twice. The first shot missed but the second hit him squarely in the sternum. His head rocked backward smashing into the wall behind and then he slumped forward, dead.

All was quiet while I assessed the situation. "Are you okay, Lola? This is Dr. Cesari."

Her voice trembled. "Yes."

I stood up and walked over to the guy to make sure he was dead. He still held a small .38 in his left hand, and I kicked it away. I checked him for a pulse but there was none.

"You can come out now. It's over."

The bathroom door opened and a nearly hysterical girl came rushing out into my arms. She wrapped herself tightly around me and I held her like that. "It's all right, Lola. You're going to be all right."

She was sobbing and could barely speak. "Why are they trying to kill me? I don't understand. I didn't do anything." She looked at the body, horrified.

"That's what we're trying to figure out, Lola. Let us try to help you, but you'll need to confide in us. We need to know everything you know, okay?" She nodded, her head buried deep in my chest, trembling uncontrollably.

"Lola, I need you to get your things. I don't think it's a good idea for you to go to Italy. I have a feeling they're watching the airports and you'd never get there. I'll do my best to keep you safe, but you have to trust me and do exactly as I say."

"I will. I'm already packed, but I misplaced my passport. I can't find it anywhere." For the sake of trust building I felt this would be the wrong time to confess about the passport so I said nothing. I would just slip it back into her suitcase when the chance arose.

"Okay, don't worry about it now. It'll turn up. We need to leave here quickly."

As she collected her things, I pulled the dead guy's wallet from his pocket. He had three hundred dollars in cash, which I took, a bunch of credit cards, a driver's license, and a Secret Service photo ID.

Great.

I picked up his primary weapon, which was the same type of pistol I took from the other guy in the trunk, a Sig Sauer .228, loaded with .357 magnums. A quick frisk revealed a cell phone and spare ammunition clip, both of which I pocketed. I now felt confident to face a new day.

"Are you ready to go, Lola?"

"I'm ready. How cold is it out there?"

"Really cold, why?"

"Helena has a closet full of winter clothing downstairs. I wasn't planning on sticking around long and didn't pack winter gear so I'll just borrow some of her stuff. I guess she won't be needing it anymore."

I nodded and thought it over. "Any men's clothing in there?"

Chapter 15

*U*sing the dead guy's cell phone, I called 911 to let them know that I heard shots fired in the house and saw someone get tossed into the trunk of a car. I didn't know what to do with him and felt it was unnecessary to let him freeze to death in the back of the Ford. I tossed the phone into the woods across the street, and we drove away as quickly as we could, given the road conditions. I had brought Cheryl a scarf, hat, and gloves from Helena's closet and although she didn't have any men's clothing a wool ski hat helped my mood. Cheryl rode shotgun, and Lola sat in the back. We'd agreed to use cash only from this point on and to remove the batteries from our cell phones.

Furthermore, the car was problematic because as soon as we dropped it off, it would ping our location. After discussion, it was decided to leave it in Syracuse and take the train into Manhattan's Grand Central Station, paying cash for the tickets. They would know we made it to Syracuse but then we would fall off the grid. Cheryl would take the week off and stay with Lola at a Holiday Inn Express on 37th Street and keep a low profile. I would call her there periodically, using a prepaid cell phone.

"Okay, Lola, now it's your turn. Tell us everything you know." I glanced at her in the rearview mirror.

She was quiet as I studied her. Cheryl said sympathetically, "Lola honey, we know you've been through a lot, but it's very important that we get to the bottom of this. Whatever it is, we won't judge you. That's a promise."

Lola sighed deeply. "I started there two years ago. I was lucky. They saw me as a natural for Cinderella so that was my main role. They didn't shuttle me around playing other characters and I didn't have to go to any of the other parks. Helena really liked me so I pretty much was Cinderella all the time. I had several understudies, and there were a few other girls trained to do my job for times when I was sick or took time off, but ninety percent of the time when you saw Cinderella it was me."

Pausing to draw a deep breath, she continued. "Helena called me into her office one night and told me that some rich big shot wanted to meet me and take me out to dinner. She told me I didn't have to if I didn't want to but that he could possibly help my career, so I thought about it for a while and said yes."

She hesitated and looked at me in the mirror. "You guys getting the picture yet?"

Cheryl turned around, naively. "Not exactly."

"You—were nice to him?" I asked gently.

"Yes—very nice." She looked down.

I glanced at Cheryl who asked, "For money, Lola?"

"Yes—a lot of money."

Cheryl finally got it and nodded. "I don't mean to be obtuse but I just want to make sure I got the facts straight, okay?" She was a lawyer through and through.

Lola nodded. "I understand."

Cheryl continued. "So, Helena pimped you out to rich guys?"

"Not just me...Snow White too, and it was all voluntary. Nobody forced anybody to do anything. I just want to make that clear. Helena was very good to me."

Cheryl looked at me and shook her head. "John, I can't believe what I'm hearing."

I agreed. "Please continue, Lola. How did we get from there to here?"

She took a deep breath and let it out. "About a year ago, a VIP started coming around. He was older, late sixties maybe even seventy, and wealthier than the usual and clearly a man of power. He wanted both of us, me and Snow White at the same time, so we became like a team for whenever he was in town. He had bodyguards and handlers too. They would even wand us for weapons before we could get near him. He scared me. I didn't like the vibe I was getting, especially from his bodyguards. They didn't like what was going on and clearly felt it was a security risk, which is why when Helena called me and said it was time to get out of town I wasn't totally surprised, even though I didn't know exactly what had happened. I thought maybe the newspapers had caught on and were going to make a big deal about it. You know, like a sex scandal type of thing, and Helena didn't want them to get near me. Then there was the real possibility of going to prison. It's not like I didn't know what I was doing was illegal."

I nodded. "Okay, that makes sense. So did this guy ever tell you his name?"

She chuckled. "Are you kidding? No, he wasn't stupid, just sick."

"Sick? How so?"

"A seventy year old man that likes to have sex with girls dressed up as Snow White and Cinderella is pretty sick if you ask me." I thought about that a little bit, trying to decide which was worse—for a guy that age to have sex with twenty year olds or to be turned on by the outfits. Tough call.

Cheryl was curious and a little more to the point. "Did you do it with the costumes on?"

"Of course, that was the whole idea."

I almost drove the car into a snow bank when she said that.

Cheryl exclaimed, "Cesari! Be careful, you almost got us killed."

"You wore the outfits? Really?" I don't know why that surprised me but for some reason it made it all seem worse.

"Not the whole time of course, but for much of it, that's why it's sick. It's the costume that turns them on, not me."

Maybe she had a point. "Were there any other girls involved besides you and Snow White, like Jasmine or Belle?"

"Not that I know of, but it was none of my business and I didn't care."

"Tell me about Snow White. What was she like?"

"She was okay. A little goofy, almost never stepped out of character. A couple of times when we were with the old guy she kind of got a little aggressive, you know? Like trying to push me out of the way. I thought she was doing the alpha female thing. I didn't care because it was less I had to do. I honestly think she thought the guy had feelings for her and she sort of resented me being there."

"How did the old guy take that?" Cheryl asked.

She chuckled. "Him? Oh he loved the idea that Cinderella and Snow White were fighting over him. Gave him a rush. It didn't matter to him that I wasn't fighting at all. In fact, it was actually an easy night for me when she got like that. Sometimes, I would barely have to touch him, which suited me just fine. Do you guys mind if I smoke a joint? I'm feeling a little tense."

Cheryl and I were silent as we digested this. I said, "Did you get along well with Snow White, Lola? And yes, I do mind so don't."

"I didn't have a problem with her but like I said I think she saw me in a two's company and three's a crowd kind of way, and you don't have to be so grouchy."

Cheryl looked at her. "He doesn't mean to be cross, but it might be better if we all stay focused. So who do you think this guy is?"

"I don't know. I guess I just assumed he was a politician or something but I don't vote or really care about those things so who knows? To me he was just another perv."

She lit up a joint despite my admonishment so I opened my window a crack, letting the brisk air howl in. She was starting to irritate me.

I said, "Did the guy ever mention taking Snow White to his castle?"

"All the time, why? He really ate up the character routine, and she encouraged it big time. I think it turned them both on so maybe they were both twisted."

"Hmm. So, where did these parties take place, Lola?" I asked.

"Here and there. Sometimes we went with him in his limo to a hotel, sometimes we did it right in the limo, but most of the time we stayed on Disney."

"We've been to Snow White's apartment, Lola." I turned the car onto the exit ramp for Syracuse as we spoke.

She chuckled. "Oh, so you've seen the love pad. I guess my humiliation is fully complete then. Well, what would you like to know?"

"Did you know there were video cameras in the room?"

"Hell no, I was supposed to get extra for that kind of thing."

Chapter 16

The train pulled into Grand Central Station at noon. Lola slept reclined in her seat, two rows back from Cheryl and me. "So what do you think about Helena?" Cheryl asked.

"I don't know but it seems highly probable that Snow White's death is related to whatever was going on in her secret bed chamber. So if Helena knew or suspected she was murdered on account of that, then she may have committed suicide out of guilt for having placed her in that situation, but before exiting this world she may have tried to spare Lola the same fate by packing her off to Italy. So maybe she told her she'd meet her there just to humor her so she wouldn't panic. On the other hand, if someone murdered Snow White and was after Cinderella, then they might have knocked off Helena as well and made it look like suicide. That wouldn't be that hard to do."

"That's not a bad theory, but why would anybody want to kill them at all? My God, it's just sex for crying out loud, and would the Secret Service really commit murder and on whose behalf—the old guy? That's hard to believe. According to Lola, he'd been coming to see her and Snow White for almost a year. If it was him then why kill everybody now?"

"Good questions, and I don't have any good answers." I thought about what she said; that it was just sex. Was it ever just sex? And what was it about sex that made people crazy, and who killed because of it?

The train doors opened and I woke Lola. "C'mon, we're here."

We parted company on the street outside the station. They took a cab to their hotel, and I hoofed it down to 42nd Street to the Kit Kat Club on the East Side just a few blocks away. It was a balmy thirty-five degrees in Manhattan and the sky was clear. Compared to upstate, I felt like I was in a heat wave. Stopping for coffee at Starbucks, I considered my situation. The seven hundred dollars I had on me wouldn't last long, and I was sure I would need more before this was over; the same for Cheryl. I had warned her not to go to a bank or ATM. I also needed a place to stay because I assumed that all the players involved would easily figure out where I lived, but most importantly, I needed a plan.

The entrance to the Kit Kat Club was on Second Avenue, near 44th Street, next to a pizzeria. The large oak door guarding the entrance was locked as the club didn't open until seven. The windows on either side of the entrance were blackened for privacy. As part owner, I had my own key but had left it with my other belongings in Old Key West. Risking a call to Vito was a possibility, but I decided against it. I had a slight advantage right now and didn't want to throw it away. Getting some prepaid phones would be my high priority once I settled in.

"Hey handsome, looking for a date?" A familiar voice broke my concentration.

Turning toward a tall, sultry woman with bright red hair that you could only get from a bottle I said, "Hi Heidi, you're a sight for sore eyes." We gave each other a warm hug.

"What's the matter? You lose your key, Cesari?"

"Yeah, something like that. Were you going in or just walking by?" I knew she lived nearby in a two-bedroom apartment. She was also part owner of the gentleman's club and its general manager, and every so often, for thrills and giggles, she would enthrall the patrons with her classic pole dance skills. The younger girls had nothing on her, and she liked to let them know it once in a while. She was thirty-nine years old, stacked, and apparently, highly skilled in the boudoir, at least according to Vito. Her stage name was Spicy Ginger.

"Baby doll, I practically live here. I should just move into the apartment upstairs. Yeah, I was coming in to do the books before we open tonight so you and Vito can get your cut. What did you need? Not that you need a reason, so come on in."

We entered the lounge, and she flipped on the lights. "Give me a sec, and I'll turn up the heat." She stepped off to the side, and I glanced around the room that I'd spent so much time in. This was Vito's preferred meeting place to avoid federal law enforcement eavesdropping. His relationship with Heidi and the girls was excellent, so he trusted them. Even though we were partners with Heidi, and Vito had on several occasions taken the plunge, we stayed out of her way for the most part and let her manage things the way she saw fit.

Heidi returned and signaled me to follow her to the back office from which she ran the place. I removed my coat and seated myself in an oversized leather chair, watching her pour whiskey into a couple of tumblers for us.

"It's a little early, don't you think?" I asked, noting the time.

She handed me my glass. "It's never too early for alcohol—or sex."

"That's very profound," I chuckled as we clinked our glasses together.

"So, am I imagining it or are you back from Florida a little early?" she asked, sitting down at her desk, facing me.

"No, you're right. Something happened down there and I'm in a bit of a fix."

"Bit of a fix? Speak English, Cesari. It's been all over television. So why'd you kill Snow White?"

We both laughed. "I didn't kill her, but my word may not be enough to prevent me from getting a lethal injection. So, I need to lay low while I sort things out."

"Really? I was just kidding. So you are involved in that mess?"

"Not really. I was just in the wrong place at the wrong time. I'd rather not go into it but I will need a place to stay for a few days. Would you mind if I crashed in the apartment upstairs?"

There was a modest two-bedroom apartment on the second floor of the Kit Kat that Heidi let some of the girls use who were down on their luck or hiding from abusive boyfriends. "No, I don't mind, but you've got company, a girl named Cocoa. She just started here at the club a couple of months ago and doesn't have a place of her own yet."

I must have made a face.

"Relax, she won't be a problem. She doesn't do drugs and I'll warn her not to ask questions."

Great, a roommate. I sighed. "Fine."

"Besides, Cesari, she's gorgeous and a great dancer. I ought to be warning you to stay away from her."

I snorted and sipped my whiskey. "Don't worry. I got bigger things on my mind; like staying out of prison."

"So, why can't you go back to your apartment? Are they watching it, whoever they are, and I assume it's not just the police you're worried about?"

She was pretty sharp and picked up on my deeper concerns. "I'm always worried about the police but you're right. It's someone else, and they are probably watching my apartment. For the same reason, I can't use my credit cards or cell phone. The people I'm involved with are very resourceful."

She nodded thoughtfully. "I see, and I guess I shouldn't ask too many questions either, so how can I help you besides letting you use the apartment?"

"I want you to call Vito, and without mentioning my name, have him come down here. Tell him you'd like to have lunch or something."

"You think they're watching him too?"

"The feds are always watching him and listening in on his calls. The people interested in me know we're friends and have contacts in law enforcement. It can really be a small world sometimes."

She nodded, understanding. "Is that it?"

"No, forget you ever saw me."

"Do you need a weapon?"

I grinned broadly. "No thanks, I'm good. Look, I'm going to go take a shower and lie down for a while. It's been a rough and really long night."

She opened one of the desk drawers, pulled out a key, and tossed it to me. "Cocoa's got the room to the left and yours is to the right. Don't get them mixed up. I like her. There are bath towels in the linen closet just outside the bathroom and a spare toothbrush in the vanity cabinet above the sink. Sorry, but no shaving equipment unless you want to ask Cocoa if you can borrow hers."

"Thanks, Heidi. I'll see you later."

I walked up the narrow staircase behind her desk and let myself into the apartment. The kitchen area was small but adequate, as was the living room. Cocoa's bedroom door was closed, and I proceeded directly to the bathroom to take a long, hot shower. I thought about things as I lathered up but really couldn't make any sense of it. So Cinderella, Snow White, and maybe others were turning tricks with rich guys in their spare time and Helena was their madam. So what? If I was a really rich and powerful guy who frequented hookers why would I suddenly want them all dead? Because of the threat of exposure? Maybe. If somebody had secretly videoed me and then tried to blackmail me with it I might be tempted to kill them.

But why kill Snow White and Cinderella? Cinderella didn't even know about the cameras, and I doubted Snow White did either. They were just kids anyway. Why take it out on them? Helena, maybe? Did she kill herself and why? I really needed to see the coroner's report.

And then there was the issue of the Secret Service. Would they really commit murder and on whose command? That was a hard pill to swallow unless they thought that what they were doing was in the best interest of their country. Honor, duty, patriotism. The only unholy trinity when it came to making innocent young men commit heinous acts. Possibly? But who would have the balls to threaten a guy so high up the food chain that he could call on the Secret Service to defend him with lethal force, and what did they hope to accomplish by threatening him in the first place? So the old guy's a pervert? Big deal. Aren't all men to some degree? In this day and age who would even care?

I stepped out of the shower, dried off, and wrapped the towel around my waist, glancing at myself in the mirror. I paused, did a quick flex, and smiled.

Looking good, Cesari.

My bedroom was small but adequate, with a small desk and chair. A full-sized bed occupied most of the room. Everything looked clean and that's all I cared about. I threw my clothes on the floor and myself on the bed. Within minutes, I was sound asleep.

At three p.m., Vito knocked on the door and bellowed. "Cesari, you in there?"

I sat up. "Yeah, c'mon in."

The door opened and the big man entered, taking a seat on the chair by the desk. Vito was a bulky, muscular man with extremely distinctive, chiseled features and jet black, wavy hair. A few years older than me, in his late thirties and tight all over, he looked like he could still play middle linebacker. He wore a silk suit and alligator shoes because he always wore a silk suit and alligator shoes. A diamond and onyx pinky ring adorned his right hand, and an eighteen-carat gold bracelet dangled off his wrist.

"I see you made it in all right, Cesari? What's with all the secrecy?"

I rubbed my eyes as I spoke. "There are lots of people who would like to know where I am right now, Vito, and I don't want them to."

He pulled a pack of camels out from the inside of his jacket and lit one up. "So Heidi tells me. Are you going to fill me in on what's going on, partner, or do I just call the cops and be done with it?" He joked and blew a cloud of smoke in my direction.

I gave him a blow-by-blow account of everything that had transpired since Cheryl and I landed in Disney. I trusted him with my life. We had grown up together in the streets of the Bronx, and our friendship had been battle tested time and again. Our life paths had diverged and I had chosen to become a physician. He had chosen to be a lifelong mobster and now ran most of the rackets in lower Manhattan. Through a confusing intertwining of our fates I had become his senior advisor, partner, and most trusted confidant. We were bound together at the hip it seemed.

"Damn, Cesari. You're wanted by the Orlando P.D. for murdering Snow White and the first thing you do when you get back to New York is kill two Secret Service agents." He started laughing just as he took a long drag on his cigarette, which sent him into a massive coughing fit.

"I didn't murder the one in the trunk, and would you mind opening a window before we both choke to death or get cancer?"

He went over to the window and opened it partway. "Did you call an ambulance?"

"Yes, I did, right before we left."

He nodded. "That was nice of you."

I detected a note of sarcasm in his voice. "Yeah, so what have you got for me?"

Vito sat back down and crossed his legs. "Okay, let me tell you what I got on that other Secret Service guy, the one you assaulted at

Disney. Phillip M. McIntosh is a thirty-two year old Eagle Scout from Kansas. He joined the service fresh out of college and has been a model citizen ever since. He has worked on numerous assignments, from protecting the first family to security for the pope. He is as they say a golden boy. Not a blemish on him, and you put him in the hospital for two days with a concussion, stole his weapon and ID, and caused him such utter humiliation that he has been put on administrative leave while his story is being investigated. Nice work, Cesari. And all this based on a hunch you had that he may have been following you."

"He was following me."

"And those guys upstate. Are you sure they were trying to kill that girl? How do you know they weren't simply trying to bring her in for questioning? They have the right to do that kind of stuff you know. If she was a hooker involved in a plot to blackmail somebody important under their protection, they may have decided to send their own guys after her rather than involve local police, who may not have understood the delicate nature of the situation."

Fuck! He was making sense.

"What you're saying sounds reasonable, but there is something very wrong about all of this, and why are Snow White and Helena dead? It doesn't pass the smell test. Besides, I know a hit squad when I see one, and that's what those guys upstate were. For Christ's sake, the asshole was creeping around that house in the dark with his weapon drawn."

"Just speculating, Cesari. That's all. By the way, where's the pistol you stole from the agent?"

"I put it in the desk drawer with the spare clip. So what about Raul? What did you dig up on him?"

He opened the desk drawer and began examining the weapon. "There is nobody named Raul Varga working for Disney as far as I can figure out. I have a guy on the payroll in the IRS and he says there are lots of people with that name but none getting a check from Disney."

"Why do you have people on the payroll at the IRS?"

"Because I want to see who's buying their health insurance and who's not? Why do you think? It's the easiest way to check a guy out."

"Relax, it was just a question. Okay, so that would make sense if he was who he says he was; some guy lurking in the background whose affairs are top secret."

"I agree. That didn't surprise me at all. In fact, I would have been more surprised if he turned up as easily as that."

"Look, Vito, I'm going to need cash and a fake driver's license if I'm going to get anything done. I want you to bring me ten thousand dollars in fifties in a duffel bag, and maybe another ten thousand in a separate bag for Cheryl."

"Cheryl?"

"Yeah, she's laying low with Cinderella for now. I think we have to assume the worst; that somebody wants this girl dead and that they're sophisticated enough to track cell phones and credit cards. I want Cheryl to have enough cash so she and Cinderella can live comfortably for a short period of time while I sort this out."

He grunted as he put the Sig Sauer back in the desk drawer. "What else?"

"Buy a bunch of cell phones with prepaid minutes so we can communicate safely, okay? I'll be staying here for a few days, but not much longer than that, and I may have to move in a hurry without saying good-bye. If these guys are as good as I think they are they'll find out all about the Kit Kat Club before too long. He knew who you were by the way."

"Who?"

"Raul. That night in Disney. He knew all about you and your relationship with me. So don't underestimate these guys."

He grunted. "I won't. I'll have the cash ready for you in a couple of hours but I'll need more time for the driver's license, at least until tomorrow morning. Give me yours now so the guy will have something to work with. All right, Cesari, let me go take care of business and I'll be back in time for dinner. Will that be all, your highness?"

"That should do it for now."

He stood to leave and turned back, grinning. "By the way, have you seen Cocoa yet?"

"Cocoa? The girl I'm sharing the apartment with? No, why?"

"She's incredible. You're going to want to tap that for sure."

"Thanks for the tip. Now get going. I got a lot of things on my mind."

He closed the door behind him, and I lay back down staring at the ceiling for several minutes, thinking about what he had said. Was I wrong about those guys upstate? Did I kill an innocent man just trying to do his job? Was Cinderella not so innocent? It was always difficult to look into the eyes of a beautiful woman and think the worst. Why was that, I wondered? I looked down at the towel I was wrapped in and realized that I needed fresh clothing and a razor. I sighed, looked at my watch, and stood up to get dressed when the door opened gently.

I held my breath as a stunningly beautiful girl with shoulder-length auburn hair poked her head in. The rest of her soon followed without an invitation. She appeared to be in her early twenties, five feet four inches tall, with big brown eyes, luscious lips, and a killer smile. She wore shorts, a T-shirt, and flip-flops, and for a second, I thought I was back in college.

"Everything okay in here?" she asked. "I heard loud voices."

I stood there paralyzed, holding my breath. There had to be some scientific explanation for why a beautiful woman could do that to a man. So this was the famous Cocoa. Wow! I said, "Yeah, everything's fine. I'm sorry if we disturbed you."

She stood at the doorway and shamelessly checked me out. I suddenly felt self-conscious and bent down to grab my shirt off the floor. As I did my towel, came undone and fell off.

She laughed. "Whoa! Look at that thing. Were you raised near a nuclear power plant or something?"

It wasn't easy to make me blush but she did. Recovering my composure, I picked up the towel and wrapped myself up quickly. "Would you mind closing the door on the way out? I'd like to get dressed," I said gruffly.

She didn't move and kept eyeing me up and down. "Don't you want to know who I am?"

I was embarrassed and felt a little helpless. If there was another way out of the room I'm sure I would have taken it. "No, not really. Good-bye."

She smiled, knowing I was off-balance. "Fine, but you don't have to be rude. It's not the first one I've ever seen."

I was getting irritated. "Well, it's going to be the last one if you don't get out."

She disappeared, closing the door behind her, and I got dressed.

Round one to Cocoa.

Chapter 17

I closed the door to my room and went out into the main living area to find Cocoa. I felt the need to clear the air between us but she had disappeared into the bathroom, so I decided to drop it and went downstairs to find Heidi.

"I need to step out and get a few things. If Vito returns before I do just tell him to relax. I won't be long."

She nodded. "Sure. Did you get a load of Cocoa yet?"

"We said hi, yeah."

"What'd you think?"

"I didn't think anything. I'll see you later, all right?"

"Sure, but why are you so grouchy?"

"I'm fine. Talk to you later."

Geez.

I left the Kit Kat Club and wandered down Second Avenue for a few blocks until I came to a small clothing store, where I picked up a shirt, jeans, a six pack of socks, and underwear. It was almost five, and I figured Vito wouldn't be back until at least six or later so I decided to risk a trip down to my office in St. Matt's. I needed to take care of a few things and figured that as long as I was nearby I might as well get a head start on the ever-present mountain of paperwork that government intrusion in health care had caused. There would be dozens of triages from my office manager and nurse, stacks of labs and pathology reports to review, and innumerable phone calls I would have to return at some point. If I knocked a few of these off now, it would be that much less of a shock when I returned to work.

A short cab ride left me off at the front doors to the hospital, and I entered uneventfully, taking the elevator to my office on the fifth floor. It entered my mind that they might be watching the hospital, but they couldn't be everywhere at once or even be sure I was in Manhattan, let alone on Third Avenue at five o'clock on a Saturday. So, although it was possible, I judged it to be improbable.

I turned the light on in my office and immediately noticed something out of place, but what? I looked around and sat down. The office was functional: a desk, couple of chairs, file cabinet, and a bookcase. My hospital ID on a lanyard lay casually on my desktop, and I picked it up and put it in my pocket. Also on my desk was my laptop, a few residual patient charts that needed to be reviewed, a legal pad, a pencil holder, a desk phone, and a small bust of Julius Caesar I had picked up for ten dollars at the Metropolitan Museum of Art. The bust was facing away as I sat behind the desk, which was odd because it always faced me. I liked to look in his face and muse about how things must have been back in the good old days. Before I left for Florida I had told the cleaning people not to enter my office, but maybe they did anyway.

I picked up the bust and examined it. On the bottom it said, "Made in China." I put it down, facing me. Something didn't feel right so I began a search of the room. In the back of one of my desk drawers I found a stack of love letters addressed to me from Marguerite Varga, aka Snow White. Each one handwritten, telling me how much she loved me and enjoyed our time together. According to the letters she was waiting for me to dump my current girlfriend and run away with her and also that she forgave me for hitting her. Damn. These guys were professional assholes. But what would be the point of planting letters like these? Obviously, they could easily be proved to be forgeries, but that could take a while and might result in me being detained. I concluded that they were simply trying to harass and intimidate me, make me uncomfortable. Well, they succeeded. I didn't like the idea that unauthorized people were hanging around my office trying to aggravate me. God knows what else they might plant here if they wanted to make me miserable, like heroin or cocaine. That would do the trick.

Looking up, I noticed the blinking light of a small video camera behind a plant on top of my bookcase. I walked over to it and saw that it was aimed at my desk. Confused and suddenly alarmed, I raced to the window just as two police cars pulled up to the main entrance of the hospital, lights flashing. I shoved the letters into the pocket of my jacket next to the stolen Sig Sauer. Shit. Why did I have to bring the pistol with me? I had a lot of reasons to move fast.

I flipped off the lights and ran down the emergency stairwell to the third floor, where I ducked into the men's locker room. A surgeon and anesthesiologist were changing into scrubs in preparation for a case.

"Hey guys, what's going on?"

The surgeon, a burly guy with a goatee named Dayton, said, "Hey, Cesari, what are you doing here? Got a case?"

"No, I live nearby and forgot something in my locker. What about you?"

"We've got a hot gallbladder in a seventy year old guy who's already septic. This should be fun."

I looked at the anesthesiologist and extended my hand. "John Cesari, gastroenterology. I don't believe we've met."

He grasped my hand. "Ashok Patel, anesthesia. Nice to meet you."

"Do you do ERCP's, Cesari?" Dayton asked. ERCP was the acronym for endoscopic retrograde cholangio-pancreatography, a specialized procedure to visualize the bile duct and remove gallstones that were sometimes too difficult for the surgeon to get at. It was used as an adjunct to surgery in specific situations.

"Yes, I do. Why?" I asked mindlessly as I fumbled with my locker combination.

"Well, this guy is a little jaundiced and may have a bile duct stone in addition to an infected gallbladder. The gallbladder can't wait so that's why I'm taking it out now. I'll shoot a cholangiogram while I'm in there, but if I find a stone stuck in the duct would you be willing to help us out as long as you're here?"

This was one of the trickiest areas in all of medicine. How to negotiate the friendly *will you do me a favor* minefield. I looked at my watch, and thought about the police downstairs. "I need to check on a couple of things first, all right? I wasn't exactly free, but if I can help you out I surely will."

He seemed satisfied with that collegial response. Guys in medicine cracked me up. They thought nothing about asking a favor on a Saturday night that might tie you up for the next eight hours just to save themselves the trouble of an extra phone call.

He smiled. "Thanks, Cesari."

After they left to do their case, I found an unassigned locker and put my coat with the Sig Sauer and the love letters inside, placing my lock on it. I didn't feel that my locker would be safe anymore. For good measure, I changed into scrubs to look more natural. If the cops weren't looking for me then nothing was lost, but I doubted that their presence was a coincidence. I walked quickly down to the main floor to see what was going on and saw two uniformed officers guarding the main entrance so I hopped on a free elevator back to the fifth floor.

The door to my office was open, and I saw the back of one of the hospital administrators standing there in conference with an officer. I turned and walked in the opposite direction. Shit. I went back to the locker room, put on surgical booties, mask, and hat and joined Dayton, who had started the cholecystectomy.

He glanced at me. "Hey Cesari, couldn't stay away, huh?"

"No, I figured I might as well hang around as long as I was here."

"Hi, Dr. Cesari." An OR nurse named Beth called out. The other OR nurse, Ellen, simply waved hello.

"Hello everyone. How's it going, Dayton?"

He never took his eyes off the video monitor in front of him. "I was hoping to do this laparoscopically but he has dense adhesions in the right upper quadrant and I think I'm going to have to open him up the old-fashioned way. In addition, I think his gallbladder may actually have perforated already. I see pus all over the place."

I looked at the screen with him. "Oh, well. Sorry about that. Looks like you're going to be here a while."

He took a deep breath. "All night probably. Well thanks for hanging around, but it looks like you're off the hook. Since I'm going to open him up, I'll just do a bile duct exploration if I think there's a stone in there."

"Okay. You don't mind if I hang around a while and watch? This is fascinating."

"Hang around all you want, just don't break the sterile field."

Distracted by what was going on outside the OR, I had taken a step too close and one of the nurses pointed a scalpel in my direction to warn me off. "Oops, sorry guys."

Dayton chastised me. "Cesari, don't ever say 'oops' in my OR, okay? Are you trying to jinx me?" Everyone chuckled.

"Sorry again."

Out of the corner of my eye, I saw the hospital administrator and one of the police officers walk by the windowed OR door, glancing in as they did. I moved closer to the video monitor and pointed at something on the screen. I was trying to give the impression that I was part of the team. "Hey, what's that?"

"It's just a loop of small bowel."

"Oh, okay. Are you going to cut it out?" I wasn't even thinking about what I was saying or how preposterous it sounded. The cop and administrator had paused in front of the door and were looking in our direction.

"Hey Cesari, have you been drinking? If you want to stay here, I'm going to have to insist you limit your questions to at least the educational level of a third year medical student, all right? No, I'm not going to cut it out. Why on earth would I do that?"

They moved on and I breathed a sigh of relief. "Sorry, I don't know what I was thinking. Well look, I hope you guys aren't stuck here too late. I'll be taking off now if you don't need me."

"Sure thing. Thanks again for stopping by, I appreciate it, and have a good night."

I waved to everyone and took off. Back in the locker room I changed quickly and hustled down the stairs to the main floor. Somebody had planted bullshit evidence connecting me to the crime in Orlando and then set up surveillance in my office to alert the police when I arrived. In the lobby, I noted that the cops had left, so I hopped a cab back to the Kit Kat Club and found Vito waiting for me in the upstairs apartment. It was well after six p.m. and closer to seven.

I sat down at the kitchen table and asked, "Where's Cocoa?" I didn't want to talk if she was within earshot.

He said, "She went downstairs to the dressing room to get ready for work. She goes on duty at eight. I see you made an impression on her."

"What do you mean?"

"She made me promise to bring you to catch her act later. She rotates through the VIP room at ten."

"Maybe. You got my stuff?"

"It's in your room already; two duffel bags, the black one has ten grand and the red one another ten. I got three phones; one for you, one for me, and one for Cheryl. Here's yours." He slid a small flip phone across the table to me. "I already charged and programmed our numbers into them. We have sixty minutes to start. Cheryl's phone is in the red bag."

I told him about what happened at the hospital and handed him the letters. He read through them and whistled. "Damn, these guys got your number, Cesari. So who do you think it was, that girl, Consuela?"

"Yeah, but how did she know I'd go there?"

"Probably just took a guess. Why did you go there?"

"It sounds stupid now, but I still have a day job, you know. I wanted to knock off some of the paperwork since I was here."

"Okay, so she set up a surveillance camera in your office and planted these phony letters. The minute they saw you they phoned it in to the police that you're a person of interest in a homicide in Orlando and that you might be trying to eliminate incriminating evidence. They ask them to check it out. Not really that hard to do but it does suggest collaboration with the Orlando police. I mean, it must have been someone on Consuela's payroll that made the call."

I nodded. "And now she knows I'm in New York."

"Yeah, along with nine million other people. Besides, if she hadn't figured out this was the first place you'd come then she'd have to be a moron, right? So relax, Cesari, she was just trying to motivate you, that's all."

"And the letters?"

"Give me a break. Any lawyer worth his salt would use these to wipe his ass. Handwriting experts would tear them apart in seconds and even though they are stamped, there are no postmarks on the letters. So how did they get here? Obviously somebody planted them." He tossed them in the trash can by the sink. It's harassment, pure and simple. She's trying to make you uncomfortable."

"Why?"

"I don't know. Maybe it's because you're off the script. You're doing things and going places she didn't plan on, and this is her way of trying to control you. You said she was pissed you left Orlando. Maybe she was trying to encourage you to go back where she could keep a closer eye on you."

I thought about that. Vito had a lot of street smart. I had to grant him that, but why take the chance of getting me locked up for who knows how long? Maybe someone didn't want this crime solved? Maybe Consuela didn't want this crime solved? Why? I stood up. "Let me change my shirt and shave and then we'll go find some place to eat."

"What about Cocoa?"

I looked at him, puzzled. "What about her?"

"I promised her you'd come see her dance."

"I heard you the first time and I said maybe."

He seemed frustrated. "I don't think you understand what she's like, Cesari."

I looked at him like he was speaking in tongues. "I really don't care what she's like. I don't even understand why we're wasting oxygen talking about her."

Chapter 18

"So what do you think, Vito? Where do I start?" We sat at a corner table in a small trattoria a few blocks away from the Kit Kat Club. The club served finger food but nothing more substantial. Alcohol and girls were the main course there.

I took a forkful of my gnocchi in a light Gorgonzola cream sauce. Vito worked on a New York strip steak, medium rare. The bottle of Chianti was already half empty. We'd had a couple of martinis to start and I was feeling very relaxed.

Vito explained. "I don't think you have a choice. You're going to have to visit this Secret Service guy, McIntosh, the one you put in the hospital, and question him more thoroughly. He's the only real lead you have. It would be great if you could find Raul or Consuela, but that doesn't seem likely. The other thing you have to do is go back to Snow White's apartment and find out who's been recording what."

I nodded in agreement. I definitely needed to go back to Orlando and snoop around some more, but first things first. "I don't suppose when you were digging into Phil's background you found out where he lives?" I asked.

"One step ahead of you, Cesari." He pushed a piece of paper across the table with Phillip McIntosh's address on it. "You're in luck. He has an apartment in D.C. but because of what just happened, he's recuperating at a friend's home in Randolph, New Jersey. It's less than an hour from here. Apparently, he has a bad headache, which is to be expected, and he also seems to have some short-term memory loss as well. He's single and his family is in Kansas. I called the hospital this morning and spoke with his discharge planner. He has an appointment set up on Monday with a shrink for post-traumatic stress counseling and a neurologist on Wednesday; very routine after an assault like that."

I was surprised. "They told you all that on the phone? That's a gross violation of patient privacy."

"Yeah, well. You'd be surprised what people will tell you if you phrase the question right. I told the woman that our friend is suspected of being a serial child molester and that his rich father pays high-priced lawyers to keep his sorry ass out of prison and that I'm a reporter representing the families of the victims and that I'm determined to see justice carried out. The discharge planner has two little kids and was practically in tears talking to me."

"Not bad, Vito. Do you know anything about this friend he's staying with and how many others might be there with him?"

"I'm working on that. First things first. Here's your new driver's license. I got lucky and found a guy willing to put a rush job on it. It's not the greatest but it should do the trick. It cost me two grand, and I'm lucky it didn't cost more. You know what it's like to get a forger to work on a Saturday? They're worse than plumbers."

I looked at the license. Benjamin P. Hendler. "It looks pretty good to me."

"Well, let's see if you can get on a plane with it. I'll have Heidi buy your ticket back to Orlando with her credit card. Which airport do you prefer and when do you want to leave?"

"I'll go visit Phil either tomorrow or Monday. So, let's say Tuesday morning out of JFK. That should give me plenty of time to do what I have to do in New Jersey and get back to Manhattan. Try to get me on JetBlue, all right? Do you have the name of the shrink, the location of the office, and the time of the appointment?"

He looked at me crossly. "What's the matter? I'm not dancing fast enough for you? No, I don't have that information but I will by tomorrow. Jesus Christ, but you're a ball breaker."

We finished dinner and paid the bill. It was almost ten. "C'mon, Cesari, let's get a nightcap at the Kit Kat and watch Cocoa dance."

"Look Vito, I understand Cocoa's a big deal at the club and all that, but I have to make a few calls and do some legwork, and to be honest, I have to sleep in the room next door to this girl. I don't think

I want to spend the next couple of hours staring at her half naked. It might blur the lines too much, if you know what I mean?"

He shook his head in exasperation. "You've changed, Cesari, you know that? All right, have it your way then. See if I care."

We entered the Kit Kat Club, and Vito made a beeline to the VIP room and Cocoa. I went to Heidi's office and shut the door behind me. Sitting behind her desk, I fired up her laptop and googled the United States Secret Service. A plan was starting to crystallize in my mind and I wanted to have all my ducks in a row. After an hour, I fatigued and changed subjects to Disney corporations. By midnight I was ready to pass out sitting up. I was going to be busy the next few days and needed to rest, so I went upstairs to my room, placed the gun on the desk, stripped down to my underwear, and got under the covers. This afternoon's events had me a little jumpy, but I soon drifted off into a heavy slumber.

Several hours later I woke, sensing another presence in the room and squinted my eyes trying to focus in the dark, not entirely sure that I wasn't dreaming. Leaning over toward the night table, I turned on a small lamp, illuminating the room. The clock read 2:35 a.m.

Sitting in the shadows on the chair next to the desk just a few feet away was Cocoa, wearing a black silk camisole and not much else. Her legs were crossed, and she was playing with the Sig Sauer I had foolishly left in the open. She didn't look happy.

"Cocoa?" I asked softly. "Is everything all right?"

"I didn't see you at the show downstairs. I was just wondering why," she pouted.

I was groggy from alcohol and exhaustion. "What?"

"Why didn't you come see me dance? You promised."

I hesitated not sure where this was heading. "I didn't promise. Vito promised for me and without my knowledge. Be that as it may, I was very tired. Maybe you should put the gun down." This particular weapon did not have a manual safety.

She looked at the Sig Sauer and then slowly placed it back on the desk as I breathed a sigh of relief. "That's what Vito said but I wasn't sure if you were really tired or just pissed off because I saw your schmekel this afternoon without permission?" She was clearly annoyed.

Jesus.

"I was really tired, and I didn't mean to offend you by skipping your act." I looked at the clock again. I couldn't believe this was happening.

She narrowed her eyes at me. "Well, you did. Especially considering how rude you were to me earlier."

She was starting to piss me off, and it crossed my mind to just physically toss her out of the room, but I thought it would be unwise to touch her. It was time to take a different approach. I sighed deeply. "All right, Cocoa, how about we start over. I admit I was a bit of an asshole this afternoon and I'm sorry. I didn't miss your show on purpose to be mean or anything. It's just that I've got a lot on my mind, and there's a lot happening in my life right now." I rubbed my eyes and yawned. I was starting to wake up and was not pleased about it.

She seemed satisfied. "That's better. So will you come and see me tomorrow night?"

For crying out loud. I was being blackmailed at three in the morning by a stripper. This was the oldest trick ever. Every woman I had ever met had this one in her playbook. *You're not going to sleep until you tell me what I want to hear.*

So I did. "Definitely. I wouldn't miss it for anything."

She smiled. "VIP room at ten p.m., okay? I already reserved a table for you. So, what's your name? We haven't actually been properly introduced." She stood up and walked over to me. Goddamn! She didn't have panties on.

"Cocoa?" I whispered, trying not to look.

"That's my name, not yours."

"John Cesari...Dr. John Cesari."

She extended her right hand to me and I took it. "Nice to meet you. So, what kind of doctor are you?"

Sitting down on the side of the bed, she gently nudged me over to make room for her. My heart rate started to pick up as I looked at her, not sure what to make of this. I stammered hoarsely. "I'm a gastroenterologist. I take care of intestinal disorders."

She smiled, sensing weakness. "Yeah, that's what Heidi told me. That sounds very interesting." She cocked her head at an angle and eyed me playfully.

I knew the look when I saw it and said, "Maybe you should, you know, go back to your room now, Cocoa."

She chuckled, wrinkled her nose, and shook her head. "I don't think so, Doctor. In case you haven't noticed I have serious control issues so why don't you just slide over and give me some room." She turned off the light and let herself under the covers, climbing on top of me.

I let out a deep breath. "Cocoa?"

"What now?"

"I have a girlfriend."

"Duly noted. Now help me get your underwear off."

"I'm serious, I really do have a girlfriend."

"Relax, so do I."

Round two to Cocoa.

Chapter 19

The next morning, I untangled myself from Cocoa's arms and legs and quietly slipped out of bed while she slept. I showered and left the apartment with the red duffel bag Vito had brought me for Cheryl. The Kit Kat Club was quiet at this hour of the day, and I stepped out onto Second Avenue unnoticed. Grabbing a buttered roll and a cup of coffee at a small deli, I walked over to the Holiday Inn Express on 37th Street to find Cheryl. It was nine a.m. and I was exhausted from my night with Cocoa. She had a lot of energy and even worse, liked to talk afterward, but I had to admit she was an interesting girl for sure. She was from Morristown, New Jersey, not too far from where Phillip McIntosh was staying in the town of Randolph, and she knew the area well. She owned a Harley, which she kept at her parents' house and had offered me its use if I needed something to get around. It was winter, but the weather in the tri-state area had been very mild the last few weeks so I kept that in mind. In fact, she offered me the use of her parents' home as well because they were out of the country touring Europe.

I entered the Holiday Inn Express and approached the attendant, asking him to ring Cheryl's room, which he did—unsuccessfully, several times. I thanked him and asked if he would tell me her room number, which of course he refused citing state and federal laws. One hundred bucks later, he wasn't as eager to uphold the constitution.

Putz.

I took the elevator up to the sixth floor and found the room uneventfully. I couldn't believe they had gone out this early so I gently knocked on the door and then more forcefully. Concern was just starting to enter my mind when the door opened partially and Cheryl eyed me through the space. She looked sleepy and just a tad cranky.

"Cesari, can't you let people sleep in the morning?"

I chuckled. "I'm sorry, and here I was worrying that somebody was in there trying to murder you."

I entered the room, swooping her up in my arms. "How was your night, beautiful?" I asked, kissing her, not a guilty bone in my body. Well, not exactly. Besides, last night wasn't my fault, and that's almost the same as being innocent, although I doubt that I could find even one woman on the planet that would agree with me. Better to just put it behind me and move on. No point in tempting fate. When I was younger I had bought into that total honesty shtick and had gotten severely burned on multiple occasions.

Cheryl said, "We slept okay. The princess had a rough night. Apparently, she's not used to keeping a low profile or going to bed before three a.m."

It was an adequately sized room with two queen beds. Cinderella squinted at me suspiciously from underneath a pillow. "Go away, I'm tired."

I turned to Cheryl. "All right, I just came to say hi and give you some walking-around money. I really don't want you using credit cards or ATM machines." I tossed the red duffel bag on her bed and continued. "There's ten thousand dollars in cash in the bag and a pre-paid cell phone with my number already programmed into it. You can pretty much go anywhere and do anything you want but stay away from your office and close friends for now."

"And what are you going to do?"

"I haven't fully thought it out yet, but you may not hear from me for a day or two. I'll try to keep you posted as best as I can. Please only call for something urgent."

"Sounds like I don't want to know what you'll be doing?"

"Probably not."

"I've started a case file for when I have to defend you in court."

I said, "Thanks, hopefully that's all you'll have to do is defend me in court and not speak at my funeral."

She laughed. "What would I say? He was a great lay, and I'll miss him, and then I'd look down at two or three dozen women all dressed in red, crying."

"Ouch, you make my life sound so shallow."

"That's because it is."

"That's not true. I'm not just a skirt chaser. I'm a very important doctor. I take out polyps and treat irritable bowel syndrome."

She laughed. "Oh, okay."

I kissed her once more, and Cinderella moaned her disapproval from under the covers. I said, "Take it easy over there. I'm leaving. Well look, I've got to run. There's a lot I have to do and not much time to do it in."

Cheryl touched my shoulder gently. "John, please be careful."

"I will. I promise."

Chapter 20

I went back to the Kit Kat Club and called my psychiatrist friend, Mark, from Heidi's office phone. "Good morning, Dr. Greenberg. How are you today?"

"I'm fine, thank you. And who may I ask is calling—Cesari? Is that you? I didn't recognize your voice. Sorry. Where are you calling from?"

"I'm at a friend's place over on Second Avenue, Mark. How's everything?" Mark was a good friend and had also been my psychiatrist in the past during difficult times. He had an office on the upper west side.

"No complaints. Getting older every day. What about you? Staying out of trouble?"

"Trying to but it's not easy. Say Mark, would you mind if I picked your brain about something?"

"Shoot, Cesari. I figured you must have had an ulterior motive for calling anyway. You always do, so what's it this time?"

I chuckled. "I have a friend who experienced a concussion recently following an assault. His employer is making him go to counseling for post-traumatic stress and he asked me what to expect. I just wanted to know what to tell him."

"Why did you assault him, Cesari?"

"I didn't say I did."

"Yeah, but you're forgetting how well I know you, so why don't you cut the bullshit and tell me the truth for a change, and then maybe I'll be able to help you. By the way, have you seen Kelly recently?"

He caught me off guard with that. "No, I haven't seen Kelly recently. Why do you ask?"

"Just curious is all. I was in Macy's last week and thought I caught a glimpse of her from a distance. It looked like she put on some weight. I figured it was post-Cesari depression. The place was jammed and I lost sight of her. So, what's going on, and whom did you give PTSD to?"

Damn, he was good, and he knew me too well. "I'd rather not go into it on the phone Mark. By the way all our conversations are protected under patient-physician confidentiality laws, right?"

"That would depend on whether you still consider me your psychiatrist and whether I have agreed to that responsibility. It would also depend on whether you tell me something that represents a real or credible threat to the well-being of another individual. So do you consider me your psychiatrist and are you planning on hurting someone?"

"The answer is yes and no."

"Okay, so what is it you really want to know?"

"What kind of questions would a psychiatrist ask a patient with post-traumatic stress?"

"It's not that simple, Cesari. Psychiatry isn't like colonoscopy where you just go in and snip out a few polyps. The human mind is complicated, both resilient and fragile, and if this is mandated counseling by his employer, he may not even have PTSD. A lot of businesses and organizations in this day and age are very quick to pull the trigger on mandatory counseling to cover their asses in court."

"Okay, fair enough, but let's pretend he really does have PTSD. What would you ask him?"

"Well, it varies from individual to individual of course and the degree of the trauma. Obviously, war veterans are at very high risk for PTSD because of the constant and prolonged stress they experienced, not to mention the life-threatening nature of their stress, but even one assault such as in the case of robbery, rape, or domestic violence can produce signs and symptoms of PTSD. Physical assault places the victims at highest risk but the assault can be emotional as well. Okay, so let's say for the sake of argument that your friend does actually have

PTSD. He may become withdrawn, emotionally numb so to speak. He may avoid discussing what happened or he may truly block it out as selective amnesia. If the triggering event was severe enough he or she may have flashbacks and nightmares. Treatment depends of course on the severity of symptoms and usually involves some combination of counseling and pharmaco-therapy. So, in a first encounter, I would take it easy with the guy and just try to get to know him in order to build trust and let him know that I care about him and that he's not just another number. I'd try to get him to open up about what happened but keep in mind that he may not be ready to. It's important to let him proceed at his own pace. If he's having trouble sleeping or coping with everyday activities I'd offer him the option of an antianxiety agent."

I thought about that. "Hmm. What would happen if the individual were to suddenly and unexpectedly come face-to-face with the individual who assaulted him? Would he freak?"

"Depending on the circumstance, yes he might, and it could potentially devastate him psychologically. It might even throw him into a crisis that he may not be able to recover from, but once again, I'm assuming worst case scenario here. It's also possible that the confrontation could provoke uncontrollable rage on his part. On the other hand, if he has amnesia he may not even remember the person who assaulted him. Everybody's different in their response to stress and their ability to cope."

"Thanks, Mark. That was very helpful. I have to admit psychiatry has always fascinated me."

"Really? Is that why you went into gastroenterology?"

We'd had this conversation before. "No, I went into GI because I like working with my hands, and using video equipment all day is like playing video games. It's fun."

"Bullshit. You went into GI for the same reason every kid graduating medical school goes into subspecialties; the pay is better. Psychiatry is the lowest reimbursed field in all of medicine. Our society thinks it's more important to pay physicians to cut things out of people rather than use their brains to solve problems."

"Feel better now, Mark?"

He chuckled. "I do actually."

"Great, I'll send you my bill."

"Let me give you one last word of advice, Cesari."

"I'm listening."

"Stay away from that guy, all right? Sounds like you've done enough harm already."

"Got it."

"So, when am I going to see you again? It's been way too long."

"I'm working on a project right now, but as soon as it's over I'll take a ride to your apartment."

"I consider that a promise, and Cesari..."

"Yes, Mark?"

"I don't know how to say this..."

"Say what?"

"It's Kelly."

I got upset. "What about her? Look, Mark, I really don't want to talk about her. I love Kelly, you know that, but she chose to end it, not me. I have to move on now, and I'm getting a little tired of people bringing her up all the time."

"I'm sorry, John. You're right, I shouldn't have said anything."

I took a deep breath. "No, I'm the one who's sorry. I overreacted. It's okay. Look, thanks for your help and I hope to see you and Sarah soon. Please tell her I said hello."

"I will. Take it easy, pal. Bye."

I clicked off. Damn. Another Kelly sighting in Manhattan. You'd think in a city this large, I'd be able to keep some distance between me and my exes. Kelly and I had dated hot and heavy for about a year or so. She ended it, and I couldn't talk her out of it. She'd told me that she didn't like my friends, but it had crossed my mind that maybe the racial divide had just been too much for her to handle. It never seemed to bother her before, but maybe that had changed for her. Until you were in those situations you really couldn't know how you were going to feel, and then there was that damned dog, Cleopatra, that we had both fallen in love with. I hoped she wasn't still brooding about that. All right, enough with this, I had to stay focused.

I went upstairs and found Cocoa sound asleep. I leaned down and shook her gently on the shoulder. "Hey, sleepy head, it's almost noon. Still feel like helping me out or is that just something you say during sex?"

She looked up at me through drowsy eyes and seemed a little confused as she looked around, as if she was trying to figure out what she was doing in my room. She sat up slowly.

I helped jog her memory by kissing her. "Remember me?"

She nodded. "It's so early. Can't I sleep some more?"

"I need your help, Cocoa, unless you changed your mind. I'd understand. I've been known to exaggerate my commitment in the heat of the moment too."

She laughed and stretched like the largest, sexiest cat I had ever seen. "No, I meant it, but I have to work tonight."

"Don't worry about that. Heidi's a friend of mine and I'm part owner in the club. It'll be all right."

That caught her attention. "You own the club?"

"Part owner. Me, Heidi, and Vito own the club."

"Cool, I didn't know that. So technically I work for you?"

"Not really. Vito and I are silent partners. Heidi makes all the decisions, and we don't get in the way. We loaned her the money some time ago as an investment."

"So if Heidi decides to fire me for not showing up at work tonight you can't stop her?"

"She won't do that. I'll explain that you're doing me a favor. She's an old friend. She'll be okay with it."

She digested that. "All right, let me take a shower and clean up."

"Great, I'll make us a pot of coffee."

She stood up and walked by me toward the bathroom, and I held my breath as I watched her. God, even with bed head, she was a knockout. How many curves could one woman have?

Thirty minutes later, I was sipping my coffee when she emerged from the bathroom wrapped in a towel. She smiled at me as she poured herself a cup, and I studied her enthusiastically. She was exceedingly distracting under normal circumstance, and I couldn't even imagine the effect she would have on a man twirling around a pole in high heels. As if reading my mind she said, "You missed quite a show last night."

I laughed. "I doubt it could have been better than the one in my room."

She liked that and wandered off with her coffee to get dressed. By one o'clock, she reemerged wearing jeans, Uggs, and a thick wool sweater.

"Ready when you are, Tarzan."

I smiled. I was starting to like her. "All right, let's go. We can grab a slice of pizza on the way."

Chapter 21

The commuter train pulled into the Morristown station at three-thirty, and we caught a cab to Cocoa's house in the center of town, about a block off the village green. I had never been to Morristown and was impressed. It was decorated for the holiday season and gave the appearance of being an affluent, well-heeled, thriving small city.

"Cute town," I commented as we walked to the front door and she fumbled for her keys. It was a modest sized, two-story home on Prospect Street a short walk from the heart of everything here.

"Yeah, it's okay. Very up and coming. It can get pretty busy on the weekends. Lots of bars and restaurants. We can have dinner there tonight if you want. There's a great steakhouse called Roots, near the park." She unlocked the door, and the alarm system started its high-pitched warning beep. Pressing in the appropriate security code, she disarmed it.

In the front foyer, we took our shoes off and hung up our coats, and I looked around. It was a very nicely decorated home, and I guessed there were at least three bedrooms on the second floor. The living room was upscale with hardwood floors, an Oriental rug, a fireplace, a sofa, and a piano. There was a menorah on the mantel piece and several nice oil paintings on the walls.

"So where are your parents and how long will they be gone?" I asked, watching her adjust a wall thermostat.

"Don't worry. They're in Greece right now and then heading to Sicily. They won't be back for another two weeks. I was supposed to check on the house for them once in a while anyway."

"Do you have any brothers or sisters?"

"Nope, I'm all there is. So, if you're planning on killing me, no one will know for at least two weeks."

I laughed. "I'm not, so let's get that one off the table."

"Well, that's good to know, and I guess since we already slept together, sexual assault is also off the table."

I very seriously said, "That would never be on my table. I don't even like to joke about stuff like that."

"Really? What are you, some sort of knight in shining white armor?"

I thought about that as I glanced at her. A nun had called me that when I was in grammar school and maybe the notion had stuck. Maybe some guys were meant to be that way and some weren't. I said, "Hardly, I just don't like to hurt girls."

She eyed me curiously before speaking. "Maybe some girls like to be hurt. You know, slapped around a little. Maybe it turns them on."

Not sure if she was just being provocative, I felt I ought to clear the air before that thought took root. "I'm not sure what you're getting at, Cocoa, but you got the wrong guy, if that's what you're thinking."

She smiled. "We'll talk about it later."

I let that pass as I busied myself walking from room to room sizing the place up like a soldier checking out his defensive perimeter.

"You're pretty paranoid, aren't you?" she asked, changing the subject.

"Yup, how about you show me the sleeping arrangements and then we'll go over things."

"I thought you'd never ask."

I followed her up the stairs, and she walked me through the bedrooms. I was right. There were three reasonably sized rooms. The master had an enormous oversized king bed and its own bathroom. The other two shared a hallway bathroom. She said, "We'll sleep in my parents' room tonight. They won't know and I'll make sure everything's clean and back to normal before they return."

I looked at the gigantic bed and was extremely tempted to take her up on it. "Cocoa, this might be a good time to talk about last night."

"What about it?"

"Well, I did mention that I have a girlfriend…"

"And I believed you."

"Yes, but last night was sort of a special circumstance and I'm not sure we should go that route again."

She looked at me puzzled. "Why not? Did I disappoint you?"

"No, no, nothing like that. You were great, but I'm sort of a one woman at a time kind of guy."

She laughed. "You didn't seem like that last night."

"That's not fair. You jumped me at three in the morning."

She snorted. "Oh, I see. You look pretty defenseless to me." She squeezed my bicep and poked me playfully in the chest as she spoke. "You know what's not fair? Dragging me to New Jersey to act as your personal tour guide, crashing at my parents' house, making me risk losing my job, and then telling me the only thing I want in return isn't such a great idea because you're suddenly feeling guilty. You can't be serious? Do you have any idea how absurd that sounds? C'mon, we're adults."

I wasn't used to be being on this side of that argument and sighed uncomfortably. "Nonetheless, I am serious and I think it might be better if I slept in one of the other bedrooms tonight. Besides, I really do need to get some rest. I haven't slept a whole night through in days."

"Look, if your girlfriend finds out, I'll tell her it was all my fault and that I overpowered you, all right?"

I couldn't help myself and chuckled. "I appreciate you taking one for the team like that but I'm afraid I'm going to have to stand firm on this."

"Seriously?"

I nodded.

She stood there for a moment thinking about it and then resigned herself, shaking her head in frustration. "Fine, but there's no need to mess up two bedrooms. We'll sleep here in my parent's bed. It's plenty big. You stay on your side and I'll stay on mine."

I studied her carefully. She seemed sincere enough so I accepted the compromise. "That will work, but we sleep with underwear on, okay?"

She chuckled. "Relax, I haven't raped anybody in almost two weeks. Besides, it's your loss anyway. I was hoping to give you a second chance after last night's lame performance." I hesitated, thinking that one over, not sure if she was being serious. She continued to goad me. "You were tired. I understand."

I didn't respond because I didn't know how to. Jesus. I gave it everything I had last night. If she was trying to give me performance anxiety she had unequivocally succeeded. I grunted and tossed my duffel bag on the floor next to the king-sized bed. It was almost five. I decided to ignore the challenge and change the subject. "Mind if I make a call?"

"Not at all. I'll go downstairs and play the piano." She turned to leave.

"You play the piano?"

She looked back. "And the saxophone and the clarinet."

This girl was full of surprises.

She left me and I lay on the bed, legs crossed at the ankles. Picking up the phone on the night table next to me, I called Vito. "Cesari, where are you and where's Cocoa? Heidi thinks you kidnapped her."

"Never mind where I am. It'll be safer if you don't know. Cocoa's with me, and she's fine. I needed her help. She'll be back tomorrow night. Tell Heidi I'm sorry but it was unavoidable and I don't want her to hold it against Cocoa." As we talked, the sound of Beethoven filled the house. I wasn't even close to being an expert on such things but it sounded pretty good.

"Fucking Cesari, you can't just pull dancers out of the lineup. They're on a schedule. Heidi's trying to run a business here."

"I said I'm sorry, but I got bigger things going on here. I'll make it up to Heidi as soon as I can. Now tell me what you know."

"Your boy McIntosh is staying with a male friend at 224 Peace Road in Randolph. The male friend owns and operates his own bakery on Route 10. His names is Herman Winkelman, and get this, he specializes in pies. The two met at Georgetown and maintained a friendship ever since."

"Friendship?"

"Your guess is as good as mine, Cesari, but I agree, it sounds suspiciously like Phillip McIntosh may be a little light in the loafers."

"Vito, you are the most politically incorrect human being I have ever met."

"I'm sorry, let me rephrase that. Our Secret Service friend may be a homo-American."

"Okay, stop. What else?"

"He has an appointment with the psychiatrist at eight a.m. at Morristown Memorial Medical Center, a Dr. Tracy Harmon. Her office is on the second floor of the medical arts building where all the outpatients are seen. It's attached to the main hospital and can be accessed either directly from the street or through a tunnel from inside the hospital."

I groaned. "Shit. The psychiatrist is a woman?"

"Yeah, so what?"

"I was toying with the idea of impersonating the shrink to get near Phil, but I'll come up with something else. So, the second floor of the medical arts building at eight, and we're sure he's never met her before."

"I can't swear to that, but he just flew in the day before so I doubt it unless he's been to her in the past, but there's nothing in his record about that. What's that racket I hear in the background, Cesari?"

"It's called Beethoven. So, out of curiosity, where does the Secret Service stand on homosexuality?"

"How the fuck would I know? I assume they're hard ass pricks like everyone else in the military and similar type organizations. They know it happens but they don't want to hear about it would be my guess."

Hmm.

I said, "You're probably right about that, which means, if I was a Secret Service agent, I probably wouldn't want to flaunt it either. Maybe that's why his apartment is in D.C. and his friend's is in Jersey. It's not that long a ride by train or car."

"Where are you going with this, Cesari?"

"Not sure yet, but I've got things to do. I'll talk to you later."

I hung up and went to find Cocoa, who was sitting at the upright piano in the living room. She had switched to ragtime and was now playing Scott Joplin's "The Entertainer." I sat next to her on the bench and watched her wail away effortlessly at the keyboard. She glanced at me and smiled. I returned the smile and politely clapped when she finished.

"That was very nice, Cocoa. You're very talented."

"Thank you."

We sat there quietly, looking at each other. I knew what she was thinking and I felt ridiculous. Cheryl and I were adults, and we weren't engaged to be married. We hadn't even promised to be monogamous, but wasn't that assumed when you were dating someone? On the other hand, she never told me about that guy she went pub hopping with in Ireland.

"What are you thinking about?" Cocoa asked softly—knowingly.

I was thinking about picking her up and carrying her back up to the bedroom. From the look in her eyes, I could tell she was hoping I would do just that but I said, "We've got things to do. Is there a shopping center nearby?"

"About five miles away on Route 202. Why?"

"I need to buy a camera and a few other things."

She laughed. "Sorry, pal, no pictures. Once you're in cyberspace, there's no going back."

I chuckled. "It's not for you, but I hope other people think like that."

"On a separate note, I wouldn't take that gun of yours to the mall if I were you, just in case you were thinking of it. New Jersey has strict gun laws and the malls sometimes have metal detectors in them. You should be aware of that."

"How do you know I don't have a New Jersey full carry permit?"

"Yeah, right. Besides, a Sig Sauer p228 with .357 ammo is not the kind of handgun you pick up at Walmart. It's used by military and law enforcement. I've been wondering all day where you stole that from."

Damn. She knew her firearms. "How do you know all that?"

She smiled, very contented with herself. "My uncle Leo has quite the gun collection. He used to take me shooting with him all the time."

"Uncle Leo?"

"He's a lawyer and he loves his guns, that's for sure. He's a card-carrying member of the NRA too. So, taking it or leaving it?"

I thought it over, weighing the pros and cons. "I'll leave it here."

"So what's going on and why do you need a camera all of a sudden?"

"It's complicated." I gave her the short version as we entered the garage, spotting a silver Mercedes sedan next to a black Harley Sportster. The bike wasn't new but looked in pretty decent shape.

"This is the bike you told me about?" I asked walking up to the motorcycle.

"Yeah, I bought it used two years ago but it runs like a top. I should probably keep it covered but the weather's been so mild I keep thinking I'm going to take it out on weekends."

I walked around it, checking it out. Grabbing one of the handles, I swung my leg over and plopped down in the saddle. The Sportster wasn't that large of a bike and felt very natural in my grip. I had ridden one or two in my day but wasn't entirely comfortable with my skills. This one was pretty light and I guessed weighed less than 600 pounds.

She saw me enjoying myself. "It's four years old but has only ten thousand miles on it. The guy I bought it from really babied it. It has an 883cc engine with five speed transmission and electric push start. Want to go for a ride?"

I got off the bike. "In thirty-five degree weather, no thank you. We'll freeze to death. Besides, I can't afford to get pulled over or take a spill. We should take the Benz, if you don't mind?"

She pouted and folded her arms, accentuating her plus-sized chest. "You sure say 'no' a lot. Aw, c'mon, don't be a wimp. It'll be fun."

"No, I'm sorry, Cocoa. Not today. Maybe some other time."

"You know, for a big guy, you're a bit of a pussy."

That was interesting. I had just been upgraded from wimp to pussy and it didn't even cost me extra. I felt my face flush as she stood in front of me, deadly serious. She was a very direct girl for sure, and I hadn't quite worked out a long-term strategy on how to handle her. She stared up at me and I looked down at her. We didn't say anything for a few seconds and just as I was about to open my mouth and tell her to knock it off she said it again.

"Pussy."

Round three to Cocoa.

Chapter 22

All said, the shopping trip took about an hour and a half. Another half an hour to reach our destination and it was just after nine p.m. by the time we parked the Mercedes in a deserted YMCA parking lot just off Dover Chester Road in Randolph, New Jersey. It was Sunday night in the suburbs and there was no one around. The township of Randolph was buttoned up tight. The temperature held at thirty degrees and without wind was very tolerable. It hadn't snowed in a week. Phillip McIntosh was staying at his friend Herman Winkelman's ranch house, just around the corner from us on Peace Road. It was a solid middle-class neighborhood, and most of the homes were on half-acre lots with attached garages and manicured lawns and gardens. I waited patiently until ten to make my move. I thought this would be a good time to swing into action. It was late but not too late. They would have finished dinner and cleaned up and would probably be kicking back with a drink to watch TV or read a book.

"Are you sure you want to come with me, Cocoa. You could just sit in the car with the heater on."

"Nah, this is more fun than I've had in a long time. I've never done anything like this before. In case you haven't noticed, I'm a bit of an adrenaline junkie."

"I noticed."

We stepped into the night air and walked several hundred yards to the corner of Peace Road and Randolph Avenue. It was a moonless night, and there were no streetlights in this section of suburbia. The area was heavily wooded, and with our dark winter coats we were well concealed. We crept around the perimeter of the house, peeking in various windows until we found them in the living room, cuddling on the sofa watching a movie on a large-screen TV.

Cocoa giggled. "This is too funny. I thought you said he was a spy or something."

We watched Herman and Phil snuggle, lips locked, caressing each other. On the sixty-inch screen, they were watching *Broke Back Mountain*. Herman Winkelman, the pie maker, was a large black man with his right arm around Phillip McIntosh's shoulder and his left up the federal agent's shirt.

"Shhh. I said he was Secret Service, not a spy, and I don't see what's so funny."

I took the Canon Rebel with the 70–200 mm zoom out of its carry bag, turned it on, and started taking photos. I loved digital cameras. They could make a total amateur like me look like an artistic genius. Now all I had to do was wait.

Cocoa crouched beside me watching intently. "They're both pretty good-looking guys. What a waste."

I glanced at her. "Waste for you maybe, not for them. Besides, it's always that way, Cocoa. All the really good-looking guys are gay. It's sad, but you women are stuck with guys like me."

"Yeah, that sucks. All we get are the leftovers."

I snorted. "Thanks. Ooh, ooh, ooh. Look. Ha, this is perfect." Herman Winkelman had slid onto the floor in front of Phillip McIntosh. Things were heating up.

I photographed while Cocoa drooled. "This is making me very horny." She whispered.

"Well, it's making me nauseated."

"Don't be homophobic. There's nothing wrong with this."

"I'm not and I didn't say there was. I was simply telling you the state of my digestive track. You chose to interpret that information with a singularly narrow—and prejudicial—point of view. Okay, I've seen enough. Let's go." I had snapped about two dozen photos when even one would probably have gotten Phil canned.

Once back in the car, I turned to Cocoa. "I don't know about you but I'm starving." It was after ten p.m. and all we had eaten today was a slice of pizza at around one.

"I thought you were nauseated."

"It passed. Let's go back to Morristown, I'm sure we can find a place to eat there. Is there a Walmart on the way? I'd like to print out some of these pictures."

"Yeah, there's one on the way into town."

"By the way, Cocoa. Thank you for acting as a guide for me. I'm sure I would have been hopelessly lost without you, and thank you also, you know, for being understanding about the other thing."

"Relax, it's okay. You have a girlfriend and you want to be loyal. I get it. Besides, I'm having fun, and I couldn't let you use my parents' house alone anyway. Giving their security code to a total stranger wouldn't have been right."

"Totally understandable."

We stopped at Walmart, made some prints of Herman and Phil, and grabbed a couple of sandwiches at a Subway. We ate while we drove and were back in the house at eleven. I set the alarm for four a.m., shut the light, and wiggled under the covers. Just in case she forgot our discussion, I rolled onto my side away from her. She was in the bathroom brushing her teeth but joined me shortly, and I heard her climb into bed. I was so close to the edge on my side that a gentle shove would have pushed me onto the floor. If she stayed on her side like she promised, there should be a solid three feet of space separating us.

"What do you think you're doing?" she whispered.

"We had an agreement, Cocoa."

"Does that mean we can't talk?"

Great. She wasn't ready for bed. I thought about it and looked at the clock. It wasn't that late and I didn't see any point in being unpleasant. "What do you want to talk about?" I was still facing away.

She was quiet for a while and then said, "You never asked me. All the guys ask me."

"Ask you what?"

"What my real name is?"

"I guess I hadn't thought about it. Okay, so what's your real name?"

"Myrtle."

"Really?" I chuckled and rolled over to face her. My eyes had adjusted to the gloom and I could see her shadowy silhouette. She was lying on her side, pillow scrunched under her head, watching me.

"Yeah, Myrtle Rosenblatt."

"That's quite a name."

She giggled. "Yeah, there aren't many exotic dancers with names like that. Guess how I picked Cocoa for a stage name?"

"I give up. Tell me."

"When I was a kid, I would only eat Cocoa Puffs for breakfast. If my parents tried to give me anything else, I would throw a tantrum. So their pet name for me was Cocoa."

I chuckled again. "You're killing me. That's pretty funny actually. So that means you spell it with an A at the end like in hot cocoa not like Coco Chanel?"

"Very good, Dr. Cesari. Not many people pick up on that."

"Speaking of your parents, how does this work? Are they aware of your career?" She had reeled me in hook, line, and sinker to a place no man ever volunteers to go. I was knee deep in pillow talk and barely conscious of the fact.

"Oh, yeah. I was very honest with them. They don't approve of course, but it's what I want to do and it makes me happy. I guess I'm a bit of a narcissist. I love it when men watch me dance. It's like I get an endorphin rush. The money's great too. I'm on the books for twenty five thousand a year with the IRS but actually take home five times that. I make five hundred to a thousand a night sometimes in tips. Heidi gets twenty percent and I get the rest tax free."

"Wow. Still, I can understand your parents' point of view."

"I know. They're solid middle-class people too. Dad's an electrical engineer and Mom's a social worker. I don't know which hurt them more. The fact that I voluntarily entered the adult entertainment industry or that I dropped out of Princeton to do it. It can get pretty uncomfortable around here at Passover."

I sat up abruptly and turned on the light, startling her. She squinted and covered her eyes in surprise. I couldn't have been more shocked as I looked at her. "You got into Princeton?"

"Full scholarship, but I only went for a year. It was too boring for me. I still read a lot though. I'm big into Existentialism. You seem surprised. Probably thought you were with some strung out whore, huh?" Her eyes had recovered and she sat up with me. As she did, her covers slipped down, partially revealing her breasts. She made no move to cover them up, but why would she? I had already seen them and so had thousands of other men.

I said, "No, I didn't think that at all. It was very obvious from the way you spoke that you must have had a fairly good education, but you don't meet club dancers every day that dropped out of Princeton. That's quite an accomplishment, Cocoa. Not everyone gets to say they earned a full scholarship to an Ivy League school."

"It was no big deal. Besides, they're all hypocrites at these places anyway. I wasn't impressed. They act all high and mighty as if they're so superior. Most of the people there are bigger whores than any of the girls I ever worked with dancing. They'd sell their souls and whatever else they had to in order to advance their careers. At least the people I work with are honest about what they're doing."

I nodded. It was hard to argue with her logic.

She studied me. "What about you? You don't look like a doctor."

"What do doctors look like?"

"Not like you. You must work out. You're very muscular, and what's that scar?"

She ran her hand along my upper chest. There was a thin line above my left nipple about three inches long where I had been slashed with a knife as a teenager.

"Thanks, I do work out. Not as much as I ought to but as much as I can. The scar—well, when I was younger, I spent too much time trying to solve problems with my fists rather than with my brain."

She smiled seductively. "You're different. I like that."

I thought about that for a while. "Well, I have to admit Myrtle…"

"I prefer Cocoa, if you don't mind."

"I have to admit, Cocoa, you are like a breath of fresh air too. I don't think I've ever met anyone quite like you."

"Thanks. I like you too."

We lay back down on our sides and quietly studied each other. There was a calmness in the room and a natural feel to our relationship. Lying next to me right now, it was difficult to believe that I had just met her. I felt as if I had known her a hundred years and yet I knew nothing about her.

She said, "You can turn off the light now. I think I'm ready to go to sleep." So, I leaned over and turned the switch, allowing the room to go dark again. I lay on my back and closed my eyes. Seconds later, she wiggled under the covers close and snuggled into me, wrapping her arms and legs around me tightly, resting her head on my chest. She wasn't wearing panties.

I sighed. "Cocoa?"

She didn't answer and made gentle snoring sounds.

"I know you're not asleep, Cocoa."

She continued her snoring.

"Good night, Cocoa," I whispered.

"Good night, John."

Round four to Cocoa.

Chapter 23

The alarm woke us at four a.m., and we quickly showered and dressed, gulping down coffee and toast as we rushed out the door. By a quarter to five we had parked the Benz in the indoor parking garage at the Morristown Memorial Medical Center and were walking in the door. We had picked up white lab coats and stethoscopes at a medical supply store in the mall the night before and looked like weary physicians coming to work for an early shift. The night security guard nodded at us, glancing casually at my ID but other than that barely took notice. It was a big hospital, which provided us with anonymity. With so many workers, individual security guards didn't expect to know everyone on sight. My ID was from St. Matt's but at this hour in the morning he didn't notice. It dangled on a lanyard around my neck and I walked with an air of authority. I was thankful I had picked it up when I was at St. Matt's the other day.

"You look great, Cocoa."

"Thanks, you too. Okay, we're in. Now what?"

"We'll just follow the signs to the Medical Arts Building where the doctors see patients. His psychiatrist is on the second floor, but I'll need to swing by the ER to get a few things."

I carried my duffel bag with the gun and a few other essential items, including a roll of duct tape I had picked up at the mall. We followed arrows on the wall to an underground tunnel that led into the medical office building. We took an elevator to the second floor and as we emerged, followed a sign directing us to Dr. Tracy Harmon's office. At five in the morning it was still dark and deserted and we arrived unnoticed. Her door was locked, but it was a simple matter of breaking in using a credit card to pry open the mechanism.

Cocoa watched me in awe. "Doctor my foot. One day, you're going to have to tell me the whole story. I told you mine."

"I will—maybe."

I closed the door behind us and gave her the duffel bag. "Just sit tight, I shouldn't be too long." I looked at my watch. "I doubt anyone will arrive before seven so you should be fine." Looking around we saw a typical medical office. There was a nice wood desk, a leather chair, diplomas on the wall, family pictures on the desk, and in this case because it was a psychiatrist's office, there was a leather sofa. Off to one side, there was a small bathroom. Perfect.

"What do I say if someone comes in?"

"Don't say anything. You're wearing a lab coat and a stethoscope around your neck. You're a doctor as far as anyone is concerned. If it's housekeeping or someone like that just say hi. If it's another doctor, say hi and leave as if you're late for an appointment."

"What if it's the doctor whose office this is?"

"Just act confused like you hadn't realized you came into the wrong office. Excuse yourself and leave. You'll be fine. Just move quickly if you're discovered. No one's going to tackle you in the hallway just because you're in the wrong office. Okay, I'll see you in a few minutes."

I turned to leave and she grabbed my arm, so I turned back to her and she put her arms around me. "How about a kiss before you go?"

I hesitated, then leaned down and kissed her.

"I've got to go now, so stay out of trouble."

She yawned and lay down on the couch. I went back to the main hospital and followed the signs to the emergency room, which I found bustling with activity. I walked in as if I belonged there and said hello to a sleepy middle-aged nurse standing next to a medication cart. She had short graying hair and looked battle-hardened from many years of clinical experience. She casually looked at my ID badge and I looked at hers; Deanna Maria Marchitellone.

"Good morning, Nurse—Marchitellone." Jesus, that was a mouthful. I smiled and added. "That's quite a name you have there."

"Yes, it is, so try not to mangle it the way you just did. You can call me DM for short. It's what I prefer and that's what everyone else calls me. Now, how can I help you Dr.—Cesari?"

"Well, I need a favor, Deanna."

"Do you have your hearing aids in?" she bristled and squared away at me, giving me a stern look.

"What?" She startled me.

"I just finished telling you, I prefer to be called DM. I hate the name Deanna. Now, are we going to be friends or not?"

I just met her and she already managed to jack me up pretty good. Okay. Take a deep breath, Cesari, and remember you're on a mission.

"I'm sorry, DM, I didn't mean anything. I'll get it straight from now on"

"You better." She was on the short, stocky side and looked straight at me, determining whether I should be forgiven or not. "So what kind of favor, Doctor, and that's not a Morristown ID you have there."

"No, it's not, DM. I'm a visiting gastroenterologist from St. Matt's in Manhattan, working with Dr. Daduvai for the week. You've heard of him?" I had checked the online hospital directory the night before. Daduvai was the head cheese around here, and I figured a little name dropping might help my cause. It also might help that DM was at the end of her shift and looked exhausted.

"Of course, I've heard of him, he's the head of surgery. So, go on."

"One of Dr. Daduvai's patients is down in radiology having an emergency angiogram. I was observing the procedure with him when the patient became combative. They were running low on sedatives, and Dr. Daduvai asked me to come over here and get some extra Versed and Fentanyl. Not much, maybe one or two syringes if you can spare it?"

She checked my name tag again, looked around for a second or two unsure, and said sympathetically, "I really can't do that, Doctor. These medications are for use in the ER only and they're counted carefully every shift. I could lose my job for giving them to an unauthorized person. You tell them they'll have to call the pharmacy if they need more meds. I know it will take longer that way and I'm sorry."

Busted. She made a valid point. Narcotics and the like were counted over and over every day to prevent theft and improper use. I thought about overwhelming her with Cesari charm but this DM character looked like a tough nut to crack. Crack she would, I had no doubt, but it might take more than the fifteen minutes I had allotted myself.

I said, "Well, thank you anyway. Have a great day."

"Sorry, Doc."

As I turned to leave, there was a scream from one of the patient rooms. Shortly following that an older woman came running out into the central work area where DM and I were talking.

"Help! Help me, please. It's my husband."

DM hustled past me and I instinctively followed. We discovered a seventyish year old man, his face and shirt covered in blood, unconscious on a stretcher. I raced in and lowered the head of the gurney so that his head was below the level of his feet. That was called the Trendelenburg position, and it allowed blood and oxygen to flow more easily to the brain.

"Who are you and what happened?" I asked the woman as I checked him for a pulse. He was breathing okay.

"I'm his wife, Doris. His stomach was upset, and we hadn't even seen the doctor yet. He was just sitting there when all of sudden he threw up a bucket full of blood and passed out."

DM quickly took his blood pressure. "80 systolic, Doc."

"Okay, do you have IV equipment in here, DM? He needs fluid in a hurry." I tilted his head to the side and suctioned blood out of his mouth so he wouldn't aspirate.

"Right behind you, Doc. Top drawer to the right. I'll get a bag of saline."

"Okay, put some oxygen on him too, and get us some help in here while I put a line in him." Doris stood in the doorway paralyzed, watching as I slapped a tourniquet on the guy's arm and started a large bore IV, attaching a bag of normal saline, which I let run in wide open.

DM said, "Everybody's tied up in the two trauma rooms with one patient in full cardiac arrest and another with intractable seizures. It's just you and me, Doc." DM was like a machine as her adrenaline surged and she buzzed about the room.

"Okay, DM, let's get some labs on him, including an electrolyte panel, cbc, INR and type and cross him for four units of packed red cells." I turned to the guy's wife. "Ma'am, does he have any cardiac history?" She stood like a deer in the headlights watching DM draw the tubes of blood.

She shook her head no.

"Does he drink alcohol or take any medications?"

"He doesn't drink at all and he's always been very healthy. He's been taking a lot of ibuprofen for joint pain, though." Doris started crying, and I thought she might faint.

"Thank you, Doris, we're going to need to work on him now. DM, could you have her sit in the waiting room. She's going to keel over." She escorted Doris out. The poor woman was barely able to stand. I looked up at the guy's cardiac monitor and saw that his heart was clipping away at an unhealthy rate of 170-180; much too fast for a man his age. He wouldn't be able to sustain that for long before something bad happened. His oxygen saturation was at ninety-two percent and he appeared comfortable from a respiratory point of view.

I checked another drawer and found a nasogastric tube. I lubricated the tip and inserted it into his right nostril. He gagged a little as it passed over his posterior nasopharynx into his esophagus and then into his stomach. In seconds bright red blood was streaming out the tube and into a plastic canister on the wall that I attached my end to.

When DM returned I said, "Take his pressure again, DM, and I'll hang another bag of saline, but we'll need to start transfusing him with blood as soon as it's available."

"I'll call for someone to pick up his blood work but it'll take at least twenty to thirty minutes to type and cross him unless you want to give him unmatched blood?"

Decisions. Decisions. Unmatched blood could result in an adverse reaction, usually not fatal, but I certainly didn't want to make things worse than they already were. "What's his blood pressure?" I asked.

DM responded. "His pressure's coming up. It's 100 systolic."

I looked at his heart rate and saw that it had stabilized and was coming down. "Good, then we'll wait for them to type and cross him, but please tell them to expedite it, and when you get the chance let's hang some IV Protonix. While you do that I'll get the GI guy on call."

There was a wall phone by the door, and as I picked it up I noticed that the guy's wife had returned to the room. "Please let me stay? I won't interfere." She pleaded and DM looked at me sympathetically. I nodded and DM stepped into the hallway to find another phone to call the lab.

I dialed the operator while Doris cradled the guy's head. He was starting to rouse a little and his color wasn't quite as bad. "Hello, could you put me through to the gastroenterologist on call? Thank you."

As I waited, I saw the old guy open his eyes and look around. "What's happening?" he asked.

Doris comforted him. "You're going to be all right, Ed. Stay calm, I'm right here with you."

"Doris, I don't understand?"

With my free hand I grasped his. "I'm Dr. Cesari, Ed. You're bleeding internally, and we're going to give you some blood soon. That should make you feel better, but I'm afraid you're going to have to stay with us a few days while we run some tests, but your wife is right. You're going to be fine."

He nodded and squeezed my hand. "Thank you."

"Hello, this is Dr. Van Arndt. Is someone looking for GI?"

"Hi, this is John Cesari. I'm in the ER with a seventy year old white male having a big GI bleed. He's going to need to be scoped in a hurry. His vitals are…"

"Slow down, champ. What's your name again?" He asked interrupting me.

"John Cesari."

"Are you a doctor, nurse, P.A., or what?"

"I'm a gastroenterologist."

"Really?"

"Yeah."

"Then why are you calling me about a GI case? Why don't you just take care of it yourself?"

"Because I'm not on staff here. I'm visiting from another hospital and happened to be walking by when the guy crashed." I saw DM rolling her eyes as she sensed he was giving me a hard time.

"Let me get this straight. You're not on staff at Morristown but you're calling a consult in the middle of the night? Give me the ER doctor right now. This is inappropriate."

"Hey, Van Arndt, there's a man's life at stake here. Let's not get hung up on technicalities. He's very ill and needs your help. The ER doctor is busy with a cardiac arrest. I'm just helping a patient in need."

The patient had perked up and both he and his wife were listening intently to my end of the conversation. DM was checking his blood pressure again as another nurse walked in with two units of packed red cells, which she handed over to her. I looked at the wall monitor and was relieved that his vital signs had stabilized and his blood pressure was now approaching 110 systolic. The situation was still critical but improving.

Van Arndt's blood pressure on the other hand was skyrocketing. "You got a pair of balls lecturing me, Cesari. Do you have any idea how many local, state, and federal laws you've broken just being in that guy's room right now?"

"It's called being a good Samaritan. Now, do you want to hear the case or not?"

I looked at Ed, who smiled at me through his oxygen mask and gave me a thumb's up. Doris also nodded her approval. DM's frown turned to a scowl as she listened. The blood was running fast into Ed's IV and his color was slowly returning.

"I'll listen, but you should know that I'm not under any obligation to come in based on anything you say. My obligation is to the ER physician alone, not to you."

Now he made me angry. "Listen carefully, Van Arndt, because I'm not going to repeat myself. You said what you had to say, and I got it. You're pissed, but let's get something straight; your obligation is to your fellow man, asshole, not to the ER physician. Your responsibility toward a patient in need trumps all other considerations; even the law. Do you understand that? Now take that stick out of your ass and pay attention."

He fumed and sputtered as I filled him in on the pertinent details, and he grudgingly agreed to come in. I turned and Doris came over to give me a big hug. "Thank you. I didn't understand completely, but I heard enough to know whose side you're on."

"Thank you, Doris. The bottom line is that your husband is going to be fine and is going to get the best possible care. You can believe that."

DM walked over to me, slipping her arm through mine. "Come with me."

As we walked out of the room she smiled. "I'd give you a hug too, but I don't want to give you the wrong idea. You're not my type. Skinny guys don't do anything for me."

Skinny?

Reaching the medication cart, she punched in her access code and a drawer slid open. She handed me several syringes preloaded with Versed and Fentanyl, both potent sedatives.

"Is that enough?"

I looked at her, surprised. "Plenty but how will you explain the missing medication?"

"Forget about it. We get the counts wrong all time. Every night someone goes home crying thinking they're going to get fired and the next morning it starts all over again. Some of these girls got the retention span of a flea. Thanks for your help in there, and just for the record, I'm going to tear that guy Van Arndt a new asshole when he gets here. I may even write him up formally to administration."

"I'd rather you didn't. Knowing how the system works, I'll be the one that gets the new asshole."

She nodded and chuckled. "Well, then I'll just have to figure out some other way of torturing him. He's on the Marchitellone shit list now and that's not a good place to be, but on that note, maybe you should hightail it out of here. It's getting close to shift change, and there's going to be a lot of fresh faces coming in asking questions."

"What about all the paperwork and documentation for what just happened in there? I don't want to get you in trouble."

"Thanks, but I never heard of you or ever saw you before, and I couldn't pull you out of a lineup if my life depended on it. You're just some doctor from the hospital who wandered in without a name tag and wandered off again when the emergency resolved. I was too busy taking care of a critically ill patient to get you to sign, date, and time all the bullshit. How's that sound?"

"Sounds like this hospital has some really sharp nurses working here. Thanks, DM. You're a diamond in the rough."

Chapter 24

*I*t was late and it was close to seven by the time I made it back to Cocoa. The building was starting to wake; the lights were on, secretaries were starting to file in, and I could smell fresh coffee brewing. The door to Dr. Harmon's office was locked and I knocked lightly. Cocoa answered promptly, pulling me in and locking the door behind me.

She looked stressed out. I asked, "What's wrong?"

"Where have you been?"

"I'm sorry. It's complicated but I got tied up with a sick patient in the ER."

She saw flecks of blood on my white lab coat. "Is that what that is?"

"Yes." I noticed that she now wore an ID badge, which was facing away so I couldn't see the name or photo. I grasped it, turning it around.

"Well hello, Dr. Harmon. Where'd you find this? In her desk?"

"No, it was on her coat."

I looked at her, puzzled. I didn't see a coat anywhere. "What do you mean?"

"Come with me." She grabbed my hand and led me over to the bathroom. Opening the door, I spotted a fifty year old woman on the floor, wide-eyed in terror with a strip of duct tape across her mouth. Her hands were behind her back, and I could see that they were duct taped as well.

"Dr. Harmon, I presume?"

Cocoa nodded, and I had to admit I was impressed.

"Okay, tell me what happened."

"I was taking a nap when she walked in at around six. I woke and we were both shocked. The lab coat threw her off and I told her that I must have wandered into the wrong office to take a nap. She almost bought it but remembered that she had locked her door last night before leaving. She noticed that I didn't have an ID badge and was about to call security. I stalled her by telling her my ID was in the duffel bag. She held up on the alarm long enough for me to pull your gun out, and now here she is."

I chuckled. "Honestly, I don't think I could have done it better myself. You didn't hurt her, did you?"

"No, she took one look at that gun and almost passed out."

I crouched to get closer to Dr. Harmon. She was thin, frumpy, with graying hair and glasses. She wore a knee-length black dress and a white lab coat, and she was very frightened.

"We have no intention of hurting you, Dr. Harmon. I'm sorry for doing this to you but suffice it to say we have our reasons. If you remain quiet, you'll be fine, we'll leave and you will never see or hear from us again. Please nod your head if you understand."

She nodded her head.

"Thank you."

Cocoa said, "What happens now? We just wait for Phil to show up? What if a secretary walks him in?"

"I thought about that? It's a massive clinic with many subspecialties all sharing office space on this floor. I counted at least thirty doctor's offices in this wing alone. The central area in the middle of the floor by the elevators is enormous and looks like it could accommodate upwards of twenty secretaries. The patient waiting area had at least a hundred chairs. The odds are that in a place this busy, the secretaries simply check you in and point you in the direction of the office you're supposed to go to."

"Wouldn't that be nice?"

"Yes, it would. We're just going to have to keep our fingers crossed." We closed the bathroom door and sat on the leather sofa together. She curled her knees underneath to face me.

"So, you like the way I handled myself, huh?"

"I have to admit. It was pretty good."

She smiled. "So, can I join your gang?"

I laughed. "Sure, every gang needs a Cocoa."

"So what time is Phil supposed to arrive?"

I looked at my watch. "Eight o'clock; in about forty-five minutes."

She was staring at me so I asked, "What is it?"

"That's plenty of time for—you know?"

"You *can't* be serious?"

"I'm always serious about that?"

"With Dr. Harmon in the bathroom?"

She smiled. "She doesn't bother me."

I shook my head but had to chuckle. "Well, she bothers me, and besides, I'm still mad at you for last night. You didn't stay on your side of the bed like you were supposed to. You have issues, did you know that?"

"And you're a pussy, did *you* know that?"

"Will you please stop calling me that?"

"Why, because it's the truth?"

I cleared my throat and ignored her. "Why don't we go over again one more time what we're going to do. This way, we won't make any mistakes."

"Fine."

"Okay, so Phil knocks on the door and you let him in. You're Dr. Harmon. This is his first visit so he won't know what she looks like or even if she's old or young. If he says anything about your age or looks just laugh it off and thank him, politely informing him that you're actually older than you look and take your work very seriously. Be warm but very business-like and then ask him to take a seat on the sofa."

I paused to take a breath and continued. "We'd like to do this without getting nasty so soften him up. Ask him about himself, his family, his work, and his friends. Gradually, lead up to the traumatic event but try to let him do most of the talking. Here's the important part. Tell him that it might help his therapy if you knew the details of what happened, such as who he worked for and why he was at Disney in the first place. Tell him that you understand the confidential nature of anything he tells you and that this conversation is fully protected by federal law and is completely undiscoverable."

Cocoa asked, "Is that true?"

"For ordinary citizens, yes, but to be honest, I'm not sure if the same rules apply to federal agents who are in therapy for things that happened in the line of duty. I have a feeling it's probably not."

She thought that one over and asked, "What if he won't talk? A lot of people don't on their first visit to a psychiatrist."

I glanced at her. "And how would you know that?"

She blushed. "I went to Princeton?"

I continued. "Anyway, I'll be listening carefully. If he tells you what I need to know, fine. If he doesn't then I'll come out of the bathroom and take over the interview—at gunpoint."

"What if he won't talk even at gunpoint?"

"One way or the other, he'll talk. Besides I have something that will loosen him up. I showed her the syringes of Fentanyl and Versed.

"What are they?"

"Short-acting sedatives I got from the ER. Fentanyl's a narcotic and Versed is a benzodiazepine. Together, they'll induce a relaxed, hypnotic state. His tongue will wag like a Boston terrier waiting for a doggy treat."

At ten minutes of eight, I went into the bathroom, closed the door and took one of the syringes of Fentanyl from my pocket. Doctor Harmon's eyes went wide. I apologized and reassured her that what I was giving her wouldn't kill her. I didn't want her to make any sudden noises when Phil came. I grabbed one of her hands firmly and was relieved to see she had decent veins. I injected the full syringe into one of the more prominent ones and watched as she gradually drifted off to sleep. I sat on the toilet and waited.

Eight o'clock came and went uneventfully. The same for eight-fifteen. At eight-thirty, Cocoa came into the bathroom. "I don't think he's coming."

The thought that he might be a no-show hadn't even entered my mind. He worked for the Secret Service, and if they ordered him to go to counseling he had better go—if he valued his career. This didn't make any sense.

"Okay, might as well give him another ten minutes or so. Maybe he got lost or something."

"Lost? He's half an hour late. He's not coming."

"Ten more minutes."

"Okay."

Cocoa went back out, but ten minutes later it was obvious that he wasn't making his appointment and we needed to leave before the next patient showed up. What could have happened? It didn't feel right. I looked at Dr. Harmon sleeping comfortably if not a little awkwardly on the floor, and I decided to leave her restrained to give us time to exit the building. I left the bathroom and signaled Cocoa it was time to leave.

"What do you think happened?" she asked as we walked into the parking garage.

"I have no idea, but he's human like the rest of us. Maybe, he got sick or something."

"He looked fine last night."

I thought about that. "Yes, he did. I think we should swing by the house on Peace Road. I was hoping to coax the truth out of him gently but I guess I'm going to have to be more direct."

"Is that why you took those photos last night—for the more direct approach?"

"Yes, people are dying and I'm not sure who the bad guys are yet so I need answers anyway I can get them."

After we pulled out of the garage I called hospital security and let them know Dr. Harmon needed help in her office. "That was nice of you," Cocoa said.

"No point in making her suffer any more than she already has. She's probably going to need her own psychiatrist after today. Thanks for helping out, by the way. Do you think you would've pulled it off? Pretending to be his psychiatrist, I mean? That wasn't what I had intended when we came to New Jersey yesterday. It wasn't until last night that I found out his doctor was a woman."

She laughed. "I guess it would have depended on how messed up he was, but if you're asking me if I could pretend to be interested in a man's life when I couldn't care less, what do you think?"

I thought about her chosen profession and nodded. "I see your point."

Chapter 25

It was ten a.m. when we rolled to a stop behind a silver BMW in Herman Winkelman's driveway. I hadn't thought about it, but if Phil McIntosh was suffering from a severe enough concussion, he may not have been able to drive himself so the pie man would have had to take the morning off from work. Okay, so what? I cradled the pistol in my pocket and hoped I wouldn't have to use it. The syringes of sedatives were in my other pocket.

"All right, Cocoa, we go up to the front door and ring the bell. They're not expecting trouble so just be casual. The sight of a woman always causes a man, gay or not, to let his guard down."

She smiled. "Trust me, I know. The question is how do *you* know?"

"I've watched a lot of shows on praying mantises and black widow spiders. It's a ubiquitous fact of nature that most males are helpless against determined females."

"What about the pictures?"

I thought it over for a second. They were in a manila envelope in the glove compartment. Two dozen glossy color photos, unmistakable, irrefutable, and in the eyes of the Secret Service brass, indefensible. I said, "We'll leave them here for now. If push comes to shove I'll come back and get them."

"Squeamish about using the pictures but not about using a gun?"

"The gun is to make sure he doesn't shoot me before he lets me talk and I guess the pictures are kind of a low blow so maybe the answer is yes, I am a little squeamish about them. I hope I don't have to use them but trust me, I will if there's no other way."

"And the drugs in your pocket?"

I didn't answer because I hadn't thought it through enough. We walked up to the front door and I pressed the buzzer. Looking around the quiet street, I noticed there wasn't much activity of any kind. Most people were already at work or at the gym working off the holiday pounds. No one answered so I rang it again and tested the handle. Locked.

From where I stood on the front porch, I noticed the side door to the attached garage slightly askew. You couldn't see that from the driveway. When no one answered a second time I pointed at it. "Let's try over there."

We walked into the empty two-car garage and looked around. It was fairly ordinary; shelves with tools, lawn mower, snow blower, ladder, and other typical items for home maintenance. There was another door inside the garage leading into the house, and I tested the handle. It was locked and I contemplated what to do next.

"What are you thinking?" she asked.

"Mostly what will happen if I break in. Phil is Secret Service, which means he may be armed despite his concussion, and we don't know anything about Herman other than he is large and black and likes to give head."

She chuckled at that as I tried my credit card trick unsuccessfully on the lock. It was a dead bolt and wouldn't yield. I walked around the garage and spotted a peg board with a mini sledge hammer and a large flat head screwdriver. Perfect. I brought them over to the door and wedged the tip of the screwdriver between the wood of the jam and the strike plate. Several serious whacks with the small sledge broke a chunk of wood off the door, freeing it from the lock and allowing it to swing inward. We paused, waiting to see if the noise had alerted anyone inside to our presence.

When nothing happened, we stepped inside furtively, recognizing that we had just entered dangerous territory. In most states we could be shot dead without warning or consequence just by stepping into the garage without permission, let alone the house. I drew the Sig Sauer out from my coat pocket and signaled Cocoa to stay behind me as we crept into the laundry room. There were a few wood steps leading into the main house and then another door at the top of these. This door opened quietly, and we entered into a modern kitchen. There was no one in sight and no signs of life. I didn't see any fresh coffee brewing or breakfast dishes. It was after ten on a Monday. This wasn't good. I started to gag. What was that smell?

Cocoa coughed. "Is that gas?"

I looked at the stove and saw all the burners were turned to the off position, but a hissing sound could be heard emanating from behind the stove. Coughing as I approached, I could see that someone had moved the appliance to get behind it and had not completely replaced it. The natural gas hose leading to the back of the oven had been disconnected and was spewing gas into the house. There was a red shut-off valve on the hose so I reached down and turned it to the off position, stopping the flow of noxious fumes. We started to get dizzy and nauseated so we ran over to a window and opened it wide, sticking our heads out and inhaling deeply.

She said, "They picked a funny way to commit suicide."

"Yeah, real funny." We stood by the windows as fresh air gushed in, cleansing the room and our lungs. Five minutes later, our heads cleared, it occurred to me that we were still in danger as there was still quite enough gas in the house that an errant spark or electrical discharge might trigger an explosion or fire, and then there was the issue of where Phil and Herman were and what condition they were in.

"Quick, open all the windows as wide as you can. We've got to clear the gas out of here."

We ran from window to window, opening them all. The gusts of cold air chilled the room but felt good as the gaseous odor dissipated. In the kitchen, we rested against the countertop and tried to understand what was happening.

As we stood there collecting our thoughts, an electric timer plugged into a wall outlet rang out and the toaster oven that was plugged into it turned on. Seconds later, there was a loud whooshing sound and a ball of flame erupted in the center of the room as the electrical discharge ignited the residual gas, and just as rapidly it dissipated. A small towel caught fire and we both ducked from the sudden heat but were otherwise unhurt. I tamped the towel out uneventfully and looked around. The ceiling and light fixtures had singed but everything seemed okay. Goddamn.

I said, "That was close. If we had arrived twenty minutes later this whole place might have been cinder."

Cocoa was speechless and I held her. "You going to be all right?"

She nodded. "I'll be fine, but we'd better find them."

Quickly walking through the home, we discovered them in the bedroom, unconscious and tied to the bedposts with rope. "Are they dead?" Cocoa asked, anxiously watching me examine them. They were in their underwear lying face up, eyes closed. Their respirations were shallow but they had strong carotid pulses.

"No, they've been drugged." I put the Sig Sauer away and checked their pupils. They were severely constricted, and neither guy responded to verbal stimulation. I undid their bonds and examined them, finding small fresh puncture wounds in their forearms. Somebody had shot them up with something much the same way I had done to Dr. Harmon, only these guys had been severely overdosed and were completely unresponsive.

I shook Phil vigorously and slapped his face a couple of times, eliciting a grunting sound. Good, he'd be okay. Just needed time for the crap to wash out of his system. His pal, Herman, didn't look quite as good. Cocoa tried slapping him and pinching him without any response. I walked around to his side of the bed and rubbed my knuckles hard along his sternum. You could wake the dead with that maneuver and in this case it worked as he groaned in response, turned to his side, and vomited on the floor as we jumped away. He was going to be fine too.

I said, "Keep stimulating them, while I open a few more windows." The smell of gas was not as strong as in the kitchen but was present throughout the house and sickening, and I hoped the brisk winter air helped them snap out of it quickly. I retrieved a towel from the bathroom and wiped Herman's face with it and then threw the towel on the mess he just made on the floor.

Several minutes later, Phil coughed and started to rouse. His eyes opened, looking around confused. "What's happening?" he asked with slurred, hoarse speech.

I brought him a glass of water from the bathroom and helped him sit up. He was very weak and disoriented. "You've been drugged, Phil.

I hate to be the bearer of bad news but somebody just tried to kill you and Herman."

His eyes registered fear and concern. "Where's Herman?"

"He's right beside you, Phil." I pointed at Herman lying next to him, being tended to by Cocoa. He looked over at his boyfriend and his memory started to return.

"Herman, are you all right?" he called out weakly, reaching over to touch him.

I said, "He'll be fine but he needs more time to wake up. Why don't we see if you can stand up, all right?"

He put his arm around my shoulder and I assisted him up. We walked around the room together a couple of times, allowing his strength and wit to return. Cocoa kept an eye on Herman, and if his respirations slowed too much or appeared too shallow, she would shake him vigorously. After about ten minutes, Phil's cobwebs started to clear. He looked at me and Cocoa suddenly concerned. "Who are you?"

"We're friends, Phil." I decided to play softball with him. I could always use the pictures later if that didn't work.

"Don't you think we should call an ambulance for Herman? And that wasn't an answer." He was still shaky but no longer needed me to stand. He stumbled over to a closet, took out a robe, and put it on.

"We can call an ambulance, if that's what you want but they won't do anything differently at this point except shoot Herman up with more drugs. Besides, I'm a doctor and my friend here is a nurse." Cocoa looked at me as I lied.

He sat down next to Herman and stroked his lover's head. Herman was starting to come around and his eyes fluttered open, staring blankly at the ceiling. Phil said, "I just want him to be all right. That's all I care about."

"He's going to be fine, Phil. I've taken care of many patients with drug overdoses, but we need to have a frank conversation about who did this and why."

"I still don't know who you are or why I should talk to you." As he grew stronger, I could see the wheels spinning inside his head as his eyes darted around the room. I surmised that he was trying to remember where his gun was and how he could get at it.

"Please don't, Phil. That would be a mistake."

"What would be?"

"Going for a weapon. I'll drop you like a ten pointer on opening day, understood?" I pulled the Sig Sauer out of my coat pocket.

He studied me carefully now, his brain finally coming into focus. I saw recognition in his eyes. "You're that doctor from Disney."

I nodded. "Cesari."

He nodded. "I remember."

Herman said weakly. "Phil, are you all right?" He reached out and they hugged. Cocoa stepped away, giving them space.

"I'm all right, Herman. How about you?"

"Tired, and sick to my stomach."

"You're going to be all right, Herman," Phil whispered and we watched them kiss tenderly.

I asked, "Feel like standing, Herman? The drugs will wear off faster if we get your blood circulating." We helped him stand up and ambulate into the living room, where we sat him down on the sofa. Cocoa brought a blanket from the bedroom for him to keep warm. The windows had been open now for quite a while and the temperature of the room had dropped considerably.

"Do you mind if I make a pot of coffee, Phil?" Cocoa asked, already filling the pot with water.

Phil said, "Please do. There are filters, coffee, and measuring scoops in the cabinet just above the coffee maker. My God, it's freezing in here."

I explained what had happened as I walked around closing the windows. Phil sat next to Herman, holding him tightly. When I was finished with my explanation he let out a deep breath. "Fuck."

"Want to tell me what's going on, Phil? I'm not your enemy."

He hesitated. "Did you kill Marguerite Varga?"

"I was going to ask you the same question, but no, I did not kill her, Phil. I was just in the wrong place at the wrong time is all. So, while we're on the subject, why were you following me at Disney?"

Shaking his head in frustration he said, "I guess my career is over no matter how I cut it." Worry lines etched deeply in his features. He was profoundly conflicted by current events as he continued. "Look, all I know is that somebody under my protection received a credible blackmail threat. I was charged to investigate it. The investigation barely got off the ground when I wound up in the hospital."

"Yeah, but why me?"

"We were watching Marguerite and saw you speaking to her just hours before you found her body. That seemed like quite a coincidence right there and the fact that everybody on the ride ran away but you also seemed suspicious. We looked up your records and it didn't jive with you just being a doctor on vacation. There were way too many shady characters and accusations in your past and then you show up hours before someone under my surveillance gets murdered. You stuck out like a sore thumb as a person of interest. So we started following you to see what might turn up."

I nodded. That seemed like a reasonable explanation. "Fine, but take a step back. So why was Snow White under surveillance by the Secret Service in the first place? Were you guys aware of what she and Cinderella were up to with that little love nest of theirs?"

"Yes, of course we knew, and obviously you do too. We never let our guy out of our sight. That's why my career is over. We were all part of it. Now that the shit's hit the fan and everything's going sideways, it's all going to come out. Anyway, so after the blackmail threat, we started watching Snow White and Cinderella. We were trying to figure out who and where they would lead us back to. When Snow White got popped, we figured whoever it was that was blackmailing our guy was on to us and was trying to silence the girls before we got to them. My first thought was that you might be some type of gun for hire, but I guess I was wrong or you wouldn't have just saved me and Herman."

Cocoa brought four mugs of black coffee on a small tray she found in the kitchen, and we thanked her. Phil took a sip of coffee and offered one to Herman who opened his eyes but declined.

"Yes, Phil, you were wrong. I didn't kill Snow White nor was I involved in any way until after her murder."

"So who are you, Cesari?"

"Apparently, I'm the victim of ethnic profiling by the Secret Service. So just to clarify, you guys were just watching the girls and not trying to knock them off to protect your boss?"

"Not a chance would we ever do something like that. We didn't think the girls were involved in the blackmail side of it anyway. We were just hoping they might lead us to the people involved."

"I'm a little slow so bear with me here, okay Phil? I want to make sure I got this right. The Secret Service is assigned to protect some old pervert who regularly cavorts with dress up whores provided by Disney. Somebody figures out just how important this guy is and sets up cameras in the playroom, filming your guy in action. They attempt to blackmail him and instead of caving in, he unleashes the service after them? Am I warm so far?"

Phil didn't respond but he didn't have to, so I continued. "You don't know who's blackmailing your guy, so you set up surveillance on his girlfriends in the hope something would turn up. Instead, Snow White goes for a swim in one of the rides and I become the number one asshole on everybody's shit list."

He nodded. "Yeah, something like that, except now we have a new problem. The rumor mill has been churning fast and furious that a couple of guys pretending to be Secret Service agents tracked Cinderella to some town in upstate New York. They were found dead with fake service IDs on them. The theory is they were going to murder her and set up the scene so that we take the fall, but something went seriously wrong and now Cinderella's gone."

This news surprised me and I took a deep breath. Fake agents? I knew one of them was dead for sure but I had called 911 when I left Geneva that night, and the guy I put in the trunk didn't look that bad. I asked, "What happened?"

"Not sure, one guy got on the wrong end of a shootout with persons unknown and the other was found stuffed in the trunk of a car with blunt trauma to the head. He died of a massive cerebral hemorrhage."

Shit!

"So what do you think, Phil?"

"Somebody's protecting her but we don't know who, and it seems like whoever it was got there just in time. Apparently, from the way it was described to me, one of the guys was in her bedroom and just about to get to her when he got fried. We're not sure what happened to the other one, but he may have been the lookout guy and got caught by surprise."

I thought about this. "Sounds like Cinderella got lucky. Is there anything more you can tell me about who the blackmail victim is or what they might be blackmailing him about? It might be helpful to me."

He laughed. "Are you out of your mind? That's a line I won't cross—ever. There is absolutely no way I would ever reveal that so go ahead and shoot me if you want. He's important and that's all you need to know. Now would you please call an ambulance?" He turned to Herman, who had nodded off again. "Hang in there Herman, honey, hang in there."

I said, "Cocoa, call 911 anonymously on their house phone. Tell them there was a gas leak here and people are ill, and then we'll leave." She gulped the last of her coffee and went to the kitchen where there was a landline.

I turned back to Phil. "One more thing. I understand that you can't reveal the identity of the victim but what about the blackmailer? You must have some clue?"

"I'm sure my client knows exactly who it is but he didn't let on to me. Whoever it is though, got moxie. He sent a go-between to our guy's home with his wife sitting right there next to him and showed them both the video of his shriveled old white butt doing a muff dive on Snow White."

"A go-between?"

"Yeah, a tall, thin woman with long black hair; very attractive, like a model, and balls of steel. There she was threatening one of the most important men in America surrounded by Secret Service agents and she didn't give a shit. She was like ice. We threatened to detain her and she told us to go fuck ourselves; that the video would be all over the Internet before we even got her in the car."

"So she just walked out, just like that?"

"Yeah, just like that. I was pissed but the boss told us to stand down."

"Did you guys get any pictures of her?"

"Of course. Fingerprints too. We ran them through our data banks but nothing came up."

"That's it?"

"She gave us a name but it's probably not real."

"Yeah, so what name did she give you?"

"Consuela."

Fuck!

I nodded and tried not let on that I knew who she was.

"Okay, Phil, thanks for talking to me. The ambulance should be here in a few minutes so we'll be on our way. Keep Herman awake as best you can." As Cocoa and I turned to leave, I hesitated and turned back. "Phil, one last question, if you don't mind?"

"Yeah?"

"Who would want to kill you?"

He chuckled. "That's easy. After Consuela threatened my guy, I walked her out of the house. When we were alone I made a promise to her that if it was the last thing I did, I would either see her in an orange jumpsuit or six feet underground. I guess she didn't take that too well because it was her with some of her friends who came to visit us early this morning."

I nodded and walked away with Cocoa, a lot on my mind. Consuela was in New Jersey and we had almost crossed paths.

Damn.

Chapter 26

"Well, Cocoa, I guess this is where we say good-bye. Thank you for all your help, and I'll see you when I get back."

"You're welcome. Are you sure you don't want company down there? I wouldn't mind coming with you."

I smiled and looked at her profile. She was driving me to Newark International Airport for my eight p.m. flight to Orlando. She had purchased my ticket on her credit card.

"Thanks, but you've done enough, and although I would love company, things are going to get a little dicey from this point on and you'd be in danger unnecessarily."

She laughed. "Wow. Dicier than what just happened? That's hard to believe but I understand. Where will you be staying in case I decide to come down anyway?"

I glanced at her. "You don't take no for an answer, do you?"

"Men don't say no to me. I say no to them. I'm surprised you haven't figured that out by now."

"Oh, yeah?"

"Yeah."

"Well, I'm not sure yet where I'm staying. I was going to figure it out when I got there. I had a room at Old Key West when this all started, and I was hoping it might still be available. I was going to check when I got there but I'm not worried I'll find someplace although I'd like to be on Disney property. It'd be a lot more convenient for what I need to do."

"Will you let me know for sure when you get there?"

"Cocoa, you're a big girl and I respect your right to make your own decisions, but you're not coming down to Orlando, okay? I'm serious. This is not a game, and even though I like you, as I have mentioned two or three dozen times now I already have a girlfriend. We call that a pre-existing condition."

"I think I caught on that this isn't a game when Herman's house almost blew up this morning, and as far as your girlfriend is concerned, I think you need to know something. Ninety-nine percent of the guys that hit on me every night are married. So, the fact that you *only* have a girlfriend makes you one of the most eligible guys I've met in a long time."

I didn't know how to respond to that bit of exotic dancer logic, but I looked at her long and hard as we pulled into a space in short-term parking. We walked to the terminal and since I was three hours early for my flight, she had decided to wait with me. I had rolled a couple of thousand dollars with rubber bands and stuffed them into my pockets, and I had left the duffel bag with the Sig Sauer and the rest of the money in Cocoa's house, planning to retrieve it when I returned.

We entered terminal A and found JetBlue, grabbing a seat on a bench near security check-in. "Do you mind if I take a quick power nap, Cocoa?"

"No, go ahead. I think I'll grab a cup of coffee and a magazine at the news stand over there."

I looked at my watch. It was five-thirty.

Cocoa nudged me, and I woke with a start. Falling asleep, I had gradually slid to one side with my head resting on her shoulder. I stretched, yawned, and rubbed my eyes. It was almost seven.

"Perfect timing," she said. "We should head to the gate."

"We? You mean me. You can't go through security."

"Yeah, just watch me." She stood up and grabbed my hand.

What was she up to?

We walked to security and I handed the officer my fake driver's license and boarding pass and watched with surprise as Cocoa did the same. The officer scanned the IDs, studied us, and I held my breath but he handed them back, waving us on.

"I see you were a busy girl while I slept."

"I got lucky, the flight's half empty. I even got a seat next to you."

"You know, Cocoa, you're starting to border on being a pest. Aren't you worried about your job?"

She laughed. "Don't worry about my job. I can always get another one. Besides, I called Heidi and told her it was all your fault. She was pissed but at least she didn't fire me."

I looked alarmed. "You didn't tell her any details, did you, about what we've been doing? She doesn't know too much and I don't want her to. Her mouth is bigger than the Grand Canyon."

"No, I just said you needed me around for a few more days for sex. She understood. She knows you're a pretty visceral guy and probably can't go more than a few hours without it."

I chuckled. "You didn't say that, did you?"

"Sure I did. Hey look, there's our gate to the right. They've already started boarding."

We landed uneventfully two hours later, and we stripped our coats and sweaters off as the hot, humid air of Orlando overwhelmed us. A short cab ride brought us to the hospitality house at Old Key West where we entered and asked for my previous room. The girl was very polite but told us that they did not rent out rooms to people who just wandered in despite having just checked out the previous week. She suggested that maybe next time we should call ahead. I thanked her and we sat on one of the oversized sofas in the waiting area and listened to the endless cycle of Disney music piped in overhead.

"What now? Are we going to sleep here?" Cocoa asked.

"No, but I can't believe that the room I just stayed in is occupied already. That girl wouldn't even check. It's only been a few days since we left and we were supposed to have the room for another week. Besides, this place usually clears out after Christmas." I looked at my watch. It was almost eleven. The Disney girl wandered over to us to let us know that they would be closing for the night in a few minutes.

I said, "C'mon Cocoa, let's take a walk."

We meandered past the pool area and onto the sidewalk that wound throughout the development. About a quarter of a mile later we spotted a sign for Turtle Pond and turned into that section. It was still relatively early, and vacationers wandered about here and there, getting on and off buses. Apartment 2525 was recessed from the main walkway on the second floor and hidden from view of the street by large trees and shrubs. I knocked gently. "This is it."

Cocoa nodded.

When there was no answer, I knocked a second time and waited. Still no answer.

I whispered. "Cocoa, wait here. I'm going around to the back."

"What's around back?"

"There's a terrace with French doors. I might be able to get in that way."

"What if there are people asleep in there?"

I hesitated. I didn't really have a backup plan. "If I see or run into anyone I'll just get the heck out of there and we'll go find a hotel off property."

"Tell me again why we just don't do that now."

"There are several places I need to check out right here on Disney property, including Snow White's apartment. I was there once but didn't spend nearly enough time. It'll be easier to get around if we're staying here."

She looked concerned as she thought about it. "Okay, but don't take too long. If anybody comes along I'll just go down and meet you at the bus stop."

Leaving her there, I walked down and around the building complex, staying in the shadows. The grass was thick and slick from a recent rain and soon my feet were soaked. It was dark and there were many bushes, tropical plants, and trees to hide my progress. In a matter of minutes, I had made my way to the rear of the apartment complex and looked up at the balcony in question. The lights were out and there were no signs of human activity like in some of the other guest rooms.

To my right and fifty yards off was a body of water with a fountain in the center and beyond that the fairway to hole number one of the golf course. To my left was a large palm tree growing at an angle next to the balcony with dense shrubbery all around. The lower edge of the terrace was slightly more than ten feet up and I quickly considered my options, making my decision. We didn't do much tree climbing growing up in the Bronx but I'd read a lot of Tarzan novels as a kid. How hard could it be?

The trunk of the tree was about a foot in diameter and its surface irregular, which I thought would allow me to better grasp and obtain toeholds. I looked up again. I didn't have that far to go. Reaching up, I wrapped my arms around the wet bark and tried to get my right foot on one of the more prominent irregularities in the trunk. The angle that the tree had grown at played in my favor, helping to support my weight, and soon I was a foot off the ground, hanging on for dear life. I took a deep breath and let it out. My pulse was racing. I had never done anything like this before.

Slowly but surely, I slid, climbed, and propelled myself upward almost as if I were climbing a rope in high school gym class. Once I was about five feet off the ground I could easily reach the lower edge of the porch railing, and with a firm grasp of the spindles in my hands, I maneuvered from the tree on to the outside ledge of the porch. From there, I swung my leg over the railing and found myself standing on the same terrace on which I'd had coffee with Cheryl on Christmas morning.

Peaking inside through the paned door I didn't see anything, though the room was quite dark. I tested the handle and it was locked, so I took out a credit card and tried wiggling it into the lock mechanism. After several failed attempts and almost destroying the card I gave up. I looked back and forth to make sure no one was in sight, took off my shirt, and wrapped it around my fist.

I prayed silently that no one was in there sleeping and then punched my hand through the pane of glass by the handle. It made a muffled sound and thankfully the carpet inside the room muted the falling shards of glass. Still, it would have been no worse than had someone dropped a glass or coffee cup. I stood there quietly in the shadows waiting to see if a light would suddenly burst on revealing a sleepy guest coming to investigate. Nothing happened so I reached in and unlocked the door, entering the room. Before turning any lights on I decided to search the apartment just in case and so quietly tiptoed from the living room to the kitchen to the bedroom. Once satisfied, I flipped on an overhead light and let Cocoa in.

She threw her arms around me and held me tight. "I was freaking out. You took so long, and why'd you take your shirt off?"

"Sorry about making you wait, but all's well that ends well. I took my shirt off because I needed something to protect my hand when I broke in." I nodded in the direction of the French door with the broken pane of glass.

She walked over to the door and inspected the floor. "Is there a broom and dust pan?"

"Yes, in the utility closet over there next to the bathroom. The apartments are fully furnished and we even have a washer and dryer."

She retrieved the utensils and busied herself with cleaning the glass off the floor as I tossed my shirt in the trash.

"What are you doing that for?" she asked, watching me as she swept glass up.

"It's filthy. I had to climb a wet tree to get onto the terrace. I'll buy a new one tomorrow. There's a small convenience store across from the hospitality house."

She walked over and made a face at me, reached into the trash can, pulling my shirt out. She then emptied the dustpan with the broken glass into the now empty container. "I'll wash this for you. That's ridiculous to throw out a perfectly good shirt. Who are you, Daddy Warbucks?"

"You don't have to do that, Cocoa."

"It's no big deal."

"Well, if you really want to, I won't stop you. Thanks."

I wasn't sure if I liked the direction this was going. It was one thing to boss me around in the bedroom. It was another to force her way onto the plane with me. But offering to wash my clothes for me sent shivers up my spine. A single woman offering to do laundry for a single man was the equivalent of a lioness crouching in the prairie waiting for a gazelle to wander by. I made a mental note to keep an eye on her and not be complacent just because she was a stripper. She was still a woman and wanted the same thing every woman wanted—me.

"John, is everything okay?" she asked, noticing me staring at her blankly.

I snapped out of it. "Yeah, sure. Look, I'm going to take a shower and lie down."

"That sounds like a good idea. I'll put this in the wash. You think they have any detergent?"

"I'm sure they do somewhere in the laundry room."

"Okay, I'll find it. Toss me your jeans and socks too. Might as well clean everything since we didn't really pack. You know what? Give me your underwear too. I'll throw my stuff in as well."

I went into the bathroom, stripped, tossed my stuff into the washing machine and stepped into the shower, thinking things over. So, the Secret Service were not the assassins I thought they were. Thank goodness for that. Consuela was a blackmailer and a homicidal maniac. Cinderella was in real danger and therefore Cheryl was as well. I knew that before, but this morning's revelations at Phil and Herman's house put a real exclamation point on it. The implication was clear; there was a high-priced call girl service being run at Disney involving Cinderella and Snow White. Helena was the madam, who made all the local arrangements with the johns, but Consuela was also involved or did she simply find out what was going on after the fact and decide to take advantage of the situation by planting cameras and trolling for opportunities?

Some muckety-muck comes along and gets his ass filmed doing the nasty and Raul and Consuela got him by the balls, or do they? He screams foul and sics the Secret Service on them. They fight back by eliminating all the witnesses, but that didn't make any sense. Snow White was Raul's daughter. He wouldn't kill his own daughter, would he? He seemed genuinely distraught over her death. And who was this muckety-muck asshole anyway? If he'd just kept his dick in his pants Snow White would still be alive and I'd be having a nice steak dinner at Epcot watching the fireworks with Cheryl. Why did anybody have to die anyway? That was a stupid question. The girls obviously knew who was or might be doing the blackmailing, that's why. But Cinderella didn't seem to know anything, or maybe she knew but didn't realize what she knew. I needed to have another chat with her at some point.

I stepped out of the shower and toweled off while Cocoa watched me from under the covers. She had the TV on. I said, "I don't suppose it would do any good to ask you to stay on your side of the bed tonight?"

She laughed. "Oh, please."

"I didn't think so. Look, I need to make a phone call, okay?" I hadn't spoken to Cheryl in a while and decided to check in on her and Lola.

"Feel free."

It was close to midnight, which was late but not that late, so I took out my cell phone, dialed Cheryl, and plopped down on top of the bed. She picked up on the third ring.

"Hi, Cesari. How are things?"

"Heating up. How are you and my girl Lola, aka Cinderella?"

"I hate the bitch. If the bad guys don't kill her I will."

"What did she do?"

"It's what she won't do, like sleep—ever. She wants to party all the time. I can't control her. Last night she said she needed some fresh air and was just going to step out for a minute and come back. That was at ten o'clock. Guess what time I finally found her?"

"I'm guessing sometime after ten?"

"Very funny. Try some time after two a.m. in some dance club two blocks away making out with two guys at the same time. I had to drag her back to the room kicking and screaming that she needed to get some or she was going to explode and then she accused me of being a prude. Can you believe that? Me—a prude? That's ridiculous."

I chuckled. "Okay, so she likes guys."

"Likes guys? Now that's an understatement. She doesn't have a clue as to what keeping a low profile means. She's exhausting me, and you didn't answer the question."

"What question?"

"Do you think I'm a prude?"

I hesitated. She could be a little uptight at times. "Well, I haven't noticed you bringing your own pillow with you anywhere—you should try it."

"Oh, shut up."

"Okay, so we've established she's a wild thing. Nothing unusual other than that?"

"Except for the fact that she chain-smokes pot, no, pretty boring mostly because she sleeps all day and I'm afraid to leave her alone because she's so reckless. I bought a couple of novels and have been reading a lot. It's actually very relaxing when I'm not chasing her around."

"Where is she now?"

"Changing. We bought ourselves some clothes with the money you gave us. I agreed to go out with her for one drink and then home it is."

I looked at my watch. "You're kidding. You're going out for a drink at this hour?"

"I know. Trust me I'm not happy about it, but it was either that or sit in a cloud of marijuana all night, and I might be doing that anyway. Besides, we're just going to a bar across the street."

"All right, be careful though, it sounds like she's a loose cannon."

"Cesari, she's not a loose cannon, she's a loose battleship. So what's the word on your end?"

"I'm back in Orlando following up on some leads. I should return to New York in a few days. You know something? I just had a thought. If she becomes too much for you maybe I can ask Heidi to take her in at the Kit Kat Club. There's an empty apartment upstairs and if anybody would know how to handle a wild cat like her it would be Heidi. She handles wild cats all the time."

"Well, let me see if she behaves tonight and lets me get some sleep. If not, I may ask you to do that."

"Okay then, well good night and take care."

"You too."

I hung up and turned off the light on my nightstand. Glancing at Cocoa, I saw she was already asleep. The remote had slid onto the bed between us so I turned the television off and got under the covers, staring at the ceiling in the dark and thinking things through.

"Are you sleeping?" Cocoa asked softly.

"Not yet. I was just thinking about what I had to do tomorrow. What about you? I thought you were out cold."

"I was just dozing, but I will be in a minute if I don't work myself up."

I smiled in the dark. "Well, then don't work yourself up."

"I think it may be too late for that."

"Tonight, I really have to insist, Cocoa. You stay over there and I'll stay over here. Let's just try it out for one night, okay?"

She slid over anyway.

Chapter 27

We left the apartment at eight to grab a bite to eat. We wore the same clothes as the day before albeit clean because of the wash Cocoa did, but I promised her that we'd stop somewhere and pick up some new clothing before the day was over. I taped over the door receptacle so the lock mechanism couldn't engage, and we walked over to Olivia's restaurant by the hospitality house and pool area. It was a beautiful morning, seventy degrees and sunny. Jimmy Buffett played overhead alternating with Caribbean steel drum music. We sat at one of the outdoor tables and ordered coffee and pancakes. Most of the other tables were occupied with families, and the servers were quite busy.

"This is fun," Cocoa commented, looking around.

I chuckled. "It would be a whole lot more fun if people weren't dying all over the place."

"Yeah, I guess."

The waitress poured our coffee and stepped away.

I said, "Okay, so do you have your bearings yet?"

"Yes, we're staying at Old Key West, Turtle Pond, room 2525."

"Good, that's just in case we get separated."

The pancakes came and we dug in with enthusiasm.

"So what's the deal with you and this girl in New York?"

"Her name is Cheryl."

She nodded. "So what's the deal with you and Cheryl? How long have you been dating?"

"It's complicated, but this time around about four months."

"One of those types of relationships—on again, off again?"

"Yeah."

"So, who's Kelly?"

Surprised, I swallowed a mouthful of pancakes and asked. "What do you know about Kelly?"

"I overheard Vito talking about her with Heidi the other night. He said she's black, beautiful, and you're still in love with her. Is that true?"

Fucking Vito.

"Kelly and I broke up about six months ago, and I'd rather not talk about her if you don't mind. It's still a sore point."

"I understand. You sure have a lot of girls in your life though. What are you going to do if it's your kid?"

I stopped eating. "What kid?"

She stopped eating too and didn't answer me. She just stared straight ahead like a deer in the headlights.

"I asked you a question, Cocoa. What did you mean?"

"I'm sorry. I thought you knew."

"Knew what? C'mon, don't do this to me," I asked, concerned and very annoyed at her evasiveness. When I asked a direct question, I expected a direct answer.

She let out a deep breath. "Vito told Heidi that Kelly looked very pregnant, like she was about to deliver. I'm sorry. I feel like such an idiot."

I was stunned and suddenly lost my appetite. "You feel like an idiot? What's that make me?" I remembered Vito saying Kelly looked "plump" and in fact, Mark too had commented on her weight. Assholes. I took a deep breath and did some quick calculations in my head. It had been six months since Kelly and I broke up. That meant she would have already been pregnant when she dumped me, but did she know at the time?

I took my cell phone out and dialed Vito. He answered on the second ring. "Hey Cesari, where are you? You should try answering your phone once in a while. I've been looking all over for you. I got your tickets to Orlando here. Your flight leaves tonight at eight p.m. out of JFK."

I had forgotten that I had asked him to get plane tickets for me. "Vito, I'm already in Orlando. It's a long story, but thanks anyway."

"Fucking Cesari. Did you know you're a pain in the ass? Can't you sit still for a minute? Heidi went through a lot of trouble getting this ticket for you. It's first class too."

"We'll talk about who's a pain in the ass when I see you, all right?" I was seriously annoyed.

"What's that supposed to mean?" he demanded, my reaction catching him off guard.

"It means I ought to kick your ass for not telling me that Kelly is pregnant."

"Oh, that," he said weakly. "How'd you find out?"

"Never mind how I found out. I thought you were my friend?"

"Hey look, Cesari, I didn't know how to tell you or even if I should stick my nose into it. I wasn't trying to keep it from you. For God's sake. What was I supposed to do?"

I was angry now. "You were supposed to tell me that I'm going to be a father, that's what, and if you didn't want to stick your nose in it why on God's earth would you tell Heidi, the human megaphone?"

He was silent at my rebuke.

After an uncomfortable minute he said, "I'm sorry."

"Okay, now pay attention, this is what I need. First off, check on Cheryl and Cinderella. Apparently, Lola has been giving her a hard time about keeping a low profile. If Cheryl tells you she can't take it anymore then I want you to set the girl up in the apartment above the Kit Kat Club so Heidi can keep an eye on her. Lock her up if you have to. She's too young and too stupid to understand the danger she's in. Then I want you to find out where Kelly is staying. I need to see her and talk about this. Even if she doesn't want to, I have to at least try."

"Okay, I'll check on Cinderella, and finding Kelly shouldn't be too hard. I'll call the personnel department at St. Matt's and ask for her contact information. I'll tell them I was her previous landlord and want to return her security deposit but she forgot to leave me a forwarding address. If they don't have it on hand I'm sure they'll steer me in the right direction. A greedy New York landlord wanting to return rent money doesn't happen every day and will evoke all kinds of sympathy. I've used that trick before. Anything else?"

"Yeah, remember those two Secret Service agents I told you about?"

"Yeah, you killed one and stuffed the other in the trunk of the car. What about them?"

"Well, apparently the one in the trunk died as a result of his injuries, but the important thing I just learned is that they weren't really Secret Service agents at all. They were just masquerading as agents. Apparently, after they dispatched Cinderella, they were going to plant stuff there to make it look like the service did it. The service has been putting heat on Consuela and Raul and I guess they figured if they put some heat back on them they would back off. In fact, Consuela tried to kill Phil and his friend Herman, yesterday."

"No fucking way."

"She's crazy, Vito. I could see it in her eyes."

"Sounds like it. Look, Cesari, there's another thing. I don't know if you heard, but it was on the news last night. The coroner in Orlando has officially ruled the death of Snow White to be an accidental drowning. I don't know if that helps you or not."

I thought that one over. "That's total bullshit. Three days ago I might have bought that but not now."

"Be that as it may, that was the determination."

"Does this coroner have a name?"

Vito chuckled. "I knew you'd want to have a chat with him. His name is Dr. Lewellyn Finch. He is a pathologist employed by the Orlando Memorial Hospital. His office is somewhere in the hospital."

"Thanks, I think I would like to talk to him."

"Okay, I'll get Kelly's address and phone number to you as soon as possible."

"Great, you can give it to me the minute you get off the plane."

"What are you talking about?"

"I need you down here in Orlando. I'm sure you can catch a flight today. There should be at least one seat available after you cancel the reservation Heidi made for me. It'll only be for a day or two. It's important and I can't say what it's about on the phone. I'm staying at Old Key West, apartment 2525 in the Turtle Pond section."

"Fucking Cesari, you think I have nothing better to do?"

"Call me when the plane lands."

I hung up and turned to Cocoa. "C'mon let's go. We just got a new assignment."

Chapter 28

The cab let us off in front of Orlando Memorial Hospital's main entrance. It was a huge complex of modern buildings, and the lobby was jammed with people. I studied the directory on the wall, found what I was looking for, and grabbed Cocoa's hand.

"This way. The coroner's office is in the basement."

"Aren't they always?" She commented, wondering why I had to check the directory.

I had never thought about it. "Why do you say that?"

"On television or in the movies, the coroner's or pathologist's office is always in the basement with the dead bodies."

I smiled. "Fair enough. I'll have to start keeping track of it when I visit different hospitals."

We took the elevator down to the basement, accompanied by nurses and orderlies. Once there, we followed signs to the pathologist's office. It was a big hospital and it took a while to get there. Pedestrian traffic slowed considerably by now and there were very few people in the hallway of this section. It wasn't deserted, just not particularly crowded like upstairs on the main floor. The pathology lab itself was quite large, and through a window we saw many technicians in white lab coats busy at work. Off to one side of the lab, I saw the door I was looking for: *Dr. Lewellyn Finch*. I was glad when I saw it was a solid wood door without a window and had a sign on it that read "Do Not Disturb."

As we walked through the lab, our approach was challenged by a young lab tech. "May I help you?"

I showed him my St. Matt's photo ID and Cocoa flashed a big Cocoa smile. I said, "We had an appointment with Dr. Finch. Is that his office over there?" I pointed at the door as Cocoa batted her eyes at him.

Thankfully, he didn't check out my ID as thoroughly as he checked out Cocoa's breasts. "Yes, that's it. Want me to get him for you?"

"We'll be fine, thank you." With an air of authority, we turned away from him and made a beeline for the door. I could feel him staring at Cocoa's ass.

She giggled as we arrived at our destination. "What's so funny?" I asked.

"I bet that kid doesn't get out much."

"Most people in health care don't, Cocoa."

"Hmm, you seem to do fine."

"Well, I'm not like most people."

"I'll say."

"Okay, ready?"

She nodded, and I knocked on the door.

"Come in," said a cranky male voice.

I opened the door and we both entered. A chubby middle-aged man with bifocals stood up from his desk. I stepped forward with hand outstretched as Cocoa discreetly locked the door behind us. "Dr. John Cesari, St. Matt's Medical Center, New York."

He studied my ID and although he was confused and annoyed, he nonetheless reached across his desk, taking my hand. He was average height and mostly bald, pushing fifty years old, wearing a white coat. "Hello, what can I do for you? As you can see I'm very busy. I'm preparing for a conference at noon." He waved at the stacks of papers and books on his desk. His eyes finally rested on Cocoa and he seemed to calm down. She wore tight jeans, and an even tighter blouse. She was very distracting under almost any circumstance, but in a hospital filled with nerds and bookworms she attracted attention like a box of donuts at a Weight Watchers meeting.

"Lewellyn Finch. Miss..."

"Myrtle Rosenblatt. I'm Dr. Cesari's assistant. It's a pleasure to meet you, Dr. Finch." It never failed. Put a pretty girl in front of a geek and he melted like a stick of butter in a hot pan.

"Please call me Lewellyn." We both watched as she sauntered up to the desk, taking a seat in one of two consultation chairs, making it clear that we weren't leaving any time soon. It was a modest sized office but big enough to have its own bathroom off to my right, which was good. I joined Cocoa in the other consultation chair, signaling Dr. Finch that it was time to talk. He hesitated but sat down, confused but not alarmed.

I said, "We won't take much of your time, Dr. Finch, and I do apologize for our rather casual attire. We just arrived from New York last night and our luggage was misplaced by the airline. We haven't had a chance to go shopping yet." I wore jeans, sneakers, and a cotton shirt. The ID around my neck gave me some credibility.

He sized us up, not quite sure what to make of this intrusion. He had the look of a guy who was used to getting what he wanted or—he might throw a tantrum. He glanced at us over his glasses. "I understand. So what exactly can I do for you both?" he asked, starting to come down from the jolt of seeing Cocoa.

"Well, Dr. Finch, this is a fairly delicate matter and I'm hoping you will extend me a certain amount of professional courtesy. I also want you to know that I am aware that I have no right to ask you what I am about to and I would consider myself deeply in your debt if you helped me out." I looked over my shoulder to emphasize the importance and clandestine nature of this visit.

"Go on," he replied, his curiosity piqued.

"A young woman died on Disney property, Christmas Eve. I know that an autopsy was performed and the results were just released. Publicly, it has been called an accidental drowning but the family, whom I represent, are not convinced and asked me to personally review the results with the coroner, so here I am. Please do not interpret this as a lack of confidence in you personally."

I saw him gulp, ever so slightly, but gulp he did. He also licked his lips, which were suddenly dry. The good doctor was nervous. He hesitated. "You're talking about Snow White, of course?"

"Of course."

"The police thought it was an accident and my findings did confirm that. So, the family can rest assured on that subject. There was nothing I found to suggest foul play."

"The trouble is, Dr. Finch, some people, including myself, are having trouble believing that."

"Why would anyone think otherwise?"

"Well, it's just that accidentally drowning in two and a half feet of water seems a little odd for a young healthy girl, and then there's the question of why she was there in the first place. Didn't that strike you as odd; Snow White wandering around in the bowels of the It's a Small World ride?"

There was an edge in my voice that he didn't miss. He sat back in his chair, and I noticed beads of sweat forming on his forehead. "People do stupid things all the time, Dr. Cesari, and die all the time accidentally as a result, and every time it's the same thing. The family won't accept it and want to blame it on somebody else."

I nodded. "This is very true. Out of curiosity, were there any signs of physical trauma on the body and was a toxicology screen performed?"

He was losing control of the conversation and didn't like it so he stood up nervously. "The results of the autopsy report are a matter of record now, Doctor. I'm very sorry for the family but I'm afraid you're wasting your time if you thought you would find out anything different than what has already been made public. Now if you don't mind as I mentioned to you already, you caught me at a very busy moment."

What a lying sack of shit.

I sighed. I hated when this happened. In our youth, Vito and I had started out by making collections for the local capos. You learned to spot a liar a mile away. "Sure, Doctor, and thank you for your time. We'll leave, but may I use your bathroom first?" I asked politely.

He calmed down a bit. "Certainly, and once again I'm very sorry I can't be of more help."

"Please, don't trouble yourself. I understand." I walked over to the bathroom and opened the door. It was a six foot square. Plenty of room. I feigned trying to open the light several times and called to him. "Is there something wrong with the light in here?"

"I don't think so. I used it an hour ago." He looked at Cocoa, who shrugged and said, "He's got prostate problems."

Finch walked over and leaned past me into the room, flipping the switch. The light came on promptly. "There you go," he said.

I grabbed him roughly by the shoulders of his lab coat and shoved him forward into the room, slamming the door closed behind us. He stumbled forward into the sink, grunting in pain as his knee hit the porcelain.

"What are you doing?" He turned around startled but not yet frightened, so I slapped him hard enough to send his glasses flying off his face and crashing onto the floor. Now he was frightened.

"What do you want?" he stammered, holding his face, which was now beet red.

"I want to know the truth about what happened to Snow White, and you're going to tell me. Please don't yell. Things will undoubtedly get much worse if you do." I started rolling my sleeves up slowly, almost nonchalantly. I learned a long time ago that the key to intimidation was to act as if what you were doing was routine, no big deal. I could sense him mulling over his options.

He said, "I don't have to tell you anything, and you're breaking the law."

"Sure you do, Lew, and you're also breaking the law. Falsifying an autopsy report is a federal offense. Did you know that? Conspiracy to cover up a homicide is also against the law, and so is obstruction of justice. You getting the picture? Snow White was murdered, Lew, and we both know it. So tell me what the autopsy really showed or you might be getting one yourself."

I finished rolling up my sleeves and squared myself in front of him. I was six feet, 220 pounds of muscle. He was overweight and maybe walked on a treadmill two or three times a week. "What's it going to be, Lew? This is your last chance."

He blinked. "I'll lose my job if anybody finds out I told you."

"Lew, maybe I haven't made myself clear. You may or may not lose your job for telling me, but you are definitely going to lose some teeth if you don't."

He was sweating profusely now and nodded. "All I know is that I had barely finished the autopsy report when the CEO of the hospital called me up and ordered me to rip it up and write a new one. He had never talked to me like that before. He was very upset, almost frantic, and I sensed that he was under a lot of pressure. The girl was already dead. Nothing was going to bring her back, and I need this job. So there it is." He hesitated.

"Go on. So what did you really find?"

"There was no water in her lungs so she didn't drown. She was dead before she hit the water. It appeared to me that she died of asphyxiation but I couldn't find any signs of physical trauma such as strangulation marks on the neck or capillary hemorrhage like when someone puts a plastic bag over your head and you struggle for air. There were no signs of a struggle."

"What about the toxicology screen? Did it show any evidence of drug use?"

"No, she was clean in that regard. Not even cannabis, at least not recently."

I nodded. "Okay, anything else?"

He shook his head no, but I watched him gulp, ever so slightly as he lied. I slapped him again even harder and dragged him over to the toilet bowl, shoving him face first down into the water. After a few seconds of letting him struggle, I pulled his head out and shoved him onto the floor against the wall. I said, "I asked you if there was anything else."

He sat there, shook water from his face and gasped. "There was a fresh needle mark in her neck."

"And…?"

"I thought it was strange because who injects themselves in the neck with anything? Then I started thinking about how she could have asphyxiated without any signs of trauma so I ran some special tests and found traces of succinylcholine in her blood and tissue."

"Succinylcholine?"

"It's the paralytic agent anesthesiologists use in operating rooms right before they intubate the patients."

"Yes, I know that. It paralyzes the patient so they can't resist and hurt themselves. They can't breathe on their own so if they are not mechanically ventilated immediately they will die."

"Exactly, if you gave that to someone on the street they would suffocate in minutes without a struggle. I think that's what happened to her. They transported her after she died and tossed her in the water to make it look like an accident."

I thought about that. "Doesn't seem like a bright idea to me. I mean figuring out that she didn't drown wasn't that hard."

He coughed up toilet water. "Just because they're ruthless doesn't mean they're smart."

I nodded. Good point. "How does the CEO fit into this? This doesn't exactly sound like good medicine."

"I don't know. To be CEO of a hospital these days doesn't have anything to do with the practice of medicine. They're practically all political appointees nowadays. Their main job is to kiss government ass and keep everybody underneath them in line. They're like the commissars in the old Soviet Union so I just assumed somebody higher up the food chain politically wanted the truth suppressed and gave him the call."

"And just like that you violated every code of ethics you were ever taught?"

He didn't say anything so I continued. "Tell me about the CEO."

"Like what?"

"How about his name for starters?"

"Paul, Paul Ashford. He hasn't been here long, maybe two years. He's fifty, just got through a messy divorce. Wife left with the kids. He got the house but she got everything else. That's about all I know. He doesn't mingle too much with the help, if you know what I mean."

I nodded. "Is that it? That's all you can tell me about him?"

"I don't really know the guy. He meets with the staff twice a year to go over budget reports and hospital finances but that's it. He's like the Great Oz standing behind the curtain. No one gets to meet him. Until he called me the other day, I hadn't seen or spoken to him in months."

"What about the woman who was found with a bullet in her head in Cinderella's Castle on Christmas? Remember her? Was that really a suicide?"

"Yes, I remember her, and as far as I can tell it was a suicide. Entry and exit wounds were consistent with that and the gun was registered in her name. There was no note but rumor had it that she was very close with the girl and may have been involved in her death somehow. She may have felt guilty over what happened. No one knows."

I was silent as I thought it over and then said, "Okay, Lew, do you have anything else to tell me?"

He hesitated again and shook his head.

I didn't believe him and stepped closer. "Do you want to take another swim in the toilet?"

He cowered as I stood over him. "No please, there is one more thing…"

"I'm listening."

His eyes darted back and forth, and I knew something bad was about to come out of his mouth. "The Varga girl was pregnant, just barely, maybe eight, maybe ten weeks was my guess."

I digested that for a moment, getting angrier by the second. I felt one of the veins in my temple start throbbing. "A young girl and her unborn child are murdered and you were going to cover it up?" I was so pissed my hands were starting to tremble.

He leaned back against the tiled wall and buried his face in his hands, sobbing. I was getting ready to kick him in the head when the door opened and Cocoa stepped in. "Hey, what's going on in here? You're starting to get loud. We didn't come here to kill the guy, remember?"

I nodded and looked at him sternly. "We're leaving now. You stay in here until the cleaning people show up tonight, and forget you ever saw us. Do you know what will happen if you don't do exactly as I say?"

He shook his head.

"I'll come back here and cut your fucking head off like some goddamn terrorist, that's what will happen."

He started crying again.

We left the pathology department uneventfully, and I was fuming. A mentally ill girl had been taken advantage of, abused, and murdered along with her child and I made up my mind that somebody was going to have to pay.

As we exited the hospital and hailed a cab, Cocoa held my arm, sensing my emotional state. "Hey, big guy, are you going to be all right?"

I wasn't sure.

I felt my temperature rising.

Chapter 29

*C*ocoa and I talked during the cab ride back to the Magic Kingdom, and I filled her in on the details of my conversation with Dr. Finch. She had heard some but not all through the door.

"What a scumbag," she commented.

"Yeah. You know, I don't know what it is but I'm a lot more upset now than I was just a day or two ago."

"Why do you think that is? Because she was pregnant?"

"Yeah, I guess, and what an awful way to die."

"Why is that? Don't you just fall asleep, like lethal injection?"

"No, not at all. Succinylcholine causes paralysis of all your muscles, including the diaphragm so you can't breathe, but you're fully conscious until you're dead. So, as your body becomes deprived of oxygen you feel the pain it causes to your tissue, but even worse would have been the terror she must surely have experienced knowing what was happening. I just feel really bad and really angry about it. There are a lot of nicer ways to end someone's life."

She put her arm through mine, came nearer and said sympathetically, "Sounds like you have feelings for this girl?"

"I don't know what it is. Before, I thought she was just some crazy girl and maybe she still is but now…"

"She's a mommy?"

"Yeah, I can't help it. It just makes me feel different about the whole thing. All of a sudden, she just seems so vulnerable and lonely. I feel a rage inside of me now like a volcano that's getting ready to erupt. If you hadn't come into the bathroom when you did I might have killed that guy Finch. I was that upset."

Cocoa hugged me. "I had no idea you were so sensitive. Maybe, it's because you just found out you're going to be a father yourself. Men get very protective with pregnant women. It's part of the male instinct... Well, I'll be darned."

"Why?"

"You really are a knight in shining armor, aren't you? I'd bet anything that you're a mama's boy too, right?"

I smiled. "Yeah, and now you're Sigmund Freud."

She chuckled. "I told you I went to Princeton for a year."

"How could I forget? There's something else though that bothers me too. It's very disturbing to me that a physician would lie like that. There are some people and professions in which we place our trust and just assume that they will always do the right thing no matter what the personal cost. It's a short list for sure but the medical profession is on top of it. The idea that Finch would falsify an autopsy report to save his job is almost too much for me to wrap my head around. Maybe I should have killed him just on principle."

She nodded. "Take it easy, cowboy, but you're right. Everybody trusts their doctor. Most people still trust policemen too, but not politicians and definitely not lawyers. No one trusts lawyers. They're all liars. It's part of their training from day one, learning how to distort and bend the truth."

I thought about that. "All of them? Do you really believe that?"

"All of them."

"You're not being fair."

She nudged me. "I have a joke."

"A joke?"

"Yeah, what do you call three hundred dead lawyers chained together at the bottom off the ocean?"

I chuckled at the image. "What?"

"A good start."

"Ouch, cut that out. That's not nice."

She laughed. "I'm sorry if I gave you the impression that I was nice."

"What about your Uncle Leo? Isn't he a lawyer?"

"He's the one who told me that joke; right after he made me promise never to marry a lawyer."

"Well, I don't know if I fully agree with you. Cheryl's a lawyer and one of the most honest people I've ever known. In fact, she couldn't tell a lie if her life depended on it."

"Really?"

"Really."

I looked into her face and saw something that made me feel different. She was beautiful in a way that could make any man weak in the knees. She was way too smart, but it was her self-confidence that impressed me the most. She looked twenty but talked like she was forty, and it was very clear that she had potential way beyond what she was doing. I could easily see her as a physician, college professor, or CEO of her own company, but she chose to do what made her happy and screw what anybody thought. I admired that. I really did. So many people were mired down in jobs and career paths that made them miserable every day because they were afraid to step outside the box.

The cab let us off near the entrance to the park. We bought day passes and since it was almost noon, we grabbed a couple of sandwiches on the way to Cinderella's Castle. Looking around, you would never know the evil that lurked just below the surface here. Crowds still thronged the streets, sidewalks, and stores making merry. Christmas trees and garland still decorated every building and street, and Santas rang bells, shouting cheerful greetings, every few hundred feet.

"Wow, look at this place."

Cocoa looked around in amazement as we stood in the center of Main Street with Cinderella's Castle directly ahead.

"First time, I gather?"

"Yeah, my parents weren't into the Disney shtick."

"What kind of vacations did you go on?"

"Oh, the usual—a week in Rome, a week in Paris, London, and of course Israel. Skiing in Vail, camping in Yellowstone, wine tasting in Napa. You know, that kind of stuff. Boring. I didn't feel alive until

I was seventeen and we spent a long weekend in Vegas. I don't think I ever came down from that trip."

I looked into her eyes for a second. She never failed to surprise me. "You are a very interesting young lady, Cocoa, did you know that?"

"*Je suis? Mercie beaucoup. Vous êtes trop amiable, monsieur.*" She said with a perfect French accent.

"Please don't tell me—I just can't take any more Cocoa surprises."

She smiled. "Well, I'm not fluent and I have a slight Parisian accent, but I could get around pretty easily if I brushed up a little. Four years of private tutoring and a full semester in Paris as an exchange student in high school didn't go completely to waste. My parents had big plans for me."

Jesus!

We finished our lunch and entered the castle. I pointed to the spiral staircase, which was cordoned off with a red velvet rope. There was a sign nearby informing the patrons that due to illness, Cinderella's appearances had been cancelled for the next few days. There was no security and the place was mobbed. I figured no one would really notice or care if we went up the stairs.

"Just act naturally as if we belonged here, okay? I'll hold the cord for you as you walk through. Don't look at anyone in particular and talk to me continuously as if we're discussing important Disney business."

We walked up the stairs together, with Cocoa chatting away at a mile a minute and gesturing with her hands as if she were making important points while I nodded, paying close attention. The spiral staircase made several turns such that by the time we reached the top we were well out of view of any curious Disney guests.

The lights were dimmed in the hallway and we waited, allowing our eyes to adjust. Helena's office and Cinderella's dressing room were off to the left, and the door marked security was farther down the corridor on the right. All three doors were closed.

"You didn't say anything about security," Cocoa whispered.

"Relax, if someone comes out we'll just say we thought the restrooms were up here."

She snorted. "Oh my God. Isn't that a bit lame?"

"Maybe, but we're paying customers. They won't want any trouble. Just follow my lead."

Helena's door was locked, and I tried the credit card trick again. No luck. It was a deadbolt.

"What now?" Cocoa asked.

"I'm thinking." If I kicked the door open, it might create a lot of noise, alerting whoever was in the security office. On the other hand, whoever was in the security office might have a key to Helena's door. Maybe I should just ask them to let me in? Maybe I should just beat them until they coughed up the key?

"Well?" she asked.

"If I kick the door open it might bring security. Then we'll be up the creek without a paddle. Right now, we haven't actually done anything wrong."

She thought it over and said, "Go hide from view on the stairs. I'll knock on the security door and see if anybody's home. I'll tell them I'm lost and was looking for the powder room. The worst they'll do is send me packing. If no one answers, you can kick the door open."

"Fine, but why do I have to hide on the staircase?"

She smiled, cocked her head, and did a head bob at me. "Don't be stupid. Most security people are men. Now go hide."

She had a point so I disappeared down a few steps while she went to the far end of the hall. I heard her knock but didn't hear a response. She knocked again and waited. Still nothing. Eventually, she returned to me.

"No one answered. Let's do it," she whispered.

We went to Helena's room. Cocoa stood to one side of the door and I stood directly in front. Taking a deep breath, I launched a full throttle kick just below the door's handle. The wood splintered, cracked, and partially gave way. A second kick caused the door to swing open. Cocoa and I entered, turning the light on, but if we hoped to find anything useful, we were sorely disappointed because the room was completely bare. It had been stripped clean, down to naked walls and carpet.

I said, "Damn, I should have searched this place better when I had the chance."

"Don't be too hard on yourself. I would've gotten out of here as fast as I could have too if I had found a dead body."

"All right, let's keep moving."

Closing the door behind us as well as we could, given the damage, we entered the hall and started toward the staircase, but Cocoa stopped and grabbed my arm. "What about those rooms?" she asked, pointing at Cinderella's dressing room and the security office.

"What about them?"

"As long as we're here maybe we should take a look? The security office might have video recordings of who came and went that night. They might even have some of Helena's stuff in there."

I thought about that. "You have a point. Let's start with the dressing room."

A quick kick opened Cinderella's dressing room rather easily, revealing that it too was completely bare. Disappointed but not surprised we moved on to the security office, where I hesitated.

"What's the problem?" she asked.

I took a deep breath. "I was just wondering if the penalty was worse for breaking into three offices as opposed to just one or two."

She shook her head impatiently. "Will you just kick the friggin' door in and stop playing Hamlet." This was the story of my life; women talking me into doing things that I knew were going to get me into trouble.

I said, "All right. In for a penny in for a pound."

As I was gearing up for a kick, Cocoa grabbed my arm. "Hey, wait a minute. The lock on this door is different than the other two. Maybe your credit card trick will work."

She was right, the lock was a little different. I examined it up close and it didn't seem to be a deadbolt like the other two, so I took my American Express card out, grabbed the doorknob, and wiggled the edge of the card into the space between the jamb's metal strike plate and latch. With some effort, the card slid past the latch, freeing it and allowing the door to open.

She gently clapped. "Nicely done, Dr. Cesari."

"Thanks."

Closing the door behind us, we flipped on the light and were thoroughly startled by what we found. "Well, well, well," I mused. "Who would have thought it? It's not a security office at all."

"It's an apartment, and quite a lovely one at that."

We scanned around a fairly large living room with a sofa, television, and recliner. Off to one side was a breakfast counter with two chairs overlooking a small but efficient kitchen. There were two doors on the other side of the living room, which I presumed led to bedrooms.

"So, who lives here?" Cocoa asked.

"That's a very good question."

The kitchen and living room didn't reveal anything interesting. The refrigerator had some milk, bottled water, and a dozen eggs. There was a loaf of bread in a bread box and the trash can revealed an empty juice container. There were a few dishes in the dishwasher and residual coffee in a mug on the counter suggesting that someone had recently been here, but who?

We walked across the room and entered a bedroom with a queen-sized bed, full bathroom, and a flat-screen television. An oversized armoire, closet, and bureau harbored an assortment of expensive women's clothing and other accoutrements. The bathroom also suggested a woman's presence. There was shampoo, bath salts, a curling iron, makeup, and tampons. Inside a linen closet, I found a small wall safe with an electronic lock. I would have loved to get in there.

"She's got nice taste," Cocoa commented from the bedroom, rummaging through the armoire and closet. "Look at all these Jimmy Choo shoes." She held up an open-toe black three-inch dress sandal with straps.

"What's a Jimmy Choo shoe?"

She laughed. "If you have to ask, you'll never understand."

"Oh my God. Will you look at this?" She held up a very pretty blue pocketbook and ran to a mirror. "It's Valentino."

While she continued her tour of what appeared to be an endless array of high-end designer ladies wear, I went through the night table drawers and checked under the bed. After a few minutes, I said, "Let's check the other room, all right? There's nothing in here."

"Speak for yourself. There's tons of stuff in here. I'll meet you there in a minute." As I left, she picked a dress out of the closet and was holding it against herself in front of a full-length mirror.

The other room was set up as a study with a desk, laptop, and bookcase. I powered up the laptop but it required a password to log on so I was stuck at the splash screen. The drawers didn't reveal a whole lot either other than a few loose pens and some blank notepaper. Who lived here and why? The thought crossed my mind that maybe this was Helena's apartment for when she worked late and was too tired to go home, but would that make sense? Consuela had told me that she had an apartment on Disney property to keep an eye on Snow White for Raul. Is this what she meant by keeping an eye on her; pimping her out to the highest bidder? I wondered how Raul would feel about that or was he in on it? I couldn't accept that. I felt sick just thinking about the depravity involved here. A search of the bookcase revealed several classics, a few modern fiction novels, and several music CDs. Nothing terribly interesting. The more I thought about it, the more certain I became that this had to be Consuela's apartment. That was the only thing that made sense.

I left the room to find Cocoa, expecting to see her modeling clothes. Instead, I discovered her sitting on the foot of the bed watching television, her face glued to the set. She barely noticed me enter the room.

"Hey, what are you doing?"

"Trying to understand what I'm looking at. Sit down with me."

I sat next to her facing the twenty-seven inch screen and realized that we were looking at the inside of Snow White's secret bedroom in the Fort Wilderness Lodge. Changing the channels brought us to her bathroom, and then to her changing room.

"That's Snow White's apartment I told you about. This must be a closed circuit TV. What made you turn it on?"

"I found an unmarked DVD in the bottom of the armoire and thought it might be important. I put it in the DVD player under the TV and was trying to figure out how to view it when you came in."

I said, "Show me where you found it."

She knelt down in front of the armoire, pulling open the bottom drawer until it tilted out onto the floor in front of her. It was filled with satin and silk underwear. Peering beyond the back of the drawer into the armoire, we discovered a hole that had been cut into the supporting wood panel beneath the drawer. This hole led into the space between the bottom of the armoire and the floor. Reaching into it, Cocoa had found the DVD. Curious, I closed the drawer and bent over to determine if I could reach or see into that space from the outside. I couldn't because the front of the armoire as well as the sides came flush with the floor. Clever. Only an extremely nosy girl would have found it. I sat back on the edge of the bed lost in thought.

"Well, are we going to see what's on it or not?" She had moved to stand in front of me and was just a few inches away.

"I already know what's on it, and it's going to piss me off."

Cocoa watched me carefully, and I looked up at her. She stuck her face right into mine, smiled, and kissed me. "Am I going to have to measure your testosterone levels? C'mon, it's just a little porn. It might be fun."

"It's not just a little porn. The girl on that DVD was an emotional train wreck and therefore the victim of abuse." Cocoa really knew how to get to me, and she knew it too.

"Fine, but we should at least confirm who's on it and what happened. Up until now it's all been conjecture and hearsay."

"I just can't." I was getting angry at no one in particular and couldn't stop myself.

She nodded. "Take it easy. I'll tell you what. I'll watch, and you close your eyes. I'll pause it when the guy's in view and there's nothing going on, all right? Win-win. I get to satisfy my curiosity and you get to confirm who it is. Now help me figure out how to use this thing."

We walked over to the DVD player and studied it. It was essentially the same as any other TV-DVD setup and all we had to do was find the right channel to use and change the video input to the TV. Returning to the bed, she sat down and clicked the play button.

She said, "Close your eyes."

I laid back down on the bed and stared at the ceiling. "Mute the sound. I don't want to hear anything."

Cocoa watched in silence for a few minutes before saying, "Oh my God, you're not going to believe this. No wonder people are starting to turn up dead everywhere. You better look at this."

She had frozen the screen on an older, easily recognizable public figure kissing a very naked Snow White. Cinderella was in the background adjusting her bustier.

I gasped in agreement. "What a piece of garbage. I can't believe it."

"Want to watch more?"

"I don't, not really. I'm starting to feel even more uncomfortable than I was. My God, she's barely an adult and he's close to seventy. This is so sick."

"Why do you think she kept the DVD there and not in the safe. Wouldn't that have been more secure?"

"By she, you mean Consuela?" I asked.

"Of course. This is obviously her apartment."

I nodded, thinking it over. "Misdirection would be my guess. Most people would focus on the safe and how to open it and not think to rummage through her clothing drawers, at least not the way you did. I know I wouldn't have found it if I were here alone. I might have opened the drawer partially and felt around a little but that's all. In fact, I was just starting to think about how I could open the safe without using plastic explosives. By the way, what made you pull the drawer out all the way like that?"

"I don't know. I was on my knees in front of it and was absolutely fascinated by how beautiful all her things are. I was excited and just wanted to make sure I saw it all so I pulled the drawer the whole way out."

"Well, good work. C'mon, let's get out of here, I need some fresh air."

"What about the safe? Don't you want to know what's in it? There might be more DVDs."

"I would love to get into the safe but safe cracking isn't one of my skills."

"Really? I thought you were Italian?" she smiled.

"That's pretty funny, but I'm Sicilian so the jokes on you."

"Isn't that just a type of Italian?"

"That's like saying a Lamborghini is just a type of car."

She chuckled and I said, "Getting the picture yet?"

"Loud and clear, but back to the safe, suppose there are other DVDs in there and we got them, don't you think we could stop all the blackmailing?"

"I doubt it, Cocoa. Even if there are other DVDs in the safe, no one would try to blackmail someone this important and only make one copy. That would be incredibly stupid. My guess is there are multiple copies running around for security purposes. The real question is what set this one apart from any others there might be. I guess at some point, I'm going to have to suck it up and watch the whole thing. I just can't do it right now."

I thought about what to do next. The question right now was that if we took the DVD we might be tipping our hand to Consuela and whoever else that we were onto them, possibly provoking a hostile reaction? How many more people would turn up dead, including Cocoa and me? I took the DVD out of the player and put it in my windbreaker pocket. "C'mon Cocoa, let's get out of here."

As we stood to leave she stared at the blue Valentino handbag and then picked it up, taking it with her.

I said, "Really? You're going to steal her purse?"

"She's a blackmailing whore. She doesn't deserve Valentino."

Chapter 30

"Thanks for coming down, Vito. Hope you had a good flight." I was a little sarcastic. He had just arrived via taxi from Orlando International Airport.

"Look, Cesari, I already apologized once for not telling you about Kelly so let it go. The flight was fine but we got another problem. Actually, you got another problem."

"Yeah, what's that?"

We were sipping whiskey poolside at Old Key West while Cocoa took a swim beneath the setting Florida sun. After we left Consuela's apartment, Cocoa and I took a cab to a nearby mall where she picked up a skimpy two-piece bathing suit and other items. I stuck with jeans and a comfortable shirt. When she took her robe off to dive in the water half of the men there came that much closer to being served divorce papers.

Vito said, "I went to check on Cheryl this morning, and we decided it might be best to have Cinderella stay at the Kit Kat Club. Apparently, she was out of control again last night. I won't bore you with the details. Anyway, the girl didn't know me and refused to come to the club without Cheryl accompanying her, which made sense. When we got there everything went fine until Heidi unloaded on Cheryl about how she should keep a better eye on you. She told her about you taking off to Florida with Cocoa, leaving her short a dancer. Heidi didn't mean to cause any trouble. It's just that she was a little frustrated."

I sighed. "Shit."

"I know—I know. Heidi's got a big mouth, but she feels terrible about it now. She's not used to straight laced women like Cheryl."

"How did Cheryl take it? Is she all right?"

"If turning white as a ghost and looking like she was going to puke is all right, then she's all right."

"That's just beautiful, Vito."

"I'm sorry."

He looked ridiculous sitting there in a charcoal-gray, two-piece silk suit, black wing-tipped, dress shoes, and a white dress shirt with gold cufflinks. He had thrown his long black, winter coat over a nearby chair. At least the shirt was unbuttoned at the top. I shook my head and sipped my bourbon. "What about Kelly? Were you able to track her down?"

"Not yet, I'm still working on that but I will. I do have something else for you, though. You know those two Secret Service agents that you said weren't Secret Service agents that you knocked off in Rochester?"

"Near Rochester."

"What?"

"It wasn't in Rochester. It was in the town of Geneva near Rochester."

"Anyway, I looked into it while I was waiting for my flight. Two guys pretending to be federal agents should have made the news, right? Well, there's been no report of anybody being knocked off anywhere in that town. I know a guy up there who works in the local papers and he said he hadn't heard anything about it. He called the local police for me and they said they hadn't heard anything about it either. The guy at the paper drove by the house as a favor to me and said everything looked fine. There was no car parked in the driveway with a body in the trunk."

"What about 911? I called it in. There must be some record of it."

"Well, I don't have access to their records but you would think the police would have said something to my friend if it had been called in? You sure you dialed the right number, and whose phone did you use?"

"Shut up. Of course I dialed the right number. What the hell is going on?" I thought about it a bit. I had used the dead agent's phone. What if someone had been wired in?

"Cesari, wake up. It means that they really were Secret Service agents. Somebody cleaned up the scene and got rid of any traces of their presence. They must have been listening in on your 911 call and ordered the police to stand down. Only certain agencies are capable of stuff like that. If those guys were just hit men hired to frame the service then whoever it was would have left the bodies there with the phony IDs. The press would have had a field day even without a dead girl. The service would have denied it but the public would just assume it was a cover-up. There would have been all sorts of heat on them and their activities. I don't know exactly what's going on but somebody's been yanking your chain about what happened that night."

I had a lot to think about. Did Phillip McIntosh lie to me? I found that hard to believe. He better not have after I saved his life. I was going to have to have another chat with him it seemed.

Vito looked me up and down. I wore blue jeans, black Nike sneakers, and a yellow Tommy Bahama beach shirt that had palm trees on it.

"You know, Cesari, I could remember a time when you had standards."

"I could say the same thing about you. Where's your tie?"

He chuckled at that. "It's been a long day."

"Okay, Vito, enough small talk."

He raised his hand in protest. "Whoa, before we get down and dirty I need to know something." He put his empty glass down on the table between us.

"What's that?"

"What's that you ask? You have a five foot, four inch bombshell, with shoulder-length hair, a size thirty-six chest, and an ass that most men would die for called Cocoa walking around Disney in a bikini waiting to give you a private lap dance later and you don't you think that requires an explanation?"

"No, not really, but if you insist, then this is it. She's a bit of an adrenaline junky and wanted to go on an adventure."

I thought Vito's eyes were going to pop out of his head. "You have got to be kidding me. Do you have any idea how many times I tried to tap that? I asked her out at least half a dozen times and each time she told me to go fly a kite. Politely, yes, but nonetheless, go fly a kite, and you just walk in like nobody's business and she suddenly wants to have your baby? How the fuck do you do that?"

I shrugged. "Maybe it's my aftershave. I don't know, and I don't care. And it has nothing to do with why we're here. So, if it's all right with you I'd like to get on with the matter at hand."

"You're unbelievable. You run away with one of the hottest dancers in Manhattan and you act like it's no big deal. Fuck. I hate guys like you."

I waited for him to settle down. He looked at his empty glass and searched around, which made me laugh. "There aren't any cocktail waitresses here Vito. If you want a refill you'll have to go to the bar and get one yourself."

He shook his head, exasperated. "What kind of a place is this? All right, so what's going on that I needed to come down here?" he asked, signaling an end to hostilities.

"I decided I had too much ground to cover alone and that I could use some backup but since we spoke this morning a lot has changed." I filled him in on my encounter with Dr. Finch and the discovery of the DVD in Consuela's apartment.

"Geez. Are you kidding me? You got proof in full color it was him with Snow White? Do you have any idea what this means?"

I shrugged. "That he's an asshole?"

"That too but what I meant is that we're dead—all of us."

I looked at him. "Aren't you being a little melodramatic?"

"Why don't you ask Snow White if she's being a little melodramatic? Can't you see what's going on here? This guy is getting rid of all the witnesses and using the Secret Service to do it. He had Snow White murdered then he used his political muscle on that coroner guy, Finch, to cover it up. Then they went to New York to find Cinderella. Fuck, anybody who knows what's on that video is living on borrowed time."

"I don't know, Vito. I spoke with that agent Phil yesterday and he seemed very sincere. He said there was no way that could happen. I'm pretty good at figuring out who's lying and who's not."

"Well, he's either lying or maybe he really doesn't know anything or maybe that concussion you gave him is whole lot worse than anyone knows."

As we spoke, Cocoa walked by with a piña colada and stretched out on a nearby lounge chair. Vito drooled ever so slightly, watching her. I said, "Take it easy, tiger." Then I called over to her, "You look great, Cocoa."

She rolled over to see me better. "Thank you, but I'm disappointed you didn't get a bathing suit and take a swim with me. I like looking at your body."

Vito muttered under his breath. "I hate you, Cesari."

I said, "I'm sorry about that, Cocoa, but I'm not in the swimming mood. Thanks for showing restraint with the suit by the way." Her initial inclination was to get a micro bikini, which is nothing more than a quarter-sized patch of material covering the pubic region and pasties attached to a string for the chest. After much discussion about Disney family values, I was able to talk her out of it in favor of a traditional bikini, which she was spilling out of anyway.

She laughed. "We wouldn't want strange men leering at me, now would we?"

I chuckled. "Right."

Vito said, "Don't rub it in, Cesari. I get the picture."

"I'm not rubbing anything in."

"Fine, so what now?"

I glanced around and slid the DVD across the table to him. "I need you to keep this in a safe place for me, understand?"

He took the DVD, looked at it, and placed in his jacket pocket, shaking his head. "Why don't you just hang on to it?"

"There are too many people looking for me, that's why."

"Great, so now they'll be looking for me too."

"Look, you're the only one I trust with it so quit your whining. Put it in a safe place and don't tell anyone about it." I looked at my watch. "You know something, it's not that late. I think I'm going to pay the CEO of that hospital a visit. Want to come along for moral support?"

He looked at his watch. It was almost nine, and he knew I wasn't asking. "Sure, I'm not tired at all, asshole."

Chapter 31

We went back to the room and waited until eleven to call a cab. At that point, Vito went outside to wait for the taxi and I hung back to say good night to Cocoa. I said, "I wouldn't wait up for us. I don't know when we'll be getting back.

She nodded. "Us? Is he staying here too?"

"I asked him to but he hasn't made up his mind. He doesn't like to sleep on pullout sofa beds."

"Well, I would rather he didn't if I'm allowed an opinion here."

"He's not so bad. C'mon…"

"It's not that. It's just that I'd rather not have anybody around interfering with us, if you know what I mean."

Boy, she didn't give up. "Well, I guess we'll just have to keep the hair-pulling and slapping around to a minimum," I kidded.

She chuckled. "You're joking but that was something I was hoping we could have a mature and uninhibited discussion about. You're going back to your girlfriend soon and we may not have many more opportunities like this."

Jesus.

I was just about to respond to that when my cell phone went off. It was Cheryl.

"Hello, Cesari. So how's Florida? Hope you're having a great time," she said, her voice dripping with sarcasm.

Uh oh. I stepped into the bedroom to speak to her privately. "Look Cheryl, I know you heard about Cocoa from Heidi, but it's not like that."

"Oh really? What's it like? Does she dance around the bed for you? Please satisfy my curiosity, when you're in a relationship with a woman like that, do you still shove twenty dollar bills into her panties?"

I took a deep breath. "I understand why you're angry..."

"Oh, you do? Now, that's funny. I'm hiding out in a low-budget hotel with an out-of-control twenty year old while you're finishing my dream vacation with a stripper named Cocoa, but that's not even the best part."

When I didn't respond she asked coyly, "Don't you want to know what the best part is?"

I really didn't. "What's the best part?"

"Well, during her tirade about you and Cocoa, Heidi also let slip that a certain ex-girlfriend of yours was in a motherly way, and that you're probably the father. Now how about that for a plot spoiler? For a girl that never went to college that Heidi was a regular fountain of information. What's the matter, Cesari, speechless? Yeah, I was too. You know what? I'm going to make this easy for you. You go your way and I'll go mine. I'm checking out of the hotel and going back to my life. Then, I'm going to find me a nice boring accountant to shack up with, and if you wind up in court, I would think twice about calling me as a friendly witness. *Capeesh, capo di tutti* assholes?"

"Cheryl, you're right to be upset but please don't overreact."

"Overreact? Why would I overreact?" She was yelling now.

I was just about to tell her why when the line went dead.

She overreacted.

I called her back twice but she didn't answer. I sighed deeply and put the phone away. I lay flat on the bed, staring at the ceiling. Damn, an accountant? Fucking Heidi. What a mouth on her. I was pissed.

Cocoa gently opened the door and poked her head in. She saw me lying on the bed and came over to sit next to me. "Are you okay? I kind of heard—everything."

I sat up and filled her in on the details as she held my hand. She said, "I'm sorry."

"Are you really?"

"Of course I am. Why would you say that?"

"Because you're smiling."

"I am?"

"Yes, you are."

"I guess I'm a happy person."

Chapter 32

Vito googled up Paul Ashford's home address and gave it to the cab driver to plug into his GPS. It was a thirty-minute ride along Route 4 to the CEO's posh, secluded suburban neighborhood just outside of Orlando, and we arrived uneventfully, after having stopped briefly at a convenience store to pick up a small flashlight.

The driver pulled to a stop about a half block away from the house and cut the engine like I told him to. "Stay here and take a nap or listen to the radio, but don't leave. We have no way of getting back to Disney." This was an exclusive neighborhood, and I doubted we could hail a cab back to Old Key West. "Here's fifty for the ride and another fifty for waiting. We won't be long and I'll give you a hundred for the ride back, okay?"

He nodded, pocketed the money, and turned on his radio. "Gracias. I wait."

Vito got out and hesitated, deciding whether to leave his coat and duffel bag in the car or not. I said to him, "I don't see why you just don't stay with me and Cocoa?"

"Because I'm not sleeping on a pullout sofa listening to you bang Cocoa all night. I made reservations at the Dolphin hotel. I might as well be comfortable while I'm running errands for you."

I raised my hands up in mock surrender. "Knock yourself out, all right? The driver looks okay. I would leave it. Nothing valuable in there?"

"No, just my toiletries and a change of clothes for the trip back. All right, I'll leave it in the car." He sized up the driver one last time and tossed his bag onto the backseat.

The house was a large villa-like two-story structure set way back on a two-acre lot. The development was dotted with similar type homes showing off their manicured lawns and pristine landscaping. There was a three-car attached garage with its door closed and a brand new forest green Jaguar sedan parked in the driveway. The neighborhood was quiet and dark as there were few streetlights in this exclusive community. I guessed that every home probably had an expensive security system and lots of guns. There might also be a private patrol, which meant it wouldn't be a good idea to linger too long.

"We'd better hurry, Vito. It's eleven forty-five. I'm guessing that sooner or later a private security car is going to swing through the neighborhood and find either the cab or us."

"So, fuck them. What are they going to do? We haven't broken any laws."

"This is Florida, asshole. They can do a lot, but at a minimum they can call the police, so let's hurry and stay out of sight."

We stepped onto the CEO's lawn and crept up to the side of the garage, keeping in the shadows. "Would you look at that car, Cesari," Vito said in amazement as we approached the Jaguar. It was sleek and had great lines.

"Shhh. Stay focused."

"I was just saying," he whispered.

I tested the garage door but it was locked. I said, "Let's walk around the side of the house and see if any windows are open."

No luck with the windows, and we slipped along the wall of the home toward the backyard, where we found a locked gate about four feet high. I glanced at Vito and signaled him to follow me over. In one smooth movement, I hoisted myself over the top and landed on my feet on the other side. Vito soon joined me and we found ourselves within a gated pool area. The pool was a twenty by forty rectangle with a diving board at the far end. Stone pavers lined the pool, and a wood deck wrapped around the back of the house, which was lined with tall windows and an ornate French door. The yard was very private and surrounded by large arborvitae and mature trees. The door and all the windows were locked.

I stood there in the dim light with Vito studying the situation. I could just smash a window but what if he had a dog or gun, not to mention an alarm system. If we just knocked he might answer it in his night shirt. I smiled at that thought. Wouldn't that be sweet?

"Jesus, Cesari, you mean you don't have a plan? In another minute, I'm going skinny-dipping. For crying out loud, it's almost midnight and it's still eighty degrees."

"Quiet down. I'm trying to think and you're not going skinny-dipping or any other kind of dipping."

I walked around a little, checking things out. The back room with all the windows had a pitched roof that jutted out from the main house by about twenty-five feet. I looked up at the second story of the house and saw the glimmer of a night-light.

"Vito, what are the odds of someone locking the windows on the second floor of their home?"

He saw what I was getting at and nodded. "I'm not sure, but the odds are zero of the house being wired up there or having motion sensors in place. People never do that especially when they have kids. They figure there's no point to it and too much of a chance of triggering it themselves accidentally in the middle of the night when they go to the bathroom or something. You got a ladder?"

"Yeah, you."

He chuckled. "That's what I figured, but you know there's still the possibility that he's got a weapon on his night table or a giant Doberman sleeping next to his bed."

"I'm going to have to take that chance. Someone ordered him to coerce the pathologist into fudging his report and I want to know who. There's no better way of getting the truth out of a guy than waking him up in the middle of the night. Okay, come to the side of the house."

I pulled up a deck chair and stood on it. Then with Vito's assistance, I climbed onto his shoulders. He leaned against the house to stabilize himself while I wobbled on top. I was six feet even and he was six feet three inches. The lower edge of the roof was nine and a half feet so I was in a pretty good position to hoist myself onto it as long as I didn't slip or run into a hornets' nest as I jostled for a footing.

With both hands firmly on the edge of the roof I stepped onto the top of Vito's head and pushed myself up, lifting one leg onto the roof and slowly maneuvering the other one on as well. Once there, it wasn't too bad. The roof was dry and the angle wasn't that steep.

I kneeled, then stood up and walked over to where the roof joined the main house. On either side of the roof's peak was a three-by-five paned glass window. I crept up to the one on my side and peered in. Looking around, I didn't see anything so I gently tried opening it. It didn't give so I crossed over the peak onto the other side of the roof and tried that window there with a better result. It slowly and quietly lifted upward, and I held my breath, waiting for an alarm to trigger, but it didn't.

Stepping silently through the window, I felt my pulse quicken and my senses sharpen as I listened for any sounds and scanned around the room. It was nearly pitch black, and I had no idea whether I was in the CEO's bedroom with him sleeping in his bed right in front of me or not.

I tiptoed gingerly around and bumped into a large sofa. I froze until I was sure there was no one sleeping on it. Next to it was a wood desk and chair. My vision gradually acclimated as I continued my search and satisfied myself I was alone. I took out the small flashlight and turned it on. It appeared that I was in his home office. I searched his desk drawers but didn't find anything particularly interesting. It was time to move on, so I turned the flashlight off and gently opened the door leading into a hallway, immediately noticing that I had to make a right or left decision. I chose right, the plush carpet muffling my footsteps as I crept along the length of the wall to the next door.

The knob turned quietly, and I entered the room. There was a low voltage night-light plugged into a wall outlet, allowing me to make out a king-sized bed in the center of the room with two sleeping figures under the covers. I considered my options and went to the side of the bed nearest the door. In the gloom, I could make out that Paul Ashford was a clean-shaven corporate-looking middle-aged guy with graying hair. The woman next to him was a brunette about twenty years his junior. Their gentle breathing was reassuring to me as I watched them.

On the night table was his cell phone, a lamp, and a glass of water. I slowly and quietly opened the drawer to the night table and found a black handgun. It was a Springfield, model 1911, .45. The old guys all loved this particular weapon. It made them feel like war heroes. Taking the weapon from the drawer, I drew a deep breath and let it out slowly. I reached under the lamp and turned it on, causing both of them to jump from the sudden burst of light.

He sat upright, shielding his eyes. "Who are you?" he asked in alarm.

She held on to him, frightened. "What's going on, Paul?"

I pointed the gun at him. I hadn't chambered a round or even checked to see if it was loaded but he didn't know that. "Everybody relax, and no one will get hurt if we all stay calm."

He demanded, "What do you want and how did you get past the security system?"

"Paul Ashford, right?" I asked, ignoring him.

He nodded. "Okay, Paul. Rule number one is that I ask the questions, all right?"

He hesitated and then nodded again.

"I didn't hear you, Paul."

"Yes, I understand." I think he was starting to anyway.

I looked at the woman. She was very beautiful. "What's your name?"

"Darlene."

"Darlene, is that the bathroom over there?" I asked, pointing at a closed door across the room from where I stood.

She said, "Yes."

"Okay, go into the bathroom over there and sit on the floor."

"But I don't have any clothes on."

I frowned at her. "Darlene, I don't like to repeat myself."

She jumped out of the bed and ran naked to the bathroom, and I followed close behind, quickly checking to make sure there were no windows, phones, or other ways out of the room. I looked at her and said, "If you don't make any noise, you won't get hurt." I closed the door, turning back to Paul Ashford, relieved to see that he hadn't moved. He wasn't totally stupid.

He stared at me as I approached his side of the bed again. "You're the CEO of Orlando Memorial Hospital?" I asked.

He nodded. "Yes, why?"

"A young girl was found dead on Disney property Christmas Eve. Remember that? She was brought to your hospital for an autopsy."

He nodded. "Yes, Snow White. I remember. What's that got to do with anything?"

"Her name was Marguerite Varga, asshole. She was a human being, a teenaged girl, not a Disney character."

He gulped and I knew I had him.

"I don't understand what that has to do with me. Her death was ruled an accidental drowning. They think she must have slipped and hit her head. What she was doing there in the first place is anybody's guess. She had a history of psychiatric illness so anything's possible."

Rather than answer him, I looked around the room until my eyes settled on an acceptable choice. I walked over to the bureau against the wall opposite the foot of the bed. There was a thirty-six inch flat-screen TV on top of it. I placed the gun down and ripped the wires out of the wall, picked the set up, and walked back over to Paul Ashford, who watched me with curiosity.

"What are you going to do with that?" he asked, eyes wide.

Without a word, I wound up like a baseball player about to hit a fastball and swung the TV full force into his face. The screen cracked and shattered as his head smashed backward into the headboard. He groaned, stunned from the pain and violence of the move. His face bled from multiple small lacerations, and shards of the screen showered the bed in front of him.

"Why...?" he stammered, fully terrified now and more than just a little fuzzy from the blow.

"Don't fuck with me again, Paul, or the next time I'll blow a hole through your knee cap. You know exactly what this has to do with you."

"You don't understand. I can't tell you. They'll kill me."

"If you don't tell me, I'll kill you right now, you son of a bitch. That girl may have had mental problems but she didn't deserve to die. Did you know she was pregnant?" I chucked the TV onto the floor and retrieved the gun, chambering a round loudly as I approached the bed.

"The DVD you stole from me. You would think that someone smart enough to get through medical school would have surmised that there might be surveillance cameras in my apartment and the foolishness to come back to the same room you last stayed in… Frankly, I'm surprised. You didn't seem that stupid."

Shit.

"I don't have the DVD."

She turned to the big guy. "Tito, hurt the girl. Just a little. Don't break anything just yet." In response, the gargantuan raised his hand.

I shouted. "Please don't hurt her. She didn't do anything. I really don't have the DVD." Tito looked at Consuela who nodded. He patted Cocoa gently on the head and she breathed a sigh of relief.

"Where is it then?"

I hesitated, and the big guy squeezed Cocoa's arm tightly, causing her to wince and squeal through the duct tape.

I said, "I destroyed it."

"I don't believe you, Doctor." She sighed deeply as she came to some sort of decision. "Have it your own way. Get on top of the covers and roll onto your stomach."

I pushed the covers off and started to roll over but Consuela stopped me.

"Take your underwear off first."

I removed them and tossed them onto the floor. "You know, Consuela, if you wanted to play all you had to do was invite me out for a drink."

Ignoring me, she said, "Lay flat on your stomach and stretch your arms out to the bed posts. We will see how funny you are in a minute." I did as she said, turning my face to look at Cocoa, who was wide-eyed with fear and apprehension.

I said, "I destroyed the DVD because I didn't want anyone else to see it. Besides, don't you have a copy?"

She retrieved something from a bag on the floor as she spoke. "You're lying and whether or not there is a copy is none of your concern. Now don't move unless you want the girl to get seriously injured."

She walked to the foot of the bed and slapped a pair of metal handcuffs around my ankles and with another pair of cuffs, attached them to the bed frame so I couldn't move my ankles more than a few inches in any direction. She then walked around the side of the bed and grabbed my right wrist, placing a handcuff on it and fastening the other loop to the bedpost. She did the same on the left side.

When she finished she said, "Thank you for cooperating."

I looked at Cocoa. "Don't worry."

The ape holding her sneered and cupped her breast just to piss me off. She shook him off and he slapped her. I decided right then and there that he was going to die first and die hard. Consuela picked my blue jeans off the floor and removed the belt, examining it. It was made of thick leather with a metal clasp. Satisfied, she wrapped it around her right hand and let the metal buckle dangle to the floor as I watched.

"One last time, Dr. Cesari, where is the DVD?"

"Does Raul know that you were pimping his daughter out to rich old men?"

She laughed. "Raul is an old fool and Marguerite was no angel. She was a horny brat. All I did was channel her energy for a useful purpose. Besides, working for me was far safer than what she was already doing, soliciting strange men for unprotected sex in park bathrooms, but that has nothing to do with here and now. You should not have meddled in my business."

"Great, so you're Saint Consuela, but I really don't have the DVD."

"That is a shame."

The strap came down quickly across my buttocks with a snapping sound, and I gasped in pain. The metal clasp of the belt felt like a claw as it struck my flesh. I arched my back and hissed through clenched teeth. She brought the belt down even harder the second time and third. I bit the pillow and felt tears stream down my face. After five strokes, Consuela paused to catch her breath, and I heard Cocoa crying. I looked over and saw her watching and becoming hysterical. I whispered hoarsely, "Cocoa, close your eyes, please."

She closed her eyes but she couldn't close her ears and I couldn't help moaning in agony. The leather belt came whipping down again and again with a ferocity and force I didn't think possible from such a slender woman. With each lash, I flopped and writhed like a fish on a trawler. The pain was intense, and I forced my mind to stay focused. I didn't want to give her the satisfaction of passing out, but I was losing the battle. Eventually, she took another breather and asked, "Have you changed your mind yet?"

"About what?" I whispered, barely able to get the words out.

She began beating me again and I soon became disoriented. It was over when I felt a small needle enter a vein in my arm. In seconds my vision blurred and my head started to swim as I watched Consuela unlock the restraints. I tried to move but couldn't. I felt like I had 100 lb. dumbbells strapped to my limbs.

Consuela stared into my face and her voice seemed miles away. "I will return in exactly twenty-four hours for the DVD. I will keep the girl until then. What you should focus on now is how many pieces you would like her returned in should you not do what I say."

My eyes fluttered and I desperately tried to keep them open. The man-beast threw a sheet around Cocoa and then hoisted her over his shoulder. Consuela swept the room with her gaze looking for something. She found it on the floor behind the chair Cocoa had been sitting in. It was her blue Valentino bag, the one Cocoa had stolen. She picked it up and glanced at me as they left. In a faraway voice, I thought I heard her say.

"Welcome home, *pendejo*."

Chapter 34

*A*n hour later, I woke up in agony, dragged myself out of the bed, and limped over to the bathroom, still groggy from the effect of whatever it was she shot me up with. I looked at my backside in the mirror and cringed at the crisscrossing welt marks and lacerations. I would have to get some antibiotic ointment for that. I took a shower to wake up and clean off. The water stung and felt like needles against the raw and wounded flesh. The pain was brutal, and it took a great deal of effort to concentrate on what I had to do. After dressing, I called Vito, waking him.

"Fucking Cesari, it's three a.m. Don't you ever sleep?"

"It's an emergency, Vito. There's been a change of plans. You're not going back to New York just yet. Consuela and company were just here looking for the DVD and they took Cocoa."

"What did you tell them?"

"Nothing, but she gave me twenty-four hours to return it or she's going to carve Cocoa up and mail her back a la carte."

"Jesus Christ. What do you want to do?"

"Not sure. I'll come get you at the Dolphin. She's one crazy bitch and there's no telling what condition we'll find Cocoa in if we don't act quickly. Do you have any weapons?"

"Weapons? Of course not. I was about to get on a plane in a few hours."

"Okay, get dressed, I'll be right there."

"What about the DVD?"

I hesitated. "Bring it. Maybe we can negotiate our way out of this, but I don't trust her. She's way past nuts. You're not going to believe what just happened here. Meet me outside the hotel in ten minutes." Twenty minutes later, I picked him up in the Jaguar and filled him in on recent events as we drove to a twenty-four-hour Walmart off of Disney property.

"Shit, is that why you're squirming like that?"

I nodded.

"Goddamn it, Cesari, you're even walking funny. You look like you just spent the night in Riker's Island lockup." He chuckled as we entered the store, making a beeline to hardware. I picked up a crowbar and Vito purchased a Remington pump action, twelve-gauge shotgun and shells. The shotgun had a pistol grip and relatively short barrel.

"You're a riot, you know that, Vito?"

"So where do you think they are? Consuela's apartment in Cinderella's Castle?"

"No, that would be too obvious. Besides, the apartment in the castle is no longer secure, and I have no doubt they've cleared out of there by now. My guess is they went over to Snow White's place at the Fort Wilderness Lodge. They'd want to keep her some place they feel they've got buttoned up. Consuela probably thinks I'll lay low until morning anyway, licking my wounds trying to regroup."

We reached the Fort Wilderness Lodge at four a.m. Vito kept the shotgun from view wrapped up in a plastic shopping bag, and I hid the crowbar up the sleeve of my windbreaker as we entered the main lobby. I still had the key to the apartment on the tenth floor that Raul had given to me so we headed straight for the elevators. The hotel was sleepy and quiet, and there were very few people around or awake enough to question our presence.

On the elevator up Vito asked, "What if she's not here, Cesari?"

"We'll cross that bridge when we come to it, but I think it makes sense for them to bring her here. They've got a naked stripper hostage. What better place to keep her than in that secret bedroom I told you about, especially since they don't know that I know about it."

He nodded. "How would they get her up there? They couldn't just bring her in through the main lobby?"

"There must be service elevators somewhere they could have accessed, and there are miles of underground maintenance tunnels running all over these parks that they could have used to get her here without any one seeing. I hope I'm guessing right, but the bottom line is if she's not here, we go check the castle. If she's not there, then we wait for Consuela to return to claim the DVD and hope for the best, but I have a hunch on this."

The elevator came to a stop and we got off and walked toward the apartment. I turned the key and opened the door quietly. The room was dark, and I turned on a light with Vito standing to the side, shotgun at the ready, but the room was empty.

"Goddamn, will you look at this," Vito said, looking around in amazement at the childish decorations.

"Shhh. I know. I've been here. It gets even worse the deeper you go." We walked stealthily through the apartment making sure no one was hiding behind the sofa or in the kitchen.

Turning to Vito, I said, "C'mon. If they have her here then it's going to be in that bedroom." In the normal bedroom, I opened the sliding doors of the closet, revealing the long row of Snow White dresses I had seen before, and Vito chuckled again.

"Will you stop it already?" I scolded him.

"I can't help it, Cesari, this is too crazy for words."

I pushed the dresses to one side enough to create an opening for us to walk through and then picked up the remote control from the nightstand. "Get ready Vito. We don't know who might be waiting for us in there."

"Got it." He stood to one side and crouched to minimize the target he might present. I pressed the button, and the mechanical sound of a garage door opening could be heard as the false wall slowly slid upward into the ceiling. There was a lamp on in the room but it was otherwise unoccupied. Vito took a few steps forward with me right behind clutching the crowbar. The bed sheets on the large canopied bed were a little crumpled as if someone had been lying on it.

"She's here," I whispered. As we entered further into the room we heard muffled sounds coming from one of the closets. I pointed at the door the sounds were emanating from.

"What's in there?" Vito asked almost inaudibly.

"The largest walk-in closet you'll ever see. I'll open the door, you be ready, okay? Take a deep breath."

He nodded and we braced ourselves for the approaching conflict. The muffled sounds stopped and I hesitated, listening. I crouched and turned the doorknob, pushing the door slowly into the dark room. Light filtered into the room from where we stood, and I made out the silhouette of a human being on the floor about ten to fifteen feet away.

Cocoa!

She saw me and got excited. She tried to say something but it was muffled by the duct tape over her mouth. We moved forward in her direction and could see that her hands were restrained behind her back and her ankles were duct taped together. A sheet partially covered her naked form, and she became increasingly agitated as we approached.

Distracted by the sight of her we momentarily let our guard down, and that was all he needed. The gorilla called Tito that had been in my apartment with Consuela stepped quickly out of the shadows on our left. Snarling viciously, he smashed Vito on the side of the head with the butt of his pistol. Vito went down like a brick, unconscious, falling on top of the shotgun. Tito pointed his weapon at me, herding me toward Cocoa and away from the door. Stepping over Vito, he flicked on the light. He was at least six foot four inches tall and solid muscle. His nose looked as if it had been broken and reset many times. He looked at the crowbar and smiled.

"How's your ass?" he sneered.

"It looks a lot like your face, only prettier."

He grinned. "Consuela said I could play with your girlfriend before I kill her. If you're nice, I'll let you watch."

"Yeah well, it looks like you're going to have to play with me first, but maybe we can negotiate."

He smirked. "I have the gun, asshole."

"But you don't have the DVD and Consuela needs it."

He thought that over. "Did you bring it?"

I could see his wheels spinning as he thought about scoring a few points with Consuela. I nodded and stepped backward slowly to give myself more room between us. I pointed at Vito. "It's in his pocket. Maybe you can just take it and we can all go on our merry way. No one needs to get hurt. You know? Quid pro quo."

He chuckled with a deep baritone voice. "Obviously, you don't know Consuela very well."

I had a feeling he was going to say something like that, but still, maybe there was a chance. "Yeah, but she's not here, and you seem like a nice guy."

He turned to face me more fully. "Obviously, you don't know me very well either."

His brain worked overtime as he tried to decide the best course of action. Before he did anything rash, he wanted to make sure he had the DVD, but to do that he would have to search Vito, which meant he would have to get on his knees, putting him at a disadvantage if I rushed him. He had a huge size advantage, but I had an 8 lb. crowbar. He had a gun, but if he killed me and didn't find the DVD, Consuela might become exceedingly un-happy. This was probably more problem solving than he'd done in years, and I could practically feel his cerebral cortex aching inside his skull.

"Drop the crowbar," he ordered. I hesitated, and he cocked the pistol, pointing it directly at my chest.

"You won't shoot."

"And why is that?"

"First of all, Consuela needs that DVD, and you can't be sure that I'm not lying to you about bringing it here. If you kill me or prevent me from getting it, you'll be the one getting his ass whipped next by Consuela. Secondly, we're in a fucking Disney hotel. What if someone hears the gunshot and calls the police? I realize it's unlikely but what if? Once again, Consuela will be pissed off. So go ahead, pelotudo, shoot."

He gulped as he thought it over, uncocked the weapon, and placed it on the floor behind him. "Okay, little man, have it your way. I want you to know that I'm going to enjoy this very much and then—I'm going to enjoy your friend." He cracked his neck and shrugged his shoulders as he got ready for battle.

He balled up his fists like a boxer and stepped cautiously toward me. I was only six feet and 220 lbs. I was a shrimp next to him. With his weight and size, all it would take would be one major head shot to end my night. I crouched and kept the crowbar raised and cocked in my right hand to discourage him from charging. There was still six feet of space between us as I sized him up and down and decided his upper body was too massive and well defended. I noticed that he approached circling slowly with the left side of his body angled toward me. He jabbed suddenly with his left hand but was still out of range and missed. He was just testing the waters, trying to see how I would react. I backed up a step but maintained my composure. We continued our methodical dance, but the gap closed steadily with each step. My pulse raced, my breathing slowed, and I'd almost forgotten about how much my ass hurt. I was worried that the next jab wouldn't miss. I glanced quickly at Cocoa who lay motionless on the floor. She watched us intently and gradually, almost imperceptibly moved her legs to position them between me and Tito, and I caught on to what she was trying to do.

Tito took another half step toward me with his left leg and I feigned a blow with the crowbar, causing him to jump back again. Cocoa's legs were in position, and it was time to spring into action. She looked at me and I nodded without taking my eyes off him. She coiled her legs together and kicked out suddenly into the side of his right knee, distracting him. He grunted and momentarily turned toward her, and as he did so I brought the 8 lb. steel crowbar crashing down with all my strength into the outside of his other knee. His leg buckled inward and he howled in pain as he staggered to the floor. Unfortunately, this move brought me within his grasp, and he latched onto my left wrist in a vise-like grip with his right hand. He balanced himself on the floor with his left hand, and I noticed he wasn't smiling any more.

He snarled and struggled fiercely, trying to pull me toward him while I resisted with all my might. He was off balance and in tremendous pain, but I knew I didn't have a whole lot of time before he recovered. In fact, I didn't have a whole lot of time before I felt the bones in my wrist snap as he tried to drag me down to the floor with him, so I raised the crowbar again and smashed it directly onto the top of his skull. I didn't hear anything break but the blow dazed him and he loosened his grip on my wrist, allowing me to tear free, panting. His eyes looked a little glassy and he fell to all fours, but he still wouldn't go down. I watched for a second as he tried to shake it off and thought about splitting his skull open with a second shot from the crowbar but decided against it. His career was about to end anyway when Consuela found out what happened. I looked at Cocoa, who was wide-eyed with fear. I looked back at this son-of-bitch Neanderthal who was planning on hurting her.

What the fuck. I was tired of being nice.

With both hands, I raised the crowbar over my head and hit him as hard as I could in his lower back toward the coccyx. A distinct crunching sound could be heard as the metal bar broke one or two maybe even three vertebrae. He groaned and collapsed flat on the floor, writhing in pain. He wasn't going to hurt anybody now. He may not ever walk again, assuming Consuela let him live. I leaned over his face to see how out of it he was. He looked at me but couldn't speak, and I watched saliva drool out of the side of his mouth onto the floor. I punched the side of his head savagely and his eyes closed.

I freed Cocoa from her restraints, and we hugged each other tightly, my heart racing wildly. "Are you okay?" I asked.

She nodded, her face buried in my chest. "What about you? That was awful what she did to you. What a monster."

"I'll be fine. I've been worried sick about you."

She looked up at me. "You have?"

"Yes, of course I have."

We stood there hugging and staring at each other for a few seconds.

I said, "You need some clothes, Cocoa. Why don't you hunt around here for something that fits and I'll tend to Vito."

We both glanced at Vito, who lay quietly where he had fallen, and Cocoa walked off in search of clothing. I knelt down next to him, rolling him over onto his back. He groaned in the process and I knew he was going to be all right. He had a lump on the side of his head the size of an apricot where he had been hit and I was sure he was going to have a massive headache.

I shook him. "Hey, Vito, wake up. It's time to go to school."

He answered without opening his eyes. "But it's Saturday, Ma."

I smiled. Too funny. I shook him again. "Get up, asshole, we've got work to do."

He opened his eyes this time and looked at me confused. "Cesari? Where are we? What happened?"

"We're in Snow White's apartment and you got cold-cocked with the butt of a 9mm Glock. Remember now?"

I helped him stand up. He was a little unsteady but was rapidly coming to. I picked up the shotgun and pistol and showed them to him. His eyes were starting to come into focus and he rubbed the lump on his temple.

He looked at the guy on the floor. "Is that the asshole?"

"Yeah."

"How'd you manage to bring him down?"

"Never underestimate me, Vito."

He nodded. "I won't. Where's Cocoa?"

"She's looking for some clothes."

I handed him the shotgun and shoved the pistol into my waistband.

"What are we going to do with him? Is he alive?"

"Yeah, he's alive, but he's not going anywhere. I broke his spine with the crowbar and probably his left knee as well. He's still breathing although I wouldn't want to be him when Consuela returns."

"Yeah, I'd bet she doesn't take disappointment well."

Cocoa joined us from one of the adjoining rooms as we talked. She had found a pair of jeans and sneakers that seemed to fit okay, but the blouse was just a little too tight, and without a bra was way too distracting. Vito's recent head trauma prevented him from noticing, but I did. I liked the look but we had to walk through the main lobby to get to the parking lot.

As if reading my mind she said, "She has a windbreaker I can wear."

"That might be a good idea. I'd rather not make a memorable exit."

Chapter 35

After collecting our gear, we gassed up the Jaguar and took off on 95 North, no longer trusting the airports now that Consuela was sure to be on the warpath. I calculated that at eighty miles an hour we could make it to New York in fourteen hours. I volunteered to take the first shift while Cocoa and Vito slept.

Traffic was light, and I really pushed it. Once we were safely out of Florida, I took out my cell phone and called the Orlando Police Department, asking to be patched through to Detective Diaz, the guy who enjoyed slapping me around so much on Christmas Eve.

"Diaz here."

"Good morning, detective. This is Dr. Cesari. Remember me?"

"Yeah, I remember you. What do you want?"

"Do you still want to solve Snow White's murder?"

He was silent and I guessed he was telling someone to turn on a recording device. "It was ruled an accident by the coroner, and I was told in no uncertain terms to let it go."

"It was no accident and you know it."

"Is this a confession, Cesari?"

"Think of it more as an epiphany. If you move fast, you'll understand better. Go to the tenth floor of the Fort Wilderness Lodge at Disney. The door at the far end of the hall is open. Have a look around and you'll see what I mean. Pay special attention to the bedroom."

"What am I going to find there?"

"I can't say without incriminating myself. I know you're recording this conversation. The other thing you need to do is visit the coroner, Dr. Finch at Orlando Memorial Hospital. He falsified the autopsy report. Marguerite Varga didn't drown. She was dead long before she hit the water. Use the same kind of persuasion you did on me and I'm sure he'll tell you all about it."

"Why are you telling me all this, Cesari? If she was murdered then you're the prime suspect again."

"Because I didn't do it, asshole. Can't you see there's a conspiracy going on here to cover up the truth? What's it going to take to get that through your head?"

"Then who did it?"

"Not sure yet, but I'm closing in on that. Now be a mensch and hustle over to Disney before someone gets there ahead of you and cleans the place up."

"Fine, but where can I find you in case you're just jerking my chain and I want to kick your ass some more?"

"You won't find me but I'll call back in a day or so to see if I can help fill in the blanks. Gotta go, big guy. Have fun at Fort Wilderness, and as long as you're there you should try to see the Hoop Dee Doo Review."

He hung up just as we reached Savannah, and I stopped at a Mc-Donalds drive-through for breakfast and coffee. It was seven a.m. and we had been on the road for three hours. Cocoa, who was sleeping in the passenger seat, roused herself and rubbed her eyes. "Want some breakfast?" I asked.

"Sure, how about an Egg McMuffin and coffee."

"How do you want your coffee?"

"Black and sweet—like my men."

I chuckled. "Hey, Vito, are you hungry?"

He didn't answer and I glanced back. He was out cold and snoring. It was a stupid question anyway. He was always hungry, so I bought him two sausage, egg, and cheese bagels.

"Should I wake him up?" Cocoa asked.

"Nah, let him sleep. He took quite the shot to the head."

I paid for the food and got back on the highway, resuming cruising speed and sipping my coffee, also black and sweet. The aroma of cooked eggs, sausage, and muffins filled the car. I watched Cocoa eat and smiled. She smiled back and asked. "Want your sandwich now or later?" I had also ordered an Egg McMuffin.

I put my coffee down in the cup holder. "I'll take a bite now, thanks."

She reached down into the bag, found the sandwich, and unwrapped it for me. I held out my hand for it but instead of placing it there, she leaned over and held it up to my mouth for me to take a bite. "Keep your hands on the wheel and I'll feed you. We don't want any accidents, do we?"

I almost said "No, mommy" but bit my tongue.

"No, we don't."

I took a bite and she leaned back into her seat. "Just tell me when you're ready for another." I nodded as I chewed and took another sip of coffee. Geez. This was just as bad as doing my laundry, maybe worse. I looked at her out of the corner of my eye. She was killing me.

"This is a really nice car," she said.

"Yeah, it's a Jaguar XJR supercharged V8 with a top speed of somewhere in the neighborhood of one hundred and seventy miles per hour. It's Jaguar's top of the line sedan. You really couldn't ask for a better ride than this."

"What do you think it costs?"

"Well over a hundred thousand, probably closer to a hundred and fifty barebones."

She thought that one over. "So what was with that apartment?"

"What do you mean?"

She rolled her eyes. "C'mon, that Snow White chick must have been cuckoo nuts."

"You tell me. You're the one who went to Harvard."

She laughed. "It was Princeton, and I only went for a year, and what's your problem with that anyway? You keep saying it sarcastically like you have a chip on your shoulder about the Ivy League. Where'd you go to school?"

"I don't have a chip on my shoulder about anything. I went to Fordham University in the Bronx and graduated with a B.S. in biology, and then I went to SUNY Buffalo School of Medicine."

"Well, I'm sorry to hear that. Maybe if you had studied harder and applied yourself you might have done better. It must have been very difficult finding a job after that." She was busting my balls and doing a good job of it too. I glanced over at her and she was smiling, waiting to see if I would pop.

Instead, I smiled. "You know, Cocoa, if I had a remote control on me right now I would point it at you and press the mute button."

"Is that all you got? You big, tough, gangster pussy."

"Oh my, you really are asking for it."

We both started laughing and I shook my head because I definitely and officially had a Cocoa problem. We reached Raleigh a few minutes after noon and were just about halfway there. Vito had woken up and we all needed a bathroom break so I pulled into a rest stop, gassed up, bought some snack food, and we headed off again. Vito drove now, and I reclined fully in the passenger seat, passing out almost immediately with Cocoa in the rear.

At five, I sensed the car pulling to a stop and woke up. "What's happening, Vito?" I yawned and stretched. "Where are we?" We were on the shoulder of I95 and it was getting dark.

"We're outside of Philadelphia. Now go back to sleep, Cesari. I'll handle this." He was looking in his rearview mirror so I turned around and saw the flashing lights of a police cruiser behind us.

"Fucking Vito. How fast were you going?"

"About a hundred. Got away with it for the last two hours."

"You are such an asshole. It's New Year's Eve and you're doing a hundred miles an hour. You couldn't just stick to a reasonable speed?"

"Relax, Cesari, we're close enough to home base that I should be able to name-drop. I know some guys in Philly."

"Great." I looked back and saw Cocoa was still sleeping. "Don't give him any reason to look in the trunk, all right?" That's where we had stored all the weapons. We might get a pass on the loaded shotgun but not Tito's handgun.

I shook Cocoa's leg. "Hey, sleepy head. There's a cop coming. Look bright and shiny. I don't want him to think we're drugged out."

She yawned. "Where are we?"

"Philadelphia. Vito decided to test the engine on the Jaguar and now we're about to get arrested if we can't come up with a good reason why we're driving a car registered to a guy in Florida who may have reported the vehicle stolen despite my best effort to put the fear of God into him."

Vito said, "Relax, Cesari. You worry too much."

Cocoa smiled. "Yeah relax, Cesari."

I gave her a look. "Thanks for sharing my concern, the both of you."

Vito said, "Okay, everybody, nice and easy, here he comes."

He rolled down his window. "Can I help you officer?" The trooper was a tall, solidly built, clean-shaven guy in his early thirties. His name tag read "Raguzza." A nice Italian boy.

"License and registration, sir, and could you please turn the engine off."

"Certainly officer, do you mind if I ask my friend to get the registration from the glove compartment?"

"Go ahead but everyone keep your hands in plain sight and move slowly."

"Hey, Cesari, get the registration, will you?"

"Sure." Neither one of us was sure if it was really there but it probably was so I reached into the glove compartment, fumbled around for a minute, and finally found it tucked inside the car's operating manual. While I was doing that, Vito unsuccessfully tried to chat up Officer Raguzza about his Italian ancestry, but all that did was make him watch us all the more carefully with one hand on his holstered weapon as he vigilantly inspected the inside of the car, including Cocoa, who smiled at him. We handed the trooper the registration and he walked back to his car to run Vito's license and the registration through his computer as we sat there holding our breath.

"Do you want me to take care of this?" Cocoa offered, and God only knew what she meant by that.

I turned around to see her better. "I don't think so, Cocoa. This kid looks pretty hard core so please don't do anything to provoke him."

"Everybody stay calm. Let's see what he has to say," Vito chimed in wisely.

After seven grueling minutes, the officer returned, handing Vito his license and the car's registration. "Sir, do you know why I pulled you over?"

"I'm not sure, officer. Was I speeding?"

"Sir, you were going one hundred and three miles an hour in a sixty five mile an hour zone. Do you realize I could arrest you now for reckless driving and impound the vehicle?" Shit. This guy was in a bad mood.

"I knew I was going a little over the speed limit officer but I can't believe I was going that fast. I apologize. This car is just so powerful, I must have lost track of the speed."

The officer thought about that. "Sir, have you had any alcoholic beverages today?"

"No, officer, I have not."

"Are you impaired in anyway?"

"No sir, I am not."

He looked inside the car at me and then at Cocoa again. "Are either of you the owner of this vehicle?"

Together, we said, "No."

"Where is the owner of the vehicle?"

Vito said, "He's in Manhattan. He paid me to fly down to Florida to pick up his car and drive it to New York for him. These are my friends who came to keep me company."

Brilliant, Vito. Absolutely brilliant.

The officer nodded, troubled by something. "Sir, would you mind stepping out of the car?" Vito glanced at me. In the time since we had stopped, the night sky had completely enveloped us and I could see the look in his eye. I gently shook my head and mouthed *don't even think about it*. A high-speed chase in a stolen car with an illegal handgun in the trunk was a losing proposition no matter how you cut it. We didn't have our backs against the wall just yet.

He said politely, "No, I don't mind at all, officer. I realize you have to do your job, but you may want to give Salvatore Montenegro a quick call before things get a little too far out of hand."

The trooper hesitated. "Who's he?"

"He's the head of the Philadelphia PBA and a good friend of mine. We went to school together."

Self-doubt clouded his features as Officer Raguzza considered this. "You were still going way too fast by any standards, sir. I can't just let you off."

Vito put his hands up. "I'm not asking anybody to let anybody off. If I was speeding then I deserve to be ticketed. I just don't want this thing to get carried away. You know what I mean? I promise to keep it within the speed limits from now on."

The officer stood there quietly staring at us and then came to some type of decision. "I'll be right back. Nobody move, all right?"

We watched him walk back to his car to check out Vito's story. I asked. "Are you really friends with this guy Montenegro?"

He nodded. "Sure."

I breathed a sigh of relief.

"Relax, Cesari. Have you ever thought about taking Xanax?"

"You should just let me take care of it," piped in Cocoa.

I said, "Cocoa, honey, please don't do anything. Things will just go from bad to worse if you get involved. Promise me you won't say anything, please?"

She folded her arms, pouting. "Fine."

Vito watched Raguzza intently from his side view mirror and I saw his right hand creep up to the ignition as the officer sat in his car.

"Don't you even think about it, Vito. You'll get us all thrown away for life if we don't get killed."

"Relax, Cesari. It's dark out so the copters will be useless and no cruiser can go as fast as this thing. We'll lose him in no time."

"You can't be serious?" I asked, suddenly becoming alarmed at the tone in his voice.

Cocoa asked, "What's going on?"

Vito turned the ignition on and slammed the car into drive, shouting. "Buckle up, everybody!" I turned around and saw Officer Raguzza getting out of his car and unholstering his sidearm.

The Jaguar lurched forward and peeled rubber as Vito slammed his foot on the accelerator. We fishtailed briefly, regained control, and sped off at full throttle, leaving a trail of smoke and dust behind. Cocoa and I were thrown backward into our seats as we reached sixty miles an hour in just under four seconds. Vito kept his foot down all the way long past eighty miles an hour and soon I watched the speedometer lunge past a hundred. In ten seconds we were at one hundred and twenty miles per hour and steadily climbing without any difficulty whatsoever. Traffic was light, and Vito was an outstanding driver but we could only keep this up so long on a busy interstate.

I shouted. "Fucking Vito. What the hell are you doing?" The speedometer was now at one hundred and fifty miles an hour and I prayed we didn't get a blowout.

"Relax, Cesari."

I looked back and saw the cruiser, lights flashing, falling back fast, but that wasn't the problem and we all knew it. It was what lay ahead. Undoubtedly, the word was spreading fast about the green Jaguar doing a hundred and fifty miles an hour northbound on I95 just outside Philadelphia.

"Is the cruiser out of site, yet?"

Cocoa and I looked back and we said "yes" in unison.

"Good, then say good bye to fucking Pennsylvania."

We were half a mile from the exit to 90E into Cherry Hill, New Jersey. At the speed we were going, we would easily pass it unless Vito did something rash, which he did. About a hundred yards from the turnoff he slammed on the breaks, and rubber screeched against asphalt. Smoke from the heat generated by the burning tires appeared in the rear and side windows, and Vito turned the car sharply into the exit causing the right side to go slightly airborne before slamming back down. We took the thirty-five mile an hour exit at seventy-five and we all held our breath as we slammed back and forth inside the car.

We merged onto 90E at a crisp eighty-five miles an hour and maintained that speed as 90E merged into NJ 73, a smaller road, as it wound its way through Maple Shade Township. We reduced our speed to a more reasonable fifty miles an hour and eventually picked up the New Jersey Turnpike toward New York. Once things had settled down, I looked at Vito. "So, would you care to tell me what that was all about? I thought you were friends with this Montenegro guy?"

"I am, but he's not the president of the Philadelphia PBA. He's a bookie in South Philly. I was hoping the trooper wouldn't call my bluff. What can I say?"

"You are such an asshole." I turned around toward Cocoa. "Are you all right?"

She was pale as a ghost. "Yeah, I'll be fine, but you should have let me take care of it."

I couldn't take it anymore. "Oh yeah, and just how were you going to take care of it, Cocoa? He didn't look like he was in the mood to flirt."

"You know, I wish you would stop underestimating me like that. I would just have called my Uncle Leo. His law firm represents the Philadelphia Policeman's Union and unlike Vito, he really is friends with the president of the Philadelphia PBA as well as the mayor of Philadelphia himself, and I personally have met them all. We could have saved ourselves a lot of trouble."

Vito and I were speechless. I looked at him crossly, shaking my head in disgust. He said, "Don't say it, Cesari. I know I'm an asshole."

"Exactly. Now drive us to Newark Airport's short-term parking. That's where we left Cocoa's car, and then you can take the Jaguar into the city. Do me a favor and bring it to a chop shop tonight, not tomorrow, for complete dismemberment now that every cop in Pennsylvania is looking for it. You'll need to lay low too when you get back because he knows who you are."

"I'll take care of the car and I'm not worried. I'll report my driver's license stolen and before the night's over I'll have a hundred witnesses who will swear I was with them all day."

Chapter 36

We picked up the Benz from the airport and drove to Cocoa's house, arriving at eight p.m. I was tired of dicking around with Phil McIntosh hiding behind the American flag. I really didn't care anymore whether he was Secret Service, homo-American, or whatever, he was going to spill his guts once and for all. I kept the crowbar and shotgun but tossed Tito's handgun into a dumpster after wiping and disassembling it.

"I'm getting kind of hungry," Cocoa said, standing in the living room of her parents' home. "Can we get something to eat?"

I looked at my watch. It was still too early to visit Phil and Herman. "Sure, how about that steak house you told me about in downtown Morristown?"

"You mean Roots? I didn't mean anything that fancy but yeah, if we have the time?"

"We have the time."

"Give me fifteen minutes to freshen up and change my clothes."

I watched her scamper up the stairs, and I took the time to look around the living room a little more thoroughly than I had the last time I was here. Then, I only concerned myself with exit strategies and defensive weaknesses. I walked over to the fireplace. On the mantle on either side of the menorah were family photos, which I studied. They were mostly of Cocoa and her parents in various stages of her childhood and early adulthood. There were several vacation pictures including one at the Wailing Wall in Jerusalem and one in front of the Colosseum in Rome. The last picture toward the end of the mantle was of Cocoa at the gates of Princeton University. She was smiling and looked genuinely happy. I studied this one for a long time. It couldn't have been taken more than five years ago. I never asked her age and had guessed she was in her early twenties. For some reason, I felt bad for her parents. She was so damned beautiful and smart. It must have broken their hearts when she told them what she wanted to do for a living. I sighed deeply. We all had to be what we were meant to be. I didn't look down on her for her decision. God knows, I had no right to do that to anybody. Still, I understood the anguish her parents must have felt. I picked the picture off the mantle to examine it more closely. Cocoa had almost perfect features: long, wavy, auburn hair; big almond-shaped brown eyes; seductive lips.

I was completely engrossed in thought and didn't hear her approach from behind, tapping me on the shoulder. "Ready when you are."

Startled, I dropped the picture on the floor, shattering the glass. I let out a deep breath. "Cocoa, you surprised me. Shit. I'm sorry."

"Some tough guy you are. I'll go get a broom."

I picked up the frame and photo and placed them flat on the mantle while she cleaned up the mess. "Can I help?"

"Yeah, there's a trash bin underneath the sink in the kitchen. Would you mind getting it for me?"

"Not at all. Cocoa, I'm real sorry. I shouldn't have been touching anything."

"It's all right. I can always get another frame."

We cleaned up and drove to the restaurant. She had put on a clean pair of jeans, a nice blouse, and some makeup. I smelled perfume and saw she was wearing three-inch black heels.

"Cocoa, I don't think heels are a smart idea for later. You know what I mean? Sometimes I have to move fast."

"I know. They're just for dinner. I put a pair of sneakers in a bag in the backseat. I'll change after we eat. I just wanted to look nice for you."

"I thought you looked nice in sneakers."

She smiled. "Wait until you see me in garters."

Jesus.

We parked the car on the street in front of the restaurant and walked in. It was forty degrees out. Cocoa wore a medium-weight leather jacket, and I wore the same thick, dark green, bulky Irish wool sweater I had been wearing all week. It was time to get new clothes. The waiter sat us at a small table by the window, and we ordered a couple of Manhattans. It was New Year's Eve and the restaurant was noisy, packed, dark, and rustic. There was a candle in the center of the table for ambience. I studied my menu but sensed Cocoa looking at me. "What are you thinking about?" I asked.

"You."

"What about me?"

"I don't know. You're kind of wild and untamed."

I laughed and put my menu down. "Talk about the pot calling the kettle black."

She grinned at that. "So, how old are you?"

I laughed again. "I should be asking you that."

"I'm twenty-five."

"Well, I'm older than that."

"By how much?"

"Too much."

"You look like you're in your mid-thirties. Am I warm?"

"Very. Why does it matter?"

The waiter set our cocktails down in front of us and asked if we were ready to order. I told him we needed a few more minutes.

She said, "They say that as a man gets older he makes less sperm and the ones he does make don't try as hard." I had just taken a sip of my Manhattan when she said that, causing me to snort. I felt the liquid shoot up my nostril, and I had to wipe my face with my napkin.

She looked thoroughly pleased with herself as I sat there chuckling. I said, "Tell me again why we're talking about my sperm counts. Did I miss something while I was sleeping in the car on the way up from Florida?"

"No, I just think about these things. So, what are you going to do about your pregnant girlfriend?"

I sighed. "Well, she's not really my girlfriend anymore so I'm not sure there's anything I can do, but I am going to try to talk to her. I mean, I'd like to be part of the child's life if she'll let me."

"Are you going to try to get back together with her?"

"I haven't thought that far ahead. I've been a little busy lately."

"Speaking of that. How's your butt? Still hurt?"

"What do you think?"

She nodded and the waiter came over again. We still hadn't looked at the menus.

"Do you mind if I order for us, Cocoa? We don't have all night."

"Sure, go ahead. I don't have any dietary restrictions."

"Somehow, I didn't think so." I turned to the waiter. "Two New York strips, medium rare, steak fries, and an order of roasted asparagus to share. Can we get a bottle of Stag's Leap Cabernet?"

He collected the menus, thanked us, and promised to return. I looked at Cocoa and could see she wasn't quite done with the small talk. She took a sip of her cocktail and studied me from across the table.

"Go ahead, Cocoa, spit it out."

"Have you ever been to a Seder?"

"I'm not coming to your house for Passover, Cocoa. Get that idea out of your head."

"Why not?"

"I couldn't do that to your parents and your family. Do you have any idea how awkward that would be for everyone?"

"It's already awkward for everyone. You have no idea what it's like for me. Everyone sidesteps me like I have leprosy. Uncle Leo, the lawyer with all his powerful friends and his son, the neurosurgeon at Columbia. There's my Aunt Myra the artist, whose works are on display at MOMA. My cousin Harold and his wife, Emily, the architects from Newport. I just sit there and smile while everyone politely pretends I don't have a life that's worth talking about."

"And so your idea to get a little attention from mom and dad is to bring home an on and off again Catholic mobster? No, thanks."

"You're a doctor. They would eat that up."

"Oh, please. And how would we tell them we met? I saw you dancing naked one night and thought to myself, now that's the girl for me."

She laughed. "What's wrong with that?"

"Listen, Cocoa girl. I agree that people have to accept you for who you are. Just because others don't share your dreams and aspirations doesn't mean that what you are doing is wrong or that you are a bad person. On the other hand, you have to accept how difficult it must be for them to accept your lifestyle. I was looking at that picture of you on the mantle, standing at the gates of Princeton, and all I could think of was how brokenhearted your parents must have been when you dropped out. It made me sad just thinking about it."

She sat back, folding her arms over her chest, pouting. "Oh brother, and I thought you were different; that you would understand."

"I do understand and I accept you. In fact, I'll go a step further. I think you're very special. You're like no other girl I've ever known, and in these last few days I've grown quite fond of you."

She liked that and smiled. "Well, what about you? I'm sure your parents must love the people you hang out with. Christmas must be a blast at your house with all the machine guns firing at the same time."

I laughed. She was killing me. "I only wish I had the choices you had when I was younger, but I didn't. My father was a casualty in a mob war when I was in the first grade, and my mother died from cancer when I was still a teenager. In those neighborhoods, it was very easy to get caught up with the wrong type of people. Fortunately, I was able to right the ship and get myself an education. You're very lucky that you have supportive and loving parents willing to stand by you despite your non-traditional career. You might want to cut them some slack and not throw me in their faces."

"I'm sorry. I didn't mean anything by that machine gun crack."

"No offense taken. Which is another thing I like about you. I sense that deep down you are a very nice and decent person and I really like that."

"Thank you and I feel the same way about you. Will you at least keep an open mind about coming? There's plenty of time between now and Passover. Just don't lock your mind up is all I'm asking."

"Fine. I'll keep an open mind, but I'm not converting. Got that? I'm not even sure what I believe in now so I'm not going to pretend to believe in something else."

She smiled from ear to ear. "What a lively imagination you have. Who asked you to convert?"

"You invited me to your house to meet your family for the holiday. That's close enough."

"I invited you as a friend and that's all. That's a very common custom."

"Fine."

"Fine."

The waiter served our dinners and the aroma of the charbroiled steaks demanded we call a truce.

Chapter 37

We finished our meal, paid the bill, and Cocoa drove us to Phil and Herman's place in Randolph. By the time we arrived it was almost midnight, and all the lights in the house were out. We parked in the driveway, and I told her to cut the lights but stay put with the engine running.

"What if they went out to celebrate? It is New Year's Eve after all." she said.

"Then they won't be home, but I doubt that after the week they've had they're in the mood to party."

She nodded. "Be careful."

I got out of the car with the shotgun and entered the garage, spotting Herman's BMW parked in its space as I walked up to the house door. The lock that I had broken hadn't been repaired yet, and I assumed they just hadn't had the time with all that had happened. When I last saw them Herman was on his way to the hospital and Phil was emotionally distraught. Unfortunately, tonight was going to be much worse if I didn't start getting some straight answers.

Quietly letting myself in, I was guided only by low-level nightlights along the lower edge of the wall, which allowed minimal visibility. It took a while for my eyes to adjust but they did eventually as I crept into the kitchen. Once in the dining room, the plush carpeting made it easier to get around without worrying about making noise. I headed straight for the bedroom and was relieved that the door was already partially open. It felt like an eternity since I was here last, not just a couple of days. I peeked in the room and tried to make out who was in the bed. In the gloom and limited vis-ibility, I saw only one body, sleeping on his stomach and a pillow over his head.

What did that mean? Was Herman still in the hospital? He hadn't looked that bad. I stepped into the room and listened to the rhythmic breathing of the sleeping figure. Approach-ing the bed, I held the pistol grip of the shotgun in my right hand and pressed it into his torso. He didn't respond so I nudged him a little harder.

I said, "Happy New Year."

He jumped around to his back, suddenly alarmed. "Who is it?"

Herman?

"The tooth fairy. Now where's Phil, pie maker?"

"He's in New York. Who are you and what do you want?"

"Why is he in New York?" I asked, ignoring his questions, puz-zled.

I turned on the lamp by his bed, and Herman cringed at the sight of the weapon. "Who are you? I don't have to tell you any-thing." I guessed he was too out of it the last time we met to remember me.

"You're wrong about that, Herman. You are going to tell me ev-erything."

"I will not and you can't make me." Goddamn, his voice was pretty high pitched for a guy his size, and I wondered if he was taking estrogen supplements.

"Look, I need to speak to Phil. It's very important."

"Speak to him or kill him?"

"That depends on what he has to say. So where in New York?"

He hesitated.

"C'mon Herman. It's late and I'm getting cranky. Where is he?" Herman was a large man naturally. He was about six foot, two inch-es tall, 250 lbs. He didn't look like he worked out very much and had chubby cheeks and a soft Pillsbury doughboy appearance. I had this image of him in the kitchen of his bakery with a white apron and chef's hat. The way he clutched the covers around him made me want to chuckle. All he needed was curlers in his hair, not that I liked to stereotype these things.

"I'm not going to tell you. I'd rather die than let you hurt him."

Jesus Christ.

I let out a deep breath and sat down in a chair near the foot of the bed, standing the shotgun up against the wall. I decided to take a different approach. "You know, Herman, you could be just a little bit more grateful."

"Why should I be grateful to a barbarian like you?"

Fucking A. Did he just call me a barbarian?

"Hey, that wasn't nice. I didn't call you any names, did I?"

He pouted. "Maybe, but you haven't been very nice either."

"Well, you should be grateful because I'm the one who saved both yours and Phil's lives several days ago."

His features softened up a little. "That was you?"

"Yes, that was me. So if I wanted to hurt you or Phil why would I have gone through all that trouble?"

He looked puzzled but was trying hard to believe me. "Then why did you come here with that nasty 'I'm a badass' weapon?"

Touché.

"Look Herman, the last time I was here the house almost exploded and Phil told me that some very bad people were after him. I didn't know what to expect so I came prepared is all. I didn't mean to frighten you."

"Humph. Maybe you're telling the truth, maybe you're not. I'm not going to betray Phil just because you're a good-looking, smooth talker."

I let out a deep breath. "What do I have to do to convince you I'm telling the truth?"

He thought that one over. "Well, if you were really here and saved our lives, and if you really spoke to Phil—then he would have told you who came that night to kill us."

"He did tell me, Herman. It was a woman named Consuela."

Herman sighed and relaxed. He nodded. "Yes, that was her. What a bitch. I'm sorry for being so suspicious of you, but you really shouldn't sneak into people's homes in the middle of the night and point guns at them."

"You're right and I'm sorry. Can we get back to Phil and where I can find him? It's kind of important."

"He's back at work for the king and queen of course."

I nodded. I knew who he meant from the video. "But I thought Phil was out on sick leave because of the concussion."

"He was but I guess something's going on and they needed every hand they could find, concussion or not. I felt so bad for him. He was in no shape to go in. He's still having headaches, but when they called, he didn't hesitate. That's Phil, a true blue patriot."

"Yeah, okay. So where is he, exactly, I mean?"

"In Mount Kisco, New York, of course. That's where the king and queen live since they left public life. I can give you the address, but you can't talk to him there, the service won't allow it. You'd have to arrange to meet him somewhere else."

"How do you reach him?"

"I don't. Too risky. If they found out about me, he'd lose his job. Phil told me they would think I'm too much of a security risk so he calls me when he can. He's pretty clever and usually finds a way at least once every day or every other day for a few minutes." He smiled at the thought.

I looked at the night table and saw a cell phone. "He calls you on that?"

"Yes, but never from his real cell phone. The service listens in on all of the agents' calls. He'll either call from a landline or from a pre-paid cell phone."

"Has he called you today?"

"No, he must have been too busy," Herman said with sadness in his voice.

"Herman, I hate to do this to you but I'm going to have to con-fiscate your cell phone for a short time. It seems like it's the only way I'll be able to reach Phil. Like you said, I'll never get near him if I just drive up to Mount Kisco unannounced."

He got upset. "But then I won't be able to talk to Phil."

"You don't have a landline that he might use as a backup?"

He shook his head no.

"Well, I'm sorry. I promise to return the phone to you right after I speak to him. I'll send it FedEx."

"I don't suppose there's any point in refusing."

I shook my head. "No, Herman, there isn't. I'm sorry."

He turned over and covered his face with his pillow. "Go away. I was right. You are a brute."

I sighed deeply and pocketed the cell phone. "Well, thank you for your time, Herman. I'll let myself out."

I left him there crying.

Cocoa looked apprehensive as I got in the passenger seat and buckled up. "How'd it go? You didn't have to kill anybody did you?"

"It went fine, and no, I didn't have to kill anybody. Is that what you think of me, that I'm some psychopathic killer?"

She grinned. "No, but you're Sicilian and that's close enough."

"Will you just drive the car?"

"Where to, boss?" She lowered her voice in a mock Brooklyn accent.

I couldn't help laughing. "I swear to God in heaven that if you don't stop I am going to spank you."

"Yeah, well I don't believe you got the moxie. So where are we going now?"

"Right now, we're going to the Kit Kat Club to drop you off and get some sleep. I got a full day ahead of me, and I need to do some research."

"What if I don't want to be *dropped* off?"

"C'mon Cocoa, you've got to get back to work some time. If you keep hanging around me sooner or later you're going to get hurt, and I don't want that."

"I know. It's just that I…"

She pulled the car onto Route 10 heading in the direction of I-80E to New York.

"What?"

"I don't know. It's just that I really like being with you."

I sat quietly for a moment. "I really like being with you too."

"I don't want it to end. You know what I mean?"

I nodded. I knew exactly what she meant, but there were a lot of women in New York I had to settle up with, and I didn't have a crystal ball to tell me what was going to happen. Cocoa was way too smart not to understand the complexity of the interpersonal relationships I was involved in. On the other hand, Cocoa was a woman, and I never met a woman who spent more than three seconds worrying about whether taking another woman's man was the right thing to do or not.

In just under an hour, we were in Manhattan looking for an indoor garage. A block away from the lounge we found one and parked the car. By the time we got to the club and let ourselves in, it was two a.m. It was dark and quiet and we were exhausted. We had spent a lot of hours on the road, and there had been way too much excitement in between, but I needed to do some research so I fired up Heidi's laptop and kissed Cocoa good night.

I said, "I'll see you in the morning, all right?"

"That's it? Good night, Cocoa? I'll see you in the morning? After all we've been through?"

"Cocoa, I'm not joining the navy, I'll still be here."

"No you won't. You're going to run to your little black baby mama and beg her to take you back. I can feel it."

I folded my arms and sat back in the chair, amused. "I don't beg, but what do you think I should do? Just pretend or ignore the fact that I'm going to be a father? I can't do that. If Kelly doesn't want me in her life I can deal with that, but my child has a right to know me and I have an obligation to try."

She came close, wrapped her arms around me and pressed her chest into me. "If this is our last night together don't you think you should come upstairs and make it a memorable one? It's the New Year. We should celebrate," she whined.

I put my arms around her waist and smiled, drawing her in. "The other night, you practically accused me of sexual malpractice."

She smiled. "I said you were pathetic. That's not the same thing."

I chuckled and looked into her face as she slid onto my lap, teary eyed. I brushed my hand lightly over her face and hair and kissed her in total surrender.

I whispered, "Let's go upstairs."

Chapter 38

At six a.m. Herman's cell phone rang crisply on the night table. I gently pushed Cocoa off of me and she rolled sleepily onto her other side.

"Hello."

"Hi, honey, Happy New Year. I'm sorry I didn't call last night. I couldn't get away."

"Phil, this isn't Herman."

There was silence on the other end.

"Who is this?" he demanded.

"It's Dr. Cesari, Phil. We need to talk."

"What have you done to Herman, asshole?"

"Nothing—yet, but that could change so be polite." I stepped out of the bedroom into the kitchen so as not to wake Cocoa.

"Where's Herman? I want to talk to him."

"He's in a safe place and you're not the one giving orders here, understood?"

He hesitated and then hissed, "Yes, what do you want?"

"You lied to me the other day, Phil."

"How so?"

"You told me that someone tried to kill Cinderella in upstate New York and frame the Secret Service. That was a lie. Those were real Secret Service agents up there and they were really trying to kill that girl. So now I want to know the whole fucking truth or I'm going to bake poor Herman in one of his own ovens in one of his own fucking pie crusts."

"You touch one fucking hair on his head and I will dismember you and your whole family. Do you hear me, greaseball?"

"Have it your own way, dickhead." I hung up. Before I could count to ten, the phone rang again.

"Hello."

"Meet me in the bar at the Crowne Plaza in White Plains at noon." He hung up this time.

I looked up and saw Cocoa standing in the doorway to her room wearing panties and a T-shirt. "What's all the cursing about?"

"Phil was upset. He thinks I kidnapped Herman."

She chuckled. "You're such an asshole. Why did you have to tell him that? Can't you see how difficult this situation is for him and Herman?"

"I didn't tell him I kidnapped Herman. He jumped to that conclusion and I didn't disabuse him of the notion."

She shook her head. "So, now what?"

"I'm going to meet him at noon in Westchester to talk it out."

"Why didn't you just talk it out now while you were on the phone?"

"Probably because he's at work and can't spend too much time away from what he's supposed to be doing or maybe he's not in a very secure place. I don't know. I'm not a spy."

"You should put on some clothes," she said.

"Look who's talking?"

"We have company." She nodded at the other bedroom door. "I had to get up in the middle of the night to pee and there was some blonde out here smoking a joint. I assumed it was that Cinderella chick you've been talking about."

I nodded. "It is. I've been so distracted, I forgot she had moved in here for safe-keeping. I thought I smelled pot in here. Let me put on some clothes. I'd like to have a chat with her."

Cocoa went back to sleep, and I took a hot shower. My ass wasn't hurting nearly as much today thankfully. Consuela and I were going to have to have a long talk about that if I could ever find her.

I shaved, dressed, and knocked on Lola's—aka Cinderella's—door. There was no answer so I gently pushed it open, peeking in. She was out cold and snoring like a sailor. How pleasant, but what really intrigued me was that there was a guy lying on either side of her. A white guy on the right and a black guy on the left. Cinderella really knew how to throw a party. The black guy opened his eyes as light flooded into the room.

"Who the fuck are you?" he demanded.

"I was just thinking the same thing."

"Shut the door, cracker, I can't sleep with the lights on."

I opened the door wider, stepped into the room, and turned the overhead light on. The guy groaned, waking up the other one. Cinderella continued snoring.

The white guy asked, "What the fuck is going on?"

I walked over to the window and opened it up fully. Brisk morning air filled the room, and everyone started to sober up, even Lola. I saw men's clothing on the floor, gathered them up with their shoes, and tossed them out the window into the street below. This got their attention, and they both sat up in the bed.

"Why'd you do that, bro?" the black guy demanded. He was about thirty-five and looked intelligent enough, but we would soon find out. He seemed reasonably fit, but he was no match for me, and I think he came to the same conclusion.

"What's your name, *bro*?" I asked.

"Omar. Who are you, her pimp? We already paid her, man."

"Omar, listen carefully. I'm going to count to three, and if you're still here I'm going to throw you out the fucking window with your clothes." I turned to the white guy, who looked about the same age and maybe slightly dumber. "Did you hear me?"

"Me too?" he asked, wide-eyed.

I sighed deeply, walked over to his side of the bed, and grabbed him by the hair, dragging him onto the floor where he landed with a thump. I said, "Yeah, you too, asshole. As of ten seconds ago, you both have been officially notified that you are trespassing on

private property for the purpose of solicitation of prostitution."
I thought it sounded good. Omar had stood up now not knowing
what to expect. The white guy was on his knees holding his head
and groaning.

They looked at each other. I said, "One."

They hesitated. I said, "Two."

They both dashed by me, naked, to the apartment door. One
of them must have tripped and fell down the stairs from the sound
of it. Lola was finally starting to come to from all the racket. Cocoa stood at the bedroom door. "John, what is going on here?
What's all the noise?"

"I'm afraid our little princess is finding it hard to break old habits.
Sorry about the commotion, Cocoa. Go back to sleep."

Instead, she stepped farther into the room. "I'd like to meet her."

Lola sat up, rubbed her eyes and yawned, looking around completely disoriented. She stretched and ran her hand through her tousled
hair. "What day is it?" she asked, her eyes half closed.

Cocoa and I both laughed.

I said, "Cocoa meet Cinderella. Cinderella meet Cocoa."

"Hi, Cocoa."

She then flopped backward onto the bed, snoring loudly.

Chapter 39

I picked up the Mercedes at the garage down the block and drove uptown to Columbus Circle, maneuvered around it, and found my way to St. Luke's-Roosevelt Hospital on West 59th Street. I parked the car in the hospital's garage and entered the main lobby.

Stopping at the front desk, I asked the volunteer where the endoscopy department was, thanking her when she told me. It was on the sixth floor of the building, and I rode the elevator up. As I approached my destination, I noticed my heart rate quickening and my hands becoming clammy. I hadn't seen Kelly in six months and could feel myself starting to unravel. Calm down, Cesari.

I got off the elevator and checked the sign on the wall, which said endoscopy was to my right. It was eight in the morning and I needed coffee. I should've picked up a cup in the lobby but I was too distracted. Stopping at the door, I took a deep breath and entered.

It was New Year's Day and except for the emergency department, services and staffing were limited because of the holiday, but it was a large hospital, centrally located in Manhattan, and couldn't afford to shut down completely. So today, services such as surgery and endoscopy would be limited to inpatients, emergencies, and urgencies. Employees would be paid double time and in some cases more for their efforts. Vito had found out that Kelly's new boyfriend was out of town visiting a sick relative and so she had volunteered to work today.

It was a very large department, and there were a handful of patient families anxiously sitting around reading magazines. It was considered the premier gastroenterology unit in all of New York. All the rich and famous came here to have their colonoscopies done. I looked around and then stepped up to the reception desk.

The forty year old nurse looked up politely. "Good morning. How may I help you?"

I smiled. "I'm looking for an old friend of mine. She's a nurse here. Her name is Kelly Kingston. I haven't seen her in a while and I was hoping to surprise her."

"Oh Kelly. Sure thing. I'll go find her. You're lucky, I don't think they've started yet. Why don't you wait in the consultation room over there. It'll be more private." She pointed to a door off to the side of the waiting room.

The consultation room was a place for doctors to speak privately to patients and their families. This one was quite small, maybe an eight foot square with a small round table and several plastic chairs. I closed the door behind me and took a seat, strumming my fingers mindlessly on the table. Several minutes later, the door opened and Kelly walked in, freezing at the sight of me. I stood up awkwardly, drying my sweaty palms on my jeans.

"Hi, Kel."

She closed the door behind her. "Hi, John."

We stood there staring at each other for a moment, and I clumsily put my right hand out, which made her laugh. She said, "I think it would be okay if we hugged."

I walked over and gave her a hug and a kiss on the cheek. "Congratulations," I said finally acknowledging the obvious. She wore blue surgical scrubs and was extremely pregnant. I felt old feelings surge to the surface as I gazed at her. She was one of the most beautiful and sweetest women I had ever known. Five feet three, dark brown skin with big green eyes and soft wavy hair—I was starting to melt. We had lived together for about a year when things went sideways for us.

"Thank you. How'd you hear?"

"Word gets around, Kel."

"Does it?"

I smiled. "Yes, it does. Please, have a seat." I held out a chair for her and she sat in it.

"Thank you, but I can't talk long. I have to get back to work."

"I know, Kel. I just wanted to say hi and see how you were. You look great, by the way." I took a seat next to her at the small table.

She chuckled. "I look fat and I feel fat. I can't believe I still have two months to go."

I hid my surprise at that one. She looked like she was going to pop any second. It was a good thing I didn't say anything. When it came to pregnant women it was always smart to keep your mouth shut and let them do the talking. "So you're seven months along?" I asked, dancing around the elephant in the living room. We had broken up six months ago. I wasn't very good at math but this wasn't that hard to figure out.

She read my mind. "Look, John, I don't know what you hoped to accomplish by coming here."

I raised my hands in mock surrender. "I don't have any hidden agenda, Kel. I heard about—well you know. I just thought I'd drop by and visit a dear friend."

Unpersuaded she said, "They are not your children, John."

I didn't buy it.

"They?"

"I'm having twins, silly. That's why I'm so big. I thought word gets around," she said laughing.

I was stunned. We were having twins. "Boys, girls, or both?" I was suddenly excited.

"I don't know or want to. I can wait and either way I'll be just as happy."

"So—you're happy?"

She got very serious. "Yes, John, I am very happy and I want you to be happy for me."

"I want to, Kelly. I really do, but it's very hard and now it's even harder, and I don't believe that I'm not the father." In for a penny, in for a pound. "I love you, Kelly. I can't help it. I will always love you and care about you and if they are my children then I want to be part of their lives."

She drew a deep breath. "I love you too, John, but you lead a very dangerous lifestyle and I will not allow my children to grow up in that environment. I know you mean well, but you're in so deep you can't even see daylight anymore. For God's sake every time I look in the mirror I'm reminded of why we can't be together." Tears started to run down her face as she brushed aside the hair on the right side of her head, revealing the scar from where her ear had been cut off by one of my enemies. "I don't want this to happen to my children."

I bowed my head. "Kelly, I'm sorry, but don't you think I can change?"

"John, I prayed for a whole year that you would change, and I know you want to but I honestly don't think you can. Walking away from you was the hardest thing I've ever done, and now you show up here. How am I going to work now?"

Full steam ahead. "Kelly—I want to be there for you. I want us to be a family, to have a house with a swing set in the backyard and a dog."

She started sobbing. "Did you have to bring up the dog? That's another thing, I miss Cleopatra. She was so sweet."

Oh damn. Why did I do that? Things were going badly enough as it was.

"Kelly, please—honey. I'm sorry for bringing it up. I agree. She was a wonderful dog and we did all we could."

"Did we? She saved our lives. What did we do to save hers?"

I was quiet. A judge had ordered Cleopatra terminated after she ripped the throat out of some guy that had attacked us. The judge had agreed to stop the euthanasia but only if we agreed to adopt her. Call it what you will but we were simply not in a position to take in a 250 lb. English mastiff, and Kelly had been racked with guilt ever since. Now, I was feeling bad too. Cleopatra had really taken to me in a big way and I to her. Maybe I did let her down.

My head bowed, I admitted, "Probably not as much as we could. If I had a time machine, I would do it over."

She collected herself and looked me straight in the eyes. "John, I don't want to see you. I can't see you. I have to move on and you have to help me move on."

I moved my chair closer, putting my arm around her. She buried her head in my chest, trembling. "I will do whatever it takes to make you happy, Kelly. I promise. I'm sorry for coming here today. I didn't mean to upset you." I could barely speak, I was so choked up.

She nodded her head into my chest. "I'll leave now, Kel." I tilted her beautiful face backward so I could look into her eyes. Her face was covered in tears and her eyes were getting red and puffy. I leaned down and kissed her on the lips.

"I love you, Kelly."

She burst out crying even worse than before and I sat there holding her. With nothing more to say, I gently started to rise in order to leave, but she held me back.

"John…?"

"Yes, Kel."

She collected herself, wiped her eyes and took a deep breath. "I don't know how to tell you this."

"What more is there to say?"

She took a deep breath and let it out slowly. "I'm getting married."

Great.

I nodded. I guessed I should have expected that but I didn't. I was speechless. She continued. "He's a good man, John. He'll take care of me and the children."

I felt the oxygen being sucked out of the room as I got lightheaded from the news. I couldn't listen anymore. When I still didn't say anything she said, "Please don't be upset."

I was so far past upset; I couldn't even find it on a map. "I'm not upset, Kel. I want you to be happy. If marrying someone you don't love will make you happy then I'm all for it."

"John, please don't be like that."

"I think I should leave now."

I stood up and tried to stay calm. Losing it here, at this moment in time, would definitely be the wrong thing to do. She stood up and wrapped her arms around me.

"Do you understand?"

Nodding, I took a deep breath. "Of course I do. Well, I know you have to get back to work so I'd best be off. Happy New Year, Kel."

Without looking back, I left her in the consultation room and hustled out of the hospital. I was hot and felt like I was going to puke. Outside, I leaned against the side of the hospital shaking and crying. I slapped my hand against the bricks several times in frustration.

Goddamn! This was only a thousand times worse than I thought it was going to be. Getting married? I couldn't believe it. I staggered into the parking garage and found the Mercedes. I leaned against the steering wheel, hyperventilating. I needed to get it back together in a hurry if I was going to function properly.

Women!

Pulling out of the garage onto 59th Street I wondered if God had deliberately made them this complicated and why he would do such a crazy thing. Maybe God wasn't a he after all.

Chapter 40

*I*t took me an hour to get to White Plains and it was only ten when I arrived so I stopped in the Galleria, the big indoor shopping mall downtown. Most of the stores were open for limited hours of operation although the place was very quiet at this hour. I had considered returning to my apartment for a change of clothes but still had lingering concerns over who might be watching and waiting for me there so I went into the Gap and bought a new pair of jeans, a casual long-sleeve shirt, a sweater, and a wind breaker. Thankfully, the weather had been hovering between thirty-five and forty degrees in the tri-state area. I left the old clothes in the dressing room.

Feeling better about myself, I drove over to the Crowne Plaza, arriving at eleven thirty. I walked into the bar and took a seat, ordering a club soda with a twist of lime. The hotel was very busy from the holiday crowds and parties, and the lobby was filled with people.

At twelve sharp, Phillip McIntosh walked into the main lobby looking very corporate in a gray overcoat and tie. He looked around, spotted me, and headed over, sitting on the adjacent bar stool. We didn't extend hands, and I watched him glance around casually, neither acknowledging me nor looking directly at me. He asked the bartender for a glass of water and discreetly passed me a small envelope about the size of a credit card. He drank the water, thanked the bartender, and walked away toward the elevators as I watched. I opened the envelope and found inside an electronic key for room 909.

Fucking spies. Always playing games.

I guess the Secret Service technically weren't spies but they had the same mentality. I threw a couple of dollars on the counter, waved to the bartender, and headed over to the elevators. Phil was already gone by the time I got there and stepped into one of the cars with a half dozen other people. I was sure we were violating the fire code judging by the size of several of the heftier guests I was crushed up against.

I got off on the ninth floor, grateful for the fresh air, and ambled over to room 909. I was about to place the key up to the lock mechanism when I suddenly had a bad feeling. Was Phil setting a trap for me? I mean seriously, would he do that? In broad daylight? In a hotel where dozens of people saw him? The room must be registered in his name, right? No way could anybody be that stupid. Still, we were talking about a government employee now, weren't we? And a pissed-off one at that. Plus, he must have given the other guys he worked with some reason why he needed an hour or two off, and they would know that this time was unaccounted for.

I rubbed my chin, and as I thought it through, a housekeeper came by pushing a cart with clean linen. I stopped her, smiling. She was Indian, about fifty years old and seemed sweet.

"Hi, I was wondering if you could help me? I just checked in and my bed hasn't been made up yet from the previous guest."

She looked upset. "I am so sorry, sir. I will change the sheets for you right now."

Using her key, she swiped it against the pad on the side of the door. The light went from red to green and we heard the door unlock with a click. She returned the key to her pocket and I followed her into the room behind the linen cart.

Phil was sitting in a Queen Anne chair by a small desk, looking out the window. He had taken his overcoat off and was wearing a two-piece suit, white shirt, and navy tie. His blond hair was neatly trimmed and combed. He was a very good-looking guy.

He stood up as we entered, startled at the sight of the housekeeper. "What's going on, Cesari? Do I have to explain the concept of discretion to you or isn't that covered in the mafia handbook?" He understandably wasn't in a good mood although from his demeanor and overall relaxed appearance I knew that this wasn't an ambush.

The housekeeper looked confused for multiple good reasons but mostly because the bed looked pristine, so I said, "Thank you for your time. I guess somebody must have made the bed while I was out."

She courteously departed and I followed her to the door, locking it as she left. As I turned back toward Phil, I realized too late that he had quickly come up behind me. He delivered a right cross to my chin. Taken by surprise, I fell back into the wall and narrowly blocked the incoming left with my right forearm.

He came in close, too close in his haste to finish me off. I jabbed my right fist under his chin directly into his larynx and he staggered backward, coughing and gasping for air. I regained my balance, hauled off, and gave him an uppercut to his jaw and he was done. His head snapped upward and he sprawled backward onto the floor. This fight was over. Cesari, one. Phil of the future, zero. I knelt down next to him, patting him down while he lay stunned and coughing. He didn't have any weapons on him. He was just venting over what he thought I might have done to Herman, and I couldn't blame him for that so without malice, I helped him up onto the edge of the bed and he shook the cobwebs out of his head.

"Do you want some water?" I asked politely.

He nodded but didn't say anything as he rubbed his throat. I brought him a glass of water from the bathroom, and he took a sip.

I said, "Okay, now that we got that out of the way, can we get down to business?"

"Fuck you, Cesari. I hate you and if you hurt Herman, I will spend every waking minute of the rest of my life hunting you down like the rabid dog that you are."

"Herman is fine. He's sitting in his house worrying about you. I just borrowed his phone."

"Then why did you say you kidnapped him?"

"I never said that I did. You jumped to that conclusion all on your own."

He looked perplexed as if he was having trouble understanding me. "You misled me, you fuck."

"I needed to talk to you."

"So, Herman's okay?"

"Probably baking you a fruit pie as we speak."

"Is that supposed to be funny?"

"Take it easy, he's at home and he's fine."

He relaxed and seemed relieved. "So why should I talk to you?"

"Because I've been thinking about things and I think you're one of the good guys. I think that you want to know what's going on as much as I do." He let out a deep breath. The stress of his job, his secret life, and his concussion were getting to him. Phil was at the tipping point. It was time to move in.

I sat next to him on the edge of the bed. "Look Phil, I'm sorry about making you worry about Herman's well-being..."

"I can't tell you what's going on, Cesari. This is way above your pay grade as they say."

"I already saw the video of your boss. I found the DVD in Consuela's apartment in Orlando."

He turned pale and looked around the room as if a fire alarm had just gone off. "You saw it? Oh my God. Do you have any idea how much danger you're in?"

"I think I do." As a matter of trust building with Phil I told him of my encounter with Consuela, down to the last detail of the strapping she gave me. He sat there in disbelief, listening. I said, "I can show you my ass if you want proof as long as you promise to control yourself."

"Fuck off, Cesari. You breeders are all the same. You think every gay guy you meet wants you."

Breeders?

"You don't?"

"I don't even want to look at your ugly face, let alone your ugly ass. Look, I believe you about Consuela. I already found out how fucking psychotic she is, but you know something, I don't believe she's the real problem." He hesitated then as if he knew he had already said too much, which was the whole point of agitating him.

"Look Phil, I'm not asking you to commit treason, all right? Just tell me what you can without giving away state secrets. I mean, at this point this really should be a criminal investigation anyway, don't you think?"

He nodded and sighed. "I'm not sure I give a shit anymore about anything. I can't stand the fact that Herman has come smack in the crosshairs of all of this because of me. I don't know what I would do if anything happened to him. Anyway, it started like I told you the other day. My guy has been visiting his girls at Disney on a regular basis for some time. Then one day this woman Consuela comes to the house and asks to speak with him and his wife. She says she has something to show him and pops a DVD into the player with all of us standing around. Within seconds, we all understood what was happening and he shoos all the agents out of the room. Thirty minutes later, they both come out pale as ghosts and he asks me to escort Consuela to her car. That's when I made the mistake of threatening her."

"Excuse me, Phil. I guess I don't understand. She just walked up to the front door and says 'I want to show him a DVD' and you guys let her in?"

"No, it wasn't that simple. Remember, he's retired and there have been no credible threats against his life. Guarding him is mostly mundane stuff like dragging him back and forth to his whores and speaking engagements. At any rate, when we told him her name he sounded like he knew her and said to send her right in."

I nodded. "Go on."

"Well, he took me aside and admitted that he was being blackmailed even though it was already obvious but he wouldn't say what she wanted, which was very understandable. He told me that he refused to submit to her demands and asked me to keep an eye on the girls to see what might turn up. You know, see who they talked to and hung out with, that kind of stuff. During this routine surveillance you came along and all of a sudden people started showing up dead. Like I told you before, my first thought was that it might be you but now I know better. Then I thought Consuela might be the one doing the killing, you know, to get rid of any witnesses, but when she came to Herman's house she accused me of killing Snow White and didn't believe me when I denied it."

"Take a step back, Phil. If your boss said that he refused to submit to her demands why didn't Consuela go public with the video?"

He took a sip of water and massaged his throat again. "He said that he would never submit to her demands but that she had given him a couple of weeks to think it over."

"Your boy doesn't have much time left, he must be going crazy."

"You don't know the half of it. In addition to all this stress, he got some sort of stomach bug and has been sick as a dog for the last several days. That's why they called me back from sick leave. I'm the only one he trusts. He doesn't like people seeing him like this, having diarrhea and vomiting. He thinks it would hurt his public image so everybody but me has to stay outside during the day or in the attached guesthouse at night."

"You're the only agent allowed in the house?"

"Yes, for the time being, I'm the *only* one in the house with him. His wife is away at a fund-raiser in D.C. but she'll be back tomorrow night. She's another piece of work; going to a fund-raiser on New Year's Eve while he's puking his brains out. He was supposed to go with her but was too sick and I guess the show must go on."

"What's the fund-raiser for? I'm not too big into politics."

"You can't be serious, Cesari? Where do you live, in a cave? She's thinking of taking a run for the presidency."

"Interesting. You would think at her age, she'd want to relax and maybe take up knitting or something."

He laughed. "Yeah, right. Anyway, he really didn't like me leaving him to come here, but he was looking a little better this morning and accepted my bullshit story about having lunch with an old friend. He's actually pretty good with things like that."

"So he's all better today?"

"Not all better, just not as sick. It's probably just a virus but his doctor insisted he have a colonoscopy to make sure everything's okay."

"A colonoscopy?"

"Yeah, where they put that tube with the light up your butt."

"I know what a colonoscopy is, Phil. So when's he supposed to have this colonoscopy?"

"Tomorrow."

"Really?" My wheels starting spinning fast and furious.

"Yep, at eight a.m., they've closed the entire OR for the morning at St. Luke's just for his security and privacy. He's starting off the New Year with a bang, slimy piece of shit that he is. I heard they had to cancel almost twenty patients because of him."

"You sound as if you're not as enamored of your boss as most of America is?"

"Well, he's not as bad as she is, but they're both hypocrites. Don't ask, don't tell, my ass. That's just their way of holding shit over your head so they own you."

"They know about Herman?"

"Yeah, and they never let me forget about it either. Do you have any idea what it's like working for people who remind you daily that they can crush you like a bug any time they want just because you love someone society says you shouldn't?"

"No, I don't, Phil, and I'm sorry. They come across as so—open-minded."

He laughed at that. "Yeah, right. Open-minded my ass. As long as the polls support them, they're open-minded. It's different when you're up close with these people the way I am. You get to see all the warts, and these two have more than most."

I nodded. "I bet they do. So what happened upstate with those two agents?"

"That's just it, I don't know. I told you the truth as I knew it the other day. I didn't lie. I've since come to realize that I was misinformed. Through the grapevine, I heard they were real agents but I don't know who they were or what happened up there."

"Best guess, Phil?"

He hesitated. "I think someone has brought a rogue team in to eliminate Consuela and everyone else associated with her little love nest to protect my guy's reputation, which is why your ass is in the frying pan now that you've seen the video and know what's at stake."

"And who would do that? Your boss?"

His brow furrowed as he thought it over and he slowly shook his head. "I don't think so. He's a degenerate womanizer but I don't see him as a murderer and I know him pretty well. In fact, if the choice was his, he'd bring all the girls home to live with him, send them all to college, be godfather to their children, etc. He'd love to be another Hugh Heffner if he could. No, he would never do something like this."

"But I bet he probably knows who might."

"I have no doubt about that."

"Phil, can I ask you an honest question, off the record, man to man?"

"Spit it out, Cesari. I got to get back to wipe his highness's ass."

I nodded. "How do you really feel about these two you've been guarding?"

"I hate their guts."

Chapter 41

*B*ack in the Kit Kat Club, I found Heidi in her office and took a few moments to berate her for blabbing to Cheryl about Cocoa and Kelly.

"You know, Heidi, I have every right to be mad at you."

"Oh, take it easy. Cheryl will get over it and from what I hear you shouldn't be complaining. A little vacation with that vixen, Cocoa. You are one lucky wop. You should be thanking me."

"I don't think this is in the least bit funny."

"Okay, Cesari, if you want to play hardball, then I'll play hardball. I'm running a business here and you're supposed to be my silent partner. Do you understand what the definition of silent is? It means you don't run off with one of my girls on the busiest night of the week and you don't throw johns out of the building before they pay."

"We're not running a whorehouse here, Heidi. This is a gentleman's club, remember?"

"You say potayto and I say potahto."

"Oh really? Besides, those guys said they paid her."

"They did?" She chuckled. "That Cinderella is one slick chick. I'm going to have to forgive her though. She is one hot dancer. She's going to give Cocoa a run for her money, that's for sure."

"You let her dance?"

"Let her? Try to stop her. Might as well channel her energy. Relax, Cesari, we don't get many Secret Service killers in here."

I shook my head. So much for keeping a low profile. "Well, I'm glad it's working out."

"Maybe it is and maybe it isn't. She's got potential but when the dust settles, we may have to get her professional help for her drug problem. She's pretty much stoned every night."

"I'll leave that up to you. Is Cocoa still upstairs?"

"Yeah, she's napping. Since it was all your fault, I decided to cut her some slack for abandoning me and let her dance tonight."

"That was nice of you. By the way, nice hair." Her hair was even brighter red than the last time I saw her.

"You like it?" she asked, smiling.

"No."

"Fuck off, Cesari, and stay away from my girls."

I watched her storm off and went up the stairs to see if Cocoa was awake. Her bedroom door was closed and I gently turned the knob, peeking in. She was lying in bed reading a book.

"Hey, what you got there?"

She was excited to see me and smiled from ear to ear. "Hi, I didn't think I was going to see you again today—or ever."

I ignored that last part, sat on the edge of the bed, and kissed her. I looked at the cover of her book. "Whoa, *The Count of Monte Cristo*, now that's a great book. I see you're halfway through."

"Have you read it?"

"Twice. It's more or less the story of my life."

She chuckled. "It is not."

"Well, maybe I haven't suffered as much as Edmond Dantes did, but I can relate to the time he spent in that prison, the Chateau D'If. I especially like the part where they beat him every year on the anniversary of his imprisonment."

She closed the book, giggling. "I missed you."

I looked at my watch. "I've only been gone eight hours."

"So, how'd it go?" she asked seriously.

"Which part?"

"The part I care about."

I nodded. "Apparently, Kelly's getting married and would prefer not having a person of my ilk hanging around her children."

Cocoa was silent for a while, sensing the land mine she had just stepped on. "I'm sorry."

"I bet."

She nodded. "I don't want you to feel bad."

I took a deep breath and let it out. "Thanks. So, there it is."

"What about the other one, Cheryl?"

"Well, she won't answer my calls, so I guess she hasn't calmed down yet."

She smiled. "So, I guess you're stuck with me."

I smiled back. "I'd hardly say that I was stuck. I think any man would be lucky to be with you, Cocoa. In fact, I'm not exaggerating when I say that I feel like I've won the lottery knowing you."

Her cheeks flushed with joy at the compliment. "Are you going to come watch me dance tonight?" Her eyes grew wide with excitement.

I didn't know how to answer that. Watching other men shove ten and twenty dollar bills into her G-string while they salivated over her wasn't exactly my idea of fun. I had lost my objectivity when it came to this girl, but she didn't seem to understand that. This was her work, her art if you will, and she was proud of it. She wanted me to share that with her. It was like she was inviting me to her gallery to see her paintings.

I said, "Sure, I'll be there at ten, all right?"

She leaped up and threw her arms around me. "Yesss. I'll be on the main stage tonight."

I nodded as my cell phone went off in my pocket. I took it out and answered.

"What's up, Vito? The Pennsylvania state police call for you yet?"

"In fact they did, but they got nothing. They're just pissed. The car's completely gone and I mean gone. They called the owner in Florida and he told them it was never stolen but that he had loaned it to a cousin of his and was expecting it back any day. What the fuck did you do to that guy anyway? I reported my driver's license stolen and I have a dozen witnesses who'll swear I was courtside with them at the Knicks game last night before we all went to Times Square to watch the ball drop. They're gonna drop the whole thing. It's way too much trouble for them."

"Sounds like you got it under control."

"Yeah, they were pissed. You should've heard them ranting and raving, but the thing that really got them going was when I asked them if they tested that officer, Raguzza, for crack use or other hallucinogens."

I laughed. "You didn't?"

"I did." I heard him laugh on the other end.

"So what's this call about?"

He got serious. "Did you watch that DVD you gave me?"

"I saw enough of it to know what was going on, why?"

"You didn't watch it to the end?"

"No, I know it shows one of the most important men in America having sex with a nineteen year old mentally ill girl dressed as Snow White. Isn't that enough?"

"No, it's not. You need to see the whole thing."

"Who told you to watch it anyway? I told you to put it in a safe place."

"Well, I did watch it and thank goodness for that. Where are you?"

"I'm at the Kit Kat Club up in the apartment."

"Okay, look, I'll meet you there and we'll watch the DVD together and then grab a bite to eat. I wouldn't mind seeing it again and you're going to thank me for it."

"What was that about?" Cocoa asked.

"That was Vito. He's coming over with that DVD from Consuela's apartment. He said that there's something on it I need to see as if what I already saw wasn't bad enough."

"Hmm, I wonder what that means?"

"I don't know. I'm not sure how much worse it can get. Anyway, after we watch the DVD, we're going to grab a bite and plan some strategy. It's time to start being a little more proactive if I want to figure things out. I'll make sure I'm back in time for your act."

"Good. I'll be watching for you and saving my best stuff for when you get there."

I thought that over. Clearing my throat, I said, "I'm just curious, I know you have a lot of dress up costumes for your dance routines—right?"

"I do. What turns you on?" she asked, suddenly animated.

"Do you think I could see them?"

"Sure, they're in the closet over there."

We walked over to the closet and peeked in. Hmm, it didn't look a whole lot different from Snow White's closet. "Do you have any nurse outfits?" I asked.

She laughed. "Oh yeah, that's pretty basic stuff. Guys love it. I'm surprised you do though since you work with them all day. I would've thought that you would find it boring."

She waded through the wardrobe, pushing stuff out of the way.

"Here they are. I have three nurse getups. One's white latex. That's this one. Latex is all the rage these days. This one here is nothing more than a white G-string and nurse's cap with a red cross on it, and the last is a real nurse's uniform for when I do a slow strip, but that's more for private parties than pole dancing. What do you think?"

I studied the last uniform as she held it against herself.

"That one, if you don't mind?"

"This one?"

"Yes, the real one."

She looked surprised. "Really? But it's kind of boring and covers up too much."

"Yeah, I know, but it's the one I like. It's very authentic."

"Okay, if that's what you want. I don't know what Heidi's going to say about it. What about the stockings? Seams or no seams?"

"Which are sexier?"

"Guys go wild over seams. I'll wear seams."

"I don't know, Cocoa, I've never been a big seam fan. How about just regular stockings tonight? I think they are way more sexier."

"Really? Okay, you're a little different than most guys. I never would have guessed."

"Yeah, I've been told that."

"I can't wait for you to see me. I'm so excited. What about shoes? I have several styles of high heels and stilettos."

I shook my head. "No, definitely not. The way to go here is with authenticity. Do you have white sneakers or flat nursing shoes? In a situation like this, Cocoa, the closer you get to the real thing, the sexier it becomes."

"Wow, okay. I had no idea. I do have white sneakers but Heidi is going to freak. She's going to think I died and my boring twin showed up." She held up a pair of white sneakers for me to look at.

"That'll be perfect. I'm getting turned on already and don't worry about Heidi. Look, I'm going downstairs to get a drink while I wait for Vito. I need to think and for some reason, I just can't seem to concentrate around you."

I gave her a kiss and went down to the bar, where there were a handful of guys sipping from rocks glasses and watching one of the girls giving an uninspired performance on the stage in front of them. Taking a seat, I ordered a scotch on the rocks and thought through my day and all I had learned. I checked my phone to see if there were any calls from Cheryl and found none. Nothing surprising there. Another hot-tempered woman. The story of my life.

By the time I finished my drink, Vito had arrived, tapping me on the shoulder and sliding onto the bar stool next to me. I looked at my watch. "You got here fast."

"Yeah, I wasn't that far away. One of the restaurants on Lexington Avenue was having some labor problems and I had to help with the negotiations."

"Is that why your knuckles are all bruised?" I asked, nodding at his hands resting on the bar counter. Self-conscious, he pulled them away.

"Yeah, well—these guys can be pretty stubborn if you know what I mean?"

"One day we'll have to look up the definition of the word 'negotiate' together. I'm curious to see what you'll think. So look, do you want a drink?"

"Nah, let's go to Heidi's office and get this over with. I'm dying to see the look on your face."

In Heidi's office, I popped the disc into her laptop and hit the play button. Vito pulled up a chair and sat next to me. For forty-five minutes, I sat there mesmerized and stunned by what I saw and heard. I couldn't have been more shocked as I glanced over at Vito.

"I told you, Cesari. It's fucking unbelievable."

I took the DVD out and replaced it back into its jacket, handing it to Vito. "Truly, it is. I don't think I would ever have believed it if I didn't see it with my own eyes. It's even worse than I thought. You better keep that someplace safe."

"Relax, I already made a copy. I hope you don't think I'm an amateur. The other one's in a safe in my apartment in Little Italy."

I nodded, still digesting all that I saw. "Good move, Vito. Okay, it's time to raise the stakes, but first we have to go see Kelly."

"Kelly? Why?"

"Because I need her help."

"I thought we were going out to eat?"

"We'll grab something from a food truck or deli."

"C'mon, you want me to eat fast food?"

"I don't mean to make you suffer like that but we don't have time and I promised Cocoa I'd catch her show tonight."

That cheered him up.

"All right, I can live with that."

Chapter 42

$\mathcal{J}$t was a fifteen-minute cab ride to Kelly's apartment on the West Side, and I took the time to fill Vito in on my interaction with her and with Phil, earlier in the day.

"Jesus, Cesari, you got balls. I don't know which is worse; you going to Kelly's apartment after what just happened or what you're planning on doing to our friend in Mount Kisco?"

"Can't be helped. Something's gotta give and somebody's gotta start talking."

The driver let us off on the corner of 62nd Street and Columbus Avenue. "Kelly lives in a nice neighborhood, doesn't she?" Vito commented, scanning around.

"Yeah, she's doing okay. I hate to do this to her, but I don't know anybody else who works in the endoscopy room at St. Luke's and I need somebody on the inside."

We walked into the impressive apartment building and took the elevator up to her floor. Vito had done some great detective work in finding out where she lived and worked. I had to give him credit for that.

I looked at my watch. It was seven p.m. We were doing well time wise. I heard the sound of a television through the door. Inside, they were watching an action movie. I knocked on the door as Vito stood by my side. My palms were sweating again, and I wiped them on my pants. No one answered so I knocked again louder.

"Relax, Cesari, she's not going to bite your head off—your dick, maybe." He started chuckling at his own joke.

"That was funny?"

"Sorry." He cleared his throat. "Did I mention that I found out who her new boyfriend is?"

"No, you didn't."

He was quiet.

"So...?"

"I heard that he's an accountant and has a peculiar first name. Let me see if I can remember it." He rubbed his chin in thought.

"An accountant? No kidding? So what's his name?" I remembered that Cheryl had said she was going to shack up with a boring accountant. Apparently, that was the default plan for all my exes.

As Vito searched his memory, a lanky, thirty-five year old black guy answered the door. His eyes went wide and he cringed at the site of me.

I said, "Omar?!" The john I found with Cinderella this morning.

Vito said, "That's his name. How'd you know?"

Before I could stop myself, I punched Omar in the nose, knocking him backward onto the floor, and immediately jumped on top of him, pinning him down while chaos erupted around me. Kelly screamed in front of me and Vito yelled behind me. Omar's nose was broken and bleeding, and he was stunned from the punch and having hit the back of his head on the hardwood floor. I gave him a quick left and was about to launch another right cross when Kelly jumped on top of me, propelling me backward with her on top. Vito had stepped in, pulling Omar out from the fracas and helping him over to the couch.

Kelly sat straddling me, grasping my wrists and pushing them back over my head against the floor. Her hair dangled in my face and her breathing came in shallow bursts. She was furious.

"What—the fuck— do you think you're doing?" she demanded.

I didn't have a good answer and I knew it looked bad. I looked over at the sofa. The white guy from this morning was sitting there, slack-jawed and wide eyed. He suddenly got up, stammered "good-bye," and ran past us out of the apartment. He wasn't as dumb as I had thought. Vito sat next to Omar making sure he was okay. Kelly squeezed my wrists even tighter, showing no signs of letting up. She picked them up a little and then slammed them back into the floor.

"Answer me, Cesari, or I will kill you dead!"

"Kelly, I'm sorry. I've been a little emotional lately." I didn't want to be the one to tell her about Omar. Fortunately, Omar took care of that for me.

From the sofa, dazed and holding his nose with a kitchen towel Vito had found for him he said, "Kelly, how do you know this creep? He's a pimp from downtown." Her grip eased up a little as she looked at Omar, puzzled, and then back at me. Her belly pressed into me pretty hard and I wondered if maybe she was having triplets instead of twins.

"What are you talking about, Omar? This is John Cesari, he's a doctor."

"Bullshit, he's a low-life pimp. I met him this morning at the Kit Kat Club."

Uh oh.

Kelly let go of my wrists and sat back on my stomach, looking at Omar. My wrists felt better, although now I couldn't breathe, but I didn't dare say anything.

"What do you mean, you met him this morning at the Kit Kat Club? What the hell is the Kit Kat Club and I thought you were visiting your sister in the hospital on Long Island last night, remember? The one who just had gallbladder surgery? That's why we couldn't go out, remember?" Omar didn't say anything.

I whispered, gasping for breath, "Maybe I can help?"

She turned to me angrily. "You keep your mouth shut and you just might walk out of here with both of your testicles." Turning back to Omar, she continued, "I'm waiting Omar." Vito sat passively on the couch next to Omar. He knew better than to say anything and looked extremely uncomfortable.

Omar's senses were clearing up and he now realized the predicament he had just gotten himself into. He started whining. "Baby, I don't know what I'm saying. I just got hit in the head. If you say he's a doctor then I guess he's a doctor. I'm all confused right now. I think I need to see a doctor myself." He turned to Vito. "Are you Santa Claus?"

I chuckled. Jesus, he was good.

"Omar, stop it." She looked at me. "Cesari, why did you punch him?"

There was an uncomfortable silence while I thought of what I should say. Kelly made a fist and punched me in the chest. "Well?"

I coughed and looked up at Omar. "Are you going to tell her or am I? I'm not going to take the fall for you, Omar."

He whimpered, "Kelly, honey, I don't know what to say."

"How about the truth? Were you or were you not visiting your sister last night? Let's start with that."

Instead of answering right away, Omar made the colossal mistake of glancing at me first. Kelly flipped out and staggered to her feet. Vito ran over to help her up and she pushed him away. Omar cringed on the couch as she hovered over him, wagging her finger. "You lied to me, didn't you? I can't believe it. You'd rather spend New Year's Eve with that pothead friend of yours than with me? That's why he ran out of here like he did. He knew what was coming, didn't he? You need to leave Omar, and we'll talk later when I calm down."

"But, baby."

"Out—now!" She turned to me in exasperation. I hadn't moved a muscle. "John, get off the floor and tell me what you're doing here and it better not be just to ruin my life." Omar slunk by me, holding his nose as I stood up. We made eye contact but that was all. I wanted to say "Don't slam the door on the way out, asshole," but resisted. After he left, I sat down next to Kelly on the sofa with Vito on the other side of her.

When I didn't answer she looked at me sternly and said, "Well, don't you at least owe me some sort of explanation?"

"Kel, I don't know what to say. I didn't come here to cause trouble for you and your fiancé but honestly, you can do better than that guy. I found him in bed this morning with a twenty year old hooker at that Kit Kat Club he mentioned. The place reeked of pot and booze and then I find him here with the woman I love. I just snapped. I'm sorry."

She softened up a bit. "What the hell is the Kit Kat Club? Some type of whorehouse? And why were you there?"

"It's an exotic dance club that Vito and I are part owners in. The girls aren't supposed to do that kind of thing but every now and then one of them gets a little—enthusiastic."

She looked at me and started weeping. "John, this is why I told you I don't want you in my life. It's this kind of stuff. It just never seems to end with you. You can't just barge in here beating up my boyfriends, bad choice or not."

"Vito, could you get Kelly a tissue and a glass of water from the kitchen?"

Kelly rested her head on me as she started crying for real, and I put my arm around her, drawing her in close for comfort. I couldn't even imagine the havoc her hormonal state was playing with her emotions.

"I'm sorry, Kel. You have to believe me. I didn't come here to cause any problems."

"I know you didn't." She punched me again, only this time in the arm. "That's the problem. Trouble just seems to follow you around." Vito returned with a small glass of water and a tissue box he found in the kitchen.

"Thank you," Kelly said, sitting up and taking them from him. Regaining her composure she said, "So why are you both here if it wasn't to break up my marriage?"

"I need your help, Kel."

She started laughing, which I thought was a good sign. "You have got to be kidding?"

"Hear me out, Kel, it's important." I paused while she wiped tears away with the tissue. Vito stood nearby like a statue.

"Fine, so tell me. How am I supposed to help you? You already knocked me up. Did you have something else in mind?"

"Okay, I know you're upset. Just keep an open mind, please?"

She sat back into a more comfortable position and took a deep breath. "I'm listening."

So I told her from start to finish everything that had happened to me since Christmas Eve. I left out nothing, including my relationship with Cocoa. It was a long story and she put on a pot of coffee while we talked. We eventually wound up at her kitchen table sipping from mugs.

Sitting next to me, inches away, it felt like old times except that Vito was also inches away on the other side, but we managed to ignore him. She was so beautiful and had a killer smile. Pregnancy really did make a woman glow. My eyes drifted down toward her breasts and I was amazed at the other thing pregnancy did for a woman. She frowned, seeing me.

"Don't get any ideas, Cesari. Nothing's changed just because I'm letting you talk."

"Wouldn't think of it." But think of it I did anyway. That's just the way men are. Always thinking of it. It took the better part of an hour to explain things fully, and after I finished she contemplated my story and plan, eventually coming to a conclusion.

"You are absolutely crazy," she said shaking her head. "You're going to get arrested, maybe even shot. Don't you see how impossible this is?"

"It's the only way to get him alone, Kel. I need your help. I'll do all the grunt work. If anything comes of it, you just say that I coerced you or threatened you. You know I'd back you up."

"Yeah, but I like him. I voted for him twice."

"Kelly, he's not a nice guy. He's an asshole; at the very least he's a sexual predator."

"Oh take it easy. You said the girl wasn't a minor. So it was her choice."

"Oh please, Kel. He's almost seventy and she was barely nineteen with mental health issues."

"But he may not have known that."

"Yeah, but he knew she was pregnant and now she's dead. Doesn't that seem fishy?"

"Why would he have her killed? Why not just pay for an abortion?"

"Maybe she didn't want one."

"Do you have the DVD with you?" she asked.

I nodded.

"Let's see it."

At least she hadn't thrown me out of the apartment, and we all moved into the living room, taking up positions around the television as she placed the disc into its compartment. Watching in silence, I noticed Kelly's eyes grow wide. After only five minutes, she looked up. "Is that the girl who was murdered?" she asked, pointing at Snow White.

"Yes, her name is Marguerite Varga, and Cinderella there on the right is Lola Lovely. She's hiding out at the Kit Kat Club. There's a death warrant out for her too." I left out the part that Lola was the girl I found Omar with. I didn't think there was any point in fanning that flame.

Kelly said, "My God. This is so sick."

I said, "Keep watching. It gets worse."

Fifteen minutes into it, Kelly covered her mouth and caught her breath. "How much more is there?" she asked.

"About twenty more minutes," I answered.

"Is it all the same, because I think I got the gist? I don't think I can handle too much more. This is so gross. I didn't know people did stuff like this to each other."

"I'll forward ahead to the critical part and spare you the details."

Using the remote, I forwarded to the last few minutes after they had finished and were getting ready to leave. Cinderella stepped out of the room ahead of our guy and Snow White. Once they were alone, Snow White tugged on his arm to get his attention. Pulling him down close, she whispered something inaudible into his ear, causing him to become noticeably upset. Angrily, he pushed her away and she stumbled, falling onto the floor. She grabbed onto his leg and he started to drag her with him. When she wouldn't let go he backhanded her viciously across the face and left her there on the floor sobbing. A short time later, Consuela came out from one of the many dressing rooms and helped Marguerite off the floor. As she did so, she looked directly into one of the cameras. The video ended abruptly.

I said, "I can't be sure but I suspect that he flipped out when she told him she was pregnant."

Kelly nodded. "It certainly looked like it. Who was that woman?"

"That was Consuela."

"The one who beat you with the belt?"

"Yes, and I think that's the reason why she was pissed about the missing DVD. She knew she could be identified on it."

Kelly held her face in her hands and sat there in disbelief. "Wow. This is so beyond anything I could have imagined. I mean, everyone knows his personal life is a mess but this is beyond description." She sighed deeply. "Okay, he's a scumbag and I'll help you. I'll go get the keys, stay here."

She left the room and I winked at Vito, who said, "Don't start celebrating yet, Cesari. This is a long way from being a done deal."

She returned with the keys to the St. Luke's endoscopy room, but before handing them to me she said, "Tell me again that you're not going to kill anybody."

"I am absolutely not going to kill anybody."

She nodded and handed me the keys. "I'll call the other nurse, Clara, right now and switch call with her. She didn't want to be in the room with him anyway. It's too much stress taking care of people like that. So I'll be the circulator for the colonoscopy, but what are we going to do about the other nurse assigned to the case? There are always two."

I cleared my throat. "We're going to tell her that our guy is bringing his own private duty nurse along who's already been cleared by the Secret Service and thoroughly trained in endoscopy. No one else will be allowed in the room other than you, the doctor, and her per service regulations. Phil's smart and will make it sound official."

"Phil, that's the Secret Service agent who hates him?"

"Yes."

"That's fine but you really will need a second nurse in the room. I can't do everything by myself."

"I hadn't gotten that far in the planning yet. I guess I thought you could handle it all." I thought about Cocoa and her nurse's uniform.

"And tell me again why this guy Phil is committing treason?"

"One, as I said he hates the guy and his wife and is sick of their shenanigans. Two, he knows that using the service as travel agents to his whorehouses is wrong, and three, somebody has been using agents as assassins and like me he suspects that this guy may know who, only Phil can't ask him directly. And he won't be committing trea-son; I'll make sure of that. By the time I'm done, he'll come out of it squeaky clean."

As I spoke my gaze unconsciously drifted down toward her breasts again. She looked at me sternly and said, "Stop it."

My head snapped up. "Stop what?"

She ignored me. "So what do you want me to do exactly?"

"We'll set up the endoscopy room together to keep the appearance of normalcy. I need you to act as a go-between to the outside so that I don't have to interact with anyone but the guy and Phil. He's been to this doctor before so I'll wear a surgical mask and pretend that I woke up with a hoarse voice as a disguise. Basically, just keep everyone away from me as best you can. The hard part will be neutralizing the real doctor. That's why we need the keys to the room. I'll set up tonight and wait for him to come in. You call him up and tell him that the case has been moved up to six a.m. at the request of the patient and Secret Service. This way he'll come in early and I'll have time to deal with him. The endoscopy department is completely closed down because of the VIP nature of this exam so there won't be any other patients or unnecessary personnel around. I promise I won't hurt the doc, okay, and he will never know you're involved."

"What about the other agents? I assume there are more than one?"

"There are four to be exact. Phil, the guy on our side, is the senior, most trusted agent. He's in charge and has things under control."

"Won't someone have to guard the doors? How are you going to get out if something goes wrong or even if everything goes right for that matter?"

"Jesus, Kel, that'll be the easy part."

Chapter 43

Vito and I returned to the Kit Kat Club just as Cocoa was being introduced on stage. I waved to her and we grabbed a seat in a leather booth not too far from the circular stage, which was already surrounded by customers. The lights went out and the room went quiet.

Suddenly, Robin Thicke's "Blurred Lines" began playing loudly and a spotlight shone brightly on Cocoa, who took off on cue gyrating, shaking, and twirling her hair. Even in the subdued outfit I talked her into wearing she was bringing the house down. Guys were fighting to see who could toss the most money at her just to get her attention for a few seconds.

A waitress approached and I ordered a club soda and Vito ordered a whiskey. "What's with the club soda, Cesari?"

"I got a long night ahead of me, Vito."

He grunted. "Yeah, I guess you're right."

"So, what's going to happen with Kelly and Omar? That was pretty messed up."

"I don't know. She's mad right now, but who knows how she'll feel in a day or two. I can't even understand why she's going to marry him in the first place. She doesn't love him."

"Well, that one's not so hard to figure out. She wants a man around for when the kids come along to provide her with all kinds of support: emotional, physical, and financial. She's having twins, Cesari. It's going to be rough. Just be glad she hates you so much she isn't demanding child support."

I chuckled. "She doesn't hate me and she's going to get child support whether she demands it or not." I paused for a second thinking it over. "So you really think that's enough reason to marry someone you don't love?"

"Cesari, what kind of a dream world are you living in that you don't know this stuff?"

I shook my head in frustration. "Well, I just don't get it. I love her and she loves me, and those are my kids. Shouldn't I be the guy providing all those things for her?"

Vito rolled his eyes. "Get over it and stop trying to figure women out. If she wanted you to be that guy she would have told you so. From what you said, she made her reasons very clear that you're not even in the running for that position despite her feelings for you, so you need to accept defeat gracefully. Besides, I can't believe you don't know the rules."

"What rules?"

"The rules that say women can do whatever they want whenever they want to and it don't matter how many guns you point at them."

Great. I was in a strip club with Dr. Phil.

The waitress placed our drinks in front of us and I caught Cocoa glancing in my direction with a devilish smile. I raised my club soda and blew her a kiss.

Vito smiled. "That's more like it, Cesari. That's what you need. Kelly's trying to move on and you need to move on too. Cocoa's a good start."

"Okay, enough with the Cosa Nostra marital advice. I'm going to need your help tomorrow morning so don't drink yourself into a coma." I noted him gulping his whiskey down way too fast.

"Don't worry about me. I'll be there with the engine running, just don't keep me waiting." He waved to our waitress and ordered another one.

The song ended and a rousing round of applause went up from the men gathered around the bar for Cocoa's performance. She thanked them, stepped down off the stage, and made her way through a throng of admirers vying for her attention, hoping for a private show either in the VIP room or anywhere else she would agree to. She politely waved them off and slid into the booth next to me.

She was beaming. "Hi guys, so what'd you think?"

I said, "You're great. How did you learn to stretch like that? It looks painful."

"I took dance lessons for ten years. Mostly ballet but a little modern, and a lot of ballroom."

I chuckled. "I should have guessed. Well, you brought the house down. When do you go back on?"

"After this next girl. She's got a fifteen-minute routine. This next one is going to be very cool. I'm doing a tango-like dance set to Deep Purple."

"Get out of here."

Vito said, "Hey Cocoa, what's with the outfit? Seems kind of—conservative, don't you think?"

I interjected. "I disagree. I think you look great, Cocoa. You look like a real nurse if you ask me and I like that."

Vito was taken back. "I didn't mean that you didn't look good; just a little—restrained is all."

"Hey Vito, this is one of those cases where less is more so lay off, all right?" I said.

"Jesus Christ, Cesari, I'm not criticizing. I'm just saying. Take it easy."

Cocoa looked at me as she responded to Vito. "John likes it and that's all that matters. I got to go now boys, her song's almost over." She squeezed my thigh, got up to leave, hesitated, and quickly leaned over to give me a kiss.

She purred, "See you back in the room."

I nodded and we watched her strut back to the stage.

"Cesari, you piss me off to no end. How do you do that?" Vito's voice dripped with frustration.

"I told you. It's my aftershave. You should try it."

"You're such an asshole."

A few minutes later, the lights went out and the room went quiet again. A booming voice reintroduced Cocoa to the audience, with cheers of approval, conservative outfit notwithstanding. The unmistakable hard rock rift from "Smoke on the Water" thundered into the room. Multiple spotlights waved back and forth across the stage, and Cocoa came flying out from her hidden position, grabbing onto and flying around the pole airborne from her momentum. The audience erupted as she moved effortlessly from classic ballroom to exotic pole dancing. The men were breathless from titillation and admiration. What she was doing was fresh and unheard of. At this rate, she was going to put the Kit Kat Club on the map. Watching her, I thought to myself that it might be worth a call to TripAdvisor or maybe even the *New Yorker*. This wasn't your average gentleman's club anymore.

After an hour of planning strategy with Vito and watching Cocoa drive strange men wild, I decided it was time to get a few hours' sleep, so I said good night to Vito and went up to the apartment. It was midnight and I fell asleep almost immediately, waking up just shy of two thirty as Cocoa joined me in bed. I didn't mind because I had set the alarm for three anyway.

I shook my head and rubbed my eyes, looking at the clock on the night table. She snuggled into me, wearing a T-shirt, and said, "I'm exhausted."

"You should be. You really put on quite the show. I don't think I've ever seen anything like that before."

"You really liked it?"

"Seriously, you raise this form of entertainment to a whole new level. I've never seen guys go wild like that."

She smiled. "Thank you. Not bad considering you tried to hide me in that boring outfit."

"I wasn't trying to hide you."

"Sure you were. You think I never dated guys who got possessive before? I let you have your way to make you happy."

Possessive?

She was a very smart Cocoa.

I was sleepy but waking up. I stretched and yawned. "How tired are you?" I asked.

"Can I take a rain check until the morning?"

I chuckled. "That's not what I meant. I mean are you up for a little adventure?"

She sat up in the bed, curious. "What kind of adventure?"

"I need someone to play the part of a nurse and you just passed your audition."

She laughed. "Right now? You're kidding, right? It's almost three in the morning."

"You don't have to do anything but stand next to me and look pretty, okay? Just wear the same nurse's uniform. It looked very authentic. I was impressed."

"It is authentic. I bought it online from a nurse's catalogue. I even got a phony ID and stethoscope to go along with it. The guys love it."

"Great, bring them along. Well, I'm sorry that you're tired but we'll need to get moving soon so how about I make us a pot of coffee."

Chapter 44

*W*e took a cab to St. Luke's and walked right in the main entrance. Cocoa wore her nurse's uniform with her ID in plain sight and I wrapped her stethoscope around my neck with my St. Matt's ID dangling from a lanyard. Nothing could have looked more natural, and the guards barely glanced in our direction.

"What's in the bag?" Cocoa asked, noting the small brown bag at my side.

"Duct tape."

She laughed and we found the main elevators, riding them up to the sixth floor. It was four thirty, and the floor that housed the outpatient endoscopy unit was dark and desolate. Cocoa and I walked to the main door, our adrenaline levels beginning to creep upward, as I fumbled in my pocket for Kelly's keys. I hadn't told Cocoa yet about what happened at Kelly's apartment. I thought it would be better if we all stayed focused.

The three keys she gave me were color coded with tape, making them easy to identify. The red key opened the main door, green opened the scope cabinet, and the blue key accessed the medication drawer. In addition to having a key lock, the medication drawer required a four-digit access code, which she gave me. It was the month and day of her birthday: 1002. I felt bad when she told me because she reminded me that I had forgotten it. I sighed. I really was a jerk. Maybe she was right. On the other hand, why should I have to remember the birthdays of girls who break up with me?

Touché, Cesari. Touché.

Proud of my logic, I felt better as I opened the door and flipped on the lights. The waiting room had about forty chairs arranged in rows facing three large reception windows. The entrance to the OR area itself was off to the right and we went in. There were six endoscopy rooms arranged in a circle around a central nursing station. The endoscopy rooms were numbered one through six, and our guy was scheduled for action in room one. The recovery room and exit were at the opposite end from where we entered, which was smart.

Patients had their procedures and were wheeled out away from the reception area into the recovery room. Families were brought back to recovery, and the patients were discharged from there out through a different door than the one they came in. You didn't want patients who had a bad experience being wheeled out through the front door where everyone could see them. This was good for us because only Phil McIntosh knew the full layout of the land, so he told his guys that there was only one way in and out of the department and that was through the front door, where he would station a guard. Another guy was assigned to stay with the car to make sure no one tampered with it, and the last guy in the detail stayed at home to watch the house and greet Lady Macbeth in case she came home early.

Cocoa followed me into room one and looked around as I searched for things and tried to get my bearings. The room was fairly spacious with a tall ceiling, sink, cabinets, a worktable, an equipment cart, and another door leading into a smaller cleaning area where the colonoscopes were sterilized in between cases. This cleaning area in turn led into the adjacent endoscopy room.

"This is so cool that you work in a place like this," Cocoa commented.

"Yeah, exactly like this. They're all pretty much set up in the same way. There it is." I pointed to the medication cart along the wall and walked up to it, inserting the key. I pressed the four-digit code into the keypad and the electronic drawer opened, revealing all sorts of fun stuff. Grabbing a handful of preloaded syringes of Versed and Fentanyl, I shoved them into my pocket and closed the drawer.

"Is that the same stuff you used on the doctor in New Jersey?"

"Yes, they're mild sedatives. They put people to sleep real quick and they don't remember anything when they wake up."

I walked over to the scope cabinet and unlocked it. It was quite large and deep, housing ten colonoscopes hanging from hooks along the back wall and a variety of other equipment on the floor. I emptied the cabinet, hanging all the scopes in the cleaning room.

"Cocoa, see if you fit in there."

She stepped easily into the cabinet and looked at me, smiling. "Is this where you're going to put him?"

"Yeah, I think so. The cleaning room might work but then he'd be out of my sight and I'm not sure I like that idea. Besides, someone might come into that area while we're working."

"So, when does Kelly get here? I can't wait to meet her."

I looked at her suspiciously. "She'll arrive at seven, a few minutes earlier than the other staff. Don't start anything, okay?"

"Relax, I know she's off limits. I just wanted to congratulate her on the upcoming wedding."

I looked at her sternly. "Whatever you do, don't bring that up. That's off limits too."

"For God's sake, you got a lot rules when it comes to your exes."

"Yes, I do."

"Okay, so who am I in all of this? You never said."

"If it comes to it, Kelly will introduce you as our boy's private duty nurse and that you are trained in endoscopy. Phil will confirm this, but the best thing is if you don't talk to anyone, just act busy, stay in the room, and do whatever Kelly tells you to. It will seem irregular but no one's going to argue with the Secret Service about something like this."

She nodded.

I looked at my watch. "Okay, we have plenty of time. I spotted the men's locker room when we entered, I'll go there and change into scrubs and be back in five minutes. Don't move a muscle."

"I won't."

I walked to the locker room, quickly changed, and donned a surgical mask and hat. I put the syringes of Versed and Fentanyl into my shirt pocket. There was an empty trash bin with a plastic liner that I removed and threw my clothes into. I hustled back to Cocoa, trash bag in hand. I couldn't have been gone more than ten minutes, but looking through the porthole of the swinging door, I found her deep in conversation with a bearded man of about forty-five. She had smartly maneuvered him so that his back was to me as she smiled and flirted her way through her predicament.

He was a good-looking, average height and build kind of guy, and I hated what I was about to do. Keep him talking, Cocoa. I saw her eyes dart in my direction as she became aware of my presence and kept him engaged, facing away from me. Placing my bag of clothes gently on the floor, I drew a ten-milligram syringe of Versed out of my pocket and took the cap off. I slowly and stealthily pushed the door open and stepped into the room. He was less than ten feet away and clearly in a Cocoa-induced hypnotic trance.

She giggled innocently and batted her eyes seductively. "I just started nursing school six months ago and I was so excited about starting my rotation today, I couldn't sleep. I just live around the block so I thought I would come in early and familiarize myself with the place."

Confused but nonetheless delighted by this extraordinary find, he continued his brazen flirtation. He was also understandably excited about his case and had come in very early. I stepped closer.

"Are you sure they are going to let you in on this case, Cocoa?" He studied her ID. "He's a political VIP. I don't know how much they told you about him."

She smiled and swayed. "I don't know anything about that, Doctor. My supervisor just told me to show up on time, look sharp and be ready to work. So here I am." She curtsied and he chuckled. I was three feet away now with the syringe in my right hand.

"So what kind of name is that—Cocoa?"

I threw my left arm around his neck suddenly and jerked him backward toward me, twisting his head violently to the left, exposing his neck. Jabbing the needle up to its hilt into the general vicinity of his jugular, I depressed the plunger fully, and before he even had the chance to register surprise, ten milligrams of Versed unloaded into him all at once. It would take a few seconds to kick in so I dropped the hypodermic and placed my right arm under his, locking my hands tightly. He struggled frantically to escape the headlock but to no avail. He clawed at the air in fear and surprise and lunged backward trying to dislodge me. Rather than let him thrash me about, I chose to fall to the ground deliberately and as I did, wrapped my legs around him. He grunted and squirmed but was rapidly losing strength as the sedative took effect so I eased up on his airway as he relaxed. Cocoa had stepped away during my attack, frozen in place by the sudden violence. She came forward now to help me up as the doctor started snoring.

"Thanks, Cocoa. Get me the duct tape. I left it on the counter by the sink."

She brought it to me and I secured his ankles and then his hands behind his back.

"Now for the hard part. We're going to lift him into the scope cabinet, but first let me get one of those colonoscopes from the other room."

He was about 180 lbs. which wasn't too bad, and although he was sleepy and out of it he wasn't totally dead weight. I wrapped a colonoscope around his chest and under his arms, tying it into a knot behind him. Then, through a combination of lifting, dragging, and begging him to cooperate Cocoa and I were able to hoist him up onto one of the hooks in the cabinet, suspended by the colonoscope tied around him. He struggled drunkenly during this process but fell asleep again, once we stopped pushing and prodding him. For good measure, I slammed another syringe full of Versed into his thigh. Dangling from the hook, his feet barely reaching the floor, I couldn't help but feel bad for the nurse that found him. She would definitely need counseling. The last thing I did before locking him in the cabinet was to slap a piece of tape over his mouth and grab his hospital ID badge off his scrub shirt.

Lawrence Brandt, MD.

"Sorry, Larry."

Chapter 45

They wheeled the patient into the room, and I stood discreetly off to one side while he flirted with Cocoa and Kelly. So far, everything had gone as planned. He had been admitted, an IV started and Cocoa's presence adequately explained. They had already turned him on his left side away from me. I had the surgical mask and hat on and had kept my distance until now. I nodded at Phil and he turned to the patient.

Phil asked respectfully, "Sir, do you want me to stay in the room or leave?"

"I think I'll be fine Phil. You can wait outside. I've been to this rodeo before. No point in you staring at my naked butt. I wouldn't want you to get all tingly," he chuckled in that unmistakable Midwestern drawl. I glanced at Phil, who bit his lip, and I made a mental note to never use that joke again.

He said, "I promise I won't, Mr. President."

"Just kidding, Phil, don't get your panties in a bunch."

Gilliam Monroe Clifton, Gill Clifton, two-term president of the United States of America. Gill to his friends, Bucky to his drinking buddies. The press called him Lucky Bucky because no matter what kind of shit he got into he always managed to come out smelling like a rose.

As Phil left the room, Kelly dimmed the lights to an appropriate level and I stepped up close behind Bucky. "How are you today, Mr. President?"

"I'm doing much better since meeting Cocoa and Kelly, Larry. You girls certainly are lovely. What about you, Larry? Phil tells me you're a little under the weather. You certainly don't sound like yourself. Of course, I haven't seen you in a year either."

Kelly stood in front of him, watching his oxygen and heart rate monitors. Cocoa stood next to me on my left. "I woke not feeling quite right but I'm okay. The mask is just a precaution. Are you ready to get started, Mr. President?"

"Well, I'd love to talk to Cocoa some more. Does she have to stand behind me like that, Lar? Can't she switch places with Kelly? No offense Miss Kelly, I like black people, I really do, especially little cuties like you, but it looks as if you're taken. Maybe when you deliver and have some time to get back in shape we can talk. And Lar, you can call me Gill." Kelly was pissed but bit her tongue.

"Why not Bucky?"

He chuckled. "Sure, why not as long as we're going to be intimate."

"Give him two milligrams of Versed, Kelly. Thank you."

We waited for the medication to take effect, and both Cocoa's and Kelly's eyes darted nervously back and forth.

"So Cocoa, you must be married, right?" he asked.

"No, Mr. President, I'm not."

"Hot damn, I knew today was going to be my lucky day. Larry, call heaven and report a missing angel."

Cocoa didn't say anything, but Kelly rolled her eyes at me and I made a serious face. "Are you starting to feel more relaxed, Mr. President?"

"I am, Larry. I definitely am, but I think I'd like one more martini before I pop the big question to Cocoa."

I nodded to Kelly. "Give him another one of Versed, please." I watched as she depressed the plunger on the syringe some more.

"Larry, I honestly don't know how you can you stand working with such beautiful women. It must be terribly distracting."

"Well, I've learned how to tune it out."

Both women chuckled.

"Oh there it is. I feel it now, Larry. Oh yeah, I'm feeling it now, baby. I'm going to Lala land for sure. Cocoa, promise me that you'll be waiting for me when I wake up."

I looked at Cocoa, nodding.

"I promise, Mr. President."

"Okay, Larry, give it your best shot, and remember, I expect flowers and a phone call from you in the morning."

With him in a relaxed twilight, I lubricated the tip of the scope and inserted it as we watched on the video screen next to Kelly on her side of the stretcher. I maneuvered the instrument with minimal effort and noted some minor findings here and there. He had diverticulosis, which were little pockets in the bowel wall, a common finding in his age group. There were also several small polyps, which I left alone. He grunted and let out a small groan every now and then as the scope made an uncomfortable turn, but I eventually made it to the cecum, the proximal end of the colon where the large intestine meets the small intestine and where the internal opening of the appendix can be found. The cecum is the thinnest and weakest part of the colon for some reason, and it is the part that could most easily be traumatically damaged.

I leaned over and shook him. "Wake up, Bucky."

His eyes popped open. "Is it over, already, Larry. Sir, you are an artist."

"Not quite over yet, sir."

I looked at the digital wall clock. It had been just under ten minutes since we started. I promised Phil that I would take no longer than thirty minutes. If he didn't check in at that point, it would seem odd. There was plenty of time.

Bucky looked at the screen and asked, "Is that me?"

I said, "Quiet now, Bucky, I need to ask you a few questions." To emphasize the point I twisted the scope clockwise, causing him to yelp as his intestines twisted internally.

"Whoa, Larry, take it easy. What's on your mind, brother?"

"Have you ever been to Disney?"

While his head cleared and he thought that one over, I had Cocoa hand me a needle injector, which I snaked through the colonoscope until it showed up on the screen in front of us.

"Why do you ask, Larry?"

"A young girl named Marguerite Varga was murdered there last week on Christmas Eve. She played Snow White in the Magic Kingdom and I was wondering if you knew anything about it?"

I turned to Cocoa. "Push the handle in, Cocoa." As she did, a very sharp needle emerged on the screen for all to see.

"I'm sorry to hear that, Lar, but why would you wake your president up out of a sound sleep to ask him a question like that?"

I twisted the scope again, only this time a little harder, and he cried out in pain as his colon pulled and tugged unnaturally against its attachments. "Because you were fucking her, asshole, and you're not my president anymore. You're my ex-president."

He caught his breath and recovered. "Easy son, you're entering dangerous waters now and I'm not sure you know how to swim."

"I've seen the video, Bucky. I know Consuela was blackmailing you. Marguerite is dead, Helena committed suicide, and someone's trying to kill Cinderella. I think you have some explaining to do."

"When did you become a Republican, Larry?"

"Have it your way. I ruthlessly torqued the scope, and he started to howl in earnest. Cocoa reached around and covered his mouth with her hand. He tried to pull her hands away but Kelly grabbed his wrists, preventing him. His heart rate monitor screeched shrilly and I eased up on the scope. He started to perspire and was breathing hard, trying to collect himself.

"Larry, you are so out of your league."

I said, "Watch the screen carefully, Bucky."

He turned his head to see better. I pressed the point of the needle into the wall of the colon, enough to draw blood but not enough to pierce through it.

"What are you doing?" he asked.

"I'm going to keep the point of the needle pressed into your colon like that. If you don't tell me what I want to hear I am going to start popping holes through the wall, allowing millions of bacteria to find a new home in your peritoneal cavity. You will subsequently develop an agonizing case of peritonitis, and at your age, I would only give you a fifty-fifty chance of survival even with surgery. So think carefully about your next answer."

"Did you know Marguerite was pregnant?"

He hesitated, looked at the needle and said flatly, "Yes."

"Who ordered her murder?"

"It wasn't me."

I started twisting the scope and he flinched. "So who then?" I demanded.

He didn't answer me.

I twisted harder and he clenched his teeth, groaning, but he didn't scream or move as he kept his eyes glued to the needle. I relaxed the scope, and he let out a deep breath and then did something unexpected. He started to cry.

Kelly looked at me, and I knew I had to end this soon. She was starting to get upset. This wasn't her style. Cocoa didn't seem as distressed. Two different personalities. I knew I had him on the ropes. He was getting ready to crack and just needed to be nudged in the right direction.

"Keep looking at the screen," I ordered.

I pushed the needle in deeply and the colon wall tented as it stretched thin, causing him to moan.

He pleaded. "Oh my God that hurts, Larry. Please stop."

"I feel your pain, Bucky. Now tell me, who ordered Marguerite's murder?" I demanded.

Silence, so I twisted the scope hard and the colon wall looked as if it couldn't take much more. Kelly looked like she was going to get sick. He finally broke and whimpered hoarsely. "It was Hildegarde." I relaxed the scope.

"Hildegarde? Your wife?" We all looked at each other in astonishment.

"Yes."

"Explain and be quick about it. I'm running out of patience." I looked at the wall clock.

He said, "Marguerite was crazy. She wanted me to run away with her and play house. She didn't understand that it was only fun and games for me. She thought it was all real. When I refused, she stopped using her birth control. She thought getting pregnant would force me to marry her. I didn't know what to do and then Consuela came to the house and showed us the video and the doctor's report that Marguerite was pregnant. Hildegarde went into a rage. I swear I've never seen her like that before."

"I don't understand, Bucky, but why kill everybody? Hurry up, I don't have all day."

He took a breath, wiping tears from his eyes. "Hil is an ambitious woman; she has her eyes set on the White House. She wasn't about to let Consuela and Marguerite upset the apple cart with a scandal like that going into an election year so she fought back with everything she had. She decided that anybody who knew anything had to be eliminated. I didn't know what was going on at first, at least not until those agents got burned up in Rochester going after Cinderella."

"So who is Consuela anyway?"

"She's Raul Varga's mistress and right hand man. They're Argentine mafia, mercenaries, gunrunners, you name it, and she's more ruthless than any ten terrorists combined. When your government wants something nasty done and doesn't want to be involved, it calls on people like Raul and Consuela, but she overplayed her hand this time. Threatening Hil's political future like that was the equivalent of lighting the fuse on a stick of dynamite."

"Have you spoken to either Consuela or Raul since the fireworks started to try to negotiate?"

"Trust me. If I could have reached them, I would have, but they're like ghosts, which is why they're so valuable to us. No one ever sees them or knows they're coming and they leave without a trace. The problem is Hil decided to act quickly and get to Consuela before she knew anything was coming, but that didn't work and now you know the rest."

"Can you call off Hildegarde? Maybe we can end this thing before anyone else gets hurt."

He laughed sarcastically. "Are you kidding? Right now she's so angry, I'll be lucky if I don't wind up at the bottom of the wave pool at Typhoon Lagoon wearing a pair of cement shoes. No, there's not a chance of calling her off. Besides, even on a good day she wouldn't listen to me. Nothing is going to stop her until she sees Consuela's head on a platter—and Cinderella's; that I can guarantee you."

"Fine, but how was Hildegarde able to swing a team of agents for this purpose? She's not president yet."

"C'mon, Larry, I thought you were smart. She's been in and out of the White House and Capitol building for more than twenty-five years. She's got more contacts and pull up there than the last ten presidents combined. You add that to the fact that she's a serious contender for the White House herself and you'll find volunteers to do her bidding crawling out of the woodwork."

I thought that one over. Unfortunately, it made sense. "Is Raul involved in this?"

He chuckled. "I doubt it."

I was about to ask him what was so funny when Cocoa nudged me to look at the clock again. Time was running out.

"Kelly, squirt him with five of Versed."

She looked alarmed. "That's a lot for an old man."

"He's not that old and we don't want him to remember anything, so please."

I watched as she emptied the syringe into his IV and I quickly withdrew the scope, tossing it onto the table behind me. I turned back to Bucky. "One last thing, asshole. What exactly did Consuela want from you?" He started to drift off again so I shook him roughly and his eyes opened.

"What did Consuela want?"

Just as his eyes closed again he whispered almost inaudibly. "She wanted us to kill Raul for her and make it look like an accident. She wants the whole enchilada for herself."

Fuck.

"Quick, Kelly, come over here and sit on the floor. I'll be as gentle as I can. I promise." I helped her get down on the floor in front of the scope cabinet and then gently and loosely wound duct tape around her ankles and wrists.

"Cesari, won't that look suspicious? I'm supposed to be a captive."

"Phil's going to be the first to come into the room, and before he does anything else he knows to unrestrain you. After that, who's going to care? We're just trying to give an illusion here in case there's someone with him when he comes in. And by the way, when the door does open don't forget you're supposed to be unconscious. Remember, I injected you with a sedative just like the guy in the cabinet."

She nodded. "I got it."

"Cocoa, give me Bucky's pillow. He doesn't need it anymore."

Cocoa grabbed the pillow from under Bucky's head and handed it to me. I fluffed and placed it gently behind Kelly's head and back.

"How's that?"

She smiled. "I'm fine, thank you. You were never this nice to me when we were going out."

"Be quiet, I have to put a strip of tape over your mouth." I ripped off a piece of duct tape and just as I was about to cover her mouth with it, I caught her looking at me. I paused, looking back. I was inches away from her face and pressed my lips against hers, giving her the most tender kiss I had ever given any woman in my entire life. She didn't offer any resistance nor say anything as I gently put the tape over her mouth, barely touching her. One sneeze and it would come flying off.

I leaned close to her ear and whispered, "I love you, Miss Kelly."

She whispered back, "I know."

I looked at the clock. One minute to go. Cocoa and I bolted into the cleaning room and from there into the central nursing station. The nurse there saw us as we rushed by and demanded, "What's going? Is everything all right in there?"

I shouted, "No. The president's in full cardiac arrest. Call a code, quickly."

She screamed "Oh my God!" and ran to her phone to call for help.

We sprinted down the hallway into the recovery room screaming "Fire!" and everybody there jumped up in panic. I saw the fire alarm on the wall, broke the glass, and pulled the lever. The entire hospital erupted in noise and flashing lights as Cocoa and I raced down the nearest stairwell to find Vito waiting for us in the Mercedes. Safely in the car, we took off down Eighth Avenue toward the Kit Kat Club. Cocoa was flushed from excitement in the backseat.

"How'd it go?" Vito asked, weaving through traffic.

"We're here, aren't we?"

Cocoa said, "That was the most exciting thing I've ever done in my entire life."

Considering her lifestyle, that was quite a statement. I turned to look at her. "Just remember one thing, Cocoa Puff."

She smiled. "What's that?"

"Today never happened."

"Got it."

Vito said, "Amen. What now, Cesari?"

"Cocoa and I need a nap."

Chapter 46

My eyes fluttered open at around three p.m. and I looked around groggily, wondering where I was. Cocoa lay next to me, the sounds of her gentle breathing told me she was sleeping soundly. My head gradually cleared and I sat up, stretching. I wasn't wearing anything and couldn't quite remember how I got that way. I hadn't been this fatigued in ages. I decided to let Cocoa sleep while I showered and shaved.

As the hot water ran over me, I held onto the nozzle for support. My butt was still sore but improving. The pain helped me wake up. For some reason, I did my best thinking—and singing, and sometimes, even a little dancing—in the shower.

The question now was what to do? Nothing I found out so far could be proven in a court of law, which meant that the guilty parties would go scot-free. This was always the problem with the rich and powerful. In some countries, you steal an apple and they cut your hand off. In others, you steal the whole damn country and live like a king the rest of your life with everybody telling you how great you are. Hildegarde was an ambitious bitch capable of murder, so in that sense she might make a great world leader, depending on which side of the aisle you fell. Consuela was also quite the piece of work, making a play for Raul's job while sharing his bed. At the same time, both of them would probably have the nerve to call Cocoa a whore. You had to love modern women.

The bathroom door opened, and I heard someone come in and sit on the toilet.

"Good afternoon, sleepy head," I said cheerfully, thinking it was Cocoa.

"What's so good about it?" a grumpy voice asked.

Fuck.

I was annoyed. "Lola, in case you hadn't noticed, the bathroom is occupied."

"I'll be done in a minute so relax."

For crying out loud.

She flushed and as she opened the door to leave, I called out, "You forgot to wash your hands." She slammed the door in response.

God, she was a piece of work.

I finished showering, dried off, shaved, and brushed my teeth. Cocoa had roused by this time and wandered into the kitchen to make coffee. I was in her bedroom tying my sneakers when Herman's cell phone went off.

"Yeah."

"It's Phil. Look, I can't talk long. Have you seen the news?"

"No, I've been sleeping all day. What's up?"

"He didn't wake up."

"What do you mean?"

"I mean he didn't wake up. He stopped breathing and had to be intubated. He's in the ICU right now recovering slowly. They think he'll be okay though. The FBI are involved now and they're calling it an assassination attempt."

I thought about that. Maybe it was. "Does he remember anything?"

"Well, he's still too critical so it's hard to say. He's starting to move around a little but he's very groggy and may have suffered a mild heart attack. This was the first chance I had to call you."

"Thanks for the update. I'm sorry about that. I didn't think I gave him that much juice. At any rate, I'm glad you called. You'll be happy to know he spilled his guts about everything."

"Well, at least we have that. So what did he say, who's responsible for all the mayhem?"

"His wife, Hildegarde."

"Get out. I knew she was a ruthless political animal but I wouldn't have guessed she'd go this far."

"Apparently, she's so close to being the leader of this great democracy that she feels murdering a nineteen year old girl is justifiable homicide at least that's the way Bucky tells it."

"So what happened?"

"Consuela had them by the balls with the videotape but the icing on the cake was that Marguerite was pregnant. Although our power couple are pretty slick and might have laughed off the hooker angle, Hildegarde realized that Marguerite's pregnancy would have been the straw that broke the camel's back in terms of public opinion, so she unleashed hell on everyone involved using a rogue team of agents she solicited through her contacts on the hill."

"Fuck, all this is about a cat fight? I can't believe it. So what was Consuela after?"

"Same thing as Hildegarde, power, of course. She was tired of playing second fiddle to Raul and thought it was time for a promotion. She wanted Hildegarde and Bucky to take Raul out for her and anoint her his successor. This way his contacts wouldn't be pissed at her. You gay guys are so fucking lucky. I have to put up with this kind of insanity every day."

He chuckled into the phone. "Yeah, I'm sure. You know, Cesari, in a different life, we might have been friends."

"We almost killed an ex-president together, Phil. I'd say we were friends right now. By the way, how are the doctor and the nurse?"

"The doc has a headache and your friend, Kelly, is fine. Everyone thinks she was a victim like he was. In all the chaos, no one's sure what the hell happened. Of course, that might all change when the dust settles. On the other hand, if we can prove that he and his wife are the scumbags we think they are I'm sure the dogs of war will be called off, if you know what I mean? Look, there's one more thing and then I have to go."

"I'm listening."

"Something important is happening at the house in Mount Kisco tonight, and I don't know what. Hildegarde called me up to tell me she's arriving at eight p.m. tonight and expecting company. She wants me and at least one other agent to meet her there and quote unquote, be loaded for bear."

"Really, she said it just like that?"

"Yeah, can you believe that? Whatever is happening is apparently more important than coming to see her husband in the ICU."

"No way. She's not going to visit him?"

"Who cares? Everyone knows their marriage is a sham anyway."

"You're right. It just surprised me to hear it like that. It seems so cold."

"It is cold, Cesari. That's what politics does to people. Anyway, I thought you'd be interested in knowing because you're already up to your eyeballs in shit."

"So what do you think it means, Phil?"

"You tell me, Cesari. You seem like a bright guy. She's in the middle of a firefight with Consuela, her husband's hospitalized, and she suddenly decides to entertain company with armed security? Obviously, somebody very germane to the current crisis is coming to town."

"Raul?"

"I don't know that for a fact and I can't tell you what to do, Cesari, but I can tell you that the cellar doors at the back of the house are sometimes left unlocked. I can also tell you that because of all of the day's confusion, someone may have inadvertently forgotten to set the home's alarm system."

"What about the other agents?"

"Two will stay here at the hospital with Bucky and there will be one other besides me at the house. I'm not sure yet what to do about him. I don't want him hurt. I may have him take the dog for a long walk to get him out of the house."

"Dog? What dog?"

"Relax, they have a big dog they use to ward off strangers. It's a rescue dog they picked up a year ago while they were pressing the flesh in some small town upstate. They were visiting some local animal shelter for a photo-op and trying to look like heroes to the local yokels. They adopted one of the dogs that was scheduled to be put down."

I was surprised by this. "Really? I have to admit, that sounds like an awfully nice thing to do."

"I guess on paper maybe, except adopting a dog, especially a big dog, is almost like adopting a child, Cesari. They're like people. They require attention and affection—lots of affection, and this one gets none of that from them. She's ignored, kept outside most of the time, and crated up when she's in the house. The agents are the only ones who spend any time with her at all, which is a shame because she's actually pretty sweet. Anyway, she shouldn't be a problem. Just be aware. I don't want you to freak if you see her. She's enormous and well over two hundred pounds, probably more like two hundred and fifty pounds. The problem is I don't know how she'll react to a stranger."

I sighed into the phone. "Fuck. What kind of dog?"

"An English mastiff."

"Really? That's interesting."

"Why is that?"

"It's complicated, but I almost adopted one myself a while back. Well, thanks for the heads up, Phil."

"Okay, Cesari, I've got to go. I don't know what's going to happen tonight but I'll do my best to try not to shoot you. Either way, this is my last night on the job so it's been nice knowing you."

"You're resigning?"

"Yes, I've had enough of this bullshit. I've had enough of politics. I've had enough of these awful human beings that claim to represent us, the people, and I don't just mean these two. These guys are just the tip of the iceberg. They're all the same these politicians, but most of all I'm tired and ashamed of hiding who I really am. Herman and I have some money saved up. We may go on a long vacation before deciding what our long-term plans are. We may even get married."

"Married?"

"Yeah, you got a problem with that? Let me guess, you're against gay marriage."

"I'm against all marriage, gay or straight. Why spoil the fun? I don't know who invented marriage, Phil, but I assure you, it wasn't a bachelor."

He laughed. "You're such an asshole, Cesari."

"So I've been told over and over. Well Phil, it may not be much consolation for you, but I believe you are a really good person and the kind of guy we need doing the work you do."

"Thanks, but I suspect after the all the facts are in, a lot of people are going to disagree with you."

"That's always how it is, Phil. When you take a stand for something, you put yourself out there for others to criticize, mock, and pass judgement on. The guys who play it safe get rewarded with big pensions and an office with a view of Central Park, but it's the guy who stands up and says I won't take it anymore who is the one that the history books remember. Some day when you have the time you should read the life story of Winston Churchill. It's very inspiring, and I think you'll appreciate it. For years, in the 1930s he warned about the rise of Hitler and the Nazis but no one listened because it was inconvenient. The liberals painted him as an out-of-touch war monger, and then one day millions of Jews, gypsies, and dissidents started disappearing into concentration camps and ovens. Almost, overnight Churchill became a hero and living legend, leading his country out of darkness. I wish I had just half the balls that guy had."

"Great. I'll tell that to the judge at my sentencing. Your honor, you're making a big mistake. I'm no different than Winston Churchill."

I chuckled. "You can always call me as a character witness."

"I feel better already," he said wryly.

"Phil, you've got more patriotism and honor in one fingertip than ninety percent of those assholes in Congress. Don't give up, all right? If you give up, what's going to happen to the rest of us?"

He was quiet for a while digesting that. "Look, I've got to go now. Thanks for the pep talk."

I walked into the kitchen and poured myself a cup of coffee, sitting next to Cocoa as she sipped hers from a mug that had *Cocoa* stenciled on it.

"Phil?" she asked, referring to my phone call.

"Yeah, he's come a long way since we first met."

She nodded. "So is everything going to be okay? I couldn't help overhearing some of the conversation."

"Well, things are uncertain but I don't think anyone's going to the electric chair just yet. Why don't you get dressed and I'll fill you in on the details over dinner. I need to make another call right now."

She finished her coffee and headed off to the bathroom to shower. Meanwhile, I dialed Kelly.

"Hi, John, I was wondering if you'd call."

"Hi, Kel, how are you feeling?"

"I'm fine. Everybody thinks I'm some sort of hero because of my *ordeal*," she chuckled.

"That's good. So you didn't go into premature labor?"

"No. Really, I'm fine. I wish I could say the same for Dr. Brandt. He is so pissed off and embarrassed. Thank God he can't recall too much. I overheard him talking to the police and FBI and he told them that he remembered talking to some student nurse but couldn't describe her or recall her name. I told them the same thing only I told them I thought it was a male student nurse to throw them off. I kept it short and sweet like you told me to. You've got to love Versed."

"It really is a great amnestic agent. Let's hope it has the same effect on President Asshole in the ICU."

She laughed, "Cesari, you crack me up. Thankfully, it looks like he's going to be okay. You heard what happened, right?"

"Yeah, I heard. I spoke to Phil just a little while ago and he gave me an update. Oh well, I'm glad you're okay, Kel. Have a good night. I guess I'll let you go now."

"John…"

"Yes…?"

"I shouldn't tell you this, and I know it's ridiculous, but—I had fun today, despite everything."

I chuckled. "Like old times."

"Yeah, a little."

"By the way, any word from Omar?"

She didn't say anything.

"That's okay, Kel. I know you have a lot to think about."

"Thank you, John, and—stay in touch."

"Really?"

"Really."

Chapter 47

"*I* saw you kiss Kelly," Cocoa said. We sat across from each other in a small Italian restaurant on Third Avenue, not too far from the parking garage that housed the Mercedes. Between my legs was the duffel bag with the crowbar and Remington pistol grip shotgun I had from Florida.

I took a sip of wine and studied her, trying to determine her mood. "I couldn't help myself. I never could resist a girl bound with duct tape."

"I'm serious. I saw you."

"So, I had to sit through two hours of watching middle-aged men shove twenty dollar bills into your garters. I think we're even."

She pouted. "It's not the same thing."

I rolled my eyes and chuckled. "Oh please. It's worse."

"No, it's not. That's my job."

"Well maybe I'm a licensed girl kisser and that's my job. Have you ever thought about that?" I gave her smug look.

She finally relented and smiled. "You'd like that, wouldn't you?"

As we laughed, our waiter served us dinner. I had penne with vodka sauce and sausage, and Cocoa had a Caesar salad with grilled chicken. An order of garlic bread sat on a plate between us next to a half carafe of house Chianti. We had time to kill and leisurely finished off our dinner with espresso and tiramisu.

Signaling the waiter for the bill, I said, "Time to go and get the lay of the land, Cocoa. Are you in?"

"I'm in."

We picked up the Mercedes from the garage, gassed up, and drove up the West Side Highway to the Bronx, merging onto 87N. By the Tappanzee Bridge, we picked up the Cross Westchester Expressway eastbound, which brought us to the Saw Mill River Parkway north to Mount Kisco. All told, the trip took close to an hour and half, and we got off the highway close to ten-thirty, parking the car on a quiet street a couple of hundred feet from the house. It was very dark with only a sliver of moonlight shining down. Cocoa was cold, and I turned the heat up in the car.

"The temperature's dropping," I noted, looking at the car's outside thermometer reading. It was mid-thirties now and snowing lightly. The forecast was for two to three inches and the temperature was predicted to drop into the mid-twenties. I wore a thick wool sweater with a black windbreaker, knit hat, and black leather gloves. Cocoa wore a medium-weight sweater and leather jacket. She was going to stay in the car where she would be all right.

"How long do you think you'll be in there?" she asked.

"Hard to say. If I get killed, then probably all night."

She looked concerned. "Don't make jokes like that. Is there anything I should be doing while I wait?"

"Not really, just stay alert and keep your phone on. If I don't come out by midnight or call you shortly thereafter, then you should get the hell out of here."

"Just leave? You can't be serious? I'm not going to just leave you here."

"Cocoa, honey, there's nothing you're going to be able to do anyway."

"Should I call the police at least?"

I thought that one over and doubted the police could do anything unless Phil requested their help. "I guess it couldn't hurt, but get yourself out of here first, all right?"

She nodded. "When are you going in?"

I looked at the car clock. "In half an hour. Phil said he was going to disarm the security system at eleven and send the other guard out to walk the dog to get them out of the house."

"Aren't you afraid of running into the dog and the other agent?"

"It's a risk for sure, but it's a big property, almost five acres, and there's a pre-defined route they always use so I should be able to stay out of their way. They'll start off on the north side of the house and I'll approach from the south. I'm worried more about the snow. Look at it."

It was coming down a lot heavier than predicted and had pretty much buried the windshield and windows so that we couldn't see out. On the other hand, that meant prying eyes couldn't see in either.

Cocoa glanced around. "So what do you think?"

"I don't know what to think, but this woman has a lot of explaining to do, and I'm way past the point of caring what the consequences are."

"That's a nice speech, but that's not what I meant."

I looked at her in the dark. "Then what did you mean?"

She unbuckled her seatbelt and got onto her knees, leaning over to put her arms around me. "I meant we have thirty minutes alone in the dark and no one can see in the car."

"Cocoa, I know I don't show it, but I'm under a lot of stress right now."

"I can help you with that." She kissed me tenderly at first and then more passionately, locking lips and tongues, and I felt my brain go on fire. I caught my breath, felt my pulse race and blood pressure rise. Damn.

Gently pushing her away I said, "Is this supposed to be the condemned man's last meal?"

She didn't say anything, just pressed her lips into mine again with even more intensity, and I could tell that she had worked herself up into a fever. We were close to the "I'm not taking no for an answer stage" that women think is their sole prerogative.

I said, "Okay, let's just say that I agree to this. How do you expect it to happen?" It was a decent sized sedan but with the center console separating the two front seats she already looked uncomfortable, and then there was the issue of clothing.

She smiled seductively at me. "Listen, if you're going to die tonight, then I want you to be thinking about me so we're just going to have to figure it out."

I chuckled. "If I die tonight it will most likely be because I was thinking about you and not what I should be doing."

She liked that and with her arms around my neck, looked deeply into my eyes. Panting, she inched and squirmed her way over the console onto me, and with her back up against the steering wheel said, "Push the car seat back and recline it as far as it will go. And then I want you to do something for me."

"What's that?"

She grabbed me roughly and said. "Shut up and kiss me."

Chapter 48

Leaning down, I looked at her through the open driver's side window. Her tousled hair and clothing hinting at what had just taken place, she looked like the cat that ate the canary.

"Great, now I'm behind schedule," I said.

She smiled. "Aww isn't that too bad."

I laughed, leaned in the window, and kissed her good-bye, waving one last time as I walked away. I forced myself to shrug her off and refocus as I jogged in the newly fallen snow toward the house, holding the duffel bag with the weapons. Cocoa was a force to be reckoned with for sure.

Once I was within a hundred feet of the property, I slowed down and stepped onto the barely visible lawn. It was a very old and wooded neighborhood with large evergreen trees and shrubbery everywhere. The lots were very large, and with the snowfall I couldn't even see another home from my vantage point so it was not hard at all to stay out of sight as I moved toward the rear of the house. I kept a healthy twenty to thirty yards away to the side of the two-story Tudor style brick and frame home, darting from bush to bush, moving closer with every step. There was some light from the house but it was getting darker the farther back I got, and I hoped I didn't trip or stumble. Kelly and I had lived in upstate New York a couple of years ago, and I had almost broken my ankle one night in a groundhog hole. I had brought a small flashlight with me but really didn't want to turn it on just yet.

Crouching behind a large arborvitae I relaxed a little and studied my surroundings. In the rear of the house, there was a detached two-car garage that wasn't visible from the road and a set of angled, partially snow-covered, cellar doors against the back wall of the house and just to the side of an enclosed wood porch. Cellar doors like that usually dead bolted from inside, but these would be unlocked tonight, according to Phil.

The only problem now was that I was still thirty yards from the house and there was no further shrubbery to conceal my approach. It was snowing pretty hard now and visibility was poor so I weighed the pros and cons. Phil was inside and wouldn't say anything if he saw a guy creeping up to the back because he knew it would be me, and the other guy was on patrol outside somewhere with the dog, but who else was in the house with Hildegarde and would they be watching? I was covered in wet, heavy snow and starting to shiver from the falling temperature. I had to act soon.

I took a step forward and slammed myself flat to the ground. The back door had opened and someone had stepped onto the enclosed porch to smoke a cigarette. The light from the house suggested a young, well-built man wearing a suit and tie. It wasn't Phil but given the circumstances he might have been the other person's security. Bodyguards were like chicks: they always traveled in pairs so there must be another one somewhere. I watched him carefully as he puffed away, casually peering into the darkness of the woods behind me. He looked very relaxed, which was a mistake because as he turned to one side, I saw the silhouette of another person suddenly rise up out of the shadows of the porch, grab him by the neck, and pull him backward off balance. Steel briefly glinted in the light from the doorway as his assailant quickly slashed his throat. He struggled briefly, futilely, and died silently, and I watched as his body was dragged away from the door and his attacker disappeared from sight again.

Shit. What the fuck was going on? I had a big decision to make now and I did. Adrenaline surging through my body, I suddenly felt warm again. I retrieved the shotgun from the duffel bag and flipped the safety to off. Things had just escalated past the crowbar stage so I decided to leave it and the duffel bag there in the snow beneath a large evergreen shrub. I cancelled the idea of going into the basement now because of what had just happened. I needed to know who was hiding on the porch. Besides, if they were still there, they might hear the cellar doors open anyway.

On my belly, I snaked carefully to the bottom of the three wood steps of the porch and gradually rose to a crouching position, ascending them slowly and quietly, all senses on red alert. Kneeling at the top in an inch of wet snow, I reached out and pulled open the screen door with care. It creaked ever so slightly as most old doors do and I froze waiting to have my throat slit, but nothing happened so I proceeded through the half open door and waited for a response as I smelled blood and saw the trail of slick fluid.

Looking back and forth, I eventually satisfied myself that I was alone. Whoever it was had left through another door off to the far side of the porch, about thirty feet away. In the dark, I could see the outline of the body partially tucked under a wood glider. My instincts told me it was time to go into action so I shook off the snow, and took a deep breath, trying to slow my heart rate.

I opened the back door and let myself into the kitchen. From a room somewhere further in, I heard the sounds of a television but nothing else. A wall clock said it was eleven-thirty.

Someone had put a pot of tea on and I thought it might have been the dead guy on the porch, otherwise it was a pretty ordinary kitchen with a table, chairs, and swinging door leading to the rest of the home. I crept forward slowly, shotgun leading the way, and gently pushed open the door, pausing as I found myself in a five foot wide, long corridor. Directly ahead was a dark, empty dining room and to my left farther down the hall was the main entrance to the house and a large archway leading into the living room on the right. There was a television set on and someone was watching the news. I felt my heart rate climbing, and I took another deep breath, letting it out slowly as I hugged the wall and inched toward the living room.

Several more steps brought me to the edge of a large rounded archway, and I heard people talking. I now had a partial view of the room and could see a large-screen television with a couple of talking heads discussing what was best for the country. There were several large, comfortable looking chairs and a coffee table, and although I was sure there was a couch somewhere, I could only see about a third of the room from my vantage point as I pressed myself tightly against the wall to minimize my exposure. So far, it seemed like an ordinary living room except for the fact that Phillip McIntosh was slumped back in one of the Queen Anne chairs with a bullet hole in his forehead. Bits of his brain and blood decorated the wall behind him.

Shit.

Ever so slightly and barely breathing, I edged forward and peeked into the room, spotting the back of a woman with long black hair facing away from me. Consuela was dressed all in black just as she had been the last two times I saw her, and she had a silenced .45 trained on Hildegarde and Raul, who both sat on the couch with their hands in their laps, staring blankly at her. I looked around and didn't see anyone else. Consuela must have gotten here moments ago because I still smelled gunpowder. Poor Phil. Herman was going to be devastated.

If I fired from where I stood, the scatter would catch both Raul and Hildegarde, injuring them. Why should I care? I should just kill them all, but I couldn't. That would make me one of them, so I aimed the shotgun at the back of Consuela's right knee. As I did, I caught Hildegarde's attention, but thankfully, Consuela hadn't noticed her slight distraction.

Consuela addressed Hildegarde. "Don't breathe or move, bitch. The same for you, Raul."

Raul hadn't seen me yet. "Consuela, my love, I don't understand? Why would you do this to me?"

"You're a pathetic fool, Raul. The thought of you touching me makes my skin crawl."

Hildegarde remained silent, hopeful, wondering who I might be and how I figured into this. I could see the wheels turning. She didn't look particularly nervous. I had to give her that. She had balls of steel. I was in the process of deciding how best to make my move when the pot on the kitchen stove, suddenly and shrilly, announced it was tea time.

The room exploded in noise and confusion as Consuela, startled, swirled around, and seeing me, fired a wild shot that shattered into the plaster wall behind my head. Dropping to the ground, I fired back. Barrel flame, gun smoke, and screams of pain filled the air. Consuela dropped her weapon, crumpling to the floor as buckshot ripped through her kneecap and thigh, tearing ligaments and blood vessels. She clutched her knee, moaning, and watched blood pour out of her onto the carpet. I quickly rose and kicked her gun away as the unattended teapot screeched eerily in the background.

She looked at me with hatred, rocking back and forth in agony. Hildegarde and Raul hadn't budged, and barely breathing, they waited for me to make the next move. Sudden recognition filled Raul's eyes. Without waiting for him to say anything I said, "Yes, Raul, it's me."

Hildegarde glanced at him suspiciously and seized the opportunity to take control of the situation. She made a move to rise off the couch and I said, "Not so fast, Madam Secretary. There are a few things we need to clarify before anybody goes anywhere."

Looking straight down the barrel of the twelve gauge, she sat back onto the sofa, suddenly realizing that I was neither friend nor foe but something else entirely, something perhaps even more unpleasant. "Who are you?" she asked.

"That's unimportant right now, but what is important is that you concentrate on telling me the truth, and don't force me to pull out a dictionary and show you what the definition of truth is."

Consuela continued to moan uncontrollably on the floor. It was a foregone conclusion that no one in this room had any intention of helping her. In the background, one of the talking heads urged stricter laws to curb the nationwide epidemic of gun violence.

"What do you want to know?" Hildegarde demanded.

I turned to Raul. "Let's start with you. Why are you here tonight?"

He looked totally bewildered. "I have no idea. I received an urgent message from Hildegarde that she wanted to meet with me in person as soon as possible. I was in Cuba at the time and flew in immediately, assuming that there was some sort of crisis that required my immediate attention. I barely arrived when Consuela burst in the room and shot that poor man over there." He nodded in Phil's direction, sincerely confused, and I believed him.

I looked at Hildegarde. "His story seems pretty straight forward. What's your version about tonight's meeting?"

"Same as his only the other way around. I received an urgent message from Raul that he needed to meet with me tonight. I was returning from a fund-raiser in D.C. and so here I am. So, who are you?"

"My name is John Cesari." I thought it over. Consuela must have set the meeting up to expedite things and bring the conflict to an end once and for all. Get rid of Raul, and then either cut a deal with Hildegarde or eliminate her in the hope Bucky would be more reasonable. I kind of admired Consuela's style; she cut right to the chase.

Hildegarde looked at me icily. "You're that pain in the ass doctor from Disney, aren't you?"

Raul glanced at Hildegarde. "You know him, Hildegarde?"

I answered for her. "Yeah, she knows me or rather—of me, Raul. In fact, she knows a lot of things, don't you, Hildegarde? She even knows who killed your daughter, Marguerite."

Raul was stunned. He stammered, "What is he saying, Hildegarde? What does any of this have to do with Marguerite?"

Consuela groaned and lay flat on her back, pale and sweaty. She was starting to lose consciousness. The rug beneath her was drenched in her blood. No one on the couch suggested I call an ambulance. That's the way sharks are. Consuela was just another slab of meat to them now.

I said, "Yeah Hildegarde, tell him. What does this have to do with Marguerite?"

From the look in her eyes, I would have to water board her for days to get anything out of her. I nodded patiently. "You're going to tell the truth, even if it's the last thing you do." I raised the gun slowly, pointing it directly into her face.

She said contemptuously, "You don't have the balls."

Shit. I counted to ten and thought about the Knights of the Round Table. As I took a deep breath and contemplated obliging her, a gun cocked loudly behind me and a dog growled. A voice said, "Slowly place the gun on the floor, asshole."

Fuck. Phil's partner, the other agent, and he brought the dog. In slow motion, I placed the shotgun on the floor in front of me. Without Phil to run interference, I was toast.

"Now raise your hands and turn around. No sudden movements, all right?"

I did as I was told, observing a clean-cut agent in his late twenties holding a 9mm Beretta in his left hand and the leash of an enormous snow-covered English mastiff in his right. The dog snarled ominously. The agent was six feet tall, and the huge, almost lion like head of the dog was well above his waist. It looked like he was standing next to a pony. I froze, staring at the dog, noting something out of place as she cocked her head, sniffed the air and studied me. She suddenly started to strain and tug at the leash, dragging the agent forward, trying to get at me.

The agent pulled back hard. "Take it easy, Cleo."

Cleo?! It couldn't be. That was the name of the dog Kelly and I had argued so bitterly about. We thought she had been put down but then I remembered what Phil had told me, that Hildegarde and Bucky had rescued the dog as a publicity stunt while on the campaign trail upstate.

The agent looked around the room confused and alarmed, trying to absorb the scene. One dead agent, a strange woman on the floor in desperate need of medical attention, another strange man holding a shotgun on his boss and her guest, and now the dog was rapidly becoming unmanageable. Hildegarde stood up as she noticed he was on the verge of being pulled off balance by Cleo.

She shouted, "Let the damn dog loose, Seth, before she drags you down."

Cleo was becoming increasingly wild now trying to reach me, but she had stopped growling and was simply pulling and leaping silently—all 250 lbs. of her. I was the only one who seemed to notice her change in demeanor.

"But she'll kill him," Seth cried out, pulling back with all his might. He was right about that, if that was what she intended. Unarmed, I wouldn't have a prayer against her and I had seen firsthand what she was capable of.

Hildegarde stepped away from me, moving closer to Consuela. "Perfect. Now, do it, Seth. I'll take full responsibility."

Seth let go of the leash, and Cleo bounded forward, leaping on top of me and knocking me backward onto the floor. She cried and licked my face in recognition and pinned me under her weight so I couldn't move. Hildegarde started to lose it.

She shouted, "Kill him now, Seth—and the dog too! Just do it."

Bitch.

Seth hesitated, and Hildegarde stepped over Consuela to grab the gun from him. As she did, Consuela suddenly reached out and grabbed her ankle, tripping her up. Hildegarde landed with a thumping sound, grunting and cursing. I pushed Cleo's head to the side to watch the macabre scene. Raul was frozen with terror on the couch as Consuela, with her last ounce of strength, pulled a syringe from her pocket and jammed it through Hildegarde's polyester pant suit, unloading its contents into her thigh. Hildegarde yelped and kicked out furiously, knocking Consuela backward causing her to strike her head on the edge of the coffee table. Her eyes rolled up and she lost consciousness for good.

I finally managed to get Cleo off me and rise to a sitting position, leaning back against the sofa next to Raul. I panted, my brain racing to figure out my next move as Cleo lay down next to me with her head in my lap. Seth was paralyzed with indecision. This situation was way over his pay grade, but I didn't have time to feel sorry for him as I searched for the shotgun, which had skidded toward Seth when Hildegarde hit the floor.

"Help me up you imbecile," she screamed and he stepped toward her, lending her a hand. The needle stuck out of her thigh and she pulled it out, flinging it onto the floor.

"Now give me that gun," she ordered.

"I don't know if I should do that, Mrs. Clifton," he stammered.

She glared at him and hissed, "I will destroy you, Seth. You and everybody you love. Now give me the gun."

The poor kid was slack-jawed, speechless, but slowly extended his hand to her.

I shouted, "Don't do it, Seth! She'll kill everybody in this room including you. She has to now." I'd been involved in enough mob wars to understand this drill. When the shit hits the fan like this, the only real solution is to get rid of all the witnesses.

Seth hesitated, thinking about what I had just said, and she lunged forward, grabbing the gun. The barrel lurched backward and upward, suddenly discharging a round through the bottom of his chin and out the top of his head, lodging in the ceiling. He crumpled onto the floor as she desperately tried to dislodge his dead hand from the weapon. I leaped for the shotgun but it was too far and I was too late.

"Stop!" she shouted, firing another shot into the ceiling.

I was flat on my stomach now near Consuela. I looked at the syringe lying inches from me.

Succinylcholine.

I looked up at Hildegarde. Suddenly, she didn't look so good. The medication was starting to kick in, and she looked like she had a bad case of vertigo. She wheezed and gasped.

Raul asked, "What is happening?"

Hildegarde seemed disoriented and stumbled backward, coughing and sucking air. She crashed into a small table, staggering face forward to the floor with the lamp from the table falling on top of her. In silence, she struggled against the effects of the medication but to no avail. I stood up quickly, kicked the gun out from her hand, and rolled her onto her back. Her eyes were open but she was completely paralyzed and had stopped breathing. I knew she could still hear me so I said, "You're not going to get off that easy, bitch."

She had a strong pulse so I tilted her head back and began rescue breathing, watching her chest rise and fall. Raul had gone over to Consuela to see how she was doing. From the amount of blood on the floor, I doubted she would make it. Buckshot must have ripped through a major artery.

I watched Hildegarde's face as I pressed my lips tightly against hers and pinched her nose to prevent any of my life-saving oxygen from escaping her lungs. The effects of succinylcholine last only several minutes, but several minutes without oxygen would be devastating to almost anyone, no matter what shape they were in. In a woman her age, if she didn't go into cardiac arrest and die immediately, she would most certainly suffer severe anoxic brain damage. Certainly, I would have enjoyed that outcome immensely, but I had a better idea in mind for her. So, I continued giving mouth-to-mouth resuscitation to a woman I despised with my whole soul.

In less than five minutes, she began to blink and breathe on her own again. I knelt beside her exhausted as she began coughing, and I watched her inhale deeply like on the first day of life and then let it out. She was going to be fine. Raul was on his knees across from me watching. "You saved her life, but why? She was going to kill you."

"Because she needs to suffer in this life first, Raul, before she goes on to suffer in the next. Spending the rest of her life in prison should do the trick."

"You must tell me everything, Dr. Cesari, but most importantly what does all of this have to do with my daughter, and why did Consuela want to kill us?"

I decided to be direct. He was a big boy.

"Hildegarde murdered your daughter, Raul. Or rather, she ordered assassins to murder her and make it look like an accident. There's not enough time right now to go through all the details, but I will later."

He put his arm out and touched me lightly. He was confused, bewildered, and teary eyed. "Please, at least tell me why she would do such a thing. My child was a flawed but innocent human being."

I was convinced he really didn't know what was going on. I hesitated. How do you summarize the life of someone like Hildegarde? I said, "Naked ambition, Raul. Plain and simple. Marguerite got in the way of Hildegarde's political aspirations and had to be removed. That's all there is to it. I promise to explain better once we're out of here."

I looked at Hildegarde. She was unconscious but breathing comfortably.

"And Consuela?" he persisted.

I sighed. "She decided it was time for a change in management in your organization, and she lured you and Hildegarde here to discuss her promotion. She was going kill you for sure and probably frame Hildegarde to use as leverage to take over your business. You may not know this, but she and Hildegarde have been slugging it out all week and Marguerite was a casualty. With you out of the way, Consuela hoped to inherit your empire, but she needed Hildegarde's support and was banking on her becoming the next president. If Hildegarde didn't agree to the plan, I suspect Consuela would have killed her too and freelanced it with whoever was in charge."

He nodded. "What was in that syringe?"

"Succinylcholine. It's a medication that causes total paralysis, including the muscles used for respiration, and will cause death by asphyxiation. It's what they used to murder Marguerite before dumping her into the water. I can't be one hundred percent sure what Consuela had on her mind tonight but maybe she was going to confront Hildegarde with her knowledge of what happened or maybe even plant it here for the authorities to find. Who knows, maybe it was for you. I don't know."

He hesitated. "One last thing, Dr. Cesari. Why would you go through all this trouble for my daughter? You didn't even know her."

I thought about that and I thought about an Irish nun from a long time ago. "You're right. I didn't know your daughter, Raul, but I didn't have to. I could feel her pain from a hundred miles away. I could hear her soul calling out to me for justice and I decided that she was going to get justice. The whole world is going to know what a monster this woman is if it's the last thing I do. If I let her die here, now, the politicians will cover up this mess. She'll get a state funeral with a horse-drawn hearse and the press will go on endlessly about what a wonderful person she was and all the good she did. I won't allow that." I glanced at my watch. "Look, there's a lot more to this story, but we need to get moving."

He nodded, trembling and suddenly burst into tears over the thought of his daughter. While he let it all hang out, I rolled Hildegarde onto her stomach and tied her hands tightly behind her back with the electrical cord from the lamp. She was still quite weak and offered almost no resistance.

"Do you have a way out of here?" I asked him.

"I have a car parked out front, but my driver and bodyguard seem to have disappeared."

"I know for a fact that one is dead and I'd guess the other one is too. Was it a rented car?"

"Yes."

"In your name?"

"Of course not."

"Good. Come with me, I have a car waiting outside. I'll drop you off at the airport of your choice and we can chat on the way."

I looked over at Cleo, who lay quietly watching us as if understanding the somber mood. When she caught my eye she picked her head up and gave a little whine.

"Are you ready to come home, girl?"

She jumped up excited and let out a happy woof.

Chapter 49

Twelve weeks later

"Thanks for driving me to the airport, Cesari. I know it's out of your way."

"My pleasure, Vito, and thank you for letting Cleopatra stay at your place until I find a bigger apartment. I really appreciate it."

"No problem, Cesari. My apartment's enormous, and I own the whole building anyway."

"Well, thanks just the same."

We were in a rental car on our way to Newark International Airport so Vito could catch his flight to Vegas, where he and Heidi were going to party like Romans. From there I was on my way to Cocoa's house in Morristown for Passover.

"I don't know if I ever said it out loud before now, but I'm sorry about everything, you know?"

I nodded glumly. "Thanks, Vito. I still can't believe it."

Six weeks ago, Kelly had given birth to a pair of healthy, beautiful baby girls, Beatrice and Gwendolyn. I should've been happy. The only problem was that I wasn't the father, or couldn't prove it at any rate. Kelly had resolved her differences with Omar and claimed that she'd had a tryst with him while she and I were still dating. I didn't believe her or my pride wouldn't let me believe her anyway. I demanded a paternity test, but since Kelly had gone ahead and married Omar against all common sense and he had acknowledged the kids as his own, the courts were unwilling to accept my petition for paternity testing, stating that it was not in the best interest of the children at this point to figure out who was sleeping with who, and when. I'd been in a lousy mood ever since.

"Can a judge really do that, Cesari? Deny you the right to find out if you're the father? It doesn't seem right."

"A judge can do whatever he or she goddamn pleases. That's one of the great flaws of our judicial system. Judges are like dictators in their courtroom. Once they rule on something, right or wrong, there's nothing you can do about it except maybe go to another judge, which I've been toying with but Kelly begged me to let it go so I don't know what I'm going to do."

Vito nodded sympathetically as he lit a cigarette. He opened the window a crack to let some air in and highway noise flooded the car.

"Damn," I said, slamming my hand on the steering wheel. "I should have thrown Omar out the window of the Kit Kat Club when I had the chance. Do you really have to smoke, Vito? We're almost there for God's sake."

"Take it easy, Cesari, I'm not the enemy. Look at the bright side. At least Kelly's not pissed about the dog anymore and you're still friends. That's something. She even said you can drop by once in a while as long as you don't make trouble."

"Great. Drop by and say hi to Omar's kids. How am I not going to make trouble? I want to kill him every time I see him."

"Yeah, I guess that would be a problem."

"Damn it, Vito, This sucks."

"Love always does, Cesari—always. By the way, I was proud of you for not making a ruckus when we visited Kelly in the hospital. You showed remarkable restraint considering how much the kids looked like you; a little dark maybe, but spot on."

"Will you shut up? Was that supposed to make me feel better?"

"Take it easy. I'm just trying to help. If it's any consolation, it was quite a thrill to see Hildegarde finally sitting in a courtroom wearing an orange jumpsuit and shackles like she deserves, and the world can thank you for that."

"The world can thank Raul for that, not me."

Vito said, "That's true."

American television had refused to play the incriminating DVD or even talk about it on the air, claiming it may have been fabricated. Hildegarde had been crowned the next president by the pundits, and they weren't about to let a sordid scandal and the death of one girl get in the way of the coronation ceremony.

With Raul's international pull, however, the DVD was shown on the Internet and on every foreign news outlet around the globe twenty-four hours a day until Hildegarde's very public arrest a few days back. The American Hispanic community had been whipped up into a frenzy and for weeks had demanded justice. The religious right had joined in when the undoctored autopsy report came to light, revealing that Marguerite had been pregnant. The CEO of Orlando Memorial Hospital resigned in disgrace and admitted that Hildegarde had personally bullied and bribed him into leaning on the coroner to falsify the original record. Phone records from the dead agents in upstate New York revealed they had received multiple calls from Hildegarde's office in the State Department. Since Marguerite was an Argentine national, that government demanded a full investigation, and several other South American countries joined in just for the fun of it. France and Russia went on record saying that Hildegarde was no longer welcome in their countries, and it didn't help Hildegarde's case that one of the dead agents in her house had been shot with his own gun and her fingerprints were all over the weapon.

"You know Vito, what bothers me most is that despite everything, it was Hildegarde's plan to hunker down as usual and weather the storm. The woman has no shame. This coulda, woulda, shoulda bullshit drives me crazy, and of all people to bring her down. You've got to love the irony there."

Vito chuckled. "Yeah, I know what you mean."

The final nail in Hildegarde's coffin, when the die-hard loyalists finally abandoned her, came when her political enemies caught up with Cinderella at the Kit Kat Club. They swooped in, cleaned her up, and with the help of Raul got her job back for her at Disney. Then, in full costume, in the middle of a beautiful spring day, surrounded by hordes of Disney guests standing outside on the balcony of the castle facing Main Street U.S.A., America's princess gave an hour-long interview with every major American news network and cable outlet, telling the world in graphic detail how she and Marguerite had been sexually exploited by Bucky on multiple occasions and that Snow White had confided in her that Bucky was indeed the father of her child and how she had feared for her life at the hands of Hildegarde.

Vito tossed his cigarette butt out the window as I got off the exit ramp to the airport, searching for his terminal. I said, "That scene at the house in Mount Kisco after Cinderella broke down in tears on national television was unbelievable. It reminded me of what it must have been like at the palace of Versailles when the mob came for Louis XVI and Marie Antoinette. The only thing missing were the pitchforks and pikes."

Thousands of protesters had swarmed to Mount Kisco demanding justice. Things got so bad that Hildegarde and Bucky were essentially prisoners in their own home. The political process in D.C. had come to a screeching halt as America held its breath. It all came to a head when a sixteen year old girl dressed as Snow White standing in front of the crowd of ten thousand strong picked up a rock and flung it through the bay window of the living room. When the police tried to arrest her, the pent-up anger of the mob broke loose and they began rioting. The justice department was finally forced to act and arrested Hildegarde the next day on charges of conspiracy to commit murder, murder in the first degree, conspiracy to falsify medical records, the unauthorized use of a controlled substance, misuse of her authority, and being a very poor dresser.

"Boy, that was great watching them bring her out of her own house in handcuffs," Vito said. "I'd never thought I'd live to see a scene like that."

I saw the sign for terminal B and steered the car toward it. "Yeah, that was good. It's a shame but it looks like Bucky's going to get off again. Did you see him on television the other night?"

"Yeah, he's something else but you know, despite everything, I'd still like to hang out with him and have a cold one or something—maybe play a game of darts."

I said, "Bowling, I'd like to go bowling with him, and go out for buffalo wings."

During his softball interview on cable news Bucky led off with a prepared statement denying knowledge of any of Hildegarde's crimes, but before anyone could ask him even one question, he complained of severe chest pain and was rushed to St. Luke's Hospital for observation. He was reportedly in good spirits when he learned that the latest polls indicated that although he was a letch, he probably had nothing to do with Snow White's murder. Another poll said that ninety percent of the country believed he was faking a heart attack and a yet a third poll had him five points in the lead for governor of New York if he decided to run.

I pulled the car to the curb and let Vito out at his terminal.

"Take it easy Vito. Have a good flight and Happy Easter."

"Thanks, and you too," he chuckled, "or should I say Happy Passover?"

"Shut up."

I pulled out of the airport and on to the entrance ramp of 280W, glancing briefly in the rearview mirror. "Are you ready for this?" Cleo, taking up the whole back row, looked at me and bobbed her head, letting out a little whine.

I smiled. "Smart dog."

Chapter 50

The Seder

I pulled into the driveway at Cocoa's house and parked the car. As I assisted Cleo out from the rear, Cocoa came running out of the house, throwing her arms around me and giving me a big hug.

"I'm so happy you made it," she said, pressing her face into my chest.

I kissed her. "Wouldn't have missed it for the world. Wow, you look great." She wore a green knee-length satin dress, high heels, and a pearl necklace. It was a fairly conservative outfit; very mature and extremely attractive.

"Thank you and so do you. I don't think I've ever seen you in a suit and tie before, have I?" I wore a two-piece charcoal gray suit, white button-down shirt, and red tie.

"Probably not would be my guess."

She grabbed Cleo's head, which was just about up to her chest. "How are you girl?" Cleo wagged her tail and licked her face. I pulled Cleo away before she could do serious damage to Cocoa's makeup.

"You told your parents about her?"

"Yes, they said she can have the whole garage. I purchased water and food bowls for her. IAMS big dog, right?"

"Perfect. Thank you. I just couldn't bear the thought of putting her in a kennel. She's going to cry a lot but I'll check on her frequently."

"She'll be fine there. You're just looking for an excuse to get away from my family."

"No I'm not."

"Yes you are. You're nervous. I can tell. Don't be scared. We stopped eating Christians years ago, everybody but Uncle Leo that is. He says it's an acquired taste."

I chuckled. She had a way with words. "How'd you know what I was thinking?"

She smiled. "The garage is huge, and we parked the cars on the street so Cleo will have plenty of room, and don't worry, if she makes a mess we'll deal with it."

I grabbed Cleo's head and looked into her eyes. "See how lucky you are?"

She woofed playfully and shook her head free.

We settled her in the garage. Cocoa helped me with my yarmulke and we went into the house together to meet everyone. There were fourteen adults including myself and six children, who had their own table. Cocoa introduced me to all the guests one at a time, starting with her parents, whom I thanked for their hospitality.

Uncle Leo was a big, serious-looking guy of about sixty. He was taller than me by about three inches, broad shouldered, and wore a slick, very expensive hand-tailored suit. His silver hair was perfectly coiffed, and a gold bracelet dangled around his left wrist. Cocoa had told me that he was a senior partner in a big Philadelphia law firm that represented the city and many of its public unions. He was a big shot, and it was clear he didn't like me.

We shook hands awkwardly, and he studied me carefully before offering me a twenty year old scotch. Turning to Cocoa, who was engaged with her dad, he asked, "Do you mind if I borrow your friend, Myrtle? I'd like to get to know him a little better."

"Sure, but don't hurt him Uncle Leo," she teased.

He put a big, muscular arm around me and I could tell that even now he must still spend a lot of time in the gym. He said, "What do you say we go outside? It's a beautiful day." We left the house and strolled down the driveway. It was almost five and not a cloud in the sky.

"So, I hear you're a lawyer," I said, trying to break the ice.

"Yeah, you could say that." At the curb he stopped at the back of a parked Bentley and popped the trunk. Reaching in, he pulled out a duffel bag, showing it to me.

"Look familiar?" he asked.

I shook my head. "Should it?"

He handed it to me. "Okay, look inside and then tell me whether it looks familiar or not."

I unzipped it, peered inside, and my heart sank. There was the Sig Sauer .228 handgun I had taken from the Secret Service agent in up-state New York, stacks of fifty dollar bills, and two left-over syringes of Fentanyl from Morristown Memorial. It was the duffel bag I had brought to Cocoa's house the night before we'd gone to Orlando. I had left it by the side of her parents' bed with the intention of retrieving it when I returned but had forgotten.

Shit.

He said, "Before you embarrass yourself by lying, let me tell you what I know already. The serial number on the gun traced back to a Secret Service agent whose whereabouts are presently unknown, but my sources tell me no one's expecting him back any time soon."

He paused, looking at me and I remained silent.

"In addition to the rightful owner's fingerprints, there was also another set of prints on the gun. Want to take a stab at who they belonged to?"

I didn't say anything. I had been to Seders before but this one was turning into a doozy. He continued. "That's what I thought." He took the duffel bag from me and placed it back in the trunk, slamming it shut.

"I don't know what to say."

"Don't say anything, just listen."

"Myrtle's father, Harry, my brother, doesn't know about this— yet. When Harry was in Europe one of his neighbors called to tell me that he saw a light on in the house when there shouldn't have been one on. When I got here, I found the duffel bag in the bedroom. Imagine my surprise. It took me a while to figure things out, but by that time everyone had become aware that Myrtle had a new man in her life, you, so I decided to keep the information to myself."

"Well thank you for that."

"Don't thank me, asshole. Myrtle's put my poor brother Harry through enough aggravation to last him two lifetimes without me having to tell him she's dating Michael Corleone from the Bronx. So, would you care to explain to me why you were in possession of a Secret Service agent's weapon or am I going to have to ruin everyone's holiday by exposing you for the scumbag you are?"

He was upset. That much was obvious, and I didn't see any point in lying to him. He was a no-nonsense street lawyer at heart and would see through any fabrications I might throw at him. "It's complicated but the guy was an assassin who tried to kill me and failed. I needed something to defend myself from his friends so I kept his gun. That's all there is to it."

"A Secret Service agent tried to kill you? And you expect me to believe that?" He looked at me in disbelief.

"You can believe what you want, but it's the truth."

"And where is this agent now, in case I want to return his pistol to him?"

I didn't say anything.

He shook his head in disbelief. "Oh, brother. You can't be serious? You know, Myrtle thinks your God's gift to the planet. How the fuck did she ever get that idea?"

"Look, Uncle Leo…"

He interrupted me harshly. "Don't call me Uncle Leo. I'm not your fucking uncle and I don't want to hear any more of your bullshit. I don't know who you are or what you think you're doing but I didn't get to where I am by being stupid, and don't let the expensive clothes fool you. I've been rubbing elbows with wise guys ever since I was in diapers so cut the crap. If Myrtle wants a mobbed up greaser as a plaything, I have no choice but to accept it but don't think for a minute you're pulling the wool over my eyes. That's my niece were talking about, and for the sake of the family, I'm going to keep this to myself for now, but the clock's ticking."

He finally came up for air, taking a deep breath and letting it out slowly. His face was flushed and he wasn't through.

"Let me explain this to you in plain English what's going to happen, paisano. That duffel bag means I own you. From now on when I say jump, you don't just ask 'How high?' you ask 'How high, *sir*?' If you step out of line even once, I'll mail that bag to the FBI with a sworn affidavit from me and my six partners that you confessed to whatever crime they want to pin on you. Are we on the same page so far?"

I nodded but didn't say anything.

He continued, "And another thing, I don't know what was going on with those syringes of Fentanyl and I don't want to know, but if I find out that you've been shooting up my niece with narcotics, I will personally cut your balls off and mail them back to Palermo."

He was going too far now. "I would never hurt Myrtle in any way. I really care for her."

"Isn't that sweet? Now listen up, Cesari, we're going back into the house and have a lovely dinner because we don't hold grudges on Passover, *capeesh*? So stop your frowning and put a big smile on your face like we're having a great time, but you got exactly two weeks to let my niece down easy, and I don't want to find out that you ever stepped foot inside this house again."

"What am I supposed to tell Myrtle?"

"Tell her they made you king of England and they need you over there in a hurry for the coronation. I don't really care what you say, but you better be out of her life the next time I speak to her. Understand?"

I nodded. "I under…"

"Shut up. I'm not finished. The next time you sleep in a bed that doesn't belong to you make sure you change the goddamn sheets."

He was angry, but I was starting to get annoyed too. Through my teeth I said, "I think you need a nap, grandpa."

"What did you just say to me?" I saw a vein in his left temple pulsating.

"Hey, you guys," Cocoa called out playfully. We both turned around abruptly to see her coming down the driveway. She seemed unaware of our heated discussion. "Don't hog my boyfriend all to yourself, Uncle Leo."

He smiled broadly and gave her a warm hug as if nothing had just happened. "I wouldn't do that, pumpkin. Johnny and I were just getting to know each other. He really seems like a great guy."

She came over and put her arm through mine, smiling. "That's because he is. Well, it's dinnertime. What were you two talking about?"

I hesitated, truly speechless, and Uncle Leo stepped in. "John was just telling me that he would consider converting to Judaism one day if he met the right girl."

This guy was a riot.

Cocoa laughed. "I don't believe it. John, you didn't say that, did you?"

Uncle Leo stood behind Cocoa glaring at me.

I held her hands gently in mine and looked into her beautiful brown eyes. Speaking softly I said, "I think what I said to your uncle was that when I met that special someone who made my heart race just at the thought of her, and who made me feel like each day was a rainbow and every night a tropical sunset, that I would consider no sacrifice too great in order to make her happy."

Cocoa put her arms around my neck and pulled me down for a kiss. "That was beautiful. I had no idea you could be so romantic."

Looking past her, I saw Uncle Leo mouth the word *asshole*.

We went into the house and seated ourselves around the dining room table, which was decorated exquisitely with the home's finest china, crystal, and silverware. There was a copy of the Haggadah next to each guest's place setting. I was lucky, I had Cocoa on my left and Uncle Leo across from me. I got to look at his mug all night. Her father sat at the head of the table and wore the traditional white robe called a Kittel. The Seder is an ancient Jewish tradition commemorating the exodus of the Israelites from slavery in Egypt. The words, rituals, and food of the Seder are a way of insuring passage of the Jewish beliefs from one generation to the next. Attending a Seder on Passover is traditional, even among those who are not particularly religious.

When everyone was ready, her father stood to say a small prayer and start the ceremony. "Before we begin, I would like to welcome into our home and our hearts a very special guest—Dr. John Cesari. John is a dear friend of our darling daughter, Myrtle, and we are pleased to share our humble home with him. All Seders are special in their own right but this year's is particularly exceptional. Our Myrtle has a very special announcement she would like to make and since I don't wish to steal her thunder, I will yield the floor."

I watched as Myrtle stood up next to me holding her wine glass. I didn't know what was coming any more than anyone else. She said, "I'll be brief. As you all know, several years ago, I dropped out of Princeton at the start of my sophomore year. This controversial decision caused much angst to everyone at this table but especially to my parents. Mom, Dad, I love you so much and am so grateful for all you have given me and all you have done for me. I am sorry for any sorrow I have caused you, and I hope that the news I bring you now will cause an equal if not greater amount of joy."

She paused for effect, looking directly at her parents. "I have decided to return to school full time to finish my education and I am delighted to announce to you all that I have been accepted into Juilliard for their fall semester and will be studying classical piano."

The room erupted in thunderous applause and cheers. Her mother and father hugged each other, tearful with joy, and everyone, including me, stood up to give Cocoa a standing ovation.

Great job, Cocoa!

As the noise died down, she raised her glass. "I would like to thank Dr. John Cesari, who encouraged me to return to school." She turned toward me and I suddenly felt like I was in a fishbowl as all eyes focused in my direction. "I have only known John for a few months but a day in his life is like a year in anyone else's. He is a man of deep conviction with an unwavering moral compass, and it is by virtue of his advice and steadfast belief in me that I was able to finally believe in myself and find the resolve to move forward with my life. He convinced me that I could do better and had so much more to offer."

Tearful, she raised her glass. "Thank you, John, for lighting a fire in me that I hope never goes out. You are truly my knight in shining armor." Everyone cheered, applauded, and raised their glasses. Everyone but Uncle Leo that is, and I tried not to notice his scowl.

Later, after all the guests had departed, I walked Cleopatra and came back in the house to find Cocoa by herself in the living room playing the piano while her parents finished up in the kitchen. She was playing Chopin and smiled at me as I sat next to her on the bench.

"Do you like?" she asked.

"Very much."

She finished the piece and held my hand. "Did you have a good time?"

"I did. That was a wonderful meal. Your mother is a great cook and you have a great family."

"Thank you. So what did you think of Uncle Leo?"

"He's quite a character."

"Isn't he though? I think he likes you. He kept looking in your direction."

"Yeah, I think we really hit it off."

"That's great because he's a very powerful man and you wouldn't want to get on his bad side. He and his partners are known as the seven savage Jews of South Philly."

I chuckled. "Thanks for the tip. Well, it's getting kind of late. I really should get going." It was after eleven, and I was sure her parents were exhausted and wanted to turn in. They didn't need me hanging around.

She looked surprised. "Go where?"

"Back to New York—to my apartment."

"Why?"

"Why?" I hesitated. "I don't know—I just assumed."

She smiled. "Don't be silly. It's late and you're staying here."

"I am?"

"Of course. Why would you think otherwise?"

"Because of—you know…" I nodded toward the kitchen.

"My parents?" She started laughing. "I think they know I'm sexually active, John. I already asked them if it's okay for you to spend the night—with me—in my room, and they said yes. Besides, they like you."

I hesitated. "I don't know Cocoa. Wouldn't that be a little—uncomfortable?"

She wiggled onto my lap and put her arms around my neck. Looking into my eyes, she shook her head and sighed in frustration. "You are truly the biggest..."

"Don't say it," I warned her.

"...nebbish, I have ever met."

The End

About the Author

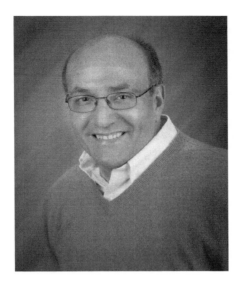

*J*ohn Avanzato grew up in the Bronx. After receiving a bachelor's degree in biology from Fordham University, he went on to earn his medical degree at the State University of New York at Buffalo, School of Medicine. He is currently a board-certified gastroenterologist in Geneva, New York, where he lives with his wife of twenty-eight years.

Inspired by authors like Tom Clancy, John Grisham, and Lee Child, John writes about strong but flawed heroes.

His first two novels, Hostile Hospital and Prescription for Disaster have been well received. Temperature Rising is the third novel in the Cesari series. The fouth novel is in the works.

Author's Note

Dear Reader,

I hope you enjoyed reading Temperature Rising as much as I enjoyed writing it. Please do me a favor and write a review for me on amazon.com. The reviews are very important and your support is greatly appreciated.

Thank you,

John Avanzato MD

Hostile Hospital

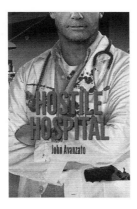

*W*hen former mob thug turned doctor, John Cesari, takes a job as a gastroenterologist at a small hospital in upstate New York, he assumes he's outrun his past and started life anew. But trouble has a way of finding the scrappy Bronx native.

Things go awry one night at a bar when he punches out an obnoxious drunk who won't leave his date alone. Unbeknownst to Dr. Cesari, that drunk is his date's stalker ex-boyfriend—and a crooked cop.

Over the course of several action packed days, Cesari uncovers the dirty little secrets of a small town hospital. As the bodies pile up, he is forced to confront his own bloody past.

Hostile Hospital is a fast paced journey that is not only entertaining but maintains an interesting view on the philosophy of healthcare. If you aren't too scared after reading, read the sequel, Prescription for Disaster.

Prescription for Disaster

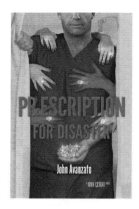

*D*r. John Cesari is a gastroenterologist employed at Saint Matt's Hospital in Manhattan. He tries to escape his unsavory past on the Bronx streets by settling into a Greenwich Village apartment with his girlfriend, Kelly. After his adventures in Hostile Hospital, Cesari wants to stay under the radar of his many enemies.

Through no fault of his own, Cesari winds up in the wrong place at the wrong time. A chance encounter with a mugger turns on its head when Cesari watches his assailant get murdered right before his eyes.

After being framed for the crime, he attempts to unravel the mystery, propelling himself deeply into the world of international diamond smuggling. He is surrounded by bad guys at every turn and behind it all are Russian and Italian mobsters determined to ensure Cesari has an untimely and unpleasant demise.

His prescription is to beat them at their own game, but before he can do that he must deal with a corrupt boss and an environment filled with temptation and danger from all sides. Everywhere Cesari goes, someone is watching. The dramatic climax will leave you breathless and wanting more.

KCM Publishing
a division of KCM Digital Media, LLC

Made in the USA
Middletown, DE
05 December 2015